REBELLIOUS DESIRE

"Don't ever try to run from me again," Stoke said.

"I wasn't running from you," Lark protested.

"Nay, you were trying to ensnare me in one of your little traps."

"I wasn't. I swear it. When I left the hall, I wanted to be alone, but *you* followed *me*. You can't believe I planned this! I was riding away to get away from you."

Stoke wanted to believe her. He stared at her, his chest heaving, every nerve in his body humming from having almost lost his life. Or was it having her in his arms again?

"Don't look at me like that," Lark whispered, nervously licking her lips. "Every time you look at me like that, you want to kiss me."

"I've discovered that when one comes close to death, it heats the blood—especially with a temptress like you in my arms . . ." He captured her chin and kissed her, hard, his lips moving across hers. He grew vaguely aware of her pounding on his chest, but after a moment, the pummeling stopped.

She moaned and he nipped at her full bottom lip, then sucked on it as he untied the thong holding her hair. Tossing it aside, he tangled his hands in her thick hair, feeling the velvety smoothness between his fingers.

He ran his tongue along her teeth and her mouth opened for him. Her body relaxed against him as her arms went around his neck. Then she was kissing him back, her hands tangling in his hair. The passion in her drove him, and he scooped her up into his arms, never breaking the kiss. . . .

Books by Constance Hall

MY DARLING DUKE

MY DASHING EARL

MY REBELLIOUS BRIDE

Published by Zebra Books

MY REBELLIOUS BRIDE

Constance Hall

Zebra Books
Kensington Publishing Corp.

http://www.zebrabooks.com

To my mother and father, whom I hope will always know I love them. To my friend Barbara, who never lets a question go unanswered. To Bob, for his engineering genius and knowledge of metals and for keeping Sandra happy.

Prologue

England, Kenilworth Castle
February, 1194

The chamber door creaked open.

Stoke de Bracy, the Earl of Blackstone, cracked open an eye. The dying embers in the hearth afforded enough light to see the dark shadow creeping toward his bed. The intruder stayed well beyond the sphere of dim light, a faceless form shrouded in night.

Since fighting in the Holy Land, Stoke made a habit of sleeping with his broadsword, Dragon's Eye, beside him. He curled his fingers around the hilt now, careful not to move his arm.

Footsteps moved closer, barely audible above the faint hiss of the embers. The unmistakable shadow of a raised broadsword eased across the floor, rising along the edge of the mattress and over Stoke's shoulders.

The attacker lunged.

Cold steel brushed against Stoke's left shoulder as he rolled to the side. The blade sliced through the mattress and a corner of his pillow.

Another lunge.

Stoke rolled off the opposite edge of the bed. His attacker's blade missed him and struck the edge of the mattress. He turned, his broadsword swinging.

His target darted back with arrow-like swiftness. Dragon's Eye's razor-sharp metal sliced through the bedpost instead of his attacker. One corner of the canopy crashed down onto the mattress. Stoke couldn't see his attacker for the wall of burgundy linen blocking his view.

He dashed around the foot of the bed with his sword raised, ready to strike another blow. The sound of retreating footsteps out in the hallway met him. He cursed under his breath and ran to the door, but it was too late. The assassin had disappeared.

Chapter 1

Two broadswords met. White sparks flashed in the sun as metal struck metal. The clank rang hollow through the crisp morning air. William Mandeville, the broader and taller of the two warriors in combat, parried and slashed again at his smaller opponent.

The smaller warrior raised a shield, deflecting the blow. William smiled, staring at the useless shield the way he would look upon a piece of rare steak he was about to spear. He brought his heavy broadsword down with a loud grunt. The crushing blow sent the scrawny warrior down to his knees in the dirt, though he managed to hold on to the shield.

Before his adversary could bring up the shield again, William kicked it out of his opponent's hand and thrust his sword close to the fallen warrior's neck. "Do you yield, Pigeon, or do I make stew out of you for the evening repast?"

"Make the stew, my lord, just take care you do not choke

on my bones.'' The smaller warrior's voice was muffled behind a helm.

William's sons, Evel, Cedric and Harold, and the fifteen knights lining the edge of the tilt yard, laughed at the smaller knight's jest.

William shot each one of them a look that could curdle milk. One by one the men grew silent.

It was so quiet in the tilt yard now that William could hear the wrens singing in the trees and the baaing of his lambs grazing not fifty feet from him. Though he felt satisfied with his dominance over all his domain, the scowl never left his face as he turned back to his opponent. Clear bright eyes, the color of hammered gold, gazed mischievously back at William through small slits in the metal.

He bent low and whispered, ''I should have you flogged and your toes broken for your insolent tongue, but I find I'm feeling benevolent.'' The corner of William's mouth lifted in a begrudging grin. He slid his broadsword into the sheath, then held out his hand to his sparring partner.

''You always feel benevolent when you best me.'' The warrior accepted William's proffered hand.

William pulled his opponent up with an indignant grunt. ''I'm destined to always feel tolerant where you are concerned, since you'll never have the strength to wield a sword as you should.''

''If you had lost the draw and we'd used lances, I might have had a better chance.'' The smaller warrior saw the frown on William's face, pulled off a helm, and smiled. A long golden braid, the tawny color of a lioness's mane and as thick as William's wrist, tumbled down the warrior's back.

William put his arm over his daughter's shoulders and pecked her on the cheek. ''You may be right there, Lark, but I'm not so stupid as to let you beat me with my men watching.''

''Are you saying you cheated on the draw?''

''I might have peeked when Evel put the straws in his hand.''

"I should have expected as much."

She hit his chest and smiled at him, a smile he always felt deep in his heart, a smile he could deny naught, not even the tilt yard. He looked into those dazzling, teasing eyes and thanked the Virgin Mother she was not like his other daughter, Helen, who padded around like a little mouse and rarely had three insipid words for her father. But Lark glowed with life, so eager to gain his favor, so willing to show her mettle. He had known she was different the moment her tiny infant fingers gripped his, and he looked into those eager, conquering golden eyes.

Even as a babe, she was unique. Unlike his other four children, she never spat upon him. He could jostle her on his knee all day long and she would do naught but laugh. Nor did she whine or cry like the rest. He'd never seen tears in her eyes, no matter how hard a blow she'd taken from anyone or anything. All metal, his Pigeon was. It wasn't natural for anyone to be so hard on the inside. One day, he knew something would breach that hardness. He just hoped the felling would leave her stalwart heart intact, for she was in a way a miracle to him. Aye, the saints broke the mold when his daughter was born. She was the stuff of martyrs. He stared over at her and grinned proudly, but the grin faded as he remembered that most martyrs died because of their courage.

She surveyed his face. That eager-to-please light in her eyes quickly dissolved into worry. "Something wrong?" she asked.

"Naught, Pigeon." William touched her cheek and smiled pensively at her.

"Oh, Father . . ." Evel called to him.

He glanced at his son and saw Evel's gaze locked on something behind William's back. William glanced over his shoulder. His wife, Elizabeth, was marching toward the tilt yard, her back as straight as St. Vale's walls, her gaze locked on him, the blue in her eyes spitting fire. Her long black braids glistened like onyx in the sun, while her brown kirtle billowed out with each stiff step.

He squeezed Lark's shoulder. "Look, your mother comes and she is ready to flay us both alive. I vowed not to let you in the tilt yard again. Now there will be no escaping her tongue-lashing. Alas, I cannot endure it without the fortification of ale. What say you we make a hasty retreat to the village until her temper cools?"

"Hurry! I'll hold her off." Lark gave him a conspiratorial wink.

"I thought you'd say that, my intrepid daughter." William pinched Lark's cheek, then took off running toward the fence. With more stamina than a man of two score and six should have, he hurdled the fence in one leap and was out of the tilt yard.

He called over his shoulder to his men and sons, "Last one to the village inn eats mud pies for a week."

The men let out a loud cheer at being given a reprieve from the tilt yard and Lady Elizabeth's temper. They ran after William, their forms a mere blur between the fence rails.

Lark watched them, a smile on her face. Taller than William, Evel easily passed him with his long legs. He was the eldest of her brothers at a score and six and favored his mother, with thick black hair and intelligent blue eyes. The younger twins, Harold and Cedric, not yet a score, looked more like William with tawny blond hair and mischievous green eyes. They were shorter than Evel and forced to stay behind, elbowing the knights around them as they tried to scramble ahead. Lark thought they looked like a pack of hounds on the hunt.

"Come back here!" Elizabeth shook her fist at William's back as she came to stand in front of the fence. She kept her gaze locked on him. When he continued ignoring her, she cupped her hands and hollered, "Don't bother coming home again—I'm throwing your bed in the moat!"

"Mother, you know you're not in earnest." Lark wiped the sweat on her brow with the back of her hand.

"Am I not?" Elizabeth squeezed her lips closed and jammed her fists down at her sides, as though trying to keep from saying something she'd regret.

"If anyone is to blame, blame me. I begged Father to let me spar with him."

Her mother blinked at her, all her fury directed at Lark now. "Are you trying to kill yourself so you can ruin this wedding? I promise you, I shall have a double wedding, even if I have to stand your corpse up beside your sister."

"Lord Avenall might have something to say about marrying a corpse."

"Go ahead, make a jest of everything. You are too much like your father. When Lord Avenall finds you sew like a blind wench, and you couldn't spin cloth if the Virgin Mother came down and blessed the loom, or you don't know a mint sauce from moldy bread, he may wish he were marrying a corpse."

"Then mayhap we should go and dig one up for him."

"Your insolent tongue will get you in trouble one of these days." Elizabeth shook her finger at Lark. "What am I going to do with you? You're hopeless." She flapped her arms at her sides, sending the long sleeves of her gown fluttering near her thighs.

" 'Twas a jest, Mother. You should try to see the humor in life. Mayhap you wouldn't get so distraught if you did."

"Humor? You speak to me of humor, while you act like a mannish savage? You could at least take some interest in your own wedding. Helen diligently helps me as a dutiful daughter should. What have you done? You stay in the tilt yard and practice, so you can skewer our guests when they arrive."

"Why should I worry? The date is not set. Lord Blackstone has yet to consent to marrying Helen."

"When he gets a look at her, he'll gladly agree to the date I've set." Elizabeth cut her eyes at Lark and frowned, obviously measuring her against Helen's perfection.

"Of course he will." The smile faded as Lark tried to keep her expression blank, though the pain went straight to the center of her core.

"Aye, but look at you. You're clearly no beauty, and you've no womanly wiles like Helen to entice a husband. She knows how to please a man and will do well in her marriage, but you . . .'' She shook her head, sending the ends of her wimple flying. ''Mark my words, Lord Avenall will grow tired of your errant ways and probably beat you daily.''

''I can promise you, Mother, no man, be he husband or not, shall ever beat me.'' Lark crossed her arms over her chest and stubborn determination raised her chin.

''You are not as invincible as you seem to think, young lady. And I'll tell you something else you had better remember— your husband will own you for your entire life. Do you think he'll want a warrior in his bed? Nay, he will want a biddable wife, someone who knows how to take care of his castle and his lands and see to his needs. Someone like Helen.''

'' 'Tis a pity you didn't have twins when you had Helen.'' Lark hid the emotion in her voice. Helen had been thrown in her face since she could remember. By now, she should be used to hearing it, but each time it drove the thorn in deeper.

''Oh, Lark, you shouldn't speak so to me.''

'' 'Tis the truth.'' Lark saw the displeasure that always clouded Elizabeth's blue eyes. ''We both know you want me to be like Helen. But I'm not, nor shall I ever be.''

''Can I help it? Your sister is the epitome of a lady. If I bring her up to you, 'tis in hopes you will follow her example. You're ten and eight now, yet you have no idea how a lady should act. You are the eldest. You should be setting the example for your sister, but what do you do . . .'' Her hand gestured angrily toward the tilt yard.

''I'm proficient at fighting, Mother. 'Tis the only thing I do really well. I'm sorry it displeases you.''

''You're proficient with weapons, for it is the only thing you work hard at doing. I'm sure you do it deliberately. You and your father love to torment me.''

''That is not true.'' Lark sighed inwardly. Arguing with Elizabeth never changed anything. In a more patient tone, she said, ''I'll try to behave as you wish. Please don't be angry with Father for letting me in the tilt yard.''

"Oh, your father! Speak not of him. Every time I think of him it makes me want to scream. Now, if you don't wish to add more gray hairs to my head, you'll come into the castle. Helen has agreed to teach you how to make soap."

"For Lord Avenall's supper?" Lark quipped.

"Hah! There you go again. Stop it this instant! If you don't start to take this seriously, I shall personally see that your armor and horse are sold while your father is swilling ale in the village. That will put an end to this incessant need of yours to learn warfare." With that parting shot, her mother flounced off, back toward the castle.

Lark stood there, frowning at her mother's back, watching her long black braids whip against her waist. If pushed too far, Lark knew Elizabeth Mandeville would carry through with the threat. Lark also knew William would get her horse and armor back. Whenever they argued, it was over her. It had always been that way. And it wasn't likely to change.

She shook her head and strode toward the castle. Baltizar, her pet wolf, trotted out of the woods and came toward her. His gray-and-white coat glistened from a swim in the pond.

Lark bent and took his face in both her hands, touching her nose against his. The tip of his cold, wet nose on her skin made her grin at him. "You coward. Though I don't blame you for hiding. I can't blame Father either."

Lark stroked Baltizar's head and glanced toward the village. If only she could be there guzzling ale with her father. Instead she must face yet another of Elizabeth's gruelling lessons— which, she knew, would go in one ear and out the other. She thought of the task before her and the smile faded. A deep sigh left her lips as she strode toward the bailey.

Lark frowned at Helen. She stood near the garden, her petite frame bent over a huge iron pot. Dark smoke spiraled upward from the thick, bubbling liquid inside and swirled around Helen's hourglass figure and along the rolling waves of chestnut hair falling down her back. Her face, usually so ivory and flawless that it could make the Virgin Mother jealous, was tinted pink from the heat, making her appear even more comely. Every time she looked at Helen, Lark was reminded of her own tanned, leathery skin, curveless figure, and thick, unruly hair. By all rights she should hate her perfect sister, but no one who knew Helen could hate her.

Helen glanced up, her large brown eyes widening with pleasure. "Oh, Lark, there you are. Why are you scowling so?"

"Mother insisted I come to learn how to make soap."

"Oh." Helen glanced down and sighed. "Mother berated you. I wish she wouldn't."

" 'Tis no matter, I'm used to it." Lark bent over the pot and made a face. "What is in there? It looks like something we should feed to the pigs."

Helen chuckled, a tinkling little sound. " 'Tis goat tallow, wood ashes, and some of Mother's lavender. We need scented soap for the guests."

Lark flopped down on a bench and crossed her long thin, legs at the ankles. She watched Helen stirring the pot, her movements graceful, somehow gentle. Her arms looked so fragile that they might break if she applied too much force on the paddle.

"Do you wish me to help you stir?" Lark asked. "You look like you're getting tired."

"Nay, I'm fine." Helen shook her head and smiled serenely.

"I do not see why we have to worry about their smelly bodies. If they stink, we can make them stay in the stream for an hour or two."

Helen smiled. "You had better not let Mother hear you say that."

"It matters not whether she hears me say it. Naught I do or say pleases her."

"You don't try hard enough."

"Should I do everything she says, she would find some fault in it. Speaking of pleasing others, I've been meaning to ask you a question."

"What is it?" Helen said absently as she raised the paddle. She closely examined the thick brown drops running off the edge into the pot. "This will need more stirring."

"Helen, are you listening?"

"Aye." Helen glanced at Lark, looking flustered. "I'm sorry. Go ahead."

"I just wanted to ask you if you are agreeing to this match with the Earl of Blackstone only to please Mother?"

Helen let the paddle slip back into the pot. In a meek tone, she said, " 'Tis the best of the offers I've received. Mother says most marriages don't start out with love. I'll surely grow to love him."

"That is Mother talking. She wants an earl in the family and will sacrifice you to get him. How can you say you'll love a man you've never met?"

"I know he is handsome and wealthy. I'm sure he is kind. What else is there?"

Lark thought of Lord Blackstone. Kindness didn't come close to describing him. She didn't want to frighten Helen by telling her the truth. Lord Blackstone had gained the name Black Dragon in the Holy Land for the many battles he had won and the sheer numbers of Saracens he had killed. It was rumored his sword had been blessed by the archangel Gabriel, and it could cut through German steel as easily as through fresh-churned butter. No doubt the mere sight of him would send Helen into a swoon.

"I don't want Mother to ruin your life," Lark said. "If you wish, I'll speak to Father and tell him you've changed your mind."

"Oh, nay, I have agreed to wed Lord Blackstone. I shall honor my promise to Mother." She looked wistful. "You are so very lucky Lord Avenall loves you."

"You're only saying that to be kind. You certainly know he is only marrying me for my dowry. According to Mother, I've no qualities a man could love."

"Of course you do. You have a great many qualities."

"Name one." Lark crossed her arms over her chest and raised her brows at Helen.

"Well . . . I-I . . ."

Helen's discomfort made Lark grin. Helen couldn't keep a straight face. They both burst out laughing.

Helen wiped the tears out of her large eyes. "I thought of one—your herbs. You help a great many people with them."

"That is only because I'm looking for unsuspecting fools on whom to try out my new draughts and balms."

"Stop it, Lark. I know you take care of people because they are in need. And you may joke about Lord Avenall too, but I know you have loved him since he kissed you that time."

Lark remembered the kiss. She was but ten and five at the time. They had been arguing after she had drubbed him in the tilt yard. He had grabbed her and kissed her . . . and kissed her . . . and kissed her. Until she was dizzy from it. He'd touched her too, rubbing his hands against her neck and her back. Avenall had the most wonderful hands, softer than her own. She'd loved him from that moment on.

Since then, she'd had a terrible fear that he would realize how much she loved him. It was a weakness in her that she despised, for it made her vulnerable. Loving makes one vulnerable to pain—she'd learned that with Elizabeth. Time and again her mother had returned Lark's love with reproaches and scorn. She couldn't bear to have Avenall do the same thing. Nay, he would never know how much she loved him.

Helen was the only person in the world to whom Lark could tell her true feelings, but she'd never voiced her fear aloud and she wouldn't now, so she said, "Aye, I care for him, but if he should ask me, I'll deny it."

"Oh, you're terrible."

"I'm convinced the only thing besides my dowry that makes Lord Avenall attracted to me is that I do not cling to him. You remember that when you meet this Lord Blackstone. Never appear over-anxious—no matter what Mother may tell you. It'll give him an advantage over you he can use."

Helen glanced over at Lark, her eyes so large and brown

that they reminded Lark of a frightened doe's. "I'll remember your advice," she said, her voice barely audible.

Lark rose and grabbed Helen's hands, keeping her from stirring the soap mixture. "Listen to me. You need not suffer Lord Blackstone. I know you're frightened. If you want, I'll speak to this Lord Blackstone and tell him you're not interested in him."

Helen shook her head and swallowed hard. "Nay, I must marry him if he wants me." She smiled serenely and squeezed Lark's hand. "All will be well. Lord Blackstone shall be the perfect husband."

"I hope you're right." Lark was unable to still the nagging feeling in the pit of her stomach.

That night, after listening to another treatise on the virtues of duty, obedience, and holding one's tongue, Lark escaped the castle. In her oldest work gown, her hair hanging in wild disarray down her back, she headed toward the village.

Her light footsteps crunched along the path. Forest trees stood like sentinels guarding everyone and everything beneath their boughs. The moon hung in the crystal-clear night, its edge so low, it touched the tops of the trees. If she reached up, she felt as if she could touch it. Stars winked at her from an inky black sky.

Above the trees, she watched bats dipping and scooping up the night insects, the flutter of their wings barely audible. She breathed deeply of the scent of spring sap dripping from the pines and listened for Baltizar's footsteps. Earlier he had gone off to hunt. He did that quite often, sometimes not returning for days.

Gradually, the trees gave way to the village. Night had settled over the wattle-and-thatch cottages. In the darkness, their ugly brown exteriors looked like crumbling walls of pox-marked rock. Not a hint of candlelight streamed from the villeins' huts.

Several foraging pigs grunted at her as she strode past them. A breeze brushed the fetid odor of the middens across her path.

She grimaced as she came upon the inn, a simple two-story structure with a yellow mortar-and-stucco exterior, in need of whitewash. She hurried behind the inn to the private room Adwid, the innkeeper, kept for her father.

Candlelight flicked beneath a crack under the door. She heard rusty hinges creak as she stepped inside. The scent of stale ale and burned turnips hit her. Embers smoldered in the hearth, shooting dim, dancing shadows along the cracked yellow walls.

Ear-splitting snores came from the men passed out on the floor, some still clutching their mugs in their hands. Evel, Harold and Cedric were suspiciously absent, probably sharing a bed with the tavern keeper's daughters. Her brothers were naught if not lusty.

Several tables sat in the middle of the room. Her father occupied the top of one of them. His snores rang out above the din of the other men. A mug rested on his chest, moving up and down with each one of his deep breaths.

Lark gingerly avoided the men littering the floor and paused near her father. She shook him and whispered, "Father."

He grunted and waved her away. "Go away, go away . . . have a care."

" 'Tis me." Lark shook him again. "Wake up."

Her father cracked open one eye. "Oh, my sweet Pigeon, there you are," he said, his words slurred.

"You cannot stay the night here. Mother is expecting Lord Blackstone, and she will make your life hell if you do not come with me now. Please, wake up." Lark smelled the strong scent of ale on his breath and wondered if she would be able to get him home. She had to try, since she felt responsible for the argument that had brought him here.

"My sweet Elizabeth doesn't want me home." He chuckled, but it came out as a snort. "If she asks for me, tell her I'm too drunk to move . . ." Her father's eyes closed.

"Father." Lark shook him, but he started snoring again.

She rolled her eyes. "I'll get Evel to help me." She pulled

the earthen mug from her father's hand and kissed him on the forehead. "I'll be right back, don't move." She smiled at the ridiculousness of that statement and went in search of Evel.

She strode through a short hall. As she did, unrecognizable deep voices drifted to her ears. A strange feeling of danger made her pause behind the taproom door and listen.

"By! Open up yer ears, lads. The messenger said he were on his way here this eventide."

"How we supposed to kill this Sassenach? He's bound ta have a whole bleedin' army with him."

"Word was he were travelin' with only one knight. Now quit your grousin', Fish, and listen. I were thinkin' we'd catch 'em down by the stream near the road. There be plenty of trees for cover."

"Two knights on horseback ain't good odds. There bein' only five of us on foot."

"Och! Are ye gettin' a yellow streak in ye now, Fish? I'm thinkin' ye shoulda stayed home."

"I ain't yellow."

"Then quit yer whining. We'll have surprise on our side. Ye and Gonnie, ye'll be opposite me and Tic—whoa there, Alard. Not too much ale. You'll be needin' to get the arrow in his heart, not his arse. We're gettin' paid to kill the bastard, not wound him."

"Aye, we need the gold. Nee doot aboot it, this'll have to be me first sober blood lettin'." A mug slammed down on the table. A round of laughter echoed through the room.

Lark eased the door open a crack. The room was empty, save for five bedraggled Scots sitting at a table in a corner. Candlelight glowed off the grubby pelts jacketing their chests. Thick beards covered their faces. Their hair hung in long straggly waves around their shoulders, definitely in need of a thorough delousing and some of Helen's lavender soap.

Lark eased the door closed, chewing on her lip. Should she save a man's life or get her father home?

She heard the bench in the taproom thunk against the floor

as the men rose from the table. Several of them burped, while others broke wind. Their laughter faded; then the front door to the inn slammed closed.

Lark didn't hesitate. She opened the door and followed them out.

Chapter 2

Enough moonlight lit the night for Lark to see the Scots' hulking shadows swaying a hundred yards ahead of her. They were on foot, their pace no more than a trot, making it easy for her to trail them. Having lived near the border all her life, she knew Scotsmen had an uncanny ability to sense when they were being followed, so she stayed well hidden as they traveled south, along a stream bordering the road.

Lark listened to the gurgle of the moving water, whispering in the night. A slight breeze wafted across her face, bringing with it the mossy scent of the stream. Clumps of grass and twigs crunched softly beneath her boots as she kept low.

The Scots approached a thickly wooded glen, where the stream widened and a bridge buttressed the road. Reeds spiked up from the boggy marsh below, whipping strange shadows over the dark, glistening water.

The Scots neared the bridge and slowed. They were still on St. Vale land. Elizabeth had demanded that William build the bridge so the wheels of her cart would not sink in the marsh. Lark smiled, remembering how her father had grumbled for a week about the demands of haughty ladies.

They spoke now with hand gestures. The one who looked like the leader motioned to the others. They parted, three of them running across the road, ducking down near the railings of the bridge, while the other two stayed on the opposite side.

The din of approaching horses' hooves took Lark by surprise. She was at the bottom of the glen, not yet close enough to warn the riders. She took off running up the glen, trying to stay clear of the Scots.

Two riders appeared on the crest of a hill.

"Hark you! Stop! You'll be killed!" she yelled, running toward them.

Twenty yards still separated her from the road. Her gaze darted between the Scots and the riders. She watched them gallop past her, sending clouds of dirt out behind them. Already they were halfway into the glen.

She reached the road, hopped the ditch, and ran after them, waving her hands and screaming, "Wait! Wait!"

The two men finally slowed near the bridge. They turned to look at her, but it was too late.

Utter chaos erupted.

The Scots attacked, their battle cries cutting through the night air. The horses reared at the sudden appearance of the attackers. Arrows whizzed past the two riders.

Lark felt responsible for the riders' lives and ran right into the middle of the fray, heedless of the danger. Instinctively, she grabbed for her sword. When her hand met only her thigh, she remembered she didn't have it.

Metal hissed as the knights on horseback drew their swords. A deep battle cry rang out, rolling through the glen. It issued from the knight fighting at the fore, a large man by the breadth of his shoulders. The knights' broadswords collided with the Scots. The vicious clank of steel tolled relentlessly.

Enthralled by the battle, Lark didn't see the Scot standing near the edge of the bridge until he lifted a crossbow. He aimed it at the large knight. She charged toward the bowman. With all of her weight behind her, she rammed his side. The crossbow sailed over his shoulder and splashed into the bog.

"Bugger me!" The man grabbed Lark's shoulders to steady himself, but they both toppled off the bridge and into the marsh.

She hit the surface of the water back first. The man landed on top of her, knocking the breath out of her, plunging her down into the murky water. Every muscle in her body clenched at the shock of the cold water. It seeped into her nose, down her throat. She tried to raise her head, but quickly realized the man's hands were fastened around her throat.

Lark grabbed his wrists and yanked, but his fingers tightened like iron spikes against her windpipe. He pushed her head deeper into the muddy bottom. Slimy mud oozed up to her ears. Her heart pounded against her ribs, the pressure crushing her lungs. If she didn't take a breath soon, her chest would burst.

With all the strength she could muster, she kicked the man's groin, a move she always used as a last resort on her brothers.

He released her neck and floated to the side. Lark surfaced and gasped for air. Through mud-caked lashes, she saw the Scot turning to attack again. She drew back and slammed her fist into his nose.

"Damn you ta hell, bitch!" He looked ready to charge her again, but must have thought better of it. He stumbled through the muck and hobbled onto shore. After a bitter glare in her direction, he hobbled off toward the woods, holding his crotch with one hand and his nose with the other.

"That'll teach you to try and drown someone!" Lark yelled at his retreating back and shook her throbbing hand. Her knuckles would probably be swollen in the morning, but the Scot's swollen parts would be much more painful. The knowledge that she'd broken his nose, among other things, brought a wide grin to her lips.

She stood up, her woolen gown so laden with water and mud that it felt like armor. Her boots made a sucking noise in the mud, each step a balancing act to keep from falling back into the water. She trudged toward the edge of the marsh, feeling her torn bliaut slapping against her thigh. The mud on her face ran down her forehead and into her eyes. She blinked and tried to wipe it away, but only managed to smear it over her eyelids and cheeks.

When she could see again, she stumbled toward the bridge, pausing near the edge. Three Scots lay dead. The fourth had the large knight's broadsword in his belly.

For a moment, the knight held the Scot aloft, suspended only by the sword and what seemed like inexhaustible strength in the knight's arms.

Lark's jaw dropped open.

The Scot was no lightweight. Indeed, he looked as large as her father, yet the knight's inhuman strength didn't waver. Lark felt sure he could hold his attacker aloft forever, if he chose to. Finally, the knight pulled back. The blade made a sucking sound as it left its victim's stomach.

The Scot's knees buckled. He gasped out a curse and crumpled into a heap on the bridge.

An eerie silence loomed in the night, coupling with the smell of blood and death. Even the night insects had fallen silent. Her ragged breaths sounded loud in her ears.

"I wanted to keep one of them alive." The large knight's deep voice split the silence. He glanced ruefully down at the fallen bodies.

"How could we?" the smaller knight said. "It was either them or us."

"I suppose you're right."

Thunk. The smaller knight's feet hit the ground as he dismounted. "I'll check on them."

Lark watched him bend over the slain men, checking for signs of life. Her gaze returned to the massive knight's back, the breadth of which could rival the oaken door to her chamber.

As if the hulking knight felt her staring at him, he whipped his destrier around and glared at her. Hair the color of coal fell in dark waves down to his shoulders, gleaming a dark, steely gray in the moonlight. Shadows blanketed his face, but she felt his eyes boring into her. The full moon hung low behind him. So large a man was he that his dark silhouette filled up the whole blue sphere.

Lark swallowed hard, hit with wave after wave of the scalding malevolence that emanated from him.

He said naught, just stared at her for a long moment. Then he spurred his horse toward her. *Clop-Clop-Clop.*

His destrier's hooves hit the wooden bridge. The steady din pierced every nerve in Lark's body. She flinched and took a step back. Then another. The knight's image grew larger and larger.

He reined in beside her, looming over her. The arm holding an enormous broadsword rested across the pommel of his saddle as he glared down at her.

Lark stared at the blood glistening on the tip of the sword and decided it might be prudent to speak first. " 'Tis too bad you didn't hear me, my lord. I was at the top of the glen, yelling, yet you rode right past me. You should've stopped sooner, for all of this could have been avoided ..." Lark paused, realizing she was babbling like her mother.

"Had you not called out at all, we would have ridden right past your friends, and they couldn't have attacked so easily." The deep voice purred with a stormy undertone.

"I was only trying to warn you ere you came close to the Scots."

"You lie to save yourself."

His large fist clenched around the hilt of the sword, and she added in a more restrained tone, "I am no liar. You can't think that I plotted this ambush with those Scots?"

"Why should I not?"

Lark licked her lips, hating this unfamiliar churning he caused in her. She gulped past the growing tightness in her throat. "I speak the truth. I'm innocent. I heard the Scots plotting to kill you at an inn in St. Vale village. I followed them so I could warn you. Who are you anyway? Why do they want to kill you?"

"You should know since you're in league with these murderers." His face moved toward the moonlight, and an odd coppery-red hue blazed in his eyes.

"I told you. I don't know these murdering swines. Would I

have saved your back from an arrow if I were with them? If I'd wanted to kill you, believe me, you'd be dead by now.''

"You are more proficient at lying than at murder."

"I assure you, I saved your life."

The knight drew himself up, the leather of his saddle creaking beneath the weight. "Aye, just like you called out to save us."

"I did! One of them had a crossbow aimed at your back. You would be dead at this moment if I had not thwarted the knave."

"I see only four dead bodies. Where is this knave?" The ruthlessness in his face softened as he sneered.

"After I broke his nose, he escaped into the woods."

"You broke his nose?" He grunted under his breath, then his voice turned sharp enough to part each hair on her head. "If this knave does exist, then you helped him and lie now to save his hide and yours. Liars deserve swift justice."

Lark was about to protest further, but the knight raised his sword. Moonlight shimmered off the long, sharp blade. After a fleeting glance in his direction, she hiked up the hem of her gown and darted up the road. It galled her to run from a battle. But she didn't have a weapon, and she had never crossed swords with a knight who wielded such a massive broadsword as this Goliath.

The destrier's hooves hit the ground like huge boulders behind her, growing louder . . . louder.

Clods of churning dirt hit her knees and calves. She felt the heavy breath of the animal on her arm as it drew abreast of her. Lark darted to the side and leaped across a ditch. Her feet never touched the other side. He grabbed the back of her bliaut, and she sailed through the air.

She squeezed her eyes closed, waiting for the blow that would hopefully send her to heaven. How long had it been since her last confession?

Before she could recall, something hit the front of her body. Her eyes flew open, only to meet with a large knee near her cheek. A thick thigh pressed against her breasts and one beneath her abdomen. Her elbow dangled near a long shin.

"Let me go! I'm innocent." She tried to turn her head and look at him, but all she could see was a corded thigh. "I didn't try to kill you. I saved your life, which I'm beginning to regret wholeheartedly."

He whacked her on the bottom with the flat of his hand. "If you try escaping again, when I'm done with you, you'll think hell a paradise."

Lark squeezed her eyes closed, feeling the blow to her bottom still stinging. Her head was filling with blood, her temples pounding. She stared at his boot in the stirrup and felt the thin tether on her patience snap. "Kill me, then. You mean to anyway."

"That remains to be seen."

Lark screwed up her face at the taunting threat behind his words. Somehow she had to escape this Goliath.

Stoke de Bracy, the Earl of Blackstone, rode back toward the bridge, feeling the wench's bony ribs rubbing against his groin. Her wet, muddy gown had soaked through his tunic and braies, and he could feel the uncomfortable wetness between his legs. She smelled too, like sour, decayed bread. Her thick, mud-covered hair slapped against the new suede boots he'd just bought. By the time he reached his friend, Rowland, he was scowling.

Rowland paused as he lined up the last of the four dead Scots along the side of the road. "That is the last of them."

"Nay, one got away," the wench said.

"Aye—you," Stoke grumbled under his breath.

"Ah!" Rowland raised his blond brows at the wench, his blue eyes twinkling. "I see you found another one."

"I'll have you know, I'm not one of them." The wench tried to raise her head so she could see Rowland.

"Either you will hold that tongue until you are addressed, or you shan't be able to sit on that bony arse of yours for a week."

"What need have I of an arse if you mean to kill me?"

"You'll soon find out."

He felt her stiffen. He couldn't tell if it was from fear or from the innate brazen arrogance in her. She had dared look him in the eye after her friends had tried to kill him, and she spoke to him as an equal. It didn't even occur to the wench to lower her gaze. Most women cowered in his presence, but not this one.

"Should we bury the bodies?" Rowland asked.

"Nay, leave them for the ravens." Stoke resheathed his sword.

"What do you mean to do with the wench?"

"I'm sure she knows who's behind these attempts on my life. I mean to get the truth out of her."

Rowland walked over to his destrier and mounted. "She looks like the type to speak naught but lies."

"I resent that remark." The brazen wench squirmed and raised her muddy head. "What do you know of my character— you, whom I've never met in all my life—"

Stoke slapped her on the bottom, cutting off her words.

"Oooo! She's a vicious one." Rowland smiled. "Better not turn your back on her."

"I don't intend to." Stoke stared down at the wench's bottom, feeling it pressing sensuously against his groin. "I'll see you on the morrow."

Rowland nodded with a crooked grin on his face. "Before you question her, I'd dunk her in the stream. She looks like she's crawling."

"I'll have you know, I had a bath just this night. When was the last time you felt water upon your own backside?"

"We can add impudence to her long list of qualities." One of Rowland's ready grins turned up the corners of his lips. "Try not to kill her ere you get the truth out of her. Good eventide." Rowland kicked his warhorse and galloped down the road.

Stoke scowled at Rowland's back, then felt the wench wiggle

against his member again. His scowl deepened as he spurred Shechem into a gallop. In moments, they cleared the glen. He found a safe spot on the edge of the wood and reined in near a stream.

"I'm warning you, if you run from me again, you'll regret the consequences." He tossed her over his shoulder and dismounted. He frowned at how much she weighed. This was no featherweight woman. She weighed as much as a man. And by the feel of her hard thighs, she was not soft like a woman either.

"Let me go—" She gritted her teeth and added, "Please."

Stoke plopped her down near the stream and stared at the lying wench. Her hair fell in dirty, matted clumps around her waist. She was taller than he had thought; her head probably reached the top of his chin. She looked more boy than woman, with the old muddy gown sticking to her flat chest and boyish figure.

"I'm a lady. You have no right to hold me prisoner." She pushed aside the hair that obscured her face and shook her fist at him.

"Aye, I can see that."

"I am, and you'll regret holding me."

He folded his arms over his chest and glared at her. "I think not, my lady." He drawled his last words through his teeth.

"I'll not be mocked by the likes of you."

"Think you I'm simple enough to believe the lies that roll off your tongue?"

" 'Tis the truth."

"If you're a lady, I'm King Richard." Stoke stared at the lying wench, at the fiery golden eyes glaring at him. The moonlight struck them in such a way to make them gleam yellow. They were the strangest color. A Tigress's eyes.

They mesmerized him for a moment; then his gaze dropped to the rip on the side of her gown. It ran all the way up to the middle of her thigh, exposing a long, thin expanse of white flesh. She had the longest legs he'd ever seen on a woman. An image of those legs wrapped around him flashed through his mind. He shook off the unbidden vision and ground his teeth together. The wench had just lured him into a trap. She was his enemy. He couldn't feel anything but loathing for her.

"Why are you scowling at me like that? Do you mean to intimidate me with your eyes?"

Stoke stared at her muddy face from behind narrowed brows. "Take off your clothes and clean yourself in the stream."

"I'll not disrobe. I don't see why you can't torture me fully clothed."

"Unfortunately, I'd like naught better, but since your clothes are covered in mud, and I wear enough of it on me already, you'll have to strip and bathe."

"I won't take off my gown, and I don't know who wants you dead." Her voice grew to a fevered pitch. "Would you have me make up a lie? I vow before the saints and the Virgin Mother, I wasn't with those Scots."

Stoke took a step toward her. "Take off your clothes, or I'll take them off for you."

She held up her hands, warding him off as if he were the devil. "I'll do it myself rather than suffer your touch."

He paused, crossed his arms over his chest, and stared at those sinfully long legs.

"Well?" She stared at him as if expecting him to do something.

"Well, what?"

"Turn around."

A smirk turned up one corner of his mouth. "Do you think me ignorant enough to turn my back on you so you can plunge a blade in it?"

"Even if I had a knife I would not kill you. You have my word of honor on that."

"Honor?" He shot her a contemptuous look. "Murderesses have no honor."

"Oh, what is the use! There is no talking to you. This is all the gratitude I'm to get for saving your wretched life. So be it. All I ask is you give me a swift death, so I can rise from the grave and haunt you for the rest of your days.''

She took off her boots and flung them at him. He ducked. One sailed past his head. As he came up, she turned and bolted into the stream.

''Murdering witch,'' Stoke mumbled under his breath and ran after her.

With one gazelle-like leap, she cleared the stream bank and raced toward the woods.

He cursed, running through the stream and up the bank, his boots slipping in the mud. The white of her leg flashed as she ran past the trees ahead of him. She was quick and strong for a woman. He increased his pace, ducking limbs, shoving leaves out of his face.

He drew close, sensing her fear. He could overtake her, but he kept the same pace, waiting for the fear to eat at her, to cause her to make a mistake. She did. She darted to the left. He dove for her. They both careened to the ground.

Stoke landed on top of her back. She twisted and hit at him with one fist, but he grabbed her wrists, pinning them above her head.

''I warned you not to run from me,'' he said between breaths. ''Now you'll learn to obey me.''

''Never! I would rather obey the devil. At least he can sense when you're not lying about something.'' Though her voice was filled with bravado, he felt her body trembling beneath him.

''I'll break you of your insolent tongue ere this night is out.'' He jerked her wrists down behind her back, then rolled off her, pulling her over on her side to face him.

''I'll not be broken by the likes of you.''

He gazed into her defiant face, the proud, stubborn chin, the rebellious golden eyes, at her lips pressed together with a determined hardness that did little to disguise a pouty bottom lip.

Her hot, uneven breaths brushed against his face and lips. He grew aware of her body pressed against him, the softness of her skin against his fingers. His hand pinning her wrists against her back rested in the hollow of her waist, his forearm meeting the bottom of her breasts. He meant to pull her up to her feet, meant to thrust her away. Instead he buried his fingers in the thick muddy hair at her nape and jerked her face to his for a kiss.

Chapter 3

Lark felt his wavy, shoulder-length hair brush her cheeks as he guided her head toward his. The strange coppery red in his eyes held her captive. An odd force, such that she'd never felt before, drew her toward him. It was so potent, so all-consuming, that it touched a primal urge deep inside her. She found herself raising her mouth to meet his. Just before their lips touched, something flashed in the corner of Lark's eye.

She turned in time to see the Scot who'd tried to drown her charging toward them, his raised dirk gleaming in the moonlight. His bulbous nose looked even larger since she'd broken it. His eyes, set deep in his bearded face, looked black and enormous with rage.

"Watch out! There's a Scot charging toward your back."

"You don't fool me with your lies."

A war cry rang from the Scot as he thrust the blade toward the knight's back.

"By Judas!" the knight growled and rolled off her, grabbing the Scot's hand.

Lark froze, her gaze fixed on the tip of the blade, a hairs-breadth from her chest. She sucked in her breath, feeling her heart slamming against her ribs. The Scot's hand wavered under the strength of the knight. She knew that only the knight's sheer will was keeping the Scot from plunging the blade into her, for the two men looked matched in strength.

Finally, the knight won the contest and shoved the Scot's hand back. Lark let out the breath she'd been holding and rolled aside. The Scot plunged the blade toward the knight's throat. Before the blade touched him, the huge knight grabbed the Scot's hand. Then a kick in the stomach sent the Scot stumbling backwards several steps.

The Scot smiled, as if enjoying the fray, and leaped toward the black knight again. As he did so, he called over his shoulder to Lark, "I'll deal with you later, darlin'."

With relentless tenacity, the Scot slashed wildly with the dirk. The knight reeled back, just missing the blade.

Lark lunged to the right to keep from being trampled. She tried to crawl away, but a tug on her collar brought her up short. Behind her, she saw the black knight gripping her bliant as he continued to fight the Scot.

Frantic to get away, she grasped the front of her gown and shift and ripped the old, worn material down the center. She stumbled forward and heard his deep growl. Without looking back, she ran into the woods and left him holding her clothes and fighting the Scot. Cold, damp air swirled around her naked skin. She shivered and kept running.

Stoke cursed, catching a glimpse of her naked body in the moonlight, feeling the wet wool of her bliaut and shift in his fist. Out of the corner of his eye, he saw the Scot's blade come at him again. His attacker was a large man, his girth and strength equaling Stoke's own.

Stoke caught the fist holding the knife before it plunged into his chest. He used the momentum of the Scot's weight, jammed his feet in the man's gut, and threw him over the side of his body. The Scot hit the ground with a loud thud.

Before the Scot could move, Stoke rolled to his feet and

attacked. The Scot was large, but he was slow. Stoke leaped on him and wrestled the Scot's arms down to the ground, pounding the one holding the knife until the Scot dropped it.

The odor of ale, blood and sweat hung about the Scot. He glared down at the snarling, heaving man. "Tell me about the wench."

The Scot's snarl turned into a wicked smile, showing his rotten teeth. "For a Sassenach, she ain't half bad when her legs are spread."

"Is she in your gang?" Stoke growled through his teeth.

"Aye."

"Does she live in your clan?"

"Nae likely, she's a Sassenach. They'd roast her and hang on her a spit." His hatred for all the English came through his voice.

Stoke jammed his elbow against the Scot's windpipe, almost crushing it. "Where does the wench live?"

He coughed and gagged out, "I dinna know."

"We shall see how much you know." Stoke kept his elbow against the Scot's neck as he shoved him on his side. He thrust his arms down behind him and pulled the Scot to his feet.

The Scot chose that moment to attack.

He rammed Stoke with his back, jerking his arms free. Stoke lost his patience and charged the Scot, shoving him forward all the way to a tree trunk.

The Scot hit the trunk, then jerked and twitched. A loud rattling breath left his mouth. His head lulled forward against the tree trunk and appeared frozen there.

Half expecting him to charge again, Stoke eyed the Scot.

Until he saw a broken, jagged limb impaling the middle of his back.

"Judas's hell!" he murmured. He had wanted to keep the Scot alive so he could question him. A small stream of blood trickled from the Scot's swollen nose. Stoke leaned closer, remembering that the wench had mentioned she'd broken the nose of one of his attackers.

Indeed, this man's nose looked recently broken, the area

beneath his eyes already turning black and blue. Stoke shook
his head. Not for one moment did he believe a woman could
possibly break a man's nose. Likely the Scot had recently
entered a fray with one of his friends and come out the loser.
Another one of her lies.

More of the wench's words flitted through his mind. She
had said there were five Scots. He recalled her warning that
the Scot was at his back. She had been telling the truth on
those two scores. It must be that she didn't feel any loyalty to
the murdering knave. Her kind never did.

Her kind. What kind was she? He had noticed her cultured
words, as if she had lived in a noble household. Probably she
had worked as a lady's maid, grown tired with it, and taken
up with the Scots. She must be a good mummer.

But not good enough. His lip curled in a predatory grin as
he strode toward his horse. He could not get her out of his
mind—the way her body felt beneath his, the heat of her lips
as she raised them up to his. He'd get the kiss that was stolen
from him. And much more. Tracking her was going to be a
pleasure.

It didn't take long for the walls of St. Vale to rise up before
Lark. The forest was a second home to her. She spent many
an hour gathering herbs in it. She knew every squirrel nest,
every stag crossing, every trail left by wild boars, every lichen
patch and hillock. And the quickest routes that would take her
home.

She left the woods and crept up behind St. Vale. The tall
gray walls shimmered blue in the moonlight. Not five feet away
the postern gate was hidden within a tangle of nettles and
brambles. She glanced longingly at the hidden portal, but it
was impossible to fight the thorns naked, so she strode past it
toward the front of the castle.

Footsteps on the parapet made her leap to the wall and press
her back against it. A guard's shadow moved across the ground
near her feet. When the footsteps faded away, she ran around

the side of the castle. As she neared the drawbridge, she heard voices echoing along the path leading to the village.

Quickly, she remembered her nakedness and darted behind the east wall. She pressed her back against it, feeling the icy stones next to her spine. Cold and shivering, she felt a wave of goosebumps on her arms and waited for the people to pass.

The voices drew closer.

"Oh, sing me to sleep, my fair maiden . . ." Lark recognized her father's discordant singing.

"You'd better be quiet, Father. You don't want to alert Mother we're home," Evel, her eldest brother, said.

"Aye, she didn't seem too happy when we left the tilt yard earlier," one of the twins said. "I would not want her to put a rat's tail in your soup."

"And she would too. The woman loves to torment me. You know she threatened to throw my bed in the moat." Her father raised his voice now, yelling, "Elizabeth, my darling wife, should I sleep in the moat?"

Lark peeked around the wall. "Shhh! Father."

"Is that my little Pigeon?" her father said. Cedric and Harold held him up by his arms, and when he turned to look at her, he pulled them with him, almost overturning the three of them.

"Whoa there." Evel grabbed his father while the twins gained their balance.

"Father, you must go into the castle and be quiet," Lark said, not wanting to face her mother at the moment. She hoped her father would listen to her. Usually, she had more sway over him than her brothers.

"Come out, come out, Pigeon. I can't see anything but your head. There's two of them—nay, three." Her father squeezed his eyes closed, then opened them again.

Lark rolled her eyes. "I can't come out."

"Why?" Harold and Cedric asked at the same time.

Lark felt a familiar eerie feeling go through her. It happened every time the twins said the same thing. After shaking it off, she said, "I have no clothes."

Her father glanced first at Harold, then at Cedric. "Have you two been playing games on your sister again?"

"Nay, Father," Harold spoke.

"You know we've been at the inn," Cedric added. "We brought you home so you wouldn't get in trouble with Mother."

"Ah! So you did." He wavered on his feet and looked back at Lark. "Where are your clothes?"

She searched for an appropriate lie. "You know how Mother hates it when I go for a dip in the pond. Well, after one of her tedious sewing lessons I went to the pond, then Baltizar—the furry beasty—ran off with my gown."

"Why is your face brown, Pigeon?" Her father hooded his eyes as if it might help him see straighter. "Is that mud? Does not look like you went swimming."

"I fell when I ran after Baltizar. When I get my hands on the wily beast, he'll regret acting the rogue." Hoping to change the subject, she turned and motioned toward Evel. "Please, may I borrow your mantle?"

"I'll let you use mine for a price." Harold snickered along with his brother.

Lark shot them a glance. For as long as she could remember the twins had tormented her. This time was no exception. "If you're not going to help me, then help Father. Please take him to his bed . . . and try to keep him quiet."

"You can't order us about," Cedric said.

"Do as your sister bids you," William said agreeably.

They glared at her, then helped William onto the drawbridge. She turned back to Evel and saw the scowl on his face.

"Here, you might need this." He threw his mantle at her.

"Thank you." Lark accepted the garment and pulled it around her. "At least I have one noble brother." She smiled at him, then fell in step beside him.

He studied the mud on her hair and face. "What have you done now?"

"'Tis a long story, which I had rather just forget." She quickly changed the subject. "Thank you for seeing Father home."

"I knew we wouldn't be able to live with Mother if I didn't."

Lark heard the din of hooves pounding the road behind her—an all-too-familiar sound. She grabbed Evel's arm. "If you care anything for me, tell the knight coming you haven't seen me. He'll leave once he knows I'm not here."

"But—"

Lark took off running over the drawbridge, then disappeared into the bailey, leaving Evel with his mouth agape and exasperation in his eyes.

Stoke reined in near the tall figure. He reached down to grab the wench, but short-cropped black hair and sharp male features made him drop his hand. "Have you seen a tall wench—blond hair, most likely naked?"

"If I had, I would have better things to do than speak to you." The slightly hostile tone in the young man's voice belied the grin on his face.

"I thought I saw her come this way."

"You're mistaken. What has this wench done?"

"She was with a group of men who attacked me."

"I haven't seen her," the young man replied too abruptly. Evidently, he realized it, for his brows furrowed while he snapped a fleeting glance toward the bailey.

Not taken in by the lie, Stoke glared down at the young man. "You know where she is. She must service you along with every other man near here. I want the wench. Tell me where you're hiding her."

"My word is my honor." The young man bristled. "I'm Evel Mandeville, heir to St. Vale. Unless you wish to face me on the field, you will have to take my word on it."

Stoke had forgotten where he was in his haste to find the wench. In a more affable tone, he said, "Your sister must be Lady Helen?"

"Aye." Evel's brows shot up in surprise. Then his gaze probed Stoke's face.

"I'm Stoke de Bracy, the Earl of Blackstone. I'm expected."

The young man looked speechless. He glanced nervously toward the bailey again. In an extremely loud voice, he said, "Then you'll be staying with us."

"How else can I meet your sister?"

The young man appeared to realize the absurdity of his own question and shifted on his feet. "That is true, my lord. My mother has been expecting you."

Stoke gave his future brother-in-law a final leer, then rode over the drawbridge, listening to the hollow thump of Shechem's hooves on the wooden planks. The wench was in St. Vale somewhere; he could almost smell her fear. He meant to find her ere the night was out. All he had to do was follow Evel. Surely he would lead Stoke to her.

He scanned the bailey as he dismounted, keeping one eye on Evel. Moonlight glistened off the gray walls, casting long triangular shadows out into the bailey. Stoke glanced at the chapel, with its pointed spire, then at the rambling, thatch-roofed stable. He scanned the long row of stalls for any sign of her. All he saw were horses, their tails swatting flies. Near the stable, a tall hay rick loomed against the night sky. His gaze moved around the base of the keep, past two hounds sniffing at a large muck pile. Near it, a row of thatched-roof workshops stood, no doubt housing a smithy, a master armorer, and a carpenter. No sign of the wench anywhere.

"What have we here? A visitor?" A man's drunken slur rang out.

Stoke glanced toward the huge doors that lead to the hall. Three men stood before them. Two men were supporting the one in the middle.

Evel strode up beside him. "That is my father and my brothers. Come. I'll introduce you. You'll forgive my father's state—he's overindulged. You can leave your horse. I'll send someone to take care of it."

Stoke said naught, only followed Evel. He paused in front of his future father-in-law. He was an older man, though he didn't have the usual paunch that accompanied age, nor was he balding. Thick, tawny blond hair covered his head; streaks of silver gray slashed across each temple.

"Father, this is the Earl of Blackstone. Lord Blackstone, this is my father, William Mandeville. And my brothers, Harold and Cedric."

Stoke nodded to the two young men holding up their father. They looked exactly alike, their blond hair gleaming in the moonlight. Twins were thought to be ill-starred, and most were drowned at birth. How did these two escape?

"Well, well, pleased to finally meet the Black Dragon," William said. "I've heard minstrels sing your triumphs. You don't really fly, do you?"

"Believe not half the things you hear of me." Stoke stared over William's head at the archway in front of the hall doors, searching for any sign of the wench.

"I'm glad to meet you anyway." William slapped at Stoke's shoulder, but missed, hitting the air in front of Stoke's chest. "Ah, but are you sure you don't have wings? I would dearly love to see you fly. It would please a jaded old warrior like me to have a winged son-in-law." He threw back his head and laughed, the deep sound bouncing off the bailey walls.

Stoke stiffened, his scowl deepening.

"Come, come. My wife will be pleased you are finally here." He leaned closer to Stoke and whispered, "I wouldn't tell her you can't fly. She has high expectations of your character. She thinks all earls can fly." William turned to Evel. "Where is my Pigeon? I want her to meet the Flying Dragon." He called louder. "Pigeon, where are you!"

"I'll get her, Father," Evel said in a placating tone.

Stoke glanced at Evel, then back at William Mandeville. He had heard the Baron Mandeville was eccentric, but keeping pigeons? And wanting Stoke to meet them? There surely was more at work within the man than eccentricity.

He waited until the twins guided William ahead of them; then he stepped in front of Evel. "Does your father keep pigeons as pets?" Stoke kept his voice low.

"Nay."

"Why then did he want me to meet one?"

Evel's gaze darted to his father's back, then shifted nervously to Stoke. A muscle in his jaw twitched as he said, "To be honest, we just lost our swine herder. Her name was Pigeon. A great loss to my father. He can't seem to accept her death." He glanced around the bailey, as if he expected this Pigeon's ghost to appear at any moment.

"Your father allows women to tend his swine?" Stoke's skepticism came through in his voice.

"Aye, he took pity on this particular simpleton. She was a creature to be pitied, always rolling in mud, losing her clothes. A nasty creature—mute too. Tending the pigs kept her out of trouble, and though she couldn't utter one sensible syllable, she could grunt and the pigs understood her." He shrugged. "She was very devoted to my father, and the pigs. I'm not sure which one she admired more."

"I see." Stoke admired William Mandeville for his compassion, but to allow a touched-in-the-head woman to herd his pigs? Stoke shook his head.

Evel remained pensively silent beside him. Stoke listened to William Mandeville's drunken humming and whistling and watched him stagger, which forced his sons to pull his listing body up straight after every step.

Stoke felt as if someone were watching him. He glanced toward what he thought must be the retainers' barracks. Something moved in the shadows. Or was it his eyes playing tricks? He couldn't be certain. The moon had slid behind a cloud, and darkness blanketed the bailey.

He frowned and thought of the wench. Her image formed vividly in his mind. She wasn't comely, he decided, nor as voluptuous as he liked his women, but as bony as a sick mule. She had little or no breasts to stir a man. Though her tongue worked well enough.

Indeed, she could rile a deaf monk. Had she employed her tongue in pleasuring a man as much as she did in vexing him, she could be a rich whore. Nor was she modest or biddable as a woman should be. She was everything Stoke loathed. Cunning.

Crafty. Brazen. Loud-mouthed. Yet, never had he felt more compelled to master or possess a woman.

He strode into the hall, scrutinizing Evel, listening to William's drunken grunts echo against the stone walls. Torches burned along both sides of a hallway. A tapestry of flowers and fruit graced one wall. Step for step, he matched Evel's strides, unwilling to let him get away from his side. Stoke knew Evel could lead him to the wench. His thoughts were still on finding her, so when they entered the hall, the sound of a woman's screech barely pierced his mind.

"No, Elizabeth, not my cup!" William yelled.

Harold and Cedric flung William aside and fell to the floor.

"Duck!" Evel yelled as he pressed himself against the wall.

Stoke didn't see the heavy gold chalice until it hit him square in the temple. He saw double for a moment. Then everything went black.

Stoke felt something cold moving across his brow and opened his eyes. A woman took the cloth away from his forehead, then stared down at him. Her thick black braid fell over one shoulder, gleaming in the candlelight. She was comely, with an oval face, and appeared to be in her forties. Worry lines flared out from the corners of her eyes and between her brows. Something in her vivid blue eyes spoke of guarded pain, a strife within her that she'd had to live with for some time.

He had witnessed the same look on his first wife, Cecily, for the whole two years of their marriage, after she had ripped his heart out and flung it back in his face. He wondered what secret hell this woman had brought upon herself as Cecily had.

"Allow me to say how very sorry I am I lost my temper. I vow, I only saw my William and when I did, I just let my temper get the better of me."

Stoke grimaced, then touched the knot on his temple. "You are the one who hit me?"

"Aye, I am Lady Elizabeth, Lord Mandeville's wife, and I'm sorely ashamed of my behavior. It was unpardonable. Had

I but known you were behind my husband, I wouldn't have thrown the chalice. Oh, you must forgive me.'' Her cheeks flushed as she glanced down at her hands.

Stoke grunted a reply and knew now William Mandeville was witless. Any man who couldn't control his wife must be touched in the head.

"How are you?" Rowland spoke from a chair near the foot of the bed, the worry in his eyes belying the grin on his face.

Stoke looked at him. "I'll live."

"Felled by a cup." Rowland shook his head. His gray eyes burned devilishly as he said, "I hope word of this does not get around. I would hate to hear a bard's song recounting the mishap." He flashed a smile at Stoke.

Stoke was used to Rowland's wry wit and glowered at him for it.

"Oh, Sir Rowland, we would never breathe a word of it," Lady Elizabeth gasped. "We cannot have your reputation disparaged so." She smiled at Stoke as her dark brows narrowed slightly. "We expected you earlier, my lord. Helen was very disappointed when you didn't join us at table. Sir Rowland said you were waylaid by business. I hope it shan't take you away from us again before you have decided upon Helen."

Stoke and Rowland shared a glance. Then Stoke noticed the all-too eager gleam in Lady Elizabeth's eyes. An abrupt trapped feeling rose up in him and made him say, "I cannot be sure, my lady."

"Oh, dear, I fear you are not pleased with us."

"He will be pleased once he sees the Lady Helen," Rowland said, grinning.

Stoke glowered back at Rowland, knowing his friend had said this to pique his interest. But Stoke found the room they had carried him to much more interesting at the moment. He glanced past Rowland's shoulder at a collection of battle-axes, displayed haphazardly and making odd-angled V's along one wall. Axes, maces, and swords of every size covered the rest of the walls. Clothes were haphazardly dumped in piles on the floor, along with a suit of armor. Bottles, with various colored liquids in them, sat on a desk next to several books. A chair was pulled out from the desk, the stuffing falling out of the cushion from the holes on the side.

"Oh, please," Lady Elizabeth gasped, seeing him looking about. "I beg you not to look at this room. It belongs to my daughter, Lark. She is not fastidious like Helen, though I plead with that child every minute of the day to tidy this room."

"Tidy," Stoke echoed, wondering if he were not in a torture chamber instead of a lady's bedroom. He thought of how alluringly perfect Cecily's room had been, how the walls were covered with bright tapestries she'd embroidered, how the chairs looked so delicate that he was afraid to sit in them for fear of breaking them. He tried to imagine what sort of woman would keep such a room. No doubt one bent on living in disorder and interested in killing. A vision of the wench formed in his mind, and his brows met. Something in the room reminded him of her. Lady Elizabeth's voice drew his attention.

"I would not have had my sons bring you in here, but 'twas the closest bed." Lady Elizabeth sighed. "I would have cleaned up this room long ago, but Lark refuses to let anyone step foot in here. To be honest, 'tis a good thing she does not." Elizabeth glanced around the room, her face screwing up.

"I see why," Stoke said. "Tell me, what does Lady Lark look like?"

"Very tall, thin, long blond hair. But why do you ask?" Lady Elizabeth looked at Stoke, perplexed.

"Just curious." Stoke held back the wicked grin that wanted to make free with his lips. "Tell me, where is your daughter?"

"I really couldn't say. She goes off on her own quite often. I've preached to her that young ladies should not do such things, but my husband lets her run wild. Heaven only knows where she has gone."

Stoke kept his expression bland.

Lady Elizabeth searched his face and blurted, "Now that I think on it, I believe she went to the inn to bring home my husband. She didn't come in with him, though." She saw Stoke's brows lower and added, "You mustn't think Helen does such things. She would never do that. She's naught like her sister.''

''I should hope not, my lady.''

''Please forgive me. I've rambled on so. I'll fix some tea for your head. I imagine it throbs. Tea will help you sleep. When you feel better on the morrow, you can meet my daughter, Helen. I'm sure you'll agree to the marriage once you see her.''

Stoke raised his hand to tell her he didn't need the tea, but his finger jammed in a hole in the coverlet. The worn material ripped as he pulled his finger out. He glanced up to find Lady Elizabeth, but she had already left the room.

Stoke dropped his hand near his side, then shook his head at the five-inch tear in the coverlet. He felt something poking his side and reached down, pulling out a dagger from beneath the sheets.

''Ah, an addition to Lady Lark's lair.'' Rowland emphasized his words by motioning around the room.

''Aye, but I don't think they should allow Lady Lark to have weapons.'' He glanced at the back of the door.

Deep indentations, the size of a dagger blade, made a choppy pattern across the oak, an indication the Lady Lark liked to practice her throwing techniques from her bed. He picked up the dagger and threw it at the door. It stuck in one of the holes in the wood and wobbled.

Rowland gazed at the dagger and asked, ''Are you thinking what I'm thinking?''

''Aye.'' Stoke grimaced, then swung his long legs down onto the floor and sat up. He held his head, waiting for the room to stop spinning.

''So she was telling the truth all along. She is a lady.''

''If you can call her that.'' Stoke frowned, then asked, ''What is the sister like?''

''More beautiful than you could dream. She's gentle, biddable, and her sweetness fills a room. I'm sure you will be pleased when you meet her.''

''Cecily was sweet and biddable . . . at first.''

''Aye, but you can't judge all women by her actions.''

"I'm already beginning to regret contemplating marriage."

"Why? You needed someone to raise your son. You cannot keep putting off choosing a wife."

"So you have tried to convince me for the past year, but I still see no need for it."

"You'll change your mind once you meet the Lady Helen. All those stories we heard at court were true. Her pleasing manner and beauty rival any lady I've ever met." A besotted grin spread across Rowland's lips.

"Those are attributes, to be sure, but all I demand of her is that she know how to run my castle, be a good mother to Varik and know how to make herself scarce." Stoke hoped Lady Helen could fill those requirements, for he had no intention of ever loving, or trusting any woman again.

"I'm sure you'll find she can do all of those things and more." Rowland grinned knowingly.

Stoke scowled back at him. If the truth be told, he had no expectations that Lady Helen would be any different than Cecily had been, for Cecily had beauty and pleasing manners. Unfortunately, her gentle facade failed to change the blackness of her heart.

At Stoke's silence, Rowland added, with irony in his voice, "You'll just have to overlook the fact that she has a sister who may want you dead."

"I'll deal with Lady Lark."

"What do you mean to do?" Rowland broke the silence.

"Find her."

"Pray, how did she get away from you?"

"You don't want to know." Stoke noticed Rowland's grin, and his expression darkened.

"It appears 'tis not your night for luck."

"I intend to change that." Stoke ground his teeth together, then said, "The Lady Lark must come home sometime."

Stoke's eye narrowed as he remembered the hot, sensual heat from Lady Lark's lips, almost touching his, and those long legs that could wrap around a man's thighs. Aye, he would enjoy facing her again. This time, she would not get away so easily.

Lark padded down the long corridor toward the hall. Torchlight flickered along the walls and seemed to follow her. Baltizar strode beside her, so close, she could feel his thick gray fur bushing her right leg. She had washed the mud off her person in the communal bath and had borrowed a tunic, braies, and a pair of boots from the retainers' barracks—after she had inspected them for crawly creatures. One couldn't be too careful. Her mother deloused the barracks every Wednesday with fleabane. Unfortunately, it didn't always drive away all the fleas and lice.

She felt her damp hair against her back. It had taken an awful lot of scrubbing to get the muck and pond scum out. The moisture seeped through the coarse wool tunic now and made her itch. She scratched a spot on her ribs and thought about that arrogant black knight. He was still here—she'd seen him walk in behind her father. They had been too far away for her to hear their conversation, for she was hiding behind the guardhouse, but she did hear her father bellowing for her.

She thought of the black knight and those mesmerizing cobra eyes. It was the power in them that made her willingly want to kiss him. How could she have done that? She loved Avenall. But the knight would never get another chance to come near her again. Her fingers gripped the hilt of her sword.

Armed with her resolve, she entered the hall. Beams as wide as her waist spanned the ceiling, aged and blackened from centuries of smoke. Tapestries, many of them sewn by her mother or Helen's hand, fanned out along the walls. Thick oak tables, bunched together in a long line, stretched the length of the room. In the middle, a fire burned in the hearth.

Evel and Sir Gowan, her father's man at arms, sat opposite each other at one of the tables. Firelight glistened off Sir Gowan's thick crown of silvery hair. He pulled on his full beard. His bushy brows met over his nose as he picked up his king and attempted to move it. Sir Gowan was the most loyal of all her father's knights, and Lark respected the old retainer as much as her father—mayhap more so. He never left the castle unattended and saw to its security while her father oft sought his pleasures in the village inn, as he had done this day. Lark felt sorry for Gowan. He had lost a wife he loved ten years back and rarely smiled after that.

They heard her footsteps and looked at her. Gowan's hand paused over the board, still holding his king.

Evel stared at her and jumped up from his seat. "Where have you been? I need to talk to you."

"Taking a bath . . ." She paused, about to say, "and finding clothes," but she noticed Gowan's suspicious look and changed the subject. "Where are the twins?" she asked, not wanting to be tormented by them for turning up naked at the castle.

"Mother thinks they're in bed, but they snuck back to the inn."

"I hope they get in before the sun comes up. Last time they shared Atwid and Mordrid's bed, I had to tell Mother they had gone out hunting early that morn." Atwid and Mordrid were the innkeeper's daughters, who were one of Harold and Cedric's passions at the moment.

"You should be more worried about yourself. You'd better hope Dame Elizabeth doesn't find you." Gowan set down the chess piece and his beard parted as he graced her with one of his rare grins. "When you didn't make it back for the eventide repast, she looked ready to flay you."

Lark turned to go and find a hiding place. Abruptly, her mother appeared, carrying a tray. Lark bumped into it. Before she could grab it, the wooden tray flew up into the air. Hot, steaming tea spilled all over the front of her mother's bliant as the mug crashed to the floor. The food-laden trencher flipped up into the air and catapulted toward Evel and Sir Gowan.

They ducked.

A whole chicken, a serving of carrots, and the trencher sailed over their heads and hit the floor. Carrots spattered, coloring the rushes with splats of orange. The chicken and trencher skidded to a halt near the hearth.

Baltizar darted over to the chicken and gulped it down, not even bothering to chew the bones.

"You!" Her mother turned a cold eye on Lark. Red-faced and trembling, she flapped the front of her gown. "Now see what you've done."

Evel jumped to her defense. "It was an accident. It wasn't Lark's fault."

"That tray was for Lord Blackstone. She's ruined it. And that beast"—she slapped the air in Baltizar's direction—"he's gobbling the last of the chicken. Now what will Lord Blackstone eat? I saved that particularly for him. Oh, what will he think of us?" Her mother grabbed her cheeks and shook her head.

"So he's here?" Lark raised a surprised brow and bent down to pick up the broken pottery around her mother's feet.

"Aye, and what do you and your father care? William was so intoxicated, he couldn't even welcome Lord Blackstone properly. And then what I did . . ." She paused and groaned loudly. "I'm sure he's already regretting coming here. Why should he not?"

"What could you have done to him but make him feel welcome?" Lark paused, her hand still clutching a broken piece of pottery.

Her mother's cheeks blew out and turned the color of bright red roses.

Lark couldn't tell if Elizabeth was too angry or too beset by embarrassment to speak. So she pulled out the bottom of her tunic and placed the broken pottery shards on it and continued. "When he meets Helen, he'll not give the rest of us a thought. Where is Helen?"

"Asleep in her chamber, where you should be instead of out roaming the woods at all hours of the night. Look at you. You've been swimming again. You look like a drowned rat, and your hair . . ." Her mother's disapproving gaze fell on the matted snarls around Lark's waist. "It will take Marta two days to get the tangles out. What a disaster these few hours here have been.'' Elizabeth turned her gaze on Baltizar as he gulped down the last morsel of chicken and strode back toward Lark.

''Ugh! Get that flea-ridden wild beast out of my home.''

Baltizar crouched at the ear-piercing tone in Elizabeth's voice, then slunk behind Lark's legs.

''You've hurt his feelings.'' Lark picked up the last bit of pottery, then stood blocking Baltizar from Elizabeth's glare.

''I should hurt something more than his feelings.'' Her mother watched Baltizar step out from behind Lark and take a step toward the bread trencher lying upside down on the floor. ''Eat that, and you will be skinned and roasted. I'm not above eating wolves.'' She hissed like a snake at him.

Baltizar crouched and retreated back behind Lark's legs. A fearless creature, he attacked wild boars, picked fights with her father's hunting dogs, even brought down wild bucks, yet when he came under the lash of her mother's tongue, he turned into the most craven creature alive. Lark couldn't blame him. Carefully, keeping the shards within the bottom of her tunic, she bent and petted Baltizar.

''Go ahead and pet him. How many times have I told you not to bring that wild creature in here! But do you listen to me? Nay, you never listen to me. Now not only will Lord Blackstone have naught to eat, he'll have fleas jumping on him because of your blatant disregard for my authority.''

''I hope not.''

Each word in the deep, familiar voice pierced Lark. Her fingers dropped the hem of her tunic. Pottery shards crashed to the floor, exploding into thousands of tiny pieces as she wheeled around. Black eyes narrowed on her, the copper fire in them branding her face. Instinctively, her hand went to her sword.

Chapter 4

Lark gaped at the huge black knight, at the broad shoulders as wide as a door, at the strong hands that looked as if they could pulverize granite. They were clenched at his sides, his thick knuckles white from the pressure. The corded muscles in his powerful thighs stretched against a pair of black braies, the same color as his tunic. Near his thigh, his broadsword rested in its scabbard. The red stone embedded in the hilt appeared to come alive and glow like his eyes.

Her gaze moved up his hip, along the rippling muscle of his flat stomach, pulling against his tunic with each deep breath, then higher still, to the wavy black hair touching his burly shoulders, to his square jaw. Thick black stubble splashed across his jaw, angled at just the proper height to condescend to the world. His mouth was wide and tight-lipped. Thick brows slashed above his straight nose in one dark line, adding a touch of menace to his face. And those pitch-black eyes, burning with that strange coppery red. Sweet Mary! They were the most intense eyes she'd ever seen, and the most potent. Already she could feel the pull of them drawing her. She fought the urge to step back. Getting a good look at him in the light made some of the bravado she'd felt earlier leave her.

When he took a step toward her, Baltizar perked up and sniffed his leg.

"Lark, put that horrible beast outside." Her mother stepped toward the black knight. "We can't have him smelling Lord Blackstone."

Lark's eyes widened as her jaw dropped open. She saw him gazing back at her, looking contemptuously smug. He couldn't be Blackstone. This had to be a nightmare from which she'd surely wake.

His eyes narrowed on her. " 'Tis a pleasure to see you again."

"You've met?" Lady Elizabeth looked incredulous.

"I know her from having seen her room." A derisive note hung in his voice.

Lark turned to Elizabeth and cried, "You let him into my room?"

"He was hurt. It was the closest place to put him. Surely you do not mind it, Lark." Her mother's tone held a warning.

"I do. You know I don't want anyone in there."

"Why? Are you afraid someone might get lost in there?" Blackstone regarded her critically.

"If I were positive that were the case, then I would gladly allow you admittance to my room anytime you desired." Lark smiled sweetly, while her eyes blazed.

"Lark, apologize this moment!"

Lark clamped her jaw shut, folded her arms, and glowered at Blackstone.

"Is there something wrong with your voice, child?" Elizabeth elbowed Lark.

She smiled woodenly at her mother. "Nay, my voice is perfectly fine."

This earned Lark a surreptitious pinch on her elbow and a smoldering glance from her mother. She leaned close and whispered, "I'll speak to you later." Then louder to the earl,

"I'm so sorry, my lord. I was just on my way up with your tea and dinner when Lark ran into me."

"Aye, Baltizar ate your dinner." Lark grinned at him behind Elizabeth's back, then bent down and patted Baltizar's head.

Blackstone easily gazed over Elizabeth's head, being a head and a half taller than she, and looked at Lark. A flash of amusement lit his black eyes, at odds with the scowl still on his face. "Mayhap I should eat the wolf."

Baltizar cut his eyes at Blackstone, as if he realized what the knight had said.

"I'm sure a bowl of gruel would be much more to your liking," Lark interpreted for her pet.

"Nay, I prefer meat at my table." His gaze slid slowly down her body.

"Father will be glad to hear it, for there is naught that he likes better than a hunt, though keeping the table stocked with meat may now prove a laborious task." Lark raked his body with a contemptuous gaze, as he'd done to her.

"And I suppose he has no trouble keeping your belly full. Being the timid, delicate lady that you are, I'm sure you eat like a bird." His gaze dropped to her baggy braies and overlarge tunic.

"To be honest, my mother has oft remarked that I have an endless gullet. Is that not true, Mother?" Lark glanced at Elizabeth, saw she was too stunned to speak, and continued, "Not all ladies eat like birds, my lord. I've seen some who can eat more than three men. Why, my aunt Isabel usually cleans out the larders when she is here, and she's considered a great lady. She'll be one of our guests for the wedding. I feel sure the two of you shall get along famously."

Lady Elizabeth gasped and turned to Lark. "I must see you abovestairs this instant!"

Evel spoke up now, looking chagrined and worried. "Would you join us for a game of chess, my lord?"

Lord Blackstone didn't answer him; his gaze was locked on Lark as Lady Elizabeth grabbed her hand and dragged her up the steps.

* * *

Elizabeth's nails dug into Lark's palm. She grimaced and listened to her mother's angry footsteps at odds with her own in the stairwell.

When they were far enough away, Elizabeth spoke, still steadily dragging Lark up the steps. "What are you trying to do, ruin your sister's chance of becoming a bride? I will not have you acting like an ill-bred peasant in front of the Earl of Blackstone. Have you remembered naught I've taught you? You wouldn't even apologize to him. What must he think of you?"

"I care not what he thinks. He's a contemptible beast. Surely you can't mean to let Helen marry him only if he desires *her*. He'll have her so frightened, she'll be cowering the rest of her days."

"You cannot judge him after having met him for only a moment." Elizabeth dropped Lark's hand, gained the last step, and turned an acid glance on Lark.

"I don't need to spend hours in his presence to know he does not suit Helen." Lark stood on the step below her, and they faced each other on eye level now. Elizabeth's whole face turned scarlet with anger, her fault-finding blue eyes leveled straight at Lark. She shook a finger at Lark's nose.

"Of course he suits Helen. And that horrible comment you made about his appetite—you never surprise me with what comes out of that mouth of yours. I was never so embarrassed in my life. How could you?"

"He deserved it."

"He most certainly did not. Whether you know it or not, a lady is supposed to hold her tongue. There is such a thing as reticence, another lesson you have yet to learn. I should have insisted you stay in that convent."

"They wouldn't have me, or have you forgotten that?"

"Pray, how could I forget it? You threatened the abbess with a knife."

"She was a witch and tried to burn my tongue with a candle."

"You provoked her—you could provoke God himself."

" 'Tis always my fault, is it not, Mother?"

"Aye, it is—and your father's. He's to blame how you turned out. He enjoyed turning you into the ill-mannered, mannish creature you are. He used to think it the best of jokes when you were little. You are a grown woman now—a lady—yet you still act no better than a churl. Just look at the way you treated Lord Blackstone. You have disgraced our family." Her mother narrowed her eyes, spitting blue fire at Lark.

"I'll always be a disgrace to you." Lark hid the emotion in her voice. "But I still do not think Helen should marry Blackstone."

"You would love to spoil poor Helen's prospects, but I shan't let you."

"I don't wish to spoil anything for her, only save her from a fate worse than death." Lark's gaze dropped to the wet spots on the front of Elizabeth's bliant. "She's like a lamb being led to slaughter, and you're sending her there just to tie this family to his wealth and title. I can't believe you're doing this. I won't let him hurt Helen."

"Helen would never give him a reason to beat her. Had he been marrying you, then I would worry, but I have no fears for Helen. She will marry Lord Blackstone and be happy."

Her mother stamped her foot. "We shall speak of it no more. Henceforth, you will be kind and amiable to him and treat him as a guest in our home should be treated. Do you understand?"

"I don't understand this ambition of yours to make Helen miserable for the rest of her life."

"I'm through arguing with you!" Her mother drew back and slapped Lark across her face.

The opened-handed slap split the air like a smithy's hammer hitting an anvil.

In the silence, they looked at each other. Her mother looked dumbfounded for a moment and appeared not to know what she'd done. It was the first time Elizabeth had ever struck Lark, and they both realized it at the same moment. Her mother stared at the red marks on Lark's cheek. Tears welled up in her eyes.

Lark blinked at her and brought her hand up to touch her stinging face. The silence that hung between them was like a wall, growing higher by the moment. That wall would never come down again. Their relationship, such as it was, would never be the same again. And they both knew it.

Lark hated being a disappointment to Elizabeth and causing her pain, but there was no pleasing her. Lark had given up trying a long time ago. She was glad to be marrying Avenall and getting away from Elizabeth, though she would miss William desperately.

Someone cleared his throat behind her mother. Lark glanced up and saw the wry-mouthed knight who had been with Lord Blackstone when he'd been set upon by the Scots. Baltizar cowered near the wall on the other side of the knight's legs, eyeing Elizabeth warily.

The knight looked uncomfortable at having witnessed the slap, and he bent down and petted Baltizar. "Please, forgive me."

"Nay, forgive me." Elizabeth looked at Lark as she spoke, then turned back to the man. "This is my daughter, Lark." She waved a trembling hand at the man. "This is Rowland of Larange, Lord Blackstone's friend. If you'll excuse me, I must needs change my wet clothes. Then I shall show you to your room."

Lark watched Elizabeth pick up the hem of her brown bliant, step past Sir Rowland, and walk down the hall. Torchlight flickered off her unnaturally hunched shoulders. Her steps were slow and labored, as if she dragged a load of stones behind her.

Rowland looked at Lark. "Please accept my apologies for not believing you earlier about being a lady."

"You'll find I forgive easily when someone realizes they have erred, Rowland of Larange."

Rowland grinned handsomely at her, two dimples beaming on his cheeks. "I hope so, Lady Lark. I would hate to have you angry with me." The teasing grin faded. "I'm sorry to have intruded upon you and your mother."

"Mayhap it was a good thing." Lark glanced at Elizabeth, then back at Rowland. She watched his long fingers stroking Baltizar. "I'm surprised you made friends with him. He doesn't let just anyone pet him."

"All wild creatures are attracted to me." He smiled at her, a princely smile that lit up his face.

"I'm sure most any creature is susceptible to your smile." As much as she wanted to dislike this charming friend of Blackstone's, she realized she was beginning to like him. But she didn't smile back at him.

"Are you flirting with me, my lady?" Rowland's grin widened.

"Nay, unfortunately, it takes more than dimples and a handsome face to tempt me. I was merely stating the obvious. And do not think to prevail upon me with your charming nature. I can tell by the way you look at me, you still think I had something to do with those Scots. Well, I didn't. Had I wanted Lord Blackstone dead, I could have shot an arrow through his heart as he entered this castle. Tell him that for me, will you, for I'm sure he still believes I plotted to kill him."

"I'll inform him, but I doubt it will change his opinion."

"I suppose not," Lark said, wondering if anything could sway a man like Blackstone once his mind was set on something.

He eyed her closely, the grin leaving his face. Something in his expression was all too clever, as if he knew the power Blackstone's eyes had over her. He couldn't possibly know that Lark had almost kissed Blackstone. Could he?

Lark bestowed an uneasy smile on Sir Rowland and noticed the twinkling blue eyes still surveying her closely. The sound of Elizabeth's chamber door closing made her glance down the hall.

"If you'll excuse me, I'm going to retire. It has been a long evening. I'll bid you good night. Come, Baltizar."

He touched her elbow. "May I say one more thing?"

"Of course."

"Do not judge Lord Blackstone harshly for his treatment of

you. There have been ten attempts on his life in the past year. Naturally, he has a right to suspect all those unknown to him, especially someone he found with would-be assassins." His gaze bored deeply into her face.

"I did not realize there were other attempts on his life. I suppose he will never believe I'm innocent now."

"I cannot say. I have known the Dragon all my life. His father was my father's overlord. Since my eldest brother inherited my father's lands, I've been floundering, trying to decide what I want to do with my life. Stoke hired me, even though he didn't need another mercenary knight." He rubbed the golden stubble on his chin, looked pensive, then continued. "Not only that, we fought in the Holy Land together. Stoke saved my life in so many battles, I've lost count. He is the bravest, most honorable man I've ever had the pleasure of calling friend. If he cares for you, then he is the best friend you will ever have. But, alas, if you are his enemy, then God help you."

"I'm not his enemy," Lark said vehemently.

"I pray that is true."

"I vow it before God and all the saints." Lark made the sign of the cross over her heart. She saw the suspicious gleam in Rowland's eyes and dropped her hand. He was as distrustful of her as his friend. Why should she try to convince them of her innocence? Let them think what they liked.

Lark left him, feeling his eyes on her back. Baltizar followed close on her heels. Her father's loud snores rumbled from his chamber and mixed with her footsteps. A little louder and the castle walls might shake. But it was a pleasant sound, like the continuous creaks of the castle, and the smell of burning tallow and wood that always permeated the air, and the way the rushes made a soft crunching sound underfoot. It gave her a sense of home and comfort. It also took her mind off Blackstone.

As Lark passed Helen's closed door, she thought of her sister. Poor Helen. Somehow she must convince her not to marry the Black Dragon. Helen would be asleep now, but in the morning she'd speak to her, no matter what Elizabeth said.

Helen must not be forced into marrying Blackstone. After

Lark made sure Blackstone realized that, she'd turn her mind to getting him to leave the castle.

She had a feeling the Dragon wouldn't leave until he was absolutely convinced she wasn't involved in the attempts on his life. With a deep frown on her face, she reached her chamber and did something she had never done before, she threw home the heavy bolt on the door.

At the sound of footsteps, Stoke glanced up from the chess board and looked over Evel's head. Rowland appeared at the bottom of the stairwell, a smile stretched across his face, his blue eyes gleaming. Stoke paused, his hand on a pawn, and watched Rowland stride over to him.

"Good eventide." Rowland bowed slightly to Evel and to Sir Gowan, who sat beside them watching the game. He faced Stoke. "May I have a word?"

Stoke stood and followed him to a corner of the room, aware of Evel's and Sir Gowan's gazes on him.

"I suppose you encountered the Lady Lark?" Rowland whispered as his grin widened.

"Aye." Stoke kept his voice low. "I heard her too, above stairs, arguing with her mother. It appears the lady does not share her mother's enthusiasm for the wedding."

"I'm afraid so. It earned her a slap from Lady Elizabeth. I happened upon them as they were arguing."

"I understand why. Lady Lark has a propensity for vexing everyone around her."

"Speaking of the lady, she told me to tell you she could have killed you when you came into the castle, but did not. She swears she had naught to do with the Scots."

"She has claimed that since I found her." Stoke paused, deep in thought, then looked at his friend. "Do you believe her?"

"Truthfully, I don't know."

"I'll find out the truth soon enough." Stoke turned and found

Evel watching him. Their eyes met for a moment; then Evel quickly turned away.

The exchange did not go unnoticed by Rowland. "Ah, it looks as if her brother may know something too. What say you, if you watch Evel, and I watch Lady Lark?"

Stoke saw the wolfish gleam in Rowland's eye. "Nay, I'll take the lady. We have unfinished business." Stoke remembered the way her golden eyes flashed when they had sparred with words. No woman had ever dared speak to him thus. Oddly, it only made him more determined to have her.

The quick glimpse he'd seen of her naked body rose up in his mind—the long legs, the charming little bottom running toward the woods. To further torment him, he remembered the feel of her hot lips almost touching his. Since he'd found her with the Scots, she had tormented him. Now it would be his turn to do some tormenting.

Deep in the throes of a dream, Lark's heart raced and she thrashed at the bed. A huge black dragon chased her through the woods, spitting fire. Flames leaped along her clothes, turning them to ashes. Naked, she ran through the trees. The faster she ran, the closer he came. His huge black wings flapped close behind. With each flap, a fierce gust of air swept past her, almost lifting her off the ground. His colossal shadow passed over her face, the shape black and ominous. His huge talons swooped toward her. Opening. Clamping onto her shoulders . . .

A noise jarred her awake. Her sweat-drenched clothes stuck to her body as her gaze scanned the room. No dragons. She let out a deep breath and touched her shoulder with a trembling hand.

At the foot of her bed, Baltizar raised his head toward the window and growled.

"What is it, my friend?" Earlier, she had set her sword near her side, for fear of having her chamber invaded by the Black Dragon. Grabbing it, she shoved back the covers and stood without the creak of one rope. Years ago she had developed the ability, for Harold and Cedric loved to sneak into her room and pull pranks. Once they had tried to cut off her hair; another time they came into her room and bombarded her with horse dung. Sometimes they were wretched pests.

The noise came again. It sounded as if someone bumped his head against the stones. A whispered curse followed. If it was the Black Dragon trying to sneak in her window, he wasn't flapping his wings very quietly. She lifted the hem of the old thin bliaut in which she liked to sleep, dodged several piles of clothes on the floor, and moved closer to the open window.

It was a warm night for March, and she'd left the shutters open. Moonlight streamed into the room. The dark silhouette of a head and wide shoulders appeared at the bottom of the window. With lightning accuracy, she thrust her sword beneath the intruder's chin, just until the sharp point met skin.

"Jesu, Lark! It's me."

She recognized Evel's voice immediately. "Could you not knock on the door?" She pulled back her sword and laid it on the desk near the window.

"I lied to get away from Lord Blackstone and his friend. They think I'm checking on an ill horse. I had to speak to you, so I crawled up on to the roof the way I used to do."

"You were a lot smaller then. You know you can't gain entrance through here. 'Tis too little." Lark stuck her head through the tiny window and came nose to nose with Evel. He lay flat across the steep roof, gripping the stone sill.

"I shan't be up here long. I was worried about you. Why were you naked and hiding from Lord Blackstone?"

"Please, do not ask me."

"You have to tell me. I risked my neck crawling up here— you can't keep the truth from me now. Tell me!"

"You promise not to tell the twins? If they get wind of this, they'll tease me until I turn into an old prune."

"Do you think I'd break a confidence?" Evel sounded wounded.

"I'm sorry, I know you would not." There had always been

a strong bond between her and Evel, in some cases stronger even than the one she shared with Helen. After a moment, she poured out her soul to him. " 'Twas horrible, Evel. Someone is trying to murder Lord Blackstone, and he thinks I'm involved.'' Lark relayed what had happened earlier and finished with, "I told him the truth, yet he refuses to believe me.''

"Surely he does not think you are behind this plot?''

"Aye, he does, and I fear there is naught I can do to make him believe me.''

Abruptly, a voice hailed from the ground, "Evel, is that you?''

Lark perked up at the voice. Every time she heard it, a smile grew inside her. She glanced past Evel's shoulder at Avenall. He stood on the ground below her window, his lanky frame outlined by the moonlight.

"Avenall!'' Lark yelled, unable to curb the excitement in her voice.

Evel glanced behind him to look down at Avenall. At that moment, he lost his footing on the steeply pitched roof and slipped. Lark grabbed his hand.

"Hold on, Evel.''

"I can't!''

Lark felt his fingers slip through her grasp. She watched him slide belly down, across the moss-covered slate tiles.

"Jesu!'' Evel's yell echoed through the bailey. He grabbed at the edge of the roof. Once. Twice. His hands missed. He tumbled over the edge, through the air, right toward Avenall.

Lark saw Avenall step back, but not far enough. Evel twisted in the air and plowed into him.

"Sweet Mary, Evel! Avenall!'' Lark drew back her head from the window and ran from the room.

Chapter 5

Lark flung open her chamber door and, not paying attention, plowed into her mother. She grabbed Elizabeth by her elbows before she fell backwards.

"Flying saints, what is the matter?" Elizabeth's brows drew together as she knocked Lark's hands from her arms.

"Forgive me." Lark stepped past her mother and took off running again. She turned and called over her shoulder, "We may not be having a wedding after all."

"What?" Elizabeth's screech echoed down the hallway.

Untouched by it, Lark took the steps two at a time. Her mother's footsteps followed close behind her.

"Lark, I demand you stop this instant and explain yourself!"

"Sorry, I cannot." But the moment Lark's foot came down off the stairs, she rammed into Lord Blackstone's hard chest. It knocked the breath out of her for a moment.

He grabbed her arms. "Tell me what is amiss. We heard someone scream."

Lark looked between Blackstone and Gowan, who stood near his side, and blurted, " 'Tis terrible. If Avenall is not crushed, may the saints be praised. He's not as sturdy-boned as Evel.

Likely he is injured. Mother will probably blame me and say I planned it to ruin the wedding.'' She knocked Blackstone's hands away and ran through the hall.

''Avenall? Hurt?'' Gowan called at her back, sounding confused, then turning suddenly pale. ''Lord deliver us from mishaps.'' The blood drained from his cheeks as he ran after her, his scabbard banging against his leg.

Scowling, Stoke turned to follow them, but froze at the sound of footsteps echoing down the stairwell. Lady Elizabeth appeared, waving a hand in the air.

''My lord, please forgive my daughter. A cloud of folly follows her. I did teach her manners, though she never uses them.'' She glanced across the hall as Lark bolted out the door, Gowan hard on her heels. She shook her fists at the door. ''Lark! I demand you stop and tell me what is going on! Lark, do you hear me?'' The door slammed shut. ''Excuse me, my lord.'' She hurried after her daughter.

More than a little curious about Lord Avenall, Stoke turned and strode out of the hall. Any man who agreed to marry such a brazen termagant as the Lady Lark must be daft—or enjoyed beating women into submission.

The thought of Lady Lark being touched by another man made him frown and pick up his stride. He followed the sound of Lady Elizabeth's screeches. Near one end of the bailey, he found the injured parties. Evel was helping Lord Avenall up to his feet. Stoke realized that all the muscles in his body had tensed. At the sight of Lord Avenall, he relaxed. The new arrival stood barely taller than Lady Lark. Moonlight glistened off the young face and the deep cleft in the middle of a weak chin. The bright blue eyes were too soft, lacking conviction, and the chestnut-brown hair, cropped short, made him look no older than a boy. It was apparent why Lady Lark had chosen this pubescent cub to wed; she could control him. He made a silent vow that she would never master him. Nay, it would be the other way around. He would do the mastering.

Rowland darted out from the shadows and fell into step beside him.

"What happened?" Stoke whispered, watching Lord Avenall waver on his feet. Gowan grabbed his other arm to steady him.

"To say the least, Evel did not go to check on his horse as he would have us believe. He must have needed to speak to his sister badly, for he fell from her window. It was quite comical. Landed right on her gallant swain, whom she seems awfully concerned about at the moment."

Stoke followed Rowland's gaze over to Lark.

"Avenall, are you all right?" Lady Lark flung her arms around his neck, almost knocking him over again.

"Yes, my dear, I'm fine."

"I was so worried."

Stoke's urge to grin faded when Lady Lark grabbed the boyish face and kissed it. Avenall's arms went around her waist and the kiss didn't end right away. He watched Avenall's thin hands move up and down Lark's back and tangle in her tawny gold hair, the same color as a tigress's mane.

Stoke's gaze strayed lower to her gown. Large worn places in the fabric, as thin as gossamer thread, barely concealed Lark's elbows and knees. The shabby state of the silk made her even more intriguing, for he could see an outline of her bottom. There wasn't much to it, but his hands itched to explore the small rounded globes. It occurred to him that, save for in the Holy Land, he'd never seen such an erotic piece of clothing.

His fist clenched as he let his gaze stray down to the ragged sides of her gown, which exposed her bare flesh all the way up to the middle of her thighs. They were not plump and rounded as a woman's should be, but sleek, coltish, and corded with muscle. He'd never seen a woman with such well-knit thighs; the power in them could go a long way in pleasing a man in his bed. A vision flashed in his mind, of her astride him, her head thrown back, her long golden hair falling down her back and tangling in his hands while he kissed her. The hours of carnal pleasure could be limitless.

He felt his body respond to the sight of her. Gritting his teeth, he wondered if the kiss would ever end. He glanced at

Lady Elizabeth. Why didn't she break up the pair? When she made no move to act, even wore a pleased grin, Stoke took a step toward them.

Abruptly, they broke apart, and he paused mid-stride.

"I've missed you so, Avenall." Those wide golden eyes dug into her betrothed's face. Her lips, still swollen and red from the kiss, stretched in a warm smile, bringing to life the dimple in her left cheek.

Stoke watched those red lips glistening in the moonlight, uneasy at the sight of that smile. He'd never seen a genuine smile on her face, nor had he seen her golden eyes glow with such sparkling warmth. It was a comely face, he decided, filled with disarming charm and hidden cunning. But he would not be taken in by her smile, as was her groom-to-be. He knew what lay beneath it. Surely, she used the beguiling smile toward her own ends, most likely on the Scots when they all plotted to kill him.

"I'm fine." Lord Avenall patted her hand, while his gaze swept the five people standing around them as if just noticing them. He cleared his throat, looked flustered, and stepped back from Lady Lark.

"Why did you not tell us you were to arrive, my lord? Shame on you." Lady Elizabeth shook her finger at the newcomer.

"Forgive me, Lady Elizabeth. I should have sent a missive, but I couldn't leave until the spring planting was seen to. Then it was too late to write, so I came straight away."

"What are you about, Evel? Were you up crawling around on the roof again? I thought I broke you of that years ago." Lady Elizabeth shot Evel a reproachful glance, then smiled at Avenall. "I hope he has not wounded you, my lord."

"Really, I'm well."

"We are so glad of it. I would not want you to miss the wedding because my son"—she cut her eyes at Evel again—"decided to act like a silly boy and crawl on the roof. We do have doors in the castle, Evel. Please use them in future."

"Aye, Mother," Evel said flatly.

"Praise be, I thought from the way Lark burst out of her

room that you were dead.'' Lady Elizabeth glared at her daugh-
ter, then looked back at the newcomer. "The things that have
happened here. Beseems no lords will want to visit us. When
Lord Blackstone arrived, I was angry with my husband—which
I sorely regret, I don't know what came over me—and I hit
Lord Blackstone with a cup meant for my husband . . .'' Lady
Elizabeth paused.

Stoke felt the lady's eyes on him and knew he'd been caught
staring at the erotic slit up Lady Lark's gown and at the long
expanse of glistening alabaster skin. It looked as smooth as
cream and glowed like a white beacon in the moonlight. Finally,
he tore his gaze away and looked at Lady Elizabeth.

She frowned at him and continued. "Of course, Lord Blackstone knows how sorry I am the mishap came to pass. And
now you, Avenall, have been pounced upon by Evel. Should
word get around that we treat our grooms so horridly, the guests
may not arrive for the wedding.''

"I doubt that, Mother.'' Lark glanced at Stoke, the smile
leaving her face.

Again he was caught staring at her legs, this time by the
object of his desire. Lady Lark's fingers tightened into the sides
of her gown, pulling them together. He let his gaze roam up
her slender hips and flat waist, further still to her small breasts
and the long, swanlike neck.

His gaze slowly rose to meet her flashing topaz eyes. She
had the audacity to shoot him a bold, indignant glance and then
blush—after she'd worn the gown on purpose to tease him and
every other man around! He'd give her one concession—she
was a good mummer, just as Cecily had been. Deep in the
marrow of his bones, he knew there couldn't be one maidenly
bone in her body. He held back a grin that twitched at the
corner of his lips. He had every intention of seducing the gown
off her later. Aye, he'd enjoy that.

"It was a blunder, but Avenall does not hold grudges. Do
you, old friend?'' Evel said, slapping Lord Avenall on the
shoulder.

"Nay, you know that." Lord Avenall turned his boyish face toward Stoke. "You must be the Earl of Blackstone."

"Aye, 'tis none other," Evel said. "And here, my lord, is Lord Avenall, Baron Listmore."

"I've heard a lot about you, my lord." Lord Avenall bowed low to him. When he rose, he was a little unsteady and had to stretch out his arms to gain his balance.

"I hope the stories you've heard were all honorable." Stoke's dislike for the young man came through in his voice.

"Aye, very. All the bards sing of you. Would you tell me what it felt like to fight with King Richard in the Holy land? I longed to go, but my father refused to allow it."

Stoke opened his mouth to speak, but Lady Elizabeth said, "I beg you to speak of war inside, where Lord Avenall can be more comfortable. Evel, please take him in and have Wira get him a cold meal from the livery cupboard. I wish to speak to your sister."

"Come then, and you can tell me what you've been doing with yourself." Evel slapped his arm around Lord Avenall's shoulders and they strode toward the hall.

Stoke cast Lady Lark one last glance. Their gazes locked. Her chin shot up in a haughty manner, the golden gleam in her eyes full of willfulness and hostility. If it was the last thing he did, he'd wipe that look off her face. His mouth twisted in a lopsided grin as he followed Evel, Gowan, and Lord Avenall into the hall. He wasn't worried that Lark would escape him— her mother would see to that.

Stoke noticed that Rowland wasn't able to take his eyes off Lady Lark and made a point of slowing down to block his view.

Rowland smiled at him and whispered, "I believe, after this night, I'll never look upon women in the same way. There is much to be said for a slender body."

"Aye, but it can be lethal on a cunning vixen such as the Lady Lark." Stoke grimaced.

"I would welcome the sting of such wiles on me, should she favor me so."

"Stay away from her, Rowland."

Rowland leveled a long look at Stoke, then asked, "Are you warning me to stay away from her because you are worried about my safety, or is it that you are intent upon having her?"

"I don't know what I intend to do with her."

"You had better do naught but watch her. You are here to see about choosing her sister for a bride. And you are too late to claim Lady Lark's hand."

"I know that. You needn't point it out. And I've no intention of marrying a termagant like Lady Lark."

" 'Tis a good thing, for she'll be marrying Lord Avenall."

The dark expression that broke out on Stoke's face made Rowland burst out laughing. Unamused, Stoke scowled back at his friend. The idea of Lady Lark marrying Lord Avenall forced an unbidden possessiveness to swirl up inside of him. He forced it back and followed Rowland into the hall.

Elizabeth waited until he and the others had disappeared through the hall doors before she grabbed Lark's arm. "How could you come running out of the house in that rag? You are half naked. Just look at you."

"If you wish to berate me again, Mother, can it not wait 'til the morrow?"

"Nay, it cannot. What must Avenall and Lord Blackstone think of you? I'm not worried so much about Avenall, for he is to be your husband, but Lord Blackstone was gawking at you as if you were a cheap whore."

"What care I for his opinion?" Lark wanted to tell her mother that he'd already seen her naked, but she said, "I'm sure his virginal eyes were not offended."

"Go ahead, make light of it, but I saw him eyeing you. You have gained his notice, and I'll not have you coming between him and Helen."

"Do you really think my intention was to gain his notice in

that way?" Lark gritted her teeth. "I'd sooner bed a spiny boar."

"You should not speak of him so. And you'll find he's not so thick-witted should he corner you and grow impassioned. What possessed you to run out of the hall without putting on a mantle to cover you? I should have burned that gown you sleep in eight years ago. 'Tis naught but a rag. When we get back into the castle, I want that gown so I can burn it."

"You know I cannot sleep without my goose-down pillow and this gown. I don't ever wear it out of my room. I was worried about Avenall and Evel and forgot I had it on. You needn't worry about me wearing it much longer, Mother. I'll be married and I'll take it with me."

"You'll not go to Avenall's home in rags. No daughter of mine is going to embarrass me in such a manner. A lady is always aware of her modesty, and I'll not have you parading around in that horrible rag—even if it is only in front of your husband."

Years of frustration exploded inside Lark. Trembling all over, she cried, "Would that I had come out naked, Mother! The saints save me from every *lady* alive." Lark wanted to scream at the top of her lungs, to pull her hair out; instead she turned and ran back to the hall before she said something she would regret the rest of her life.

"Do not forget he is to marry your sister!" Elizabeth's voice rang across the bailey.

"How could I forget?" Lark muttered under her breath.

She had to speak to Helen and convince her not to consider Blackstone should he propose. If Elizabeth made it unbearable for Helen, she could come and live with her and Avenall—if he hadn't changed his mind. Lark doubted it. Avenall needed her dowry to fill his coffers, and surely he must care for her if he wanted to marry her. But first, she had to somehow convince the Black Dragon that she was innocent of any wrongdoing. She frowned at the thought. Determined dragons weren't easily convinced of anything.

* * *

When Lark reached the hall, Evel, Lord Blackstone, Avenall, Gowan, and Rowland were standing in the middle of the hall, chattering like a group of squirrels. Maybe not all of them. Blackstone wasn't speaking, only wearing a grim, brooding look and standing several steps back from the others.

The soft tread of footsteps made Lark pause in the shadows and glance toward the stairwell. Helen came hurrying down the steps, her long brown hair flowing down around her, looking like a sleepy-eyed nymph. Her green samite bliaut and mantle flowed out around her perfect curves. She didn't see Lord Blackstone until she reached the bottom step. Then color stole into her cheeks. Immediately, she lowered her gaze and executed a graceful curtsy.

"M-my lord."

Lark crossed her arms over her chest, waiting Blackstone's first reaction to Helen. His expression remained cryptic, not giving any emotion away. Most men faced with Helen's beauty panted like hard-run hounds. Blackstone's reaction was odd in the extreme. Lark narrowed puzzled brows at him.

Blackstone stared at Helen for what seemed like ages, taking in every rounded curve beneath her beautiful green bliaut and the thick, dark hair waving down over her full breasts to her waist. A strange, disquieting grin moved across his lips as he stepped toward her.

He touched Helen's chin and lifted her face to look at him. " 'Tis a pleasure to finally meet you. You are indeed as comely as the rumors said." His tone remained unmoved as he spoke.

No man had ever spoken to Helen without fawning all over her, and the surprise showed in her face. She looked too shy and too bewildered to say anything, only staring at Blackstone with her large, doe-like eyes.

Lark felt every muscle in her body tighten as she fought the urge to shake Helen and make her say something. It was the first violent thought Lark had ever had toward her sister. In the past, she'd always protected Helen—especially from the twins.

Never had Lark lost her temper with Helen or wanted to hurt her. A sudden rush of shame poured over her and she shifted on her feet.

At that moment, Elizabeth came into the hall, her face still flushed with anger. After one disparaging glance at Lark, she noticed Helen and Blackstone and ran to them.

"My lord, you've met my daughter." Elizabeth put her arm around Helen's shoulder. "Is she not comely?"

"Aye." He stared down at Helen, towering over her. The top of her head barely reached his chest. Surely just the sheer size of him would send Helen to the hinterlands to hide.

"I thought you would be pleased." Her mother's eyes glowed proudly at Helen. "I had not meant for you to meet my daughter until morn. Why are you up, my dearest?"

Helen turned to her mother and found her voice. "I heard a loud yell. Is everything all right?"

" 'Twas I." Avenall stepped toward Helen.

"Lord Avenall, you've finally come." Helen stretched out a trembling hand toward him. Some of the anxiety Blackstone had caused in her melted from her face.

Avenall took her proffered hand and squeezed it. "Aye, it took longer than I anticipated in the spring planting, and I had to discharge my overseer. When I looked at the books, I found the man was robbing me blind."

"How horrible. I know how you dislike unpleasant situations. I hope you've found a new man."

"Aye, but he is still learning. Alas, let us not speak of him now. I left all that behind me to come here."

"And we are so glad you have arrived." Helen's eyes brightened. She granted him one of her warm smiles, but then her expression turned anxious. "I hope you were not hurt—I mean, when you yelled."

" 'Twas not really me, but Evel doing the yelling."

Helen glanced at her brother for an explanation.

"I fell from the roof," Evel said tonelessly.

"I hope you are not hurt."

"Fear not, I have experience in that feat and Avenall broke my fall." Evel elbowed Avenall in the ribs.

"You are not hurt?" Helen peered anxiously at Avenall.

"Nay, he's fit." Evel slapped Avenall on his shoulder.

Lark looked at the two men she loved second only to her father. She envied the ease between them. Since almost the moment Avenall came to St. Vale as a gangly youth, Evel had befriended him. At times, Lark grew jealous of their friendship. Evel understood Avenall's quiet moods. Quite often Avenall invited Evel to walk with him, excluding her. Her envy only lasted as long as she could see them on the path. It didn't take her long to find other distractions to keep her mind off being ignored. And Avenall always made it up to her by spending time with her.

"Well, he looks fit enough to be at his wedding," Gowan said, smiling at Avenall.

"Aye, as you say." Avenall's smile lagged just a little and he appeared to remember Lark. When he spotted her standing near the hallway in the shadows, his smile broadened.

Lark smiled back at him, wanting very much to kiss him again. It had been so very long since she'd last seen him, and it had left an empty ache in her.

For no apparent reason that Lark could see, Blackstone stepped between them, blocking her view. All she could see was his broad back and the wavy black hair hanging down to his shoulders. She frowned at his back. She should walk over to Avenall, but she didn't want Blackstone gawking at her body through her old nightgown again.

"Come, Helen, to bed with you," Elizabeth said. "That is all the visiting you can do for one night. You and Avenall can chat on the morrow. Evel, please show everyone to their rooms. Gowan, would you rouse Wira and order her to bring a cold tray to Avenall."

" 'Tis done, my lady." Gowan nodded and strode toward the servants' quarters, his boot thudding on the stone floor.

Elizabeth appeared to have forgotten that Lark was in the hall. She locked elbows with Helen, and they climbed the stairs.

That was fine with Lark. She was glad to be spared her mother's notice, though, if she cared to admit it, it pricked what little vanity she had that Blackstone also seemed to have forgotten she was there. The least he could do was scowl at her. But he still had his eyes trained on Helen, watching the seductive sway of her long hair brushing against her full, rounded bottom. He watched her every move until she disappeared up the stairwell.

Rowland and Avenall looked equally enthralled by Helen's backside, until Evel clapped his hands together and said, "Follow me, if you please."

Blackstone glanced at Lark, hitting her with that penetrating black gaze. His gaze dropped to the threadbare gown, slowly skimmed her flat chest, and paused to ogle her legs, exposed on the sides by the open seams, then lower still, to her bony ankles and long bare toes. With a contemptuous slowness, his eyes moved up again to meet her face, obviously comparing her to Helen.

This wasn't anything new. Men had always compared her to Helen and found her wanting. But she didn't see the usual revulsion or indifference in Blackstone's eyes, only a kind of devouring hunger that made the blood rush to her cheeks and her body tingle all over. It made her aware of how dangerous he was.

As if he read her mind, a wicked grin lifted one corner of his lips. The dark, sensual look in his gaze said, "You'll soon be mine." He turned and, without a backward glance, followed Evel and Rowland up the stairs.

Before attempting to follow him, Lark waited until he'd gone all the way up the steps. She was well aware that she would probably not get any sleep tonight. He had thrown down the gauntlet and she must be ready to pick it up.

Several moments later, Lark paused in the stairwell, waiting for their footsteps to die away, listening to their conversation.

"If you have need of a wench, I can wake one of the servants, my lord," Evel said.

"Nay, just show me to my bed," Blackstone said in his deep baritone.

"I am not of the same turn of mind as my friend. I would like a wench to warm my bed." Rowland's voice had a smile in it.

"I'm sure I can find one to suit you . . ."

Lark was thankful that Blackstone's room was in the lesser hall. A year ago, when Elizabeth had decided upon a double wedding, she had harped at William to build a much-needed wing to accommodate the guests. After a month of constant nagging, her father finally agreed. A long hallway connected the new wing to the main hall. Blackstone's room was in the new wing, far away from her chamber. Praise the saints.

Their voices and footsteps faded. As Lark lifted her foot to tread on another step, she heard her mother bid Helen goodnight in a loving tone, which she rarely, if ever, bestowed on Lark. Not until the soft footsteps ended abruptly and a door closed did Lark dare climb the steps. When she reached the top, Helen's door creaked open.

"Psst!" Helen waved Lark toward her room. "I must speak to you."

Lark stepped into her chamber and Helen gently closed the door. Neatness invaded the whole room. Not a wrinkle marred the flowers embroidered on the counterpane that was turned down and tucked neatly around the mattress. How Helen could sleep in a bed without it looking as though she had slept in it, remained a mystery to Lark. Her gaze strayed to a desk sitting against one wall, glistening with wax, so much so that she could see her reflection in it.

Above the desk, a large wooden rosary hung from a nail, where Helen knelt for prayer every morning and evening. The sewing box by a small chair was closed, everything tucked neatly inside. The grassy scent of new reeds mingled with the fragrance of lavender and filled the room. Lark sighed at the perfection of it. It felt like a church altar; she didn't dare trespass long upon it. Like her mother's room, this room made her uncomfortable.

"Oh, I'm very pleased with Lord Blackstone." Helen threw her arms around Lark in her excitement. "I just had to tell you."

"You like him then?" Lark asked incredulously as she hugged her sister back. "Belowstairs you looked too overcome to speak to him." She stepped back, noticing the glow in Helen's wide umber eyes. She had never seen her sister so animated.

"Aye, well, Mother says he's abrupt, but nice. It's just his way. I hope he chooses to wed me. He is handsome too, do you not think so?"

"I suppose, if you like large dark things."

"You do not mean it." Helen grinned. "And his eyes—they are so black and perfectly shaped. Did you not notice his long lashes? Are they not comely eyes?"

"Debolt's are prettier."

"Stop it." Helen clamped her hand over her mouth, muffling a giggle. "You know your destrier does not have pretty eyes."

"If you were a knight, I'd challenge you for that remark." Lark struck an indignant pose, at odds with the grin on her face. "Alas! I'll not have Debolt disparaged. I can't think of a more gallant way to die than defending the honor of my mount. What say you? Shall you choose your weapon, or shall I?"

Helen caught herself before she laughed again. "Lark, you must be quiet or Mother shall hear us. I am sure you are comparing Lord Blackstone's eyes to Lord Avenall's."

The lightness left Lark's voice as she said, "No one has blue eyes like Avenall's. They sparkle like flawless sapphires. Remember when I used to tease him and call him Sir Lord Sapp and Hire."

"Aye, you teased him unmercifully."

"I know." Lark sounded proud of herself. "I doubt you will get away with teasing Lord Blackstone."

She paused for a moment, and the smile left Helen's face. "You speak as if you do not like him."

Lark gazed at her sister. How could she tell her the truth

about Lord Blackstone? She asked, "Do you honestly like him?"

"Aye, he will make a fine husband." Helen paused, then said more to herself, "And I liked it when he touched my chin." She put her fingers up and ran them over the spot he had touched.

"He'll touch more than your chin on your wedding night. Will you be able to stand him rutting over you like a randy goat?"

Helen's face turned the same scarlet as the embroidered roses on the coverlet.

Lark realized she'd just addressed Helen as she would have her father's men and her brothers. Clearing her throat, she added, "I'm sorry. You know what I mean."

"I'm sure the first few times will be awkward." Helen stared down at her hands as she twisted them.

"Worse than awkward, if he's a clumsy oaf." A vision of Blackstone rose up in her mind, of him tackling her to the ground, right before he had tried to kiss her. Lark found the chase exhilarating. Helen would never survive that kind of treatment.

"I'm sure he is not. He was married before me."

"Aye, and probably to a biddable meek lamb like you. She probably couldn't keep him from his marriage rights. You will be forced to bed him as well."

"I suppose I shall, just as you will bed Lord Avenall." A slight frown marred Helen's brow.

"Unlike you, I can defend myself. If Lord Avenall hurts me the first time, I shall never allow him in my bed again. If he should order me to sleep with him, I'll just inform him I'm not his chattel. Should he persist, I'll skewer him with a lance." Lark grinned as a vision rose up in her mind of her chasing Avenall around their chamber with a lance. She couldn't help but smile.

"You would never forbid Avenall your bed," Helen said, aghast.

"I would."

"You don't mean that. You love him—surely you'll not turn him away."

"There is love, and there is self-preservation. I can still love him, but it will be courtly love. But you"—Lark touched her cheek—"will not even have love. You'll be owned by Lord Blackstone, property to be done with as he sees fit. Mark my words, he'll order you about and you'll not be denying him your bed either. He's domineering. He'll take what he wants."

"Mother says I shall be glad when he comes to my bed after the first few times."

"Did she?" Lark raised a golden brow at Helen. As a child, she had been curious about procreation. She spied on her brothers enough to know that some women enjoyed being bedded. And Elizabeth Mandeville certainly seemed to enjoy her husband's bed. Lark's room was across the hall. Most any night of the year, Lark could hear the pantings and groanings that sometimes went on for hours. It could be that Lord Blackstone would treat Helen differently—after all, she was comely and he did not suspect her of trying to murder him. Still, the idea of Helen enjoying the Black Dragon in her bed seemed so far-fetched it made her frown.

"I feel we shall have a good marriage." Helen sounded as if she were trying to convince herself of that fact.

"Does not his sheer size frighten you? His shoulders are as wide as Debolt's haunches, and probably as hairy."

Helen had to cover her mouth and catch another laugh. "I don't mind his size. I shall always feel safe with him."

"Aye, that broadsword he carries is large enough to kill three men with one blow." A hint of esteem and envy came through in Lark's voice. She recalled how he'd fended off the attack of the Scot in the woods. She couldn't help but admire his battle skills—just a little.

Helen looked disturbed by Lark's description of his sword. In a forced confident tone, she said, "See, I shall always be protected."

"I doubt any brigand with half a brain would attack him."

"So you do find some merit in him?"

"Aye, how could I not admire him as a fellow warrior? Even the bards sing of his prowess in the Holy Land. But if you dare speak of it to him, I'll deny it."

Helen smiled at her. "I shall never tell him, but I hope your opinion of him will change."

"If you're sure about marrying him and he treats you well"—Lark made a face—"I'll try to tolerate him. Most likely, when I see you with him I'll be smiling openly, thanking the saints he's not *my* husband."

Helen's dark brows furrowed slightly, and she looked confused, not knowing how to take that comment. Russet eyes stared at Lark pensively for a moment. Finally, a grin fluttered back onto Helen's lips. "You will come to have brotherly affection for him, I'm sure of it. That is all I ask of you. Should Lord Blackstone choose me, I'll want you and Avenall to come and visit us, so please don't do anything to anger him."

"I believe just the sight of me annoys him," Lark said dryly.

"Why would you say that?" Helen's voice grew suspicious. "You haven't done something to anger him?"

"I've tried my best to." Lark saw Helen's dark brows meet in worry. She quickly amended, "You know most men are intimidated by me. I can't imagine why they don't like brazen shrews." Lark's lips split in an impish grin.

Helen didn't return the grin. Her wide brown eyes remained grave. "If you strove to be a little more affable, they would like you. You know how lasting first impressions can be. Mother says—"

"If you spout some of Mother's harping wisdom at me, I'll be ill right here in your pristine room." Lark grabbed her stomach, feigning sickness. "You would not want me to be sick all over your new rushes, would you?"

"I'm sorry." Helen touched her arm. "I know how you abhor hearing Mother's scolding."

"Better she ridicule me than you. I doubt you could endure it." Lark hid the hurt behind a nonchalant tone. She'd learned to conceal the scars her mother had left on her heart.

"I would gladly take your place if I could."

"I know. That is why you are my favorite sister."

"I'm your only sister," Helen said, grimacing.

"And I've been blessed to have such a caring and considerate one." Lark hugged her. The grimace on Helen's face faded into a smile as Lark drew back. "Now you must go to sleep. If you have dark circles under your eyes in the morn, Lord Blackstone will be displeased. If that happens, I'm sure Mother will blame me. I'd best go. Try not to dream about Blackstone over-much." Lark smiled at Helen and gingerly pulled the door closed behind her, not making a sound.

Lark thought of their conversation. Who would have believed Helen would favor Blackstone for a husband? He was a little handsome—if one liked brutish dark bears. If she didn't know better, she would swear Helen was well on the way to caring for Blackstone. How could that be? Helen preferred gentle, kind men like Avenall. A thought crossed her mind that made her pause in midstep. Why had Avenall not chosen Helen for his bride? Most men would have.

She did not ponder it long. A memory flashed in her mind, of Blackstone, of that menacing look on his face right before he'd turned and followed Evel up to his room. He would probably try to torment her again. But when and where would he strike? Her gaze combed the long hallway. Torchlight flickered along the empty walls. Sighing under her breath, she moved down the hall, feeling her thin bliaut brush against her ankles and the cold stones beneath her feet. Her mother did not believe in wasting rushes in the hallways.

Her father's resounding snores followed her down the hall. When she reached her room, she quickly opened the door, stepped inside, and threw home the bolt.

The metallic sound creaked in the silence . . . an unusually heavy silence. She sensed something and paused, her hand still on the bolt. Her ears pricked at the slow steady rasp of breathing behind her. Though the sound was barely audible, hardly more than a whisper, it grated against every fiber of her body.

"Baltizar, I hope that's you." Her whisper sounded like a scream in the silence.

"I'm insulted."

At the familiar deep, derisive voice, she whipped around. Moonlight streamed in through the small window, outlining Blackstone's huge, dark form. The softness of the moonlight enhanced the glowing black eyes, the coppery fire in them beaming out at her.

She turned and grabbed for the lock. A beefy hand clamped over her mouth and the other clenched her waist. Abruptly, her back hit his hard, unyielding chest.

"You're not taking your leave of me so soon," Blackstone said, his voice deep and rough near her ear.

Chapter 6

Fear had always been an abstract concept for Lark. But with the Black Dragon's hot breath scorching her neck, sending goosebumps down to her belly, and the unrelenting strength of his brawn holding her, she finally understood why warriors retreated to safe havens after battle.

A memory rushed back to her of her previous response when he had fallen on top of her and she'd raised her mouth to meet his. Those eyes. They wielded some sort of power over her that she loathed. This new-found chink in her mettle goaded her no end, for like a wolf with a still-struggling prey caught in its mouth, she knew the predator in him enjoyed the fear in her.

Lark ordered him from her room, throwing in several expletives to bolster her courage. Unfortunately, her voice came out mumbled behind his palm.

"Alas! Is that any way to greet me?"

She told him she'd like to greet him with the tip of her dagger, but again his hand muffled her words. As she threw out more incensed barbs, the calloused skin on his palms brushed against her lips. She grew keenly aware of the sheen of perspiration on her own skin, melding with the heat of his hand. The coarse slickness where their flesh touched made her lips moist and hot.

Not only that, she could feel his sinewy chest against her back and his thick, corded thighs pressed against the back of her legs. To make matters worse, his hips ground tightly against her backside, and . . . Holy Mother! There was no mistaking the erection intimately prodding her bottom.

The last of her mumbled tirade became lost in a maze of jumbled thoughts, chief among them, why was he aroused? She didn't know whether to feel indignation or pleased. Helen was the one who excited lust in men. Even with Avenall, she had always felt his kisses could be more robust in their ardor. Sometimes it was she who wouldn't end the kiss when she knew very well he wanted to.

Blackstone stood there a moment, holding her, then leaned close to her ear. "Does this sudden silence mean you have surrendered, tigress? I would not want to wake up the castle with your screaming. If I take my hand away, will you hold that tongue of yours?"

Lark closed her eyes, fighting the unbidden stir of sensations his hot breath caused on her ear and neck. After a moment, she gathered her wits and nodded.

The moment her mouth was free, she turned and hissed at him, "How did you get in here, Blackstone?"

"We are acquainted enough to be on a first name basis. Call me Stoke."

"I don't want to be on a first name basis with you. What have you done with Baltizar? If you have harmed him, you'll know what the tip of my sword feels like in your belly—"

He clamped his hand over her mouth again. "Your sweet threats endear you to my heart. For such kind words, I'll tell you, your pet is unharmed. I lured him outside with a piece of meat. Judas's blood, but you feel good in my arms!" He began to nibble on her ear, running his tongue along the lobe.

Lark felt a shiver go down her back. She thought of screaming down the castle walls, but she'd rather face the Black Dragon's lips on her neck than try to explain to Elizabeth what he was doing in her room—especially after she had accused Lark earlier of trying to seduce him.

His lips moved lower on her neck. She felt the hot, moist tip of his tongue glide along her skin, while the hand that had cupped her mouth slid down over her chin, then her neck, to touch her breast. His other hand moved from her waist and closed over her other breast. Lark arched her back, her body no longer her own but under the power of his large hands. The heat of them burned clear down to the very core of her, making her knees grow weak. Lark's head lulled back against his shoulder. Something drawn to the fire in him made her face turn toward his.

The moment their lips touched, she gasped at the tantalizing feel of them, soft, scalding, and seducing. The taste of him filled her all the way to the tips of her fingers and toes. His tongue slid into her mouth. As she felt the drugging silkiness, the sensual way his tongue molded and caressed every crevice of her mouth, her haze-filled mind wondered why Avenall had never done this to her. He could at least have tried it.

Without ending his exploration of her mouth, he whisked her up into his arms. Lark grew vaguely aware of the mattress against her back as he eased down on top of her. She could feel his powerful body covering every part of her, his hard erection urging the soft flesh between her legs, a tantalizing feeling that made her heart pound. The masculine smell of leather and horse, and his own clean, musky scent filled her senses. His long black hair waved down along the sides of her face, tickling her temples and cheeks as he continued to kiss her.

Lark wrapped her arms around him and kneaded the muscles in his back, awed by the way her fingers molded to the steely brawn there. It was like running her hands over sculpted rock.

"You drive me mad," he groaned. One of his hands slid down her bare arms. The callouses on his palms brushed against the tender skin on the inside of her forearm, making tingles shoot to her wrists and up to her shoulder. Her silk nightgown bunched against the inside of her arm as he slid his hand up it, then along the side of one breast. His hand moved up to cup her breast again; then he flattened and molded the pliant flesh.

He rubbed her nipple between his thumb and first finger. She sucked in her breath, feeling heat flowing through her. Her breathing grew rapid and heavy. She could think of naught but him, his hand on her nipple, his tongue moving against hers in a primitive undulation, the warmth of his body pressing against hers. Avenall had never made her feel like this.

His thigh eased between her legs, even as his hand moved from her breast and glided down her ribs, along her flat waist, to her hips. Her gown was tangled up around her hips, and when he touched her naked thigh, a tingly sensation shot down to her toes. With tormenting slowness, he slid his hand up her leg. She felt his finger dip into the soft folds there.

"Sweet Mary, you mustn't," Lark cried out, trying to close her thighs, but they wouldn't oblige her. All she could do was writhe beneath the sensations shooting through her as he stroked her.

"Aye, my tigress. Let me feel you."

"I shouldn't."

"Why shouldn't you? Are you afraid to have a real man?" He continued to stroke her while he kissed her, his tongue thrusting into her mouth, keeping rhythm with his finger.

Lark's hips began to move against his hand, and she wanted to cry out from the pleasure of it.

A howl rent the air.

The discordant din hovered in the hallway for what seemed like ages.

Lark's wits returned to her in a flash. She tried to push him off her. When he didn't move, she grabbed the back of his hair and gave it a good yank.

Stoke broke the kiss. "By Judas," he muttered as he grabbed her fingers and squeezed until she dropped his hair.

"Get off me!" Lark fought him now, using all the strength in her body, but he easily pinned her wrists above her head.

The howl came again. This time Baltizar's dirge carried

through the whole castle. It boomed down the hallway with the intensity of a blast from a hunting horn.

"I thought I got rid of that flea haven," he said near her ear.

"I hope he wakes the entire castle."

Her hope came true. Abruptly a door opened out in the hall. "Lark!"

Lark flinched at the sound of Elizabeth's voice and glanced toward the door.

"That wild creature is in the hall." Elizabeth's words were muffled through the door. "I thought I told you to put him outside. What is he doing in here and howling?"

When he didn't seem inclined to move, she hissed, "Get off me."

"Lark! I hear whispering. You're talking to someone. Open this door!" The pounding began and grew insistent. "If you do not open this door, I'll get Gowan to do it."

Stoke growled low in his throat. "Do not think you can get away from me that easily. You owe me some answers about the Scots, Tigress, and I mean to get them." He rolled off her and stood.

"I know naught about them."

"Lark! Open this door! Who is in there with you?"

Lark turned to him and whispered, "Get under the bed."

"I'll not crawl beneath a bed." He splayed his legs and crossed his burly arms over his massive chest. A stubborn grin pulled at his lips.

Lark took in his size and knew he couldn't fit beneath her bed even if he were willing. "Very well, but I'll not forget this. The next time you try to come into my room, you can be sure I'll set a trap." Lark scooped up a pile of old shirts and braies her brothers had outgrown and she'd confiscated years earlier. They made great camouflage for times such as these. She dove beneath the bed and pulled down the counterpane. As she scooted over against the wall, she mounded the clothes over her.

Her mother's pounding never let up.

She heard Stoke pass by the bed and pause before the door. Metal scraped against the bolt; then hinges creaked as he opened the door.

"Oh, my lord!" Her mother gasped loudly. "What are you doing in Lark's room? Where is she? I thought I heard voices."

"I know not. I seemed to have gotten lost when I went to visit the garderobe. I thought this was my room."

Lark held her breath, wondering if Stoke would give her away.

"Have you seen my daughter? That creature of hers is generally always near her."

"Nay, but I wish you luck in finding her." Lark let out the breath she'd been holding. "If you'll excuse me, it has been a long night. Good eventide."

The dust sticking to the side of her face and hair tickled the inside of Lark's nose. She clamped her fingers over her nostrils and stifled a sneeze as Stoke's footsteps faded down the hallway.

A small crack between the mattress and the counterpane allowed Lark about half an inch of space in which to see her mother. Elizabeth's long blue gown swished past Lark's face and paused. Her mother stepped closer to the bed . . . closer . . . bending. She was going to look under the bed! Every fiber in Lark's body froze. She held her breath and flattened her spine to the floor.

Elizabeth peered directly beneath the bed. Lark couldn't see her face, but she felt her mother's penetrating gaze.

After a long, tense moment, Elizabeth sighed loudly and stood. In a flurry of blue silk, she whipped around and stormed out of the room. The door slammed behind her. Lark felt something hairy brush her thigh. She glanced down her side and saw Baltizar crawling on all fours toward her. He paused and laid his head on her hand.

She drove her fingers into the thick gray fur on his neck. "That was close, my friend. I owe you more than you know. You saved me from the clutches of the Black Dragon. I suppose I'll have to face Mother though. What say you we sleep under the bed for the rest of the night? At least she'll not find me 'til morn. Though, 'tis not Mother I'm worried about so much, but the other.'' Lark frowned up at the bottom of the mattress and knew she must be ready the next time he surprised her.

If she cared to admit it, she liked his kind of surprises. Every part of her body still throbbed from his hands. If she closed her eyes, she could still feel his hands caressing her breasts, his finger between her legs. . . .

Nay, she mustn't think of such things. She loved Avenall. For that very reason, she couldn't allow Stoke to get near her again. If he had proceeded, she hated to think what would have happened. He would have taken her maidenhead. How could she have explained that to Avenall? To Helen? Nay, the Black Dragon might have some wicked power over her, but she would conquer it. She had to.

At dawn, Lark dressed in a pair of brown braies and a tunic. She reached beneath her sleeve and strapped a leather sheath around her forearm. The dagger in it was turned so the hilt lay near her wrist for easy access. Lark rubbed her hand over the smooth, inlaid-pearl hilt. She loved this particular weapon, for it was a gift from William on her twelfth birthday. He'd said it was to protect her should her sword ever fail her.

She slid another dagger into her right boot. This knife she had won from Avenall in a chess game seven years ago. She'd beaten him three out of four games. He'd never played her since.

Smiling from ear to ear at the memory, she strapped on her broadsword and straightened the scabbard. Ready for an encounter with Stoke, she strode toward the door. Baltizar hoped off the bed and joined her.

Lark checked the hall for signs of Elizabeth or Stoke. She let Baltizar out and gingerly eased the door closed behind her. As she strode down the hall, her gaze warily eyed each chamber door she passed. Her loose hair brushed her bottom, the slight sound melding with her light steps. It was too much bother to braid it, so she had pulled it back with a leather thong and left it to straggle down her back.

She grew aware of male voices drifting up the stairwell. For as long as Lark could remember, the familiar sound of her father's men breaking the fast had greeted her morning. This was where she usually smiled in anticipation of joining them. But this wasn't a usual morn. Stoke could be down there waiting for her. At the thought, her brows furrowed.

She approached the stairwell just as Marta climbed the last step. Marta looked at her and clutched her panting chest. Wisps of gray hair had escaped her braid and bunched out around her face and ears. With a gnarled hand, she shoved them back from her eyes. The thick wrinkles stretched across her parchment-thin skin, giving her the ancient look of a sage. Lark had asked Marta her age once, but her response was, "Old as these castle walls." And she looked it too, with her hunched, frail frame.

Her old nursemaid squinted at Lark. The wrinkles above her cheeks stretched, the blue veins beneath her sheer skin protruding. "Where ye been, child? The mistress had me searching the castle over for ye. Have ye no care for an old woman?" Marta's hand moved up and clutched the base of her throat, the slight tremor in her frail hand worsening. Her panting grew louder.

Lark loved the old nursemaid as a grandmother and was wise to Marta's artifice. Whenever she wanted to make Lark feel guilty, she mentioned her age. They knew each other far too well for Lark to be taken by such tricks. "I'm sorry." Lark touched her arm. "Mother should not have asked you to look for me."

"O' course, she should. Ye are my responsibility 'til they lay me in the ground. I've nursed all the master's whelps and him besides, and I love ye like me own. I don't mind tellin' ye, ye might be the cause of me death yet. I thought the twins would do it with their mischief, but yer just as bad. But I won't scold ye, for yer mother will do plenty of that." She pointed one gnarled finger at Lark's chamber. "Just march yer backside back there. The mistress says yer not to go below without having on a pretty bliaut befitting a proper lady. Lord Avenall is with us.''

Lark jammed her hands on her hips. ''I've no need to wear finery for Avenall, he's seen me looking much worse in the tilt yard. And I've no desire to make an impression on Lord Blackstone.''

''Maybe ye haven't, but some of his knights have arrived and brought a wain of gifts with them. Yer mother might not be wantin' ye to look like such a ragtag in front of them. Ye should see all the trinkets they brought for yer sister. The mistress is beaming. And Helen, bless her sweet face, is beside herself with joy. She fairly preens when that big hulkin' lord is near her. They be belowstairs now going through the wain. Some o' the finest fabric I've ever seen. Some with silver and gold threads running through it. And gold and jewel-studded cups and platters. He must be richer than the king himself.''

''I'm sure Mother will be requiring an inventory of all his wealth. Has he agreed to marry Helen yet?'' For some reason, Lark's stomach clenched into knots as she waited for Marta's answer.

''Nay, but he will. He wouldn't have given her the cart of gifts if he wasn't agreeable. Yer mother expects he'll claim her this morn.''

''I'm glad Helen has made such a fine match.'' Lark had tried to sound pleased for Helen, but her words had come out tonelessly. ''And since he is Helen's betrothed and not mine, why should I dress to impress his lordship, or his knights?''

Marta shook her head, sending out clouds of wispy gray hair. She paused and stared deep into Lark's eyes. ''Ye wouldn't be jealous of yer sister, now would ye?''

Lark could never feel the brunt of those too-intuitive gray eyes without feeling uncomfortable. She fought the feeling now and gazed back at them. ''Why should I? I'm glad Helen is happy.''

''Ye don't seem to like him very much.'' Marta's bushy gray brows touched the lids of her small eyes as she asked, ''Have ye a reason?''

Lark couldn't reveal that Stoke suspected her of trying to kill him, so she said, "He is arrogant, brutish, and thick-witted. That is my only complaint."

"Ah! He's no more arrogant than any handsome, rich earl. And no man with such black, sharp eyes as he can be thick-witted. Nay, yer usually a good judge of character, but ye've got the wrong of this lord, ye have."

"I'm glad you find him so gallant and pleasant."

"I'm wondering if ye don't as well." Marta raised one gray brow at her.

"Nay, Marta. Why should I find him attractive? You know I'm to marry Avenall."

"Aye, but do ye love him like ye think?" Marta's eyes grew wide in her head for a moment.

"I wouldn't be marrying him if I did not."

"It might just be a girlish fancy ye have for him. Lord Avenall is pretty enough to turn yer head, but do ye really love him here"—Marta thumped the spot over her heart—"where it counts?"

"Of course I love him."

"Nay, I think ye like to bedevil him like ye did as a child, and ye may look upon him as a pretty bauble, but ye don't really love him. Ye know not what it means to love a man body and soul. When ye do, it'll show on ye. Ye'll be sick with wantin' him. But it might be too late to find true love, if ye marry the wrong man."

"That is utter nonsense, Marta. I love Avenall. I've always loved him."

"I ain't never said this 'fore now, but I've never felt he was the right one for ye. That one's too gentle a soul to be dealing with the likes of ye. Ye'll make him a miserable being with your strong ways, and he'll lose his respect for himself and ye for him. Ye remember when ye was little? The moment ye wanted something and got it, ye didn't want it anymore. That's how it'll be with yer betrothed. Ye'll grow tired of him soon enough with his poetry and gentle ways."

"How can you say this?" Lark stared at her old nurse, trying to look indignant, while a small part of her feared that what Marta had said might be true. Nay, she loved Avenall.

" 'Tis the truth and ye know it, and I'm about the only one who loves ye enough to tell ye."

"I shan't discuss this any longer." Lark stepped past Marta and headed down the steps.

"Where do ye think yer going? Yer to put on a bliaut and later yer to try on yer weddin' gown."

"I'm sorry, Marta, but I've been wearing braies and shirts for years now, and I do not intend to change now. I'm not interested in pleasing Lord Blackstone. Father is the only one I wish to please, and he doesn't mind my braies and tunic. After I eat, I'll come back up and try on the gown." With those parting words, Lark headed down the steps, feeling Marta's gaze digging into her back.

How could Marta think that her love for Avenall wouldn't last? Of course it would. She loved him as much as she did her father. And this nonsense about Marta believing Lark was jealous of Helen and Stoke. How ridiculous.

Lark entered the hall frowning. Dozens of men filled the cavernous room, some seated at the table, some standing. The strangers, who mingled with her father's men, all wore black tabards with small dragons embroidered on them. Three serving maids scrambled around the room trying to keep cups filled and food flowing.

Wira, one of the serving maids, paused long enough to speak to her. Lark looked at the tall, buxom woman before her. Her thick black hair fell down to her waist in long braids, stark against her white skin. By far, she was the comeliest of the serving maids, though her eyes held a wariness that belied her ten-and-nine years and made her look older than she was. Lark had a feeling the wariness had to do with a passion for Evel, for Lark had caught her sneaking into his chamber on several occasions.

"Lady Lark, ye should see the cart of presents Lord Black-stone's men brought with 'em. They be gifts for Lady Helen."

"Where are Lord Avenall and Lady Elizabeth?"

"They're with Lady Helen goin' through the cart." One of the men banged his cup on the table. Wira frowned. "I'd better see to fillin' that one's thirst 'fore he pounds a hole in the master's table."

Lark watched her slip through the maze of men, dodging pinches on the bottom and groping hands. Two of the Dragon's men, who stood several feet away, spotted Lark. One was a grizzled man with a patch over his eye and scars slashing across his face. Close-cropped blond hair covered the other man's head. He looked younger than his friend, about a score and ten, and had one drooping eye.

Scar Face's gaze raked her from crown to toe. A slow venomous smile parted his lips. He punched Droopy Eye in the elbow. "Look what we've got here. I think 'tis a woman in man's clothes."

"Could be a boy, bony and lanky as it is. Ain't got breasts nor an arse to speak of neither. Does have hair like a woman." Scar Face walked a slow circle around her. "I wonder if it ain't a eunuch." He reached out to touch Lark's hair.

Chapter 7

Baltizar leaped from the stairwell, his teeth bared. He hunched his back and growled low in his throat. Saliva glistened on his fangs.

Scar Face's eyes widened as he leaped back.

"Aye, look, the eunuch has a protector." Droopy Eye kicked at Baltizar, trying to tease him.

The wolf growled and snapped at the heckler's boot.

"If you don't get away from him, I vow you will regret it." Lark looked at them as she would a cockroach that needed to be crushed.

They both laughed heartily.

Scar Face sobered. "It does have a mouth on it. We should take down those braies and see what's beneath 'em. Aye, whatta you say? It might teach the thing a lesson." Droopy Eye elbowed his friend again.

Lark's fingers tightened around the hilt of her sword. "I advise you not to get near me again, for I'm not feeling benevolent this morn and Baltizar has not been fed."

"You scared?" Droopy Eye elbowed his friend.

"I be shaking in me boots."

They threw back their heads and guffawed.

In one fluid movement, Lark pulled her dagger from her sleeve and drew her sword. Before they brought their heads back down, she had thrust the tip of her sword beneath Scar Face's neck, and the dagger met the hollow of Droopy Eye's throat.

Their laughter died. Unable to lower their chins for the razor-sharp steel pushed against their necks, they looked down their noses at her, a bewildered, surprised expression on their faces.

"Good, I have your attention. For your own well being, I hope you've decided against your present course of action. Aye?"

Neither of them spoke.

"Come, surely you have something to say." Lark shoved the blades tighter against their necks and smiled when they flinched. "Only moments ago, you were men of so many words. Have you no words now?"

"We were mistaken." Droopy Eye's cheek twitched wildly.

"Aye, you were mistaken. Should you wish to continue this assault on my person, I would gladly welcome it in the tilt yard."

"Nay, we don't wish it." A layer of sweat shimmered on Droopy Eye's brow and his Adam's apple bobbed against the blade.

"Hark you well—the next time you insult someone in her own home, you'd better be ready to defend yourself."

"Who *are* you?" Droopy Eye asked.

"Lord Mandeville's daughter," Lark said proudly.

They shared a haggard glance, then grew even paler.

At their silence, Lark continued, "I feel sure the two of you will mind your manners while staying under Lord Mandeville's roof."

"Aye, my lady," Scar Face said through his teeth, his beady eyes narrowing on her.

Lark realized it was so quiet now that she could hear the flutter of a feather. She turned and saw that every eye had turned her way. All of Lord Stoke's men watched her, some with interest, others with disgust or suspicion. She quickly withdrew her blades and met the gazes of the thirty men.

Lark caught sight of her father, seated in the center of the dais. He didn't look at all as though he was suffering from a night of debauchery. His cheeks were rosy and his green eyes twinkled as he smiled proudly at her.

Her gaze moved to the Black Dragon, who occupied the chair next to her father. In the light of morning, he looked very different. Even handsome in a brutal, dark way. His hair was pulled back and bound at his nape. He wore a black tunic. A large green dragon embroidered on it spanned his wide chest, and his metallic red eyes seeming to glow with each inhalation. He wore a black velvet mantle lined in red silk. Two golden dragon pins held his mantle at his shoulders. Lark hadn't noticed before, but he had a devil's peak on his forehead. His black eyes pierced her face for what seemed like decades. Abruptly, his gaze dropped to the dagger and blade still in her hands, and his lips tightened with suppressed emotion.

"Daughter, shame on you, making enemies of Lord Blackstone's men the moment you enter the room." The laughter in her father's voice belied the reproachful words.

"I just pointed out"—Lark lifted her sword and ran a finger over the sharp edge—"to these men the correct deportment for guests here at St. Vale."

Her father laughed and so did his retainers. They'd grown accustomed to her behavior and wry sense of humor. Some of the tension left the faces of Stoke's men, and they too joined in the revelry. But the brooding scowl didn't leave their leader's face. Stoke stood and leveled those black eyes at Scar Face and Droopy Eye.

Abruptly the laughter ended, the silence again so heavy that it blanketed the hall.

"I'll not have my men acting like ill-behaved curs," Stoke said, his voice laced with a menacing softness that bounded through the silence like a shout. "Get out of my sight before I see to your punishment myself."

Both men stared at their liege for a moment. Scar Face opened his mouth to say something, then looked into the scowling face of his master and abruptly clamped his jaw closed. Without a backward glance, he turned on his heels and stormed from the hall. His companion shot Lark a malignant look with his one good eye and trailed after his friend.

Stoke turned his gaze Lark's way. There was censure in his expression, as if he blamed her for the incident. She met his gaze squarely. In no way would she take the blame for the crude behavior of his own men. With a succinct thrust, she resheathed her sword and dagger.

"Come and break the fast with me, my brazen daughter!" William's voice boomed through the silence.

Lark glanced up at him, catching the faded green eyes beaming with love and pride. The region near her heart warmed, as it always did when her sire looked at her like that. She lived daily for one of those looks. To be looked upon without scorn or ridicule, as her mother usually did, was like feeling the sun burning inside her. Even though Stoke was at the table spoiling the occasion—she could feel his simmering gaze upon her— she would not let him sully the pleasurable moment with her father.

She kept her gaze on William, held her head high, and marched over to the table. Baltizar followed close on her heels. Stoke occupied her mother's usual seat to the right of her father. On the other side of William, Evel sat next to Harold and Cedric.

As she drew near the twins, they turned and smiled derisively at her. The only way to tell them apart was by the scar on Harold's right cheek, a mark he had received when they were sword-playing with sticks as children. He had jabbed Lark one time too many. She'd lost her patience and attacked. After that, they had never asked her to join in another round of mock swordplay.

Harold raised his hands and applauded her silently now, taunting her as she strode past him.

"You've done it again, little sister," Cedric whispered. "You'll have the whole of Black Dragon's army at our throats."

"Better at our throats than our backs," Lark said through a tight smile.

"Here, take my seat." Evel stood, but Rowland was quicker. He was already up and pulling out his chair.

He swept her a gracious bow. "Nay, I insist you take my chair, my lady." His deep blue eyes gleamed, and his dimples came to life as he bestowed a wide grin on her.

Lark looked at the chair, then at the back of Stoke's wide shoulders next to it. As she stared at the black, glistening hair curling near his shoulders, she remembered the feel of it against her face when he had kissed her.

"Thank you." Even though Lark forced out the words, they still sounded tremulous.

The grin never left Rowland's lips as he slid the chair in for her. After another smile in her direction, he left her and joined a group of Stoke's men who stood near a wall.

Stoke turned. His penetrating gaze slid down her body, then snapped up again. She felt the tension oozing from him and moved as far away from him as she could without falling out of her seat.

William leaned past Stoke to look at Lark. "Where have you been, Pigeon?"

Stoke's eyes narrowed at the sound of her nickname. He glanced over at Evel, who looked enthralled by the curves of his spoon.

Her father continued. "It is not like you to fly away from the roost when we have guests. Your mother has had the whole castle out looking for you. She roused me at dawn."

"I'm sorry, but I didn't want Mother to find me, so I slept beneath my bed."

William didn't look at all surprised by her confession. He merely shrugged his shoulders. "Aye, well, I suppose you had good reason. I believe your mother wanted to make a good impression on our guest." He nodded at Stoke. "Have you met the Black Dragon?"

"We've met." Stoke turned the full force of his black eyes on Lark.

"Aye, we have." Lark didn't flinch beneath that obsidian gaze.

"She's probably quizzed you on all the battles you've fought in the Holy Land. If you have not guessed, my daughter's interests lie in war. She is naught like her sister."

"I have heard about battles before." No longer able to stare into those probing eyes, Lark gazed at the trencher she was forced to share with Stoke. Glad to have something to do, she picked up three large slabs of roast pork and threw them beneath the table.

Baltizar caught them in midair. In three bites, he gulped them down. At the smell of the meat, she felt her mouth watering and heard her stomach growling. Ignoring Stoke as best she could, she picked up a piece of dark bread. She spooned some scrambled eggs on it, rolled it up, and bit it.

Her father took a sip of his wine and studied her. "Are you ill? I have never seen you so indifferent toward war talk—especially concerning the triumphs of a knight as famous as our guest here." He clapped his hand on Stoke's shoulder.

Lark swallowed. "I am perfectly fine, Father. I just do not wish to discuss warfare." She jammed the rest of the bread into her mouth and chomped on it.

Her father blinked excessively at her, staring at her as if she were a stranger sitting at his table. After a moment, he leaned back in his chair, his brow wrinkled with worry lines. "My daughter may not be of a mind to hear your war stories, but I for one would like to know how your sword can cleave granite walls without a scratch."

"That is an exaggeration." Stoke looked pleased in spite of his modest words.

"I only know of what the bards sing." William grinned. "Their facts may be slightly skewed, but most of their tales are based on some truth. Pray, tell me where you got such a sword. Did the archangel Gabriel appear unto you and bless it, as rumor would have it?"

In spite of feigning indifference, Lark found herself leaning over in her chair to eavesdrop.

Stoke drew close to William's shoulder and whispered, "Since I may soon join your family, I suppose I should let you in on my secret. I dabble in the metal arts. I forged my own sword." He lovingly stroked the hilt of his weapon.

"You could be a rich man if you opened up an armory. You must tell my armorer your secret."

"The world is not ready for such a secret. Can you imagine the damage such hard metal can have should the secret be leaked to King Philip, or any other of our king's enemies? In good conscience, I cannot divulge my forging process, but I shall forge a sword for you in my own workshop first thing when I return home."

"I believe you'll work out as a son quite nicely." William bestowed a warm smile on Stoke and slapped him on the back. "Have you decided upon my youngest daughter yet?"

The muscles in Lark's chest clenched as she waited for Stoke's reply.

"Nay, I'm in no hurry to marry. I must get to know her a little better."

"What is there to know? Either you want her or you don't." William shot Stoke a curious look.

"I shall decide in a few days."

Lark realized she'd been holding her breath and let it out. For some odd reason, which she hated to think about, it mattered to her that he had not yet committed himself to Helen.

Evel was arguing with the twins about whether barbed arrowheads shot truer than pointed ones. In frustration, Evel turned to William to settle the matter. "Which do you think it is, Father?"

William answered the question. "Barbed, of course."

Stoke seemed to lose interest. He straightened in his chair and glanced over at Lark.

When his shoulder brushed against Lark's arm, she remembered that she'd been leaning toward his chair. She jerked away, the contact still shooting a warmth down her arm.

He bent over until his shoulder was tight against hers and whispered, "I am surprised by your indifference to war stories.

Surely anyone as well versed in the arts of cunning as you, and as deft as you are at irritating my men"—his gaze slid down her body with annoying slowness—"would certainly long to speak of war."

"Not when you are involved in the speaking." Lark tried to listen to the conversation between her father and Evel, but she could not concentrate, for her skin was still tingling where her arm touched his.

"I find it hard to believe you dislike me so much after last night." He cocked a dark brow at her. He obviously knew what his touch had done to her, for a wicked dark light shone in his eyes.

"I lost my head. 'Twill never happen again."

"Won't it?" One of his black brows shot up and a lazy, sensual grin turned up the corners of his mouth.

"Stay away from me. I told you, I know naught about those Scots who attacked you."

"If that were true, why did one of them swear to me you were involved and had spread your legs for him?"

"He was the man whose nose I'd broken. Naturally he'd besmirch my character."

"You really don't expect me to believe you broke his nose."

"I did. He was the one I stopped from putting an arrow in your heart. If you go to the swamp, you'll find the crossbow in the bog."

"How do I know you didn't put it there?" He gazed at her with distrust gleaming in his eyes.

"Is there no way to convince you I'm innocent?"

"Nay, though I'd be wounded if you stopped trying," he drawled.

Lark gazed into those black, swirling eyes, enthralled by them, so she wasn't aware of his hand slipping beneath the tablecloth until he touched her thigh. His long fingers began kneading her flesh.

Warmth spread from toe to thigh and pooled somewhere deep inside Lark. The protest she was about to make died on her lips. She was lost in the feeling of his hand moving up her thigh, the way his wide palm covered the whole top of her thigh, the heat of it penetrating through her braies. Those wonderfully long fingers began to massage her thigh muscle. A memory flashed in her mind, of the way he'd kissed her last night and how it felt to have his hands on her breasts. Her breathing grew rapid and shallow. She slumped back against her chair, trying to fight the heat flowing out his hand, burning her skin.

"You won't stop trying, will you?"

"Move your hand or you shall lose your fingers," Lark managed to say, but her words sounded more like a caress than a threat.

"If you think to use those puny weapons of yours on me as you did on my men, think again. I'll eat them and spit them back at you."

"Beseems that would be very hard on your teeth," Lark said, feeling a languid feeling crawling over her.

"It keeps them sharp for when I come across fiery hot flesh like yours."

"You'll never get another chance to sink your teeth in me as you did last night." Lark felt his long fingers dip down between her legs and rest there.

"As I recall, you enjoyed my touch," he said, his breath hot against her ear. "Especially when I touched you here." He stroked her through her braies.

A shudder went through her. She reached down and grabbed his hand to pull it away, but his fingers pressed deeper into her soft folds. Her breath caught in her throat and her hand paused on top of his. She couldn't think. Her whole body trembled. Inadvertently, the grip she had on his hand eased.

Her free hand dropped beside her and felt weightless beneath the onslaught of his touch. It was almost impossible to concentrate on looking as if naught was happening. She could feel his fingers moving against her palm, stoking the fires already burning in her. The ache in her loins grew unbearable. She arched her back against the chair slightly, groaning inwardly, wanting to press her body against him.

She turned and glanced at him. He gave her a roguish grin, picked up a thick slice of pork with his free hand, and ate it as if naught was happening under the table. He even turned and spoke to her father. "Aye, Lord William, I'll have to agree, a barbed arrow is much more accurate and travels further."

"What say you, Lark?" William bent forward and looked at her.

Lark didn't answer him right away. She was busy trying to makes sense of her jumbled thoughts and not writhe beneath the raging sensations Stoke's fingers were sending through her. After a moment, she said, "I—I know not."

William stared at her strangely. After a long moment of contemplation, he sat back in his chair.

After that, she couldn't follow the conversation at all. Her thighs relaxed, opening fully for him, giving him free rein of her body.

He bent near her ear and whispered, "Shall we continue this in my chamber?"

"Nay. I hate you." Lark felt his hot breath on her neck, sending tingles down her throat.

"So you say, but I think not. You're afraid of me."

"I fear no man," Lark said in a breathless whisper.

"You should be afraid of me, Lark."

"I'm not."

"That is a lie. I can almost taste the fear in you. You're afraid to experience real passion with me, lest your appetite wane for that meek lamb you are to wed. He's never touched you like this, has he? He doesn't make you shudder all over, does he?"

"He does—that's not true. It's not!"

His comment stabbed Lark's wits and reeled them back from the sensual blur that had held her prisoner. She knocked his hand away and tried to leap up and jerk back at the same time. Her chair fell over with her in it, causing her to tumble backwards.

The loud bang as oak met stone brought everyone's attention to her.

Silence reigned over the room once again. Lark had landed on the floor, the chair between her legs. Her bottom throbbed where she'd hit the back of the chair.

Stoke offered her his hand. "Here, let me help you up." A lopsided grin twitched his lips.

She glowered at him. "Nay, but thank you." She knocked his hand away and stood.

"What is the matter, Pigeon?" William turned and looked at her, his bushy brows drawn in worry.

"I lost my balance and fell backward," Lark said, her chest heaving so much she could hardly get out the words.

"Are you sure you are well? You don't look it." Her father glanced at Stoke, then back at Lark.

"Aye, Father, I'm just not very hungry."

Stoke turned and eyed her, that infuriating grin on his face. She didn't take her eyes off him as she bent and righted the chair. Footsteps sounded behind her. She turned and gazed into Elizabeth's furious face.

"Where have you been? Do you know I've had everyone searching for you?"

The screech brought Stoke around in his chair. Rage screwed up Lady Elizabeth's face. Across from her, Lark stood her ground, her yellow-gold eyes wide with a kind of vulnerability he'd never seen in them. It was the first outward sign of weakness he'd ever glimpsed in her. He should enjoy seeing her defenseless like this, yet for some reason it afforded him no pleasure.

"I slept out in the woods last night, Mother. I'm sorry it caused trouble."

"Trouble! Do you know how I've worried? Have you no sense of propriety? Sleeping out of doors like a common villein! And just look at you. You look like a boy in those clothes. At least a gown would hide your curveless frame, but you insist upon going around in braies, exposing your thin hips and legs to the world. I'm surprised Avenall sees anything to love in you—'' Lady Elizabeth appeared to realize that Lord Avenall and Helen stood at her side and clamped her mouth closed.

Lady Lark hunched her shoulders and flinched as the words struck her. For a moment she looked like a martyr standing there, taking a beating. Her gaze darted between her mother and Lord Avenall; then she took off running, dodging Stoke's men.

''Come back here!'' Lady Elizabeth stomped her foot. ''You have to try on your wedding gown! I'll not have you running off again.''

Her only answer was the slamming of the heavy oak door.

''I'll go after her,'' Helen said.

''Nay, I'll go.'' Lord Avenall looked down at Helen.

''Nay, 'tis my fault, I'll go after her.'' Lady Elizabeth turned to run after her daughter.

Lord Mandeville leaped up from his chair. In three long strides, he grabbed his wife's arm and said, ''Let her go, Elizabeth. Have you not done enough to her?''

''Oh, you always take her side. Since she's every bit your daughter, you go after her and see if you can do anything with her.''

''You could do more with a kind word than with your barbed tongue.'' William thrust her aside as he hurried to catch his daughter.

Stoke stood, respecting William Mandeville more than he previously had. At least he could put his wife in her place when need be. And Lady Elizabeth needed to be reproached for continually squawking at her daughter. Something smoldered behind the scolding, something more than mere rancor, a kind of canker that festered deep within Lady Elizabeth. Stoke wondered what had caused it as he strode toward the door. He couldn't help but feel a stab of sympathy for Lark. He didn't understand this unbidden feeling. After all, she was involved with his enemy.

Lady Elizabeth stepped in his path, barring his way. ''I'm so sorry you must witness the behavior of my unruly daughter. She disgraces us all. Please finish your meal, my lord.''

"All the disgrace does not rest with your daughter, my lady." Stoke pointedly eyed her, watching a blush creep over her face. When she looked too distressed to speak, he said, "Forgive me, but I have business to attend to."

"But Helen so wanted to eat with you," Lady Elizabeth said, finding her voice. "She will be disappointed."

"I shall speak to her." His gaze flicked over to Helen, who stood near Lord Avenall.

She looked comely in a yellow kirtle that hugged her hour-glass curves. Two thick, long braids fell to her waist. A circlet of tiny clover blossoms ringed her head. She was the essence of loveliness and grace, everything cunning in a woman. When he'd first seen her, he had been struck by how much she looked like Cecily. It was hard for him to look at her and not remember the painful memories Cecily had engraved in his mind. Granted she was not like her brazen sister, but still it was hard for him to even gaze upon her.

Lord Avenall shot Stoke a knowing glance and grasped Lady Elizabeth's arm. "May I escort you to the table?"

"Aye." Elizabeth patted his hand and looked flustered.

Stoke watched their progress for a moment, then turned back to Lady Helen. He lifted her chin so she would look at him. "I'll not be able to break the fast with you this morning, but I shall speak to you later."

She blinked up at him with wide brown eyes and smiled timidly. "I know Lark and Mother argue, but please, do not judge either of them over-harshly. Mother should never have spoken to Lark as she did, and she knows that."

"Does she always speak thus to your sister?"

"Not always, only when she is very angry. And Lark took it so bravely. I don't blame her for running out. Please do not judge her harshly. In spite of the hard facade she puts forward, she really is hurt very easily, though she hides it well. And if she does not like you now, she will. She's not one to warm to people easily, but once you gain her love and respect, there is not a more loyal heart in all of Christendom."

"I wish I could believe that." Stoke looked toward the empty hallway through which Lark had recently exited.

"I feel sure you'll love her as I do, once you get to know her."

Stoke glanced back at Lady Helen. The naive expression on her face looked genuine. It stung his conscience. The last thing he wanted to do with her errant sister was love her. His hand dropped from her chin. "I should go. When I return, we'll take a long walk together."

"I would like that—oh, and thank you for the gifts. They are so lovely."

"You are quite welcome. I could not come here empty-handed." Stoke bent and kissed her hand. He felt her fingers trembling against his lips. It brought a frown to his face as he straightened and dropped her hand.

Had he not been taken in by the same shy beauty Cecily possessed? No woman was what she seemed on the outside. There was always a secret, cunning part of her she hid well. He gazed into Lady Helen's eyes and wondered what secret she hid behind that sweet facade.

Rowland cleared his throat near them. The frown deepened as Stoke eyed his friend and said to Lady Helen, "If you'll excuse me."

She curtsied gracefully, then strode over to join her mother. Stoke watched the sensual sway of her hips beneath her gown, then turned to Rowland. "Watch her brother, I'm going after Lady Lark." He glanced over at Evel and locked gazes with him.

Evel quickly glanced away, but not before Stoke noticed the worried frown on his face.

"I was stuck with Evel last night, and I had to oust a wench from my bed just to watch his chamber door. He didn't move after he settled in. I had hoped you'd let me follow our little mischief-maker while you stayed here and wooed your intended." Rowland's eyes twinkled.

"Nay, I find I have other things on my mind."

"Alas! See that they do not make you forget your business here." Rowland glanced at Helen and frowned pensively.

"I'll not forget it." After a quick glance in Rowland's direction, he strode out of the hall. He took his time. After all, he didn't want Lady Elizabeth to think he was following Lark.

When he reached the bailey, he found William Mandeville scratching his head and frowning toward the gates. Stoke followed his gaze and caught a glimpse of Lady Lark on a huge white destrier, galloping over the drawbridge. She rode bareback, bent low over the animal's neck. Her thick straight hair bounced against her wool tunic and formed a golden cloud of disarray down her back. Her pet wolf followed closely on her horse's hooves.

"I tried to stop her," William said, more to himself. " 'Tis better she has some time alone."

"Does she often ride out alone?" Stoke asked, not bothering to hide the suspicion in his voice.

"Aye, when she can stand no more of her mother's sweet words." William's voice was thick with regret.

Stoke started toward the stable.

"Are you taking your leave of us?" William yelled at Stoke's back.

"I have urgent business to see to. I'll return shortly."

"Have you no one who can see to your business?"

"Not to this particular problem."

William leveled a sidelong look at Stoke's back, and a knowing grimace marred his face. He shook his head as he turned and strode back into the hall.

Lark gave Debolt his head, feeling the thud of his hooves deep within her chest and the pumping of his sleek muscles against her thighs. She didn't rein in until she felt him tiring. They slowed and she patted his sleek neck, feeling the warm, foamy sweat clinging to her fingers.

At a craggy cliff, she reined in and glanced down into the

Constance Hall

glen that separated St. Vale's property from that of Malgore, owned by one of her father's vassals, Sir Joseph Montfort.

This was her favorite place to come when she needed to be alone. How could Elizabeth humiliate her like that in front of everyone? She was used to her mother's furious tirades in front of her father and his men, but to suffer such an affront before Stoke and his retainers! She would rather have been boiled in oil.

And that comment Stoke had made about Avenall not making her shudder. Of course Avenall did—well, maybe not so much as that wretched Black Dragon. Avenall had never touched her like that. He worshiped women, he'd never be so forward, and she felt quite sure he had never lain with a woman and was saving himself for his wife. If she cared to admit it, she had often wanted him to be a little more aggressive in that area. Aye, she did. She'd even rubbed her body against him to entice him. He had said they should wait until they were married and gently nudged her away.

Lark scooted back and slid off Debolt's rear to the ground. His sleek white head dipped down and he began cropping grass. She too, bent and yanked up a handful of grass, only she twisted the thin blades until it shredded in her hands.

Her gaze strayed down into the glen as she tugged another clump of grass from the ground, snagging it before Debolt had a chance to eat it. The morning sun hit the dew-covered granite stones embedded in the steep sides of the valley. They glistened like jewels. A slight morning breeze wafted through the hollow, swishing the thick field grass beside the rocks. Tiny yellow buttercups swayed within the green patches. Closer to the bottom, near a meandering stream, the white and red flowers of dead nettles harkened the coming of spring. Lark breathed in the clean, moist morning air and took comfort in the seclusion.

Lark heard the thunder of hooves and turned. Stoke galloped toward her, his huge destrier eating up the distance between them. He was the last person she wanted to see. Frantic to get away, she reached for Debolt's reins. Stoke's black horse pranced to a halt, blocking her way.

Lark leaped out of the way and took a step back. "Why did you follow me? Can you not just leave me alone!"

"Unfortunately, I can't do that." He dismounted and came toward her.

"You must leave me alone." She continued to back away, feeling her feet slipping on the slick stones beneath her kid boots.

"Stop it, Lark. Don't take another step. You're near the edge." He froze midstride.

"I don't care! Stay away. Do you hear, I can't get near you. I hate you!" Again she stepped back. Her foot slipped on the edge of a rock.

"Nay!"

Lark heard his loud bellow as she felt herself falling over the side of the cliff.

Chapter 8

Stoke dove for Lark and caught one of her ankles. With both hands, he hung on, feeling the leather of her boot bunched against his palm. For a moment, her arms and one leg dangled over the edge of a jutting rock.

"Sweet Mary," she gasped, her voice shaky.

"Hang on, I'll get you up." Stoke crept backwards on his knees and carefully pulled her up onto the rock.

He lay there, clutching her to his chest, feeling her body trembling all over. He grew aware of the pounding of her heart against her back. All the blood had drained from her face. Her head was tight against his chest. She had grasped handfuls of his tunic and was twisting the material in her fists. Stoke stroked the back of her head, reveling in this defenseless side of her. He didn't dare speak, for he sensed this was a rare moment in her life, one which few people were allowed to glimpse or be a part of.

As if she became aware of what she was doing, she pulled back from him. "I'm fine now." She didn't look him in the eyes as she struggled to control the fright still possessing her.

Stoke felt the loss of her closeness right away. He stood and held out his hand. "Can you get up?"

"Of course I can." She tried to look indignant, though her body shook all over. She stared at his outstretched hand, then reluctantly put her hand in his.

Stoke knew what it cost her to take his hand. He gave her an encouraging smile. Her sweaty palm felt slick against his own as he pulled her up.

Suddenly, her legs crumpled beneath her, and she fell against his chest. "Forgive me," she said, gazing up at him.

He clamped his arms around her waist, steadying her. "What is there to forgive, save perhaps being so headstrong you don't know your own limitations?" He felt her fingers splayed against his chest and looked down into the golden depths of her eyes. A man could get lost in them.

"I know them, all too well." She gazed up at him, nibbling her bottom lip to keep it from trembling.

"Do you, my tigress?" Stoke touched her chin and felt the soft skin of her jaw against his fingertips.

The womanly scent of her filled his senses. He hadn't noticed before, but she had high cheekbones and a sleek, perfect nose. Her brows were a tawny gold and finely arched, blending into tanned skin, making them barely noticeable. Long lashes, the same color as her brows, framed her large eyes, proud unconquerable eyes, yet very bewildered at the moment. Her bottom lip, fuller than the top, glistened from where she was biting on it.

"You've no right to be so comely," he whispered. His fingers tangled in the thick hair tied at her nape, and he bent to kiss her.

The moment he tasted her lips, he groaned deep in his throat. The feel of her in his arms filled him until he wanted to burst.

He knew the moment she succumbed to her own passion— the trembling stopped, her lips softened, and she melted against him. He drove his tongue into her mouth, the sweet heady taste of her like manna to him.

His hands dropped to her bottom, and he pulled her hips

closer, rubbing his erection against her. She wrapped her arms around his neck. He felt her fingers twine in his hair, sending a shudder down his neck and spine.

As Stoke was about to ease her back onto the ground, he heard the thunder of hooves. Before he could break the kiss, the riders came to a stomping halt.

"Lark! For the love of God, what are you doing?"

Stoke broke the kiss and looked at Lord Avenall. Rage filled his boyish face, turning it bright red. Evel sat on a mount beside him, his jaw agape.

Lark scrambled to get out of Stoke's grasp, color seeping into her face. "Oh, Avenall, I can explain."

"If you have an explanation, I'd like to hear it." Avenall stared down at her, gripping the reins in his hand as if he meant to shred the leather.

"This was my fault." Stoke stepped toward him.

"Stay out of this." Lark shot a warning look at him, then turned back to Avenall. " 'Twas my fault. I fell over the side of the cliff. Lord Blackstone merely saved my life. I was a little shaky and he helped me to stand. I fell into his arms."

"And then you kissed him." Avenall leveled his gaze at Stoke.

"Nay, I kissed her." Stoke enjoyed the slow grin he aimed at her betrothed.

"Go away! You're making matters worse." Lark waved her hand at Stoke, but didn't bother looking at him.

"How can the truth make matters worse?"

"Sweet Mary! Shut up!" Lark whipped around and glared at Stoke.

Stoke crossed his arms over his chest and grinned wickedly back at her. The perverse part of him enjoyed every moment of this.

"You, sirrah, are supposed to be settling on Lady Helen. How dare you take liberties with my betrothed." Avenall's gaze blazed at Stoke. "If you ever touch Lark again, I'll meet you in combat."

"Nay, you shall not." Lark shook her finger at him. "He'll kill you with one blow. If anyone meets him, 'twill be me."

"I look forward to it." Stoke raised his brow at her.

She shot Stoke a smoldering gaze, then touched Avenall's hand, which made him stop glaring at Stoke. "Listen, it was just a moment of weakness. It was no one's fault."

"How could you kiss him?" Lord Avenall looked like a hurt boy as he gazed down at her. "And to think I rode out here to see if you were all right."

"It should never have happened. I felt naught. 'Tis already forgotten."

Stoke snorted under his breath, which earned him another flash of her golden eyes. Her betrothed didn't appear too happy either, his expression ripe with repressed jealousy.

"Believe me, you are the only man I shall ever love. He means naught to me," Lark pleaded.

Avenall gazed into her eyes for a moment, then he knocked her hands away. "I no longer wish to discuss it." He jerked back on the reins. His horse pranced to the side, almost knocking Lark over, and then he rode away.

"Wait! I can explain!" She ran a few steps after him and paused. Her shoulders slumped. She stared down at the ground, shaking her head.

"That was a very good job of wheedling, Tigress. I admit, I never expected such a display from you." Stoke gathered Shechem's reins as he spoke.

She turned. If her eyes could shoot spikes, he'd be mesh by now. "I hate you! You've ruined everything!"

"Could you let me speak to my sister ... *alone?*" Evel glared at Stoke.

"Very well, but we shall finish what we started, Lark."

At the sound of her name, she glanced at him, her golden gaze still filling him with holes. "We've naught to finish. I've said all there is to say to you. I didn't try to kill you, and I wasn't with those bloody Scots. And if you ever come near me again, I will skewer you and cook you over a slow fire!"

"Is that any way to speak to someone who just saved your

life?'' Stoke graced her with his most devilish grin as he mounted his horse.

"I wouldn't have fallen if you hadn't come near me."

"Are you that afraid of me?"

Her chin shot up. "Not when I have a weapon in my hand."

"I'll be sure to oblige you, when next we meet." A grin twisted one side of his lip.

"You needn't favor me with your kindness."

He rode past her, the creak of his saddle leather mingling with her heaving, exasperated breaths. The smile on his face widened. His prey was a challenge, and he so loved goading her. He was going to enjoy conquering her, every last inch of her. Aye, and he would make her forget that fool Lord Avenall. One way or the other, he would have her. Then he would get the truth out of her and find out who was trying to kill him.

Evel waited until Stoke had ridden down the side of the glen ere he spoke. "I came to warn you that Lord Blackstone rode out after you, but I see it was a futile endeavor."

"Why did you bring Avenall with you?" Lark watched Stoke's dark form getting smaller and smaller as he galloped across a sloping field, his destrier's hooves kicking up clods of grass.

"I didn't. I came upon him on the way here. What the devil were you doing, kissing Blackstone?"

"Evel, please." Lark rubbed her temple. "I don't need you berating me."

"By my fay, someone needs to. Avenall will never forgive you."

"It wasn't my fault he followed me here. He refuses to leave me alone."

"From what Rowland told me, Blackstone has had ten attempts on his life. He has every right to follow you, since he found you with the Scots."

"I'm sick to death of his suspicions." Lark turned and strode toward Debolt, where he was busy cropping grass.

"Lark! Lark! Evel!" Their names echoed across the glen.

Pausing, she followed the din to the adjacent cliff and saw Sir Joseph waving. He was a large man in his middle years, as round as he was tall. His long, bushy gray beard narrowed to a point that touched his barrel-sized belly. He wore his hair cropped short, which made his square face appear wider than it was. On the cart next to him sat his wife, Lady Lucinda. A long green veil covered her hair and hung down the sides of her moon-shaped face. She too, waved at Lark, her massive breasts jiggling against her round stomach.

"Good morrow, Sir Joseph and Lady L!" Lark called back to them, using the pet name William used for Lady Lucinda.

"That's all we need," Evel mumbled under his breath.

Lady Lucinda cupped her hands and shouted, "We were just on our way to visit your mother and see if she needed help in preparing for the wedding feast. Come and join us. We have need of pleasant company."

Lark made a face, not sure how pleasant she could be, but she could not appear rude and refuse them. With her resolve firmly in place, she called back to them, "We'll go with you."

"Now you've done it." Evel looked askance at her as she mounted. "We'll not have a moment's peace on the way back."

" 'Tis better than hearing your reproaches." Lark kicked Debolt and trotted off, feeling Evel's gaze on her back.

It took only a quarter of an hour to traverse the glen and meet Lady Lucinda and Sir Joseph where it leveled enough to cross. Lark cantered up to their wain and welcomed the sight of their globe-shaped, smiling faces.

Evel drew alongside them and bowed to Lady Lucinda and Sir Joseph. "Good morrow."

"Well, Evel, aren't you the handsomest creature to grace these old eyes," Lady Lucinda teased.

"How are you? I hope we find you well." Sir Joseph got off a few words before his wife interrupted him.

"Of course they are well. Why, just look at them, riding the hills so early. What are you two about? Granted it is a lovely morn for a ride. I just spoke those very words to my husband."

Lady Lucinda beamed a wide smile at Lord Joseph. "Did I not, my love?"

Sir Joseph opened his mouth to speak, but Lady Lucinda cut him off. "He said as much to me when we decided to come and visit your mother and father. I thought it looked like rain, and my knees have been paining me, but there is not a cloud in the sky. Imagine that. So we set out for St. Vale. I had hoped to glimpse someone along our journey to break the monotony. You know how it can be. Husbands"—she smiled again at Sir Joseph—"rarely make good conversationalists—unless of course they are thinking of wars." She chuckled, jiggling her two chins. "Aye, is that not true, my love?"

Sir Joseph's jaw opened to speak, but his wife beat him to it, so he merely shrugged and clamped his mouth closed.

"I must tell someone about the beautiful gown that I had made just for your wedding. Such a wonderful wedding it will be . . . when the day is set. And Helen will be getting married with you. Has the Earl of Blackstone arrived? I'm sure he has, what with Helen's beauty to be gazed upon. And what a wonderful prospect your mother has found for your sister—and you as well. I've oft told Sir Joseph that Lord Avenall was perfect for you." Lady Lucinda took a breath.

Lark saw her chance to change the subject. "How did the cream I sent you work on your joints?"

"Praise Mother Mary, you are such a fine one with your herbs—a natural healer. Sir Joseph knows this. Indeed, he and I fight over your potions. We are so lucky you dabble in the healing arts. You could certainly teach those leeches a thing or two. Yes, indeed."

Lark felt someone watching her. Her gaze traveled up the brow of a grass-covered hill. She caught sight of Stoke, a rigid figure of masculinity, massive even at this distance. Rowland sat his mount next to him. They had paused in the middle of field, deep in conversation, though Stoke had his gaze trained on her.

"What are you looking at, my dear?" Lady Lucinda craned her neck around toward Blackstone. "My, oh my! Who is that hulking knight all in black? What a fine line he cuts in the saddle.''

"That is Lord Blackstone," Evel said flatly.

"The Lord Blackstone who's come to see our Helen? How wonderful." Lady Lucinda clapped her hands.

"If you'll excuse me, I'll meet you all back at the castle."

"Lark, don't." Evel grabbed her arm. "He won't like it. You're asking for trouble."

"I'm sick to death of him following me everywhere. Do you think I care what he likes?" Lark shook off Evel's hand and kicked Debolt into a gallop.

"What did you mean, he wouldn't like it?" Lady Lucinda asked, her curiosity brimming from her eyes.

Evel ignored Lady Lucinda and watched Lord Blackstone jerk on the reins. His horse reared. The huge black animal's plate-sized hooves pawed the air. Horse and rider sped down the hill after Lark. Evel watched them and shook his head.

"What did you mean?" Lady Lucinda tried again. "I really must insist you tell me, dear boy."

"All I meant was Blackstone has a dislike for Lark."

"A dislike?" She clucked her tongue. "Not like your sister? Pishah! He must not know the real Lark. Everyone who knows her loves her. She might be a little rough around the edges, but there is silk inside her, and the best kind. Aye, I've often said that. I have."

"I don't think he's come across the silk yet." Evel screwed up his face and watched Blackstone ride out of sight.

Lark knew every inch of St. Vale land as she knew every scar on her body. She took the fastest, flattest route to the castle, along the main road that would take her by the village. She meant to hide in the village until he'd passed by. That would teach him to follow her. When she glanced over her shoulder, she saw him—his back sword-straight in the saddle, his dark, brooding gaze intently on her.

Her heels dug into Debolt's sides. She loosened the reins

and let him set his own pace. The wind whipped past her face as she bent low over his back.

The pounding of his destrier's hooves grew louder. She kicked Debolt again. They galloped uphill now, Debolt's heavy breathing growing labored. He was one of the fastest stallions in the stable, but still Blackstone's horse was gaining on her.

A stand of trees stood off to the left of the road. As Lark came abreast of them, metal flashed in the top of a tree. She saw a man standing on a limb, a crossbow aimed at Stoke.

It all happened at once. Before Lark could scream out a warning, the man shot the arrow. She glanced behind her in time to see Stoke leaning over the side of his saddle, the arrow already whizzing past his horse. Stoke whipped out a dagger. With a lightning flick of his wrist, it left his hand and flew toward the tree. In the process of reloading, the bowman didn't see the dagger until it was too late. He moved. The dagger plunged into his neck. Arrow and crossbow fell from his hands.

He tumbled forward, and his dead weight plummeted through the branches . . . crack . . . crack . . . crack. He landed on the ground in a tangled, limp heap. Lark was about to jerk Debolt to a halt, but when she saw those black eyes fix on her and the searing flame in them, she decided against it and flicked Debolt's rump with the reins.

The thunder of his destrier's hooves pounded close behind her. Lark felt the shoulder of his horse bump the side of her leg. Rough fingers dug into her waist. Then she was sailing through the air.

Chapter 9

Stoke reined in as he grabbed Lark and plopped her in front of him on the saddle. She struck out at him with her fists, but he easily grabbed her wrists. "Don't ever try to run from me again."

"I wasn't running from you."

"Nay, you were trying to ensnare me in one of your little traps."

"I wasn't. I swear it. When I left the hall, I wanted to be alone, but *you* followed *me*. You can't believe I planned this! I was riding away to get away from you."

Stoke wanted to believe her. He stared at her, his chest heaving, every nerve in his body humming from having almost lost his life. Or was it having her in his arms again?

"Don't look at me like that. Every time you look at me like that, you want to kiss me." She nervously licked her lips.

"I've discovered that when one comes close to death, it heats the blood—especially with a temptress like you in my arms . . ." He captured her chin and kissed her, hard, his mouth covering her tight lips. He grew vaguely aware of her pounding on his chest, but after a moment, the pummeling stopped.

She moaned, not a sensual sound, but one mourning the inner war she was losing. He nipped at her full bottom lip, then sucked on it as he untied the thong holding her hair. Tossing it aside, he tangled his hands in her thick hair, feeling the velvety smoothness between his fingers.

He ran his tongue along her teeth and her mouth opened for him. His tongue slipped between her lips to plunder the sweet, moist depths while he moved his hands down to massage her bottom. Her body relaxed against him as her arms went around his neck. Then she was kissing him back, her hands tangling in his hair. The passion in her drove him, and he scooped her up into his arms and dismounted, never breaking the kiss. She was good at the art of seduction, and this was probably a ploy to get him off guard, but if he did not have her now, he would burn up with wanting her.

As he headed toward the wood with every intention of sating his desire, he heard riders approaching. He cursed inwardly as she broke the kiss.

Lark stared up at him, confusion on her face, as if she couldn't believe she'd been kissing him. He glanced down the road. Evel and Rowland galloped toward them, her pet wolf bringing up the rear.

"Halloo!" Evel waved his arm at them.

"Is there no place I can find to be alone with you?" he grumbled under his breath.

"I hope not." Her golden brows met in a frown, and a slight blush seeped into her cheeks.

"We shall be alone, and you needn't fight the passion you feel for me."

"Oh! I feel only loathing for you!"

"If 'tis loathing, then I would not want your love."

A cloud of thick dust blew across the road as Evel and Rowland reined in near them. Evel spoke first. "We saw the dead man and left Sir Joseph with the corpse. Are you all right?" He addressed his question to Lark.

"I'm fine. The assassin only shot at Lord Blackstone."

"Then why is he carrying you?" Evel leered at Stoke, then at Lark in his arms.

"Not because she is wounded," Stoke said under his breath, staring at her lips.

"You can put me down now." Stoke's grip on her tightened and she added, "Please."

As Stoke plopped her on the ground, he was wearing a frown of frustration.

"Do you think he had accomplices?" Rowland asked, a grimace marring his expression.

"That remains to be seen." Stoke looked at Lark.

"Surely you don't think Lark had something to do with this?" Evel jumped to his sister's defense.

"Don't speak to him, Evel. 'Tis no use. He's made up his mind about me, and naught we say can change that." Lark extended her hand up to him. "Please, give me a ride back to the castle. I'm sure Debolt has gone home."

"I'll give you a ride, but I should give you a thorough flogging." Evel grabbed Lark's hand and pulled her up behind him. "Now see what you've done. He thinks you are involved. Why should he not? I told you not to ride off like that. . . ." Evel's voice faded as he kicked his horse into a gallop.

Stoke stared after them and mounted Shechem.

"I don't believe Evel is guilty of anything but caring for his sister," Rowland said, staring at Evel's back.

"You may be correct in that quarter, but I still believe his sister is somehow connected to all of this." Stoke gestured toward the fallen assassin.

"What do you intend to do? How can you pursue her and devote time to your would-be bride?"

"I'll get the truth out of her tonight."

Rowland shot Stoke a dubious glance and shook his head.

Stoke mounted and thought of her. Aye, he would have the truth, and the tigress. One way or the other.

* * *

The moment Lark stepped foot in the hall, her mother cornered her and forced her to stand for the final fitting of her wedding gown. It was a grueling hour of gibes.

"Lark, stand still."

"Must you slouch like an old woman?"

"Will your breasts ever grow?"

"We'll have to take the hips in—you have none."

"How did your arms and legs get so long? I believe they have grown overnight."

Lark would have preferred another slap, but she had a feeling Elizabeth would never lose control like that again. She favored torturing Lark with words and well-placed pin pricks. Through it all, Lark had been forced to listen to Lady Lucinda's constant chatter about the wedding plans.

By the time it was over, Lark wished she had run away and married Avenall at his holding. Elizabeth had sent Helen out to find Stoke, so Lark saw her chance and bolted out of the hall with her. Lark watched a young girl chase a flock of chickens across the bailey as she and Helen walked side by side.

"Are you sure you will not accompany me to the tilt yard?" Helen said. "Avenall will be there."

"Nay. If he wants to see me, he knows where I am. And should I go, then I might want to ride against someone, and I doubt my body can take it after meeting the points of Mother's pins." Lark rubbed her bottom. "I'll forgo the tilt yard and spend my time in the garden. I've neglected it of late and the weeds are mounting a counterattack against my herbs." Lark hid a frown behind a wooden grin. She wanted very much to join in the harassing of Blackstone's men, but their liege would be there. And after she had melted in his arms and kissed him earlier—after vowing never to do it again—she didn't relish being subjected to those black, hungry eyes.

"Do you think I should bother him in the tilt yard? Mother said I should and that he's only forgotten he promised to walk with me. But I know not how he will feel should I disturb him.

I would not want to appear to be pestering him." Helen stared down at her hands as she wrung them.

"He needs pestering, if you ask me."

"Oh, Lark, how can you still dislike him, after what happened this morn. It was horrible! Someone attacked him when he was riding out on business. Lady Lucinda could not stop talking about the man they found with Lord Blackstone's knife in his throat. Why would someone attack him?"

Lark held up her hand and counted off her fingers as she spoke. "He's arrogant, brutish, stubborn, impulsive, and hears only what he wants to hear." Lark ran out of fingers and held up her other hand. "He accuses others ere he bothers finding out the facts, he tries to dominate those weaker than he, he has an annoying habit of staring at people. I'd say those qualities generally do not instill admiration."

"Lark, be serious." Helen half-frowned and half-grinned at her.

"Very well." The grin left Lark's lips. "I have no idea why someone would attack him." Lark didn't tell Helen about the other attempts on his life, or that he thought she was involved in them. "The man must have been a thief, waiting by the road for some unsuspecting traveler."

"But you could have been attacked too. Lady Lucinda said you had raced ahead of them. You must have seen it all happen. Did you?" Helen stared at Lark in rapt attention.

"Aye, I saw it."

"Did you see any sign of more thieves?"

Lark shook her head.

"What if there are more waiting to attack us?"

"If it eases your mind, I'll speak to Father and we'll ride out, though no gang of thieves will stop the guests from arriving. No doubt they will come in droves, eat our larder clean, and send Mother scurrying about to look the part of a noble hostess."

The tenseness left Helen's expression as she smiled and said, "Thank you, Lark, I knew speaking to you would make me feel much better. I had better go and find Lord Blackstone."

Helen strode toward the gates, her strides graceful, her long, dark hair swaying against her back.

Lark turned and headed in the opposite direction. The mid-morning sunlight beat directly down on her scalp as she strolled through the bailey. A breeze brushed her face, redolent with the fetid mold from the moat, at odds with the scent of newly-strewn hay in the stable. Two unshod, dirty-faced villein children passed her, batting a rock with sticks.

The green gown and linen undersmock Elizabeth had forced her to wear tangled around her ankles. She paused in mid-stride to keep from tripping, grimaced, and pulled the offending silk from between her legs. Like the rest of her gowns, it was too short. Her mother refused to make her new clothes, hoping Lark would sew her own, but Lark wouldn't embarrass herself by picking up a needle. Her aim with a sword and lance was much straighter than any line she could sew. It didn't bother her that some of her gowns were three and four years old. She rarely wore them anyway, and when she did, it was only to quell Elizabeth's harping.

Lark felt her hair swinging against her bottom with each stride. Since Avenall's arrival, Lark allowed Marta to take a comb to her tangles. Her hair fell down her back, tangle free, but still straight and unruly, dressed with a beaded leather circlet, a present from her father. She didn't like to leave her hair unbraided—the thick mass only got in the way—but Marta said it would catch Avenall's attention worn loose. Not that Lark cared if it caught Avenall's attention or not. What was the sense of trying to look alluring, when he was already her betrothed? To her way of thinking, she should be able to go about as she pleased. But she did not argue the point with Marta. The elder woman rarely lost an argument when she had a comb in her hand.

She passed two young women servants standing over a huge cauldron, boiling clothes. Sweat dripped from their brows, and they paused to wave and swipe their sleeves across their faces. Lark called a greeting to them. Across the bailey, the smithy stood at his forge, hammering a piece of iron. The steady beat echoed against the stone walls and pounded in her ears.

"Good morrow, Daith," Lark called to him.

He paused and glanced up from his forge. Daith's bulky shoulders and arms were at odds with short, thin legs and made him look as if he would topple over at any moment. Red curly hair covered his bean-shaped head, and a flat nose spanned a pair of kind gray eyes. He raised a surprised brow at her. "Aye, what are ye doing here, me lady? I thought ye'd be out in the yard testing the mettle of the Black Dragon's men." He jabbed a hammer toward the gates. "Are ye not going out to join them? I thought for sure ye'd be the first in line to knock one of the knaves on his arse." He grinned at her.

"I'm foregoing that pleasure. The garden needs my attention," Lark said, skirting several honking geese.

"Aye, well, later then." Daith leveled a curious look her way.

"Aye." Lark waved and hurried around the back of the hall, not wanting to make more excuses.

She passed beneath a trellis and stepped into the medallion-shaped garden. Stepping stones formed two paths that cut a large X through it. The triangular plots of dark, rich earth overflowed with neat rows of herbs and flowers. Apple, pear, plum, and cherry trees lined the perimeter, providing shade along the path. The sweet scent of mint and sweet bay wafted through her senses and made her smile.

When not in the tilt yard, or working on her herb potions, Lark could be found here, in the tranquility of the garden, where she could escape Elizabeth's verbal attacks and critical eye. Elizabeth did not like to work in the garden for fear the sun would turn her skin the color of tanned leather. This was a boon for Lark, for she found solace here. And silence.

As she reached a patch of marigolds, she noticed Avenall sitting on a stone bench. His legs were stretched out in front of him, the green edge of his cotte peeking out beneath a bliaut made of fustian. Both garments showed wear on the hems, and she noticed a hole in his left stocking. Until this moment, she hadn't realized how badly he needed to fill his coffers. Sunlight glinted off his head, setting on fire the streaks of red in his chestnut hair. The quill in his hand made a scratching noise as it moved across a page of a book.

At the sound of her footsteps, he glanced up and slapped the book closed. "Oh, Lark, I thought I would be alone here."

"If you wish, I can leave."

"Nay, nay." His frowned at her and stood. "I hoped to find you alone so we could discuss what happened earlier."

"I suppose we must." Lark grimaced and tried to change the subject. "Why are you not in the tilt yard with Father?"

"I begged leave to come here."

"Penning poetry again?" Lark smiled at him, drawn to the frail, compassionate side of him. It always aroused a tenderness in her she didn't know existed otherwise. That was why she loved him so much. She could appreciate his gentle nature even more since meeting the Black Dragon.

"Aye," he said, staring pensively down at his book.

"Will you read me what you've written?"

"I really wanted to speak to you about what happened. Please, sit with me." He took her hand.

Lark hoped he would try to kiss her. If he would just kiss her, everything would be all right. But he merely scrutinized her with those brilliant blue eyes. After a moment, he brushed the bench off for her, then touched her elbow and helped her sit, as if she were a precious, breakable object.

"I've missed you." Lark squeezed his hand, basking in the tender way he always dealt with her. His fingers felt oddly clammy against her palm. She stared at his hands, thinking they were small compared to Stoke's, hardly wider than her own.

"Lark, please, you are trying to change the subject again."

"Can we not forget the Black Dragon for a moment?" Lark's fingers tightened around his hand. "I haven't seen you in over six months. Have you naught to say to me but to bring up Blackstone? Forget him. Have you not missed me?"

"Of course I have." He squeezed her hand. "And you look

lovely today in your gown. I like your hair worn that way too. 'Tis like a golden waterfall flowing down your back.''

Avenall always made free with his compliments, and as usual, they made Lark feel self-conscious. To break the awkward moment, she said, "Harold and Cedric have always said my hair looks like rotting straw—but thank you for noticing it.''

His bright blue eyes met hers, and he frowned. "Why can I never admire you without you always turning my compliments into jests?''

"I know you only say them out of kindness, but you don't have to lie to me. I know what I look like. I'm no beauty like Helen.''

"Both of you have qualities that rival the other's.'' He stared pensively down at his book.

"Well said, Oh, King Solomon.'' Lark bowed at the waist.

He raised a brow in surprise. "That is the first time you've ever shown me any deference.''

"I lost my head.'' A teasing grin pulled at her lips.

He remained silent a moment. His expression grew somber. Usually Lark could tease a grin out of him, no matter how angry he was with her, but he continued to look sulky.

In a patient tone, he said, "You made me digress. We must discuss Lord Blackstone.''

"Nay, we mustn't. 'Twas a spur of the moment mistake. I've forgotten it. Surely you know that he means naught to me. You are the lord I'm going to marry. Please forgive me?'' Lark touched her hand to his cheek and gazed into his deep blue eyes.

His brows drew together in a frown. After what seemed like ages, but must have been only a few moments, he finally shook his head. "I suppose so, since I believe he tried to take advantage of you. I know you would never have allowed him to kiss you in that way.''

"Never.'' Lark added too much emphasis to the lie and realized it. She gazed down at her hands.

"He needs to be taught a lesson. He just cannot kiss whomever he pleases."

"Please, let it drop."

He gazed long and hard into her eyes. "I have this strange feeling that you belong to him now and not me."

"I'm not his." Stoke only owned every lustful fiber in her body. Lark knew she would have an awful lot to confess to Father Kenyon on Friday. "You are the man I chose to marry, not him. I despise him. Can we not just forget about him? If not, I'm going to leave." Lark knew she'd better go before she told more lies. She stood, but Avenall grabbed her hand.

"All right, Lark. We'll forget it for now. We must address another issue."

"What?" Lark let him ease her back down beside him.

"We have never spoken of our married life, but I wish to do that now. My hope is that when we marry, you shall be able to obey and respect me."

"I'll always respect you, though I'm not sure about the obeying part." Lark teased him with a half-hearted grin.

"This is no jesting matter, Lark . . ." His words trailed off. He again frowned pensively down at the book in his hands.

"You needn't take it so seriously."

"We must speak of it in earnest. You'll be my wife. To have peace between us, I must have the final word in all matters. You must realize this."

"I had not thought of it until this moment. Why must you have the final say?"

"Because I'll be your husband. A wife must submit to her husband."

Lark thought of Stoke and said, "What if he is pigheaded? What if he bullies all those around him? What if he cannot discern truth from lies? Should a wife submit to someone like that?"

"Are you saying I have these attributes?" Avenall stood, crushing the book against his thigh.

"Nay, not you. I was merely speaking in general."

Some of the emotion left his face. "I'm glad of that. We should have spoken of this sooner."

"Aye. Why did you never tell me you felt so strongly about this?"

He moved one lip over the other, then said, "I knew it would be a struggle." He shrugged. "It always is with you, when someone tries to sway your opinions."

"Since I'm so obstinate, why are you marrying me?"

Avenall was never one to stay angry, and he proved that now by wrapping his arms around her. "I'm marrying you because I love your strength and beauty and wit. I'm sorry if I've made you angry, but you know I speak the truth."

Lark knew he was right as she stared back him, unable to think of one good retort on her behalf.

He smiled in his usual patient manner. "So we have reached an agreement?"

Lark pouted back at him, unsure she wanted to concede so easily.

"There is that stubborn look I love." He pulled her close for a kiss.

When their lips touched, all Lark could think about was how bland the kiss felt compared to Stoke's lusty, devouring assaults on her mouth. Avenall's mouth softened against hers. He wrapped his arms around her and pulled her closer. His kiss grew passionate, more so than she'd ever experienced.

She should have reveled in the feel of his hands touching the back of her head and the satiny softness of his lips against her mouth. But something was missing. Stoke's kisses forced fire to erupt inside her, encompassed her like a giant wave, taking with it all her wits; Avenall's kisses left only a warm spark, hardly enough to light a fire. Before she felt even a warm glow, he drew back and grinned, his long-lashed sapphire eyes gleaming.

He looked pleased with himself as he said, "Now have we reached an agreement. You'll submit to me in all things. I'll have no wife of mine doing as she pleases without consulting me."

Lark gritted her teeth and pulled away from him. A realization hit her all at once. In the past Avenall had always swayed her by kissing her once, and she would give in to anything he wanted. Having been taken advantage of with such ease, and perceiving just how blind she'd been since the first time he'd kissed her at the tender age of ten and five, made her brows furrow. She asked, "And are you to seek counsel from me on matters?"

"That is different." Impatience slipped back into his voice.

"Nay, 'tis not. You believe me such a simpleton that my opinion is worth naught to you."

"You know that is not true. I value your opinion, obviously much more than you value mine," he said abruptly. "We'll discuss this when you've had time to reflect and cool your temper." He turned and strode away from her.

Lark opened her mouth to say more, but knew Avenall would not stay to argue with her. It was his way to run from adversity. In that respect he was like William Mandeville, and she could find no fault in his behavior. But it irritated her when she was ready for a good argument and he walked away.

She stared at his back the way she would look at a stranger. At the moment, he was a stranger. They had never discussed how their marriage would be. She only assumed it would be a partnership, in which they would share in making decisions. After all, she considered herself equal to him in every way, and in some cases a little above him—especially when it came to warfare and weapons. He would soon learn that one kiss from him would not sway her as it had when she was young and innocent—a time that seemed so distant now, a time ere Stoke entered her life and ravished her. She now knew real passion. It was gritty, all-consuming, and scalded her alive. It was incredible.

"Sweet Mary," she mumbled and fell to her knees near a patch of marigolds. How could she have these feelings about a man who was supposed to marry her sister? Immersing her hands in the stubborn, encroaching spring grass, she tried to put Stoke's face out of her mind and think of Avenall, but all she saw in the rich black earth were those fiery dark eyes.

Lark finished weeding several rows before Stoke's eyes disappeared at last. The soft murmur of voices drifted toward her. As they grew louder, clearer, she paused, her hand still on a clump of grass. The low-pitched baritone made her squeeze the clump of grass. Rich black earth crumbled in her hand as she leaned past an apple tree and saw Stoke.

Chapter 10

Lark hunched down behind the tree and the bench in front of it, hoping neither he nor Helen had seen her.

"I wonder where Lark could be," Helen's tinkling voice carried over the garden. "She said she'd be here. I did so want her to join us. I thought an encouraging word from you might persuade her."

"I'm sure she is about tormenting someone or something," Blackstone said.

Lark sneered at his comment.

"Oh, my lord, Lark would never torment anyone. She does her best to help others. Just look at her garden. She uses the herbs to make salves and potions to cure everyone's ills. Why, I remember just a sennight ago, she went into the village to help a little boy who'd broken his arm."

"Somehow I cannot picture your sister in the role of a healer."

"But she was so wonderful! I accompanied her, and when she had to wrap the limb, I could not stand to watch. She didn't berate me for being ill, only sent me outside."

"How noble of her."

At his last snide remark, Lark raised her head and peeked around the bench. Blackstone was staring into Helen's eyes, a pensive, aloof mask on his face. He looked wickedly handsome with his hair pulled back from his face, so black it glistened blue in the sun. His profile to her, she could see the dark stubble on his square chin, the point of his widow's peak touching the top of his brow. A fine sheen of sweat glistened on his forehead, the result of exercising in the tilt yard. He wore the same black tunic and braies that he'd had on earlier, the embroidered dragon stretching across his wide chest. A bee buzzed around Lark's face, drawing her attention away from Blackstone. She swatted it away, then glanced back at them.

"Do you mind, my lord, if I ask a question?" Helen asked, looking sheepish.

"Nay, what is it?"

"I just wondered . . . what happened to your first wife?"

"I do not like to speak of her." The hard mask dissolved for a moment, and a hint of pain flashed over his face. It faded quickly behind a carefully guarded expression.

"Oh." Helen stared down at her hands.

"But I will tell you she gave me a son."

"I believe someone mentioned that to me. I've forgotten how old he is, though." Helen looked pleased that he'd spoken to her and smiled timidly at him.

"Almost three."

"Have you no other children?"

"None." For a moment he stared pensively at Helen, scrutinizing her. In a blink, the hard mask returned as he asked, "Has your sister been acting strangely?"

"I know not what you mean." Helen cocked her head at him. "I've noticed no change in her."

"Have you seen her speaking to any strangers?"

"Nay, but Lark likes taking walks at night. I suppose she could speak to anyone she chooses then."

"I see." Stoke rubbed his jaw, looking deep in thought. Suspicion gleamed in his eyes as he said more to himself, "I wonder what else she does?"

''Why do you inquire? Has Lark done something wrong?''

''Nay. She is such a brazen creature, I just wondered what her habits were.''

''Lark is very different from any lady you might have encountered, but I hope that does not offend.''

''She is very much like every one of her kind, just a bit more open about it.''

Helen stared at him, a look of confusion on her face.

He gave her a strained half smile. ''But you need not worry about your sister pleasing me. Luckily, she is not here now.'' He gazed at Helen and studied her.

Lark ground her teeth as she watched him. He didn't thrust Helen against his chest, or wrap his arms around her as he had done to Lark, but stood back from her and continued to gaze into her large brown eyes. The hardness never left his eyes, but his expression softened ever so slightly. In a way, it was a tender display, the first Lark had ever seen from him.

It was obvious how he felt about Helen. She was to be prized and gazed upon, while only three hours ago, Lark had suffered his groping hands and burly caresses. He thought of her as no more than a whore who had tried to kill him, to be used as so much chattel.

Lark picked up a clod of dirt with every intention of hitting him with it, but the bee landed on her nose. When she batted at it, the insect plunged its stinger into her.

''Ouch!'' Lark realized she'd spoken aloud when Stoke turned and their eyes met.

His lips stretched in a contemptuous grin, as if he'd known she'd been in the garden all this time. His face turned slightly into the sunlight, setting the copper specks in his eyes on fire.

His grin and those glowing eyes taunted her, and she stuck out her chin defiantly.

''Lark!'' The surprise on Helen's face melted behind a scarlet blush.

Lark scrambled to her feet and strode toward them. ''How

dare you ogle my sister?'' She shook the clod of dirt at Stoke, punctuating each word, then turned on Helen. "Mother should never have let you come here alone with him in this deserted garden. I'm sorely ashamed of you."

"But he was just talking. And I came here to find you." Tears filled Helen's eyes.

"You found me a bit too late. I did not hear you enter the garden."

"I'm so sorry. I—I thought it would be all right to walk with him. I—I—" Helen looked too flustered to speak. She hurried down the path, sobbing.

Lark stared after her, abruptly feeling like the worst kind of shrew. Why had she taken her ire out on Helen?

"I hope you are pleased with yourself."

She turned and fixed him with a level stare. "Don't try to lay the blame on me. You should never have lured Helen here."

"I'm supposed to be here getting to know her. Are you saying I shouldn't be alone with her?"

"You are too dangerous to be left alone with any woman."

"Be careful, tigress, your claws are drawn, or is it jealousy that has you hissing?" He cocked a dark brow at her, looking smug.

"Pray, why should I be jealous? Were you the last man on earth, I would gladly give you to Helen. But don't think you can use her as you have tried to use me. And if you ever come near me again, I vow it will be the last time."

"Don't threaten me."

Glancing back at his face, Lark raised the clod of dirt still in her hand and threw it. He ducked. She darted to the left, skirted the apple tree, and ran down the path. Expecting him to follow her, she didn't stop running until she reached the hall. When she didn't hear his footsteps, she sighed and glanced behind her. Not a sign of Stoke, but the wash women had paused from their chore and regarded her closely.

Lark shot them a sour look, opened the heavy oak door, and ran into the hall. He'd come for her again. Aye, he would. If

she cared to admit it, she didn't know how to defend herself
against his lips and his touch. They turned her into a pliant
jellyfish. She strode into the hall, knowing she had to avoid
him at all cost. But first she must find Helen and apologize.

Later that night, Lark heard a knock on her chamber door.
She stiffened and thrust the tray of food aside. "Who is it?"
   "Your sire."
   She slid off the bed and slowly strode to the door. Metal
scraped as she threw back the bolt and opened the door.
   "Hello, Pigeon." He wore a worried expression on his ruddy
brow, belying the smile on his face.
   "To what do I owe this honor?" She knew something was
terribly wrong. He never came to her room just for a visit.
   He sauntered past her, careful to avoid a mound of clothes
near her bed. His gaze swept the messy room with an accepting
nonchalance as he turned toward her. "Well, Pigeon, when
your mother told me you would not come down to table and
join Avenall and me, and that you asked for a tray to be sent
up to you, I thought to come up and see if you are well. 'Tis
not like you to take to your room, and you've never been sick
a day in your life."
   "I've just an ache in my head." Lark peeked out into the
hall, checked for signs of the "ache," but Stoke was not to be
seen. She slammed the chamber door closed and bolted it.
   To strangers, William Mandeville came across as the worst of
fools, but Lark knew that below his merriment-loving demeanor
lurked the brightest, shrewdest mind she'd ever encountered.
When he watched her pointedly as he did now, with his perceptive grass-green eyes, she knew trouble was soon to follow.
Observing her hands still clutching the lock, he asked, "Why
are you bolting your door?"
   "I don't wish to have any of Blackstone's drunken men
barging into my room unannounced."
   "Is it the Black Dragon's men you worry about, or the lord
himself?"

"Why should I worry about him?" Lark tried to sound disinterested.

"I may be old, but my eyes work. I saw the way he rode after you this morn. And he has been preoccupied all day. You should have seen it when the quintain almost unseated him." Her father threw back his head and guffawed. When he noticed Lark wasn't smiling, he sobered. "He keeps his eyes on the stairwell and not on Helen, as he should. Do you know I'm starting to believe he's more interested in you than your sister— not that I'm surprised." He touched her arm. "You are infinitely more amusing than your sister and a much better companion for a warrior."

"I would rather die than be anything to him. It sickens me to know he will be Helen's husband."

"Why this disdain?" Her father gently squeezed her arm. "This is not like you to find fault in such a fine knight. The man is a bit taciturn, but legendary when it comes to winning battles. And he was kind enough to agree to gift me with a sword. He could not be all bad. Now, what is between you two?" She opened her mouth and her father added, "Mind, I want the truth."

Lark had never lied to her father before and she wouldn't start now. She explained what had happened, leaving out the part about the power Stoke had over her. "So you see why he suspects me—especially after this morn."

"I do." The wrinkles at the corners of his eyes deepened as a frown invaded his features.

"Please do not tell Mother. She will blame me."

"You should know better than to ask me to keep it from Elizabeth. I never tell her anything of significance, and you know that. I confide in only two people, you and Gowan."

"I wish you would not tell Gowan either, Father. The fewer people who know of this unfortunate circumstance the better."

"They will know soon enough. Your mother has the eyes of a hawk, as does your sister."

"I'll try to stay away from him."

"Why should you have to hide from him?" William's lips

hardened and his eyes burned with a green light that usually shone only when he meted out punishment to thieves.

It prompted Lark to add, "Only until he's gone."

"When will you face him? I taught you better than to run from trouble." A note of disappointment rang in his voice. "This needs to be brought out into the open so he can know of your innocence."

"It would do naught but provoke him. He suspects me and naught will change his mind, and Helen seems to care for him, though I know not why. Please do not intervene on my behalf. Promise me you will not."

"I make only one vow, and that is to wait until Blackstone makes up his mind about Helen and leaves us. If you have not persuaded him of your innocence by then, I shall speak to him. I'll not have him believing you are guilty of trying to kill him because of some twisted turn of fate. I'll have no daughter of mine falsely accused. Should he choose Helen to wife, he could bring discord to my family from his ill-conceived notions. I'll not have it."

"Please, don't. I wouldn't wish bad blood to rise between you and Lord Blackstone because of me. Let me handle this. 'Tis my problem. I'll settle it with him. When he finds the person behind these attempts, he'll know 'tis not me."

Her father said naught, only rubbed the stubble on his chin. "I wish we could be sure of that."

"I am." She grabbed her father's hand and squeezed it. "Please say you'll let me deal with him."

He stared into Lark's eyes for a long moment, then said, "How like you to want to handle this. All right, I'll agree. But should he not act with honor and fairness, I'm going to step in and see that he does."

"All right."

"And Lark, be on your guard. I know you didn't jump up from breaking the fast this morn and ride out of the castle for no reason. He did something to you, did he not?"

Lark quelled a blush that threatened her cheeks. She couldn't tell her father Stoke had touched her and aroused her until she wanted to scream, so she said, "He only said things to anger me."

Her father shot a skeptical look at her. "See to it that is the only thing he does to you, Pigeon. Now, are you coming down to table?"

"I prefer to stay here. I have this bee sting on the end of my nose, and I look ridiculous." Just then Lark saw Baltizar grab the whole trencher off the tray and gobble down the scooped-out loaf in three bites.

William watched him too as he said, "You look fine, the bump on your nose is hardly noticeable, but I understand when one's vanity is involved. Even if you didn't have a sting on your nose, you'd probably prefer the company of your pet to your father's."

"You know that is not true." Lark pecked him on the cheek.

This brought a smile to his lips and a gleam to his eyes. He tweaked her chin. "If I can't cajole you into coming with me, then I should go and endure your mother's displeasure." He turned to leave, but paused. "I'm glad you spoke to Helen earlier. I was growing tired of her bursting into tears when ere I looked at her. What was ailing her?"

"Something I said." Worry furrowed Lark's brows. "I lost my temper and became over-harsh. I couldn't find her to apologize right away."

"Aye, well, I'm finally glad you soothed her. I pity the Black Dragon should he look at her wrong." With that, William unbolted the door, shot Lark a warm smile, and left her chamber.

Lark paced the length of her room, stepping over several piles of clothes along the way. Her glance strayed to the vials and concoctions of herb potions on the desk. The thought of sitting idle for another few hours and working on them was like torture. Five hours was too long to be cooped up in her room. The walls were beginning to close in on her. She would have liked to speak to Avenall, but he was belowstairs with the others. It would be hours ere they all retired and she could finally be alone with him.

"I have to leave this room. Come, let's go."

At the word "go," Baltizar paused from licking the last bit of grease off his mouth and perked up. He hopped down off the bed and stood waiting for her at the door.

She checked the hallway and left her chamber. Baltizar brushed her leg as she headed toward the servants' stairs. Hopefully, she wouldn't meet Stoke.

As she stepped out into the bailey, thousands of stars winked at her. Voices came from behind her, and she hung back in the shadows, waiting for a group of knights to pass. They entered the hall. The door slammed, and their chatter died away.

She started toward the stable, her footsteps whispering in the strange silence that night always brought upon the bailey. A slight breeze wafted across her face, carrying with it the odor of the dung heap by the cow brye. She wrinkled her nose and hurried to the stable.

The better destriers and palfreys stayed inside the covered stable, not outside where the lean-to housed the retainers' and guests' horses. She strode down the stable, passing Evel's and the twins' mounts. She paused near William's stud, Tencendur, a dappled gray imported all the way from Gascony. He whinnied and bobbed his head at her. She patted his forehead and moved to Debolt's stall. Her beloved stead was one of Tencendur's superior offspring, fleet of foot, square of breast, and tight-rumped like his dashing father.

When Lark drew near, Debolt nudged her side, sniffing her pocket. "Looking for your treat, are you? You're rotten, you know that?" She pulled out the apple and stuck out her hand, palm up.

She felt his large, soft muzzle brush her open palm as he snatched the apple between his teeth and chomped down on it. Her hand moved up and rubbed the sleek white neck. Muscles rippled beneath her palm, while his coarse white mane brushed the back of her hand. "Would you like another treat? Shall we take a night ride?"

"Not unless you want company."

The deep-pitched, velvety voice penetrated through the darkness of the night and sent shivers down Lark's spine.

Chapter 11

Lark turned to see Stoke's hulking form blocking the stable door. The moonlight behind him hid his face in dark shadow, making his shoulders look even larger than they were. If she didn't know better, she would swear Goliath stood before her. If she only had a slingshot.

"So where were you planning to go?"

"If you must know, I wanted only to get away from you, but I see my efforts are all for naught."

"You'll never get away from me unless I wish it."

Lark's contemptuous look was lost on him, for his gaze was on Baltizar, who sniffed the air and walked toward him. "How did you know I was in the stable?"

"After your father said he could not persuade you to join us, I slipped away from the hall and went to your room. I knew you couldn't stand to stay there very much longer, and I was correct." He waved a piece of meat beneath Baltizar's nose, then tossed it out the door. "Go and get it, wolf."

As big as you please, the traitorous beast strode up to Stoke, let him pet him, then ran outside to find the meat.

Stoke slammed the stable door closed, making her jump in

the pitch blackness. She heard him jam something in the wooden latches as he spoke. "Now, where were we?"

"We were nowhere. I'm leaving this moment." Lark wanted to step toward the door, but she couldn't see him. Frantically, her gaze scanned the pitch blackness. Her senses pricked for some sign of where he might be. The only thing she could sense was those blazing black eyes staring at her.

"I cannot let you go now that I have you all to myself."

Lark glanced to her left. By the sound of his voice he stood but a few feet from her. She took a step back. "Has anyone ever told you that you are like a persistent nightmare?" The straw crunched as he took another step.

Instinctively, she eased the dagger from the leather sheath around her wrist.

"I don't mind being your nightmare."

"I mind it."

Another barely audible rustle of hay.

"Go away," she warned, gripping the dagger, her heart pounding in her chest.

"I shall when we finish what we started earlier."

"We didn't start anything earlier."

"How soon you forget the way you trembled in my arms after I saved your life. I could have taken you then, or later before Rowland and your brother interrupted us, or last night. Have you forgotten how you writhed beneath my touch? I've not forgotten it."

Lark opened her mouth to speak. As if he could see her in the dark, he cut her off. "Do not deny it, for it would be yet another lie out of your mouth. Let me prove it to you. Let me touch you."

"Nay. I'm engaged to Avenall." Lark clenched her fists and stepped back. "Stay away, or I vow you'll not leave here standing."

"We both know you don't mean those sweet threats." He took another step toward her.

The movement didn't make a sound, but she felt him through the darkness coming closer, his powerful aura almost a tangible thing. She stepped back. Her bottom connected with a stall door and she flinched.

"Keep your distance." She raised the knife and inched her way around the stall.

"I think not. I've wanted you since the night we met. I've wanted to strip you and run my hands over your naked body until I feel you quivering, taste those fiery lips of yours, and run my palms over your breasts. I've wanted to suckle your breasts and stroke that hot flesh between your legs—"

"Stop it." Lark fought the warmth his words caused within her. She began to tremble all over, remembering how he touched her beneath the table, how helpless she was to stop the wild sensations he sent through her. A film of perspiration broke out all over her body. Her voice wavered as she said, "This is your last warning. Stay away from me."

He laughed, a heavy, rich sound that filled the stable. Annoyed by the unfamiliar sound, Debolt and Tencendur stomped their stall walls. Not at all taken in by the laughter, Lark moved back into an empty stall.

Abruptly, Stoke dived for her.

His weight hit her full force. Her fingers inadvertently loosened around the dagger, and she felt it leaving her hand. With a quick flick of her wrist, she snatched it back. She thanked the saints she didn't lose it and tumbled on her back into a pile of straw.

He landed on top of her, his hands supporting most of his weight. She slid the dagger deeper into the straw at her side.

"When are you going to learn you cannot threaten me?" He touched her chin with surprising gentleness. His finger traced the curve of her jaw, moved up to slide slowly across her bottom lip. The roughness of his skin, the heat of his fingertip, sent a tingle coursing down her face and throat.

"I've learned it. Now let me up." Lark felt her palm sweating against the smooth ivory handle of the dagger. The weight of his body pressed her down into the straw, not an oppressive feeling, but one that she was beginning to welcome.

"Nay, I have to prove it to you." His hot breath brushed

her face. "I'm drawn to that willful stubborn streak in you. It makes my blood burn as I've never felt it burn for a woman."

"Then I wish I were the meekest woman alive." Lark hated the fear in her voice and the quaking inside her. The spineless jellyfish was coming back.

"You may be a lot of things, but meek is not one of them, no matter how hard you may wish for it." He lowered his face and captured her mouth.

The potency of his hot lips against hers made her breath catch. She could feel her insides quivering, surrendering to him and the power he had over her. It would consume her soon. There would be no saving herself from him. "I am not his . . ." The very words she had used to Avenall came back to haunt her. They played over and over in her mind. In a blurring panic, she raised the dagger and plunged it into his back.

He tore his lips from hers and growled deep in his throat. Every muscle stiffened as he moaned, "Damn you . . ." He collapsed on her, his head banging against her chest, his body feeling like a slab of iron pressing down on her.

Lark froze, her hand still on the dagger, unable to believe what she'd just done. Hardly able to breathe, with his dead weight on her, she used all the strength in her arms and legs and shoved him off her. Trembling, her breaths coming in great raw gasps, she lay in the hay, recoiling in horror at what she'd done.

It occurred to her he might still be alive. She squeezed her eyes closed, and with a shaking hand reached over and felt his body. When her wrist brushed against the dagger, she involuntarily jerked back. It took her a moment to regain her nerve. She forced herself to lay her hand on him. The tempered ridges of muscle along his back brushed against her quivering fingertips, and something else . . . the thready rise and fall of his chest.

"Oh, God, you're alive. Thank you, Sweet Mary," she mumbled as her fingers found the hilt of the knife. She pulled, squeezing her eyes closed at the sucking sound.

With one final tug, the dagger left his back. Something warm and sticky stuck to her palm and seeped between her fingers. When she realized it was blood, his blood, she flung the blade aside, glad to be rid of it.

It hit the stable wall. In the silence, it sounded like the strike of a mace against armor.

She put pressure on the wound and used her free hand to pull the dagger from her boot and cut several strips of linen off the bottom of her smock. Working quickly, she made a bandage and placed it over the wound. She strained against the weight of his arm and shoulder as she wound the strip around it. When she finished, she let out an exhausted sigh.

She heard him take a breath. It came from deep within his lungs and sounded like a moan. Then nothing more.

"Nay, you cannot die . . . you hear me?" She leaned over him and felt frantically for a pulse in his neck.

Nothing.

"Wake up! Do you hear me, wake up!" She smacked the side of his face and beat on his back. "Stay with me! Do you hear! Surely you want to come back and finish harassing me— not that I don't deserve it now. I wouldn't blame you if you did."

She felt his back. Not a bit of movement. Using all the strength she could muster, she rolled him over on his back. She slapped his face as hard as she could, feeling the coarse stubble there like a file against her hand. "You cannot die. Do you hear?"

Lark felt his neck again.

A pulpy deadness met her fingers.

"You cannot die! You're supposed to settle on Helen, and she cares for you. Please don't let this be on my conscience the rest of eternity. How like you to torture me this way." She pounded on his chest. "Wake up!"

He didn't stir.

Lark collapsed back into the hay, tears of frustration burning her eyes. She drew up her knees, buried her face in clammy palms, and rocked back and forth. In all the time she'd spent training with weapons, she'd never taken a life. It was only sport. The image of plunging the dagger in his back flitted across her mind, the way it felt when it met his flesh. Worse yet had been the feel of pulling it out of his back.

Lark bent over and heaved, throwing up what little of her supper she'd just eaten in her room. When the retching stopped, she sat and buried her face in her hands. She rocked back and forth, while her whole body trembled. She had never wanted to kill him, but she'd been afraid of that power he held over her. Sweet Mary! He'd saved her life on that cliff too. She had never thanked him. She had thanked him now.

"Lark, where are you?"

She froze at the sound of Evel's soft whisper. Her head came up as she heard the stable door rattle.

"I'm here," Lark whispered back, the gritty, terrified quality in her voice sounding foreign to her ears.

"Open the door."

"Are you alone?"

"Aye, but I won't be for long."

His words stirred her into action. She rose, trying to stay as far away from Stoke's body as she could. She stumbled her way to the door, her knees feeling like wobbly stilts. Her hands shook as she pulled the pitchfork from the wooden brackets where Stoke had jammed it.

Before she could open the doors, Evel shoved them open, banging one into her side. "Ouch!" Rubbing her hip, she backed away and watched him step into the stable.

He grimaced as his gaze met hers. "I noticed that Blackstone had disappeared from the hall, and I went to your room to find you, but you were gone. I've only got a moment. Rowland follows me around like a hungry puppy. I asked Wira to entertain him for a moment, so I could slip away from him."

"Evel, you've got to help me!" Lark threw herself at him and hung on to his neck.

He made a choking sound and pulled her arms from around his throat. "St. John's bones! What is the matter with you, Lark? You're choking the life out of me."

"I've killed him."

"Killed who?"

"The Black Dragon."

Evel regarded her behind narrowed lashes. "You didn't kill the Black Dragon. This is no time for one of your pranks. Save those for the twins."

"It's no prank." Lark dug her fingers into the front of his tunic. "You've got to listen to me. I've killed him."

The seriousness in her tone made his jaw drop open. He looked unable to speak, only staring at her, dumbfounded.

Lark grabbed his hand and pulled him through the stable. "I'll show you."

"Jesu! I don't want to see." Evel barely lifted his feet as Lark dragged him forward.

Debolt and Tencendur and several palfreys stirred as they moved down the middle of the stable. Lark flinched and shied away from the horses, every movement, every sound amplified in her ears. Her nervousness was contagious and Evel jumped too.

"Damn it, Lark, stop it. It was just the horses."

"I can't help it. Any moment, I expect Stoke's ghost to leap out at me." Her hand went to her neck as she pulled Evel along.

"Don't be irrational."

"I'm not . . ." Lark words died in her throat as she reached Stoke's booted feet, jutting out from the stall. She stared down at them and pointed. "There he is. Dead as a rock."

Evel bent over and stared into the stall. Enough moonlight streamed in through the door for him to see who it was. "Jesu!" His jaw dropped open again.

"I didn't mean to kill him." She spoke past the strangling tightness in her throat. "He fell down on top of me. I had my dagger in my hand . . ." Her voice trailed off.

"You have to tell Father what you did."

"I cannot. I just spoke to him and asked him to let me deal with Stoke. What will he think of me? Nay, I can't bear to see the disdain on his face should I tell him I stabbed the Black

Dragon in the back. He would never forgive me for such cowardice.''

''He'll know someone did it when the body is found. You know Father will not give up until he finds out who. King Richard will send someone to investigate. Likely, you'll hang for the murder. Blackstone's supposed to be one of Richard's closest friends.''

''Not if he doesn't know I did it.''

''Everyone will know.''

''They will if you don't keep your voice down,'' Lark hissed at him.

''How can you hide what you have done?'' he asked, lowering his voice.

''I need your help.''

He held up his hands to ward her away. ''You're not involving me.''

''But you're the only one I can trust to help me.''

''Don't ask it of me.'' He backed away from her.

''Please, Evel. Have you forgotten the time I saved you from that boar? It would have gored you. What about that time at Uncle Jamus's, when you stole into Lady Jane's bedchamber? 'Twas I who lured her husband's guard from the door. That knave chased me all night. And remember that time when you needed a reason to see Lady Katherine so you could seduce her, and you made me pose as your mad sister who needed her tender care?''

''All right, all right!'' He waved his hand to cut her off. ''But should we both hang for this, I hope you will be satisfied.''

''Thank you, Evel.'' She stepped toward him and raised her arms to hug him, but he stepped back.

''Don't think your caresses will make me approve of what you are about to undertake. I abhor it. You could get us both hanged. Do you understand? I'm only doing this to pay you back for what you've done for me. But after this, do not ask me for any more favors.''

''All right, I'll never ask another favor. Just help me out of this disaster.'' She picked up Stoke's feet. ''Come on, help me put the body on Debolt's back. We have to get rid of it, before someone comes looking for him.''

''Where are you planning on taking the corpse?''

''You'll see.''

Evel backed her destrier out of his stall. After much shoving and grunting and cursing, they finally succeeded in getting the heavy body slung across Debolt's back.

Lark wrapped leather thongs around the corpse's hands and feet, securing the limp body on the horse; then she threw a blanket over it. Evel lead the horse while Lark walked on the side of it and balanced the body so it didn't fall. They waited until the bailey was clear and the watch guard had moved to the opposite side of the castle. Then they snuck across the bailey and out of the gates.

It didn't take them long to cross the road and enter the woods. Neither of them spoke. The soft thud of their footsteps and the plod of Debolt's large hooves braided with the hum of nightly insects, filling that void of tension-filled silence that stood between them.

She smelled the scent of cedar and decayed leaves as they trudged deeper and deeper into the thick forest. The clean scent of the woods used to hold a wealth of pleasure for her, but from this moment on she was sure it would sicken her. The memory of this whole night would haunt her the rest of her days.

Something rustled overhead.

They jumped at the same time and glanced up into the bright yellow eyes of an owl. A relieved glance passed between them, but neither spoke. What they were doing required the solemnity of silence and it followed them deep into the woods.

Lark paused and whispered, ''This is far enough, do you not think so?'' Her next words made her grimace and look at the body. ''I think the ravens will pick the flesh clean ere someone finds it.''

''I think that if you sailed the corpse over the sea to Ireland and dumped it, it would still not be far enough away, but I guess this will have to do." Evel went to work untying the thongs.

"I'm really sorry to involve you." Lark helped him heave the body down onto the ground. "Perhaps, if the body is found ere the ravens get it, they will believe an assassin killed him and left him here."

"They may. And should that happen, they will speak to Rowland, who believes you and I are in league with the assassins." His hand sliced the air angrily. "Favor me with no more of your suppositions." Evel grabbed a pile of leaves and tossed them on the body in an irritated manner. He grabbed more leaves, scowling as he worked.

Lark helped him, the cold leaves feeling like dead wrinkled skin against her fingers. She couldn't bear to look at Stoke's face while she worked. When she was through, she stared down at the mounded leaves, shadowed by moonlight, and bit her lip.

"Come on." Evel grabbed her arm.

"Shouldn't we say a prayer over him?"

"I think you had better save your prayers for your own soul—and mine." Evel pulled her behind him.

He picked up Debolt's reins, leaped on the stallion's back, and helped Lark mount behind him. She squeezed her eyes closed and prayed silently, asking the saints to spare Evel should she be caught. Resting her face against Evel's stiff back, she listened to the pounding of his heart as they rode back through the forest.

The din of hooves died away. A heavy silence hung over the forest, until it was broken by the sound of leaves rustling. And a ragged groan.

At dawn the next morning, tension as thick as a druid mound shrouded the very air in the hall. Lark watched her mother pace before the hearth, the crisp crunch of Elizabeth's footsteps on the rushes a counterpoint to the hiss and crackle of the fire.

Lark heard one of Helen's barely audible sobs. She glanced

over at her sister, who sat next to her. A steady stream of tears flowed down Helen's comely face, each tear stabbing at Lark. Worse yet, she could not get the image of stabbing Stoke out of her mind. It had played over and over in her mind, each time growing more vivid than the last. She would gladly have traded places with Stoke, if it would bring him back.

When Helen hiccuped, Elizabeth paused in her pacing and turned to look at her. In a voice tight with restraint, she said, "Please, Helen, you must stop crying. You've been crying for hours. You'll make yourself sick. You don't want to be sick, do you?"

"But what if something has happened to him?"

"Naught has happened."

"But he disappeared. And I overheard some of his men speaking about the attempts made on his life. What if he were murdered?" A fresh wash of tears flowed down Helen's pale cheeks.

Lark couldn't look at Helen any longer and glanced down at her hands, the tightness in her throat strangling in its intensity.

"You have been unusually quiet since Lord Stoke's disappearance, Lark. Do you know anything of these attempts on his life?"

It took Lark a moment to find her voice. "Only what I've been told."

"And what is that?"

"I've heard that ten attempts have been made on his life."

Helen and Elizabeth gasped at the same time.

In a vexed tone Elizabeth reserved only for Lark, she said, "I wish you had told us."

"I'm sorry, Mother."

"You should be, but I cannot lay the blame solely on you. He should have had the decency to inform us of this. We had other suitors for Helen's hand. Lord Lovington wanted her. Now he may not even look at her after she spurned his proposal. Lord Blackstone could at least have informed us if he wanted to marry Helen, instead of stringing us along. And most likely 'twas because he knew someone wished him dead. Should I ever meet this cur, they will hear a piece of my mind. I'm sure they know not the trouble they have put me to and how we've spent months planning for this wedding. I've promised everyone we know an invitation.''

''If this person is found, Mother, I doubt they will live long enough for you to speak to them,'' Lark said flatly, a sick feeling roiling in her stomach. She had not yet confessed her sins to Father Kenyon, their local priest. But taking Stoke's life and the way in which she had done it was so wretched, so craven, that she didn't think she could speak it aloud even to a priest.

''Oh, dear, I shall never see him again. . . .'' Helen's words died away behind a large gulp, then more tears.

Elizabeth touched Helen's shoulder. ''Do not despair, child, all may not be lost. He may still be alive and if he is not, you are pretty enough to find another husband. And now that I think on it, there is Lark's wedding. All our preparations need not be for naught.''

''Say you don't mean that.'' Lark's eyes widened at her mother.

''Of course I do, why should I not?''

''Surely you do not expect me to think about marrying Avenall when Helen's prospective husband may be lying dead somewhere.''

''I see no harm in it.''

Helen jumped out of her chair, ran across the hall, and up the stairs, her sobs trailing behind her.

''Now see what you've done.''

''It was you. How could you be so insensitive? We may be attending Lord Blackstone's funeral.''

The doors to the hall swung open. Loud voices boomed down the hallway. Her father and a whole party of men appeared. Evel, the twins, and Avenall entered the hall last.

Her father plopped down in a chair and his head dropped back. Lark had never seen him look so exhausted, or his face so drawn with worry. He looked older to her, too, and not as stalwart as she had always thought him.

Elizabeth ran toward him. "Did you find him, my dear?"

"Nay." William rolled his tired eyes. "It wasn't for lack of trying. We looked for him most of the night. By my teeth but I did not know the forests had grown so dense! In some places it was so thick my horse couldn't get through the underbrush. When I could no longer keep my eyes open, I called the men home."

"What of Lord Stoke's men?"

"They are still out there. They refuse to give up. We need food and a lot of ale."

The worn-looking men sat down at the tables.

"I'll get a servant." Elizabeth rushed from the hall.

William placed down his elbows on the table and rested his chin on his hand. Gowan leaned over and spoke to him in a hushed tone.

Lark heard footsteps and glanced up. Evel strode toward her, his blue eyes glazed over with worry. Instead of moving to the table to sit with her father, she stayed seated near the hearth. He sat down in the chair Helen had occupied and bent near her. "You're never going to believe this."

"What?"

Evel gulped, making his large Adam's apple bob in his throat. "The body is gone."

"It couldn't be." When the twins looked at Lark, she realized she'd spoken too loudly. She lowered her voice and said, "You must be mistaken."

"Nay, I went right over the exact spot where we left it. The body was gone."

"Could an animal have taken it?"

" 'Twould have to be an awfully big beast. Nay, an animal didn't take it."

"Then who did?"

"I know not, but something is amiss. I feel it."

"What are you two gossiping about?" Harold said, striding up to them, Cedric hard on his heels.

Firelight danced in their golden hair as they cornered Lark

and Evel between them. They crossed their arms over their chests and eyed her.

"What do you two want?" Evel demanded.

Harold ignored Evel and bent near Lark. He whispered, "The question here is, what have you and Evel been up to?"

"I don't have time for you two," Lark said, grimacing.

"You're hiding something," Cedric said in his usual snide tone as he touched her arm.

"Nay, we're not." She jerked her arm out of his grasp.

"We know." Cedric tossed the two words out like boulders, looking pleased with himself, matching Harold's expression.

"Know?" She looked at them, keeping her expression as cryptic as she could, while her stomach clenched into knots.

"We saw you and Evel sneaking out of the castle last night. You had something large slung over Debolt's back. 'Tis going to cost you to keep us silent."

She stared at both of them. Their chief goal in life had always been to torment her. But they had never had the upper hand before. She regarded them with cold speculation and said, " 'Twas naught more than an old rug Mother asked me to move for her."

"She's never been much of a liar." Harold playfully hit his brother's shoulder.

"We just can't figure out why you did it." Cedric said.

"She didn't do anything," Evel said.

"You're involved too, so you'd better smile when you speak to us." A smug smile spread across Harold's lips.

Lark ground her teeth.

"Have you told anyone?" Evel's fists clenched at his sides, and he shot Lark a censorious look, as if it were all her fault.

"Nay, and we won't if you meet our demands." Cedric smiled at Evel and tweaked Lark's nose.

She knocked his hand away. "What demands?"

"That the two of you be our slaves."

Lark clamped her jaw so tightly together that her neck and teeth ached. It killed her to say her next words, but she forced them out. "All right, but I warn you, I won't forget this."

"We didn't think you would," Harold said, adding a saucy smile.

"You can start tomorrow by currying our horses." Cedric's grin grew devious, matching Harold's.

"And I'm to see to the cleaning of the moat. You can do that too."

"After that, the stables need mucking out."

The twins paused, staring pensively at each other, as if one couldn't think without the other.

"Is that all?" Lark stood now, fists on her hips, glowering at them.

"Probably not. Give us a day." Harold grinned. When he saw Lark's mouth crimped in annoyance, he added, "Ah, ah, ah! I know what you're thinking. You are our slave now. Get used to it."

"That is if you don't want everyone to find out about what you did." Cedric finished the thought for his brother.

"You'd better not tell anyone," Evel said between his teeth.

"Just do what you are supposed to and no one will ever know." Harold wore a self-satisfied grin.

"What are you four whispering about?" William's loud bawl gained the attention of all his children.

"Naught, Father," Cedric blurted.

"Then I suggest you break the fast and rest, for we'll be leaving in a few hours to go and relieve Lord Stoke's men."

The twins' golden brows snapped together in a frown as they turned and strode toward the table. Evel cast Lark an annoyed look and followed them.

Lark rose and noticed Avenall, who stood below one of the tapestries. The top of his head just touched the sewn image of William's spear, thrusting into the Saxon King Harold at the battle of Hastings. His head blocked the fallen King Harold. It looked as if the point were about to pierce Avenall's skull. He stepped away and glanced around the hall, looking preoccupied. When his liquid blue eyes alighted on Lark, he strode toward her, his brow heavy with distress.

She couldn't speak to Avenall. Not now. If she didn't get

out of the hall this very moment, she might break down and tell her father everything. She ignored Avenall, kept her head down, and strode past the tables, the conversation of William's men low and solemn compared to their usual boisterous jabber. She heard snippets of conversation about the attempts on Lord Stoke's life and what they would like to do when they found the culprit. In spite of trying to hold her shoulders erect, they sagged, and she had a hard time not running out of the hall.

"Lark, wait!"

At the sound of Avenall's voice, she swung around. She watched him hurry over to her. He took her hand and asked, "Do you know where Helen is?"

"She ran to her room, crying her eyes out. Why?"

"I'm worried about her. I know how sensitive she is. I'm sure she is overwrought with worry. I wanted to speak to her and see if there was anything I could do."

"By all means. Mayhap you can get her to stop crying. I could not," Lark said, waving her hand toward the stairs.

"We will talk later." He patted her hand and dropped it.

"Very well." Lark turned again, surprised by her lack of desire to speak to him.

She hadn't missed him at all since the argument in the garden, nor did she wish to bring that up again—especially when she could not get Stoke's face out of her mind—nor her thoughts that Evel might hang right along with her for helping her dispose of the body. Everything had gone so terribly awry. Worse yet, the twins knew.

That afternoon, Lark stood on the bank of the moat, watching two castle servants dragging a net through the brownish-green water. The film of scum stuck to the net, making it glisten like the slimy skin of a snail. Everything considered waste went into the moat, including the excrement from the garderobe. Overseeing the cleaning was no pleasant task, but the sludge made good rich earth for the herb garden. At the moment, she deserved all the distasteful tasks the twins could heap on her.

There would have to be many more ere her conscience stopped punishing her.

She paced the edge of the moat and nervously braided a reed between her fingers. The wind rattled the last of the stubborn fall leaves still attached to the nearby oaks. She jumped, the sound like the rattle of a thousand bones to her overly sensitive ears. But every sound lately grated against her. She even jumped when there was no sound.

She scanned the road and the wood near it. Any moment she expected to see William emerge with Stoke's body thrown over a horse. Her gaze strayed to a massive red oak. A vision of her and Evel, hanging by their necks from one of its thick boughs, rose up to plague her. Where was Stoke's body? What could have happened to it?

The reed in her hands snapped. She frowned down at it and tossed it away. Abruptly, one of the men near her gasped. He dropped the net and pointed at something in the wood. The worker next to him threw up his hands, his face ashen.

The net slid down into the moat with a loud splat.

Lark turned. Her breath caught, her eyes widened, and her mouth dropped open. Muscles in her throat constricted. She grabbed the base of her neck and in horror, fused with a certain amount of relief, she watched Stoke emerge from the woods.

Chapter 12

His muscular arms thrust aside the low-lying brush along the road. The dragon on his tunic flapped its wings with each prowled step toward her, its eyes glowing ominously. Dirt covered the hem of the tunic and the front of his braies as if he'd risen straight from the grave. The bandage she'd applied cut across his shoulder and the tip of one of the dragon's wings. Pieces of leaves, embedded in the linen bandage, stuck to it like misshapen brown teeth. Stoke's coal-black hair waved around his pale face and wide shoulders.

Her relief was short-lived, giving way to an impulse to flee. But the frigid fury emanating from him impaled her, freezing her limbs and turning her insides colder than a gravestone marker. The red in his eyes flared and kindled like two altar candles.

He wavered a little on his feet, yet continued toward her. Pain masked his expression, making him look even more forbidding. She wanted to go to him, to help him, but the expression on his face made her step back.

He kept coming.

She kept backing away.

"Be gone!" He glared at the two servants.

They bowed, crouched away, then took off running back toward the drawbridge.

Lark licked her lips, tasting the spittle collecting at the edge of her mouth. A vision of being drawn and quartered rose in her mind. By his expression, he'd find something worse yet to do to her. Swallowing hard, she felt her foot catch on a tuft of grass. Her feet slipped. She screamed and rolled down the bank.

Face first, mouth open, she hit the swill in the moat. Her arms and legs flailed for a moment, until she realized that where she'd landed the water was only knee-deep. Bile rose in her throat at the fetid odor that was now a part of her. In her mouth. In her nose. Melting into her skin. Even her soul felt filth-ridden, not so much from the moat ooze, but from having stabbed Blackstone in the back. She rose out of the water, pulled something long, green, and slithery from across her nose and left eye, and glanced up.

From the top of the bank, he stared down at her as an executioner might look upon his next victim. "I can see you are delighted to see me."

Lark took one look at him and could no longer hold back the bile. She wretched until her ribs were sore. After a long moment, she held her middle, panting. She gasped, "Dear Mother Mary knows I didn't mean to hurt you. You shouldn't have come near me. I told you to stay away."

"Aye, but your lips and body said something different. I underestimated you. 'Twill never happen again."

Had the devil ever spoken to her, she imagined he would have sounded exactly as Stoke had just sounded. She turned and saw him trudge down the bank, the coppery glow in his eyes piercing all the way down to the marrow of her bones.

The yip of hounds echoed off the outer castle walls, bouncing across the moat, growing louder by the moment. He turned and glanced behind him.

"Praise be! There he is by the moat!" Lark heard William's loud yell.

Hound after hound appeared near Stoke's legs and swarmed around him in a large circle, tongues sagging and tails wagging.

William, Rowland, her brothers, Avenall, and Gowan all reined in near the moat. Evel saw that Blackstone still lived, and a relieved smile broke across his face. Rowland and Gowan scowled at the bloody bandage on Stoke's back. Avenall appeared oddly detached from the scene, resting his hands on the saddle's pummel, a blank look on his face as he stared at Blackstone. As if Avenall felt Lark's gaze on him, he glanced at her standing in the moat and frowned.

"My God, what a stench." Harold leaned over his mount's neck to peer down at Lark.

"Aye." Cedric mimicked his brother's snide tone. "I thought the moat had a stronger odor than normal."

"Do you enjoy bathing in the moat, sister?" Harold asked, grinning devilishly.

"That is enough." William drew himself up in the saddle, shot a glance at the twins, and looked down at Lark. "What are you doing, Lark?"

William never used her name unless he was irritated. In a placating voice that wavered, she said, "I—I tripped."

"Here . . ." William threw her one of the reins in his hand and turned to Blackstone. "Where have you been, sirrah? Do you realize we have scoured the whole countryside looking for you?"

"Someone stabbed me and left me for dead. When I came to, I wandered aimlessly in the woods in the dark, then I passed out again. I woke up only an hour ago and walked here."

"I'm surprised the dogs did not find you ere now." Avenall's voice was laced with suspicion.

William spoke before Blackstone had a chance. "Do you not remember the first time we turned them loose and they flushed out a stag?"

"Aye, I remember," Avenall said.

"But why did they keep circling back to the castle? That one puzzles me?" Gowan pulled on the tip of his silver beard.

"They must have become confused and lost the scent."

William eyed the dogs with disgust. "It wouldn't be the first time it happened."

"Do you know who stabbed you?" Rowland addressed Blackstone, all the while staring at Lark.

"I did not see the poisonous viper's face."

At the unexpected words, Lark's glance whipped over to Blackstone.

His gaze cut into her face for what seemed like years, but had been only seconds. He meant to torment her until he chose to seek revenge—she could see it in his eyes. Lark cringed inwardly.

Unable to look him in the eye, she glanced down at the green film sticking to her gown. Then she used the rein in her hand to pull herself from the moat. Green slimy reeds stuck to her person as she stepped on the other side of Tencendur, putting something solid between her and Blackstone.

The exchanged eye-fire between Lark and Blackstone did not go unnoticed by William as he said, in a voice only they could hear, "I hope you are sure you have the culprit and not someone who is innocent."

"Be assured, I only punish the guilty."

The words were directed at Lark, and she felt them like stabs to the back. She didn't dare look at Stoke, but watched a hound sniff at her own leg. The animal hung back several feet, crouched on his haunches. He raised his nose and sniffed, afraid to approach her.

Tencendur must have decided he'd had enough of her rankness, too, for he laid his ears back and the whites of his eyes flashed as he sidestepped.

"Whoa there, old man." William patted the stallion's neck. "Hand me the rein, Lark, then go and bathe in the lake ere your mother finds you."

"Aye, Father." Lark cast him a quick glance as she strode toward the lake. The dogs parted, giving her and the noxious odor a wide girth.

"Oh, and Lark?"

"Aye?" She turned to look at William.

"Burn those clothes."

Lark nodded.

Harold and Cedric chuckled.

William turned and glared at them. "You two can go and find your sister some clothes and soap, then see to the rest of the cleaning of the moat. I thought your mother told you to do it days ago."

Harold stammered and Cedric gulped, his Adam's apple bobbing in his throat.

"Save your excuses," William bawled. "Go and do as you are bid, or you'll answer to me."

Harold and Cedric shared a sheepish glance, turned, and rode toward the drawbridge.

Lark felt Stoke's eyes on her, the enmity pouring from them like hemlock. She quickened her pace toward the lake. When would he come for her? The worst part was the anticipation. And he knew that. He enjoyed making her squirm. She grimaced, feeling her insides already squirming.

William watched his daughter's long-legged strides, her head hanging almost to her chest. Green scum stuck to her braid and turned the tawny gold the color of tarnished brass. Her dress hung between her legs in dripping folds. Her feet dragged with each step. Something was dreadfully wrong with her. He turned to Blackstone and saw him studying Lark the way a hawk watches its prey.

Blackstone wavered slightly on his feet, and Rowland dismounted and steadied him. "Can you make it back into the castle?" he asked.

"Aye. Then I'm going home."

William shared a glance with Gowan, then frowned at Blackstone. "You're taking leave of us?"

"Aye, I'm sorry to say, I'm going to have to delay any wedding plans so I can find the culprit who stabbed me." Blackstone glanced back at Lark. "Of course, I shall pay you for any inconvenience you and your wife might have suffered."

William grunted under his breath. ''Aye, well, I have suffered very little, though I cannot say the same for my coffers. My wife insisted upon emptying them to prepare for this anticipated wedding.''

''Be assured I shall fill it again.''

'' 'Tis a known fact double weddings bode ill.'' William glanced at Evel, who had not said a word. He appeared enthralled by a horsefly on the ear of his mount. ''I told my stubborn wife as much when she conceived of this idea, but I understand your reasoning. I wouldn't want to enter a marriage knowing my life was in danger.''

''But I shall never understand it,'' Avenall blurted. ''Why did you decide to marry when you knew someone was trying to kill you?''

''I needed a wife, but I see now it was unwise of me. I should have found my nemesis ere I thought of marriage.''

''Helen will be overwrought.'' Avenall's voice raised to a fevered pitch. ''Your wealth will not buy back her happiness.''

Blackstone's dark gaze locked with Avenall's. For the longest time, he didn't speak, only stared at him, taking his measure. Then he said, ''I will speak to her.''

''Speaking to her will do naught,'' Avenall said. ''She's been crying her eyes out for hours while you were gone. Now if you tell her this, she will never recover.''

William saw Blackstone's fist tighten at his sides, and he inched Tencendur between the two. ''Of course Helen will recover. You have forgotten her forgiving nature. Now I'll hear no more of it.'' He leveled his gaze at Avenall, a look that had sent him scurrying from William's presence as a lad.

But the young man only glowered back at William. He opened his mouth to speak, thought better of it, then turned his horse and cantered toward the drawbridge.

''Wait!'' Evel called to Avenall's back as he followed him.

''Avenall is young.'' William spoke his thoughts aloud and listened to the clatter of hooves as Avenall and Evel took the planks on the bridge.

"Aye," Blackstone grumbled under his breath. "But I have no patience with boys." He turned to Rowland. "Let us go."

William watched Blackstone lean heavily on his friend's shoulder as they strode toward the drawbridge. A large bloodstain on Blackstone's back drew his gaze. The size of a horse's head, it spread across his right shoulder. A crudely tied bandage covered the wound high up near his arm. Blood had soaked the bandage and dried to a dark brown.

Gowan leaned over and grabbed the reins to Rowland's destrier. He edged his horse near William. "Something is amiss here."

"That would be the truth if it ever came to my ears. And did you notice the bandage? Who would stab someone and put a bandage on the wound? Not Blackstone—he couldn't reach his own back in that kind of pain."

"A villein could have done it for him."

"He didn't say he'd seen anyone. And did you not sense something between Lark and the earl?"

"One would have to be a dullard not to." Gowan glanced past Blackstone, toward Lark as she jumped a ditch and headed into the woods. "Do you think it was she who stabbed him in the back?"

"I know not, but I shall question her ere the sun sets." William's frown matched Gowan's. "If Lark did stab Blackstone, she must have had a good reason for it, and I mean to hear that reason."

"What will you do when Lady Elizabeth gets wind of the earl deciding not to marry?"

Abruptly, a loud shriek came from the bailey.

William looked over at his longtime friend. "I believe she knows. A prudent retreat to the village is in order. Time will bear out her disappointment, and I shan't be here to suffer the brunt of it. I leave that to you, my good friend. I'll be back ere the sun sets." William spurred Tencendur down the road toward the village. The five hounds followed behind him.

Gowan watched him through a cloud of dust. Another screech split the air. He hunched his shoulders against the piercing sound. Frowning, he looked longingly in the direction of the village.

Several hours later, Lark gained enough nerve to come home and face the Black Dragon's fury. When she entered the hall, her footsteps rang hollow in the empty, cavernous room. She strode past the long oak tables, her gaze scouring every corner and shadow for any sign of Stoke.

She heard another set of footsteps behind her and wheeled around, half expecting Stoke to jump out at her. "Oh, Marta!" She grabbed the base of her throat. "You shouldn't sneak up on a person like that."

Marta paused with a tray in her hands. The wrinkles sagging over her sharp cheekbones stretched as she said, "I wasn't sneaking. I'm taking a tray up to yer mother and Lady Helen. They took to their beds when the earl up and quit us."

"He's gone?" Lark gaped at Marta in surprise.

"Aye, gone. Said he couldn't marry 'til he caught the person who be trying to kill him. I don't blame him, but the mistress didn't take it well. After she screeched her head off, she took to her bed, moaning. Ain't never seen her so distraught. I made her some tea. She's been asking for ye and the master."

"I suppose she means to try and keep my marriage on schedule." How could she go through with the marriage, while the threat of the Black Dragon hovered at her back?

"All of that." Marta pursed her ancient lips and snorted critically. "She spoke as much to Lord Avenall."

"Well, if it pleases Mother—the saints know I do very little to please her—I shall go through with the marriage. Mayhap Father can gain a little peace from it."

"I think ye should not marry to please others, but yerself."

"I shall be pleased." Lark's voice lacked conviction, and it made Marta stare deep into her eyes.

Marta looked ready to say something, but appeared to change her mind. After a moment, she said, "I wish ye'd speak to yer sister. She's still crying. I'm worried she'll make herself sick. Ain't like her to cry this way."

"I'll speak to her." Lark would never understand Helen's attraction to Stoke. He didn't suit her at all. Oil and water, that's what they were. On top of that, he would make Helen a terrible bully of a husband. She glanced around the empty hall and asked, "Where is everyone?"

"After the twins fetched yer clothes, they all went off to the village to join the master."

Now Lark knew why Harold and Cedric were in such a hurry to leave her in peace by the lake. When William left for the village, they knew they could swill all the ale they liked and bed the innkeeper's daughters at no expense to themselves. All the burden of expense fell on her father. But she knew Avenall would not be with them. He never went to the inn. So she asked, "And Lord Avenall, where is he?"

"He's in his chamber, resting. The search for the earl done him in."

Lark noticed the tray shaking beneath Marta's frail arms. "Here, I'll take it up." She grabbed it out of Marta's grasp. "Where is Wira?"

"She's up with the mistress rubbing her neck." Marta's lips grew tight, and she rubbed her fingers over the protruding veins and paper-thin skin on one hand. "These old fingers are too gnarled for massaging, so I went for the tea."

The familiar heavy thump of footsteps behind them told Lark that William was home. She glanced back at him. His eyes were glassy, his cheeks a bit ruddy, though his walk was steady, and his nose not overly red, as when he was intoxicated.

His green eyes lit up at the sight of her. But then he appeared to remember something, and the light went out of them. He frowned and said, "I want a word, Lark."

He'd used her name. She was surely in trouble. "I'm taking this tray up for Marta."

"Where are all the servants whom I feed and clothe?" William's gaze swept the empty hall. "I told Elizabeth that Marta was not to do fetching."

172   *Constance Hall*

"Wira is busy with Mother. And the others are helping Cook prepare for the evening repast."

Some of the exasperation left William's voice as he looked at the elderly woman who had raised him and his children. All the concern and respect he felt for her came through in his voice as he said, "Marta, go up and have Wira get this tray. You are not to carry a thing, is that understood?"

"I'm not so old I can't do—"

"Cease your grumbling, old woman, and do my bidding." Though William's words were gruff, he said them with a lop-sided grin on his face.

Marta, like most who served William, had never been able to resist that grin. She turned, shook her head, and hid a grin of her own as she hobbled up the steps.

Lark set the tray on a table.

"Sit, Lark." William took her hand. He kicked out two chairs with his foot and pulled her down next to him. "I must needs speak with you."

"I confess, 'twas my fault." Lark let out a long sigh, the burden of guilt that had pressed on her heart for hours lightened.

"You confess and know not what I'm about to ask." He blinked curiously at her.

"I do know, and I did it."

"When have you taken to sorcery and reading minds?" He raised a brow at her and leaned close to look in her eyes.

Lark detected ale on his breath, mixing with the stale odor of the inn and saddle leather issuing from his clothes. "It does not take a sorcerer to know what of you speak. 'Tis Lord Blackstone, and I did it."

"I had hoped you'd deny it." He leaned back and ran his hands through the sides of his graying golden hair. "But I should have guessed you'd be honest with me. You've never lied to me."

"Nay, Father, I could never do that."

"That is why you are so special to me." William reached out and touched her chin. His eyes gleamed with a depth of emotion that came from somewhere deep inside him.

"I'm sorry, Father. I didn't mean to stab him in the back."
Lark gazed down at the golden hairs on her father's thick wrist.

He dropped his hand and said, "I blame you not."

"You don't?"

"Nay." His eyes turned a darker green as he said, "He wanted you, did he not?"

Lark nodded and felt a blush start in her cheeks and burn all the way down her neck.

"His touch didn't disgust you, did it? You wanted him and you panicked enough to strike out at him."

Lark's eyes widened. "How did you know that?"

"Human nature and the workings of women and men are not foreign to me. And I happen to know you, Pigeon, better than you know yourself. You should realize that by now." The lopsided grin came back.

"Aye, I should, but 'tis disconcerting that you know me so well." Lark couldn't help but smile back at him.

"I know only the part of you that is like me."

"Like you?" Lark cocked her head to the side at the compliment and studied William.

"Aye, you have all of my good and bad qualities."

"You have no bad traits, Father."

He smiled as he used to when she was a child and touched her shoulder. "Aye, I have them, and you are about the only person in the world blind to them. Like you, I'm stubborn—especially when it comes to matters of the heart."

"I don't understand."

"One day you will." He dropped his hand, leaned back in his chair, and stared pensively at the hearth across the room.

When he didn't seem inclined to speak, Lark said, "If you mean Mother, I've often wondered why you married her."

"I took her to wife for the dowry and lands she brought. I had naught to recommend me but a claim to being the youngest son of a baron—which you know left me naught, having five brothers. All my sire's wealth went to your Uncle Egbert." He shrugged, accepting his destiny. "There has never been want of sons in the Mandeville line—not that I'm complaining. I wouldn't have traded one of my brothers for my father's wealth and lands. And I'll never regret marrying wisely.''

Lark remained silent. The moment needed silence to digest it.

William broke the quiet. ''I knew she was a shrew when I married her, but she was beautiful, and I sensed a passion in her that answered my own. Had she been cold and unresponsive, I would never have wedded her. There were other ladies from whom I could have chosen.''

''So you married without love.'' Lark voiced her thoughts aloud, having sensed this since she was old enough to contemplate the unusual relationship between her parents.

''Never underestimate the power of desire. It goes a long way in making a marriage.''

''But lust is not love.''

''Nay, but eventually it leads to love. Never think I do not love your mother. At times she could vex the blood from my veins, but should she die this moment, and I could never again feel her lying next to me and feel her warmth against me, I would mourn the loss all the days of my life. I have done things I heartily regret in my life, but marrying your mother is not one of them.''

Lark knew this for the truth. She had never seen William stray from his wife's bed. Even when he went to the inn and the wenches rubbed against him in invitation, he had always sent them on their way with a good-hearted pat on their backsides.

At her silence, he continued. ''I have oft wondered at your choice in Avenall. He is certainly not what I had pictured for you as a husband.''

''Who did you picture, Father?''

''If you want the truth, someone like Blackstone.''

''Pray, not him.'' Lark squeezed her eyes tightly together.

''You wanted the truth, and there it is. When you first blossomed into womanhood, and I saw the attraction between you and Avenall, I thought it no more than a passing infatuation on your part, so I did naught about it. Then when your mother pressured you to get married, and you announced you wanted him for a husband, it was too late. I hoped you'd change your mind, ere you married him.''

''But I love him,'' Lark said, realizing her voice held too much fervor.

William stared down at the fat ruby ring on his finger and said, ''When you kiss him, does he stir your blood as the Black Dragon does?''

Lark hesitated and gulped deep in her throat. Finally she said, ''Nay, but I love him in a different way.''

''How many ways are there to love? Speak not of that notion of courtly love, for 'tis twaddle if ever I heard it. If there is no passion between you, what is there?''

''Love.''

''Love? When I doubt seriously if you can respect him?''

''Father, that is not true.''

''He is an insipid soul. Even as boy, he lacked zeal in the yard. I thought he would never learn to hold a sword properly, or even to polish my saddle as it should be. As a squire, Marta could have done a better job—and I knew you and Evel took up most of his chores.'' He wagged a finger at her. ''The most fight I ever saw from him was when he stood up to Blackstone on behalf of Helen's feelings. And such a paltry issue at that.'' William grunted under his breath.

''That would be just like him. He looks upon Helen as a sister. Naturally he'd defend her. He is the noblest man I know. I don't care what you say, Father, I do love him.'' Lark stubbornly raised her chin.

''Aye, but do you love him enough to commit your life to him?'' He put his hand over hers. She opened her mouth and he raised his hand to still her. ''Don't commit yourself yet. Think long and hard on it. In a sennight, if you still feel the same, the wedding will go on, but should you decide against it, I'll call it off, for I can manage your mother's ire, but the thought of you being unhappy for the rest of your life is more than I can bear.''

She smiled at him, then leaned over and kissed his cheek, feeling his bewhiskered face against her skin. ''I'll think on it.'' She rose and left him staring after her. Lark knew the next week would be the longest in her life.

Six nights later, Lark thrashed at the covers. The dream that had plagued her sleep for days was back. Avenall stood in the garden. The moon, at its zenith, hovered above his head. His blue eyes sparkled at her through the shadows of the garden. The sweet scent of coriander and brown earth hovered in the air. He stood on the path in front of her, hands stretched toward her. With raised arms, she tried touching him, but a force held her back. Try as she might, she could not reach him. His fingertips were inches from her, but this dark force stood between them. . . .

Abruptly, something clamped over Lark's mouth and jarred her awake from the dream. Before she could fully open her eyes, someone jammed a rag in her mouth and flipped her over. A knee plunged into her back. Her face dipped into the pillow. Strong fingers clamped around her wrists and jerked her hands behind her. Struggling to breathe, she felt leather thongs biting into her wrists.

She turned to look at her attacker, but a sack was jerked over her head, down over her shoulder and body. Someone tied it around her thighs. Large unyielding hands bit into her waist and swept her up. Her belly hit a rock-hard shoulder. The dark force in her dream had come for her.

Chapter 13

For the next two hours, hell visited Lark. The pounding of the horses hoove's vibrated in her chest, and Stoke's body touched her everywhere. His thick legs pressed against her bosom and across her hipbones. His loins were tight against her right side. As the horse galloped, the friction between their bodies added to the heat, increasing the blood pounding in her temples and the roiling in her stomach.

Cool, damp air swirled across her bare feet and up the back of her thin nightgown. Through the open weave in the burlap sack over her eyes, she could see a blur of darkness and a hint of moonlight. Would he ever stop to rest the horse? This torture had to end sometime.

As if he read her mind, he slowed his mount. She thanked the saints for the respite. He reined in and dismounted. Abruptly his hands were on her waist and she landed in his arms. Dizziness overwhelmed her at the sudden righting. To keep the world from spinning, she leaned her head on his shoulder.

He stiffened. Each of his strides pounded the ground and reverberated through her with the same shock as a sword smashing against her shield. Ten long, agonizing strides, and he placed her on the ground.

Leaves crinkled beneath her bottom and bare feet. Dampness seeped through the burlap sack and her thin nightgown. She shivered, listening to him walk away.

So this was to be her punishment. Left in the woods. Bound. Gagged. Stuck in a sack. Easy prey for predators. A punishment equal to when she'd left him in the woods, stabbed in the back, easy fodder for the ravens. But there was a difference. She hadn't known he was still alive; he knew she was. The thought of becoming a meal for a pack of wolves made her pull at the thongs on her wrists and bite down on the gag.

"So you've still got fight in you?"

She heard his deep voice behind her and froze. The panic slowly ebbed. He rolled her over, cut the bindings on the sack, and with a quick jerk snatched it off her. Next, he pulled the gag out of her mouth. An aftertaste of dirt, beeswax, and wool lingered on her tongue.

She spat out the little fibers stuck on her tongue and glanced at the thick elms and oaks around her. A patch of starlit sky winked at her through the spiraling forest boughs overhead. Spring leaves were just starting to emerge, like feathers sprouting along the naked bark. She noticed Venus's beacon in the eastern sky. By the position of it, she knew they had traveled southwest, and by the height of the moon it looked to be close to midnight.

He stepped in front of her, towering over her, arms folded across his chest. Tentacles of swirling deep-purple clouds passed over the moon, and his face was thankfully hidden from her. Darkness totally eclipsed his eyes, sparing her the brunt of their burning intensity. He stood, peering down at her, a massive monolith of indignation.

Lark shifted and felt the thongs chafing against her wrists. When she could no longer stand his scrutiny or the silence, she asked, "Would it help to say I didn't mean to stab you in the back?"

" 'Tis best you not speak at all." He stepped back from her.

In spite of his warning, she asked, "Would you punish me for protecting my honor? You had no right to come near me again. I warned you to stay away."

"You don't kiss a man the way you did and expect him to believe you when you warn him away."

Lark didn't have a verbal parry for that one, so she nervously shifted and changed the subject. "What do you mean to do with me?"

"Make you my prisoner."

"But you cannot do that."

"But I can and have."

"My father will never allow it. And Avenall will come for me. You've ruined everything now. We were to wed on the morrow."

"Your father and fiancé have no say in it. If they come for you, they will have to deal with me first."

"Please, don't cause a war with my father."

"I'll do what it takes to keep you my prisoner."

Her expression fell. She watched his silhouette take form as part of the moon peeked out behind him. With his sable hair hanging down around his massive shoulders, his body looked like an arch above a finely-chiseled granite pillar. If there was an ounce of compassion in that hard, unyielding form, she knew she would never find it.

He eyed her a moment longer and turned abruptly. His mantle whipped around him as he stalked toward his destrier. She watched the scabbard at his side thump against his long thigh. Moonlight caught the red stone embedded in the hilt of his massive broadsword. For a moment, the glazed orb looked like the eye of a dragon awakening, the sleepy lids opening and closing.

She blinked at the uncanny reddish haze beaming from the stone, thinking it greatly matched the hue in its owner's eyes. Feeling a sharp twinge in her shoulder blades, she twisted the bindings holding her wrists behind her back and said, "At least untie me. If I'm to be your prisoner, I'll need my hands."

"I have seen what you do with your hands. When I wish to

be bludgeoned in the back again, then I'll untie you." He didn't bother turning to address her, but continued to rummage through a satchel hanging from his saddle.

"If you do not untie me soon, I shan't be able to move my arms." She frowned at the pleading tone in her voice.

With mute indifference, he pulled a flask from the satchel and strode toward her. He sat across from her and tipped up the flask. When he finished drinking, he eyed her over the top of it, as if he were trying to figure out what to do with her. His gaze moved down her body in a hungry perusal, pausing at her breasts. Her waist. Lower still, between her legs.

Lark glanced down at herself. Her threadbare gown hid very little from his view. Her hardened nipples protruded through the fabric, and her dark gold woman's mound shone beneath the almost transparent linen. Heat seeped through her and warmed her from the inside out. Whether it was from a blush, or the heat of his gaze, she didn't know.

He stared at her a moment longer, put aside the flask, and pulled out a knife from his boot.

Without taking her eyes off the glistening blade, and in a calm voice that surprised her, she asked, "Will you kill me now?"

He didn't say a word, only leaned toward her with the knife in hand. The sharp steel came toward her, as his dark eyes never left her face.

To keep from begging him not to kill her, she gritted her teeth and tensed. If she were to die, she'd die with honor. She met his gaze with all the courage she could find.

To her surprise, the hand holding the blade veered off and around to her back. His shoulder brushed her arm as he leaned behind her. She flinched at the contact.

"Hold still." He grabbed her wrists and cut the thongs. "Think not that I'll kill you. I much prefer to keep you as a prisoner." A wicked grin pulled at his lips.

Where his arm touched her, she felt a tingle shoot down to her wrist. She jerked away from him. With a slight tremor in her hands, she rubbed the chafed skin on her wrists. "Thank you," she said, not sounding at all indebted to him.

"See that you keep them where I can see them." He didn't move away from her, but sat so close that she could feel the heat of his knees singeing her thigh.

"I have to relieve myself." Lark glanced at the dagger in his hand.

"Very well, but I shall accompany you." He thrust the dagger back in his boot, stood, and pulled her to her feet. Momentarily, he stared into her eyes, wearing a strange, unreadable expression. She didn't know if he wanted to strike her or kiss her. He chose neither. He dropped her arm, then motioned toward the woods. "Lead the way, I prefer not to turn my back on you."

She shot him a glance and strode past several thick-trunked trees and paused. When he only stood there, staring at her, she said, "Must you watch?"

" 'Tis either that, or hold it." One corner of his lip twisted.

"Very well, I'll hold it. I hope my bladder bursts, for then I'll die, and you'll be cheated out of the satisfaction of having me for a prisoner." Squaring her shoulders, she turned and took a step back toward the horse.

He grabbed her arm and pulled her around to face him. "Very well, go behind this tree, but should you try to escape, you'll not like the punishment I have in mind." His gaze snapped down her body.

Glad to escape his scrutiny, she stepped behind an impressive beech, with an enormous smooth gray trunk. Perfect for privacy. Glancing around her to make sure he was not peeking at her, she yanked up the hem of her gown and hummed loudly while she emptied her bladder. When she was done, she strode back around the tree and found him, ankles crossed, arms folded, one shoulder propped against the trunk.

"You surprise me. I thought you would run." He straightened and blocked her path.

"I'm not that much of a simpleton. You could easily capture me. When I escape, it will be when I have the advantage."

"Think you I will ever give you that advantage?"

"You may not give it, but even great warriors as yourself make mistakes. When you do, I'll be gone."

His fingers bit into her arms. "Do not make threats you'll never keep." His deep silken voice cut through her like a blade.

He stood so close that she felt his hot, stormy breaths scorching her face. In a calm voice, belying the fluttering his nearness caused in her, she said, " 'Tis no threat, only the truth. Would you have me lie and tell you I'll not try to escape?"

"Are you getting a conscience now?"

"I had a conscience. I'm not as wicked as you believe."

"Nay, you're worse than I could ever image." He dropped his hands. "Get moving. Shechem has rested long enough."

"Where are you taking me?" Lark walked ahead of him and rubbed at the chill bumps on her arms.

"You'll know when we get there."

She felt something heavy fall on her shoulders and realized it was his mantle.

"Keep that around you. I wouldn't want you to catch a chill and die from a fever." His words came out laced with sarcasm.

She clasped the thick velvet around her, his scent and warmth heavy upon it. If only she could fling it back in his face. But she was cold and would not give him the satisfaction of savoring her discomfort.

Baltizar stepped out of the shadows and strode up to her. She paused and patted her shoulders. He jumped up and rested his paws on her chest.

"You should not have followed me," she said, running her hands over the coarse gray hair at his neck and allowing him to lick her face.

Stoke paused and watched her.

She turned toward Stoke. "I hope during my imprisonment I'll be allowed to keep him."

"You should be denied any pleasures, but since I've grown to respect the animal, I'll allow it." He reached over and patted Baltizar's head.

The wolf licked his hand.

Stoke's forearm brushed against her left breast. Her pulse quickened. An ache grew in her breasts as both nipples hardened. A memory flashed, bringing with it the feel of his hands caressing her breasts, the taste of his tongue as it twined with hers, the weight of his body and how it molded to her own. She remembered being in the hall, feeling his hand when he stroked her beneath the table. Heat flared in her breasts and flicked down to her loins. How could the mere touch of a man stimulate her so? She loved Avenall, but his touch never had this power over her body.

She pushed Baltizar aside and moved away from Stoke's arm. "Beseems he's more loyal to you than me." She strode toward the horse, leaving Stoke and Baltizar to follow.

Somehow she had to escape and get back to Avenall. She loved Avenall. Wanted to be his wife. This passion for a lord who was bent on imprisoning her was absurd. Surely 'twould pass. It had to.

Two hours later, Stoke watched her head drop onto her chest and her body list to the side. He grabbed her shoulders and pulled her back against his chest. She snuggled into the curve between his neck and shoulder and mumbled something unintelligible in her sleep.

Her lips moved against his neck, the softness burning his skin. Strands of golden hair stuck to the bottom of his chin, tantalizing his throat like caresses from gentle fingertips. The sensual, earthy smell of her, braided with the scent of herbs in her hair, filled his senses. Her bottom rubbed against his loins, making his body throb against her soft woman's flesh. He felt the curved line of her spine tight against his chest, pressing against his taunt nipples and rubbing against the hair between them. He cursed inwardly. She was his prisoner, yet it was he who was being tortured.

The desire to throw her on the ground and sate his long-held lust clawed at him to be appeased. With every intention of having his fill of her, he slowed Shechem.

A memory sparked, of kissing her in the straw, feeling her lips and body working their cunning spell on him . . . then the blinding pain as the blade pierced his back. His blood ran cold at the recollection now. He had thought she wanted him as much as he wanted her. She had encouraged him with her ardent kisses, then played the standoffish tease at other times. He had thought it was a game she played with all her victims. Too late, he realized it was no game.

He recalled the vow he'd made never to fall prey to her cunning feminine wiles again. As he'd done with Cecily, he'd let down his guard around a woman and paid for it dearly. It was true Cecily had never stabbed him in the back. He would have preferred it rather than having had his heart ripped out and trod upon. Something soft brushed his chin, and he realized he was stroking Lark's hair with his jaw. He jerked his head up and scowled down at the top of her head.

He drew himself up and concentrated on the moon disappearing behind thick clouds. The road ahead melted into a barely penetrable gray mist. A gust of wind blew past his face, the scent of sheep and rain heavy in the air. Lightning bolted across the sky, illuminating the cleared fields lining the road. Off to his left, he noticed the Abbey of Bardney, the crenelated walls bare against the brilliant sky.

He urged Shechem off the road and into the field. Heavy drops of rained pelted his head and face. More lightning arced the sky. Thunder rolled.

His prisoner started and bumped her head under his chin. She must have realized she was leaning against him, for she stiffened and scooted forward. "Forgive me." She rubbed her head. "I must have dozed off. Where are we?"

"At the moment, we're heading for shelter."

The sky opened up. Sheets of rain beat down on them. She huddled beneath his mantle as blasts of wind drove her back against his chest. For the first time in two hours, he welcomed her warmth pressed against him.

The abbey gates blurred before him. Stoke bent over and pounded on them. After a moment, a small oval window in one of the gates opened. A face peered out at them. Everything about the face was pointy—the nose, the chin, the cheekbones, even a conical head rose up from a tonsure. The monk's slanted eyes studied them. Finally, he said, "Who goes there?"

" 'Tis the Earl of Blackstone. We need lodgings."

The gate opened and Stoke led Shechem into the courtyard.

The tall, pointy-faced monk peeked out at them from a hooded leather cape as he grabbed Shechem's reins. "I'll stable your animal, my lord. You can go in. Brother Duncan will see you to a room."

Stoke dismounted. When Lark made a move to jump down, he grabbed her in his arms and ran to the door.

"My legs are not broken," she said, keeping her face lowered against the rain.

"Aye, but I prefer not to have your muddy feet sully my chamber."

He opened the door and stepped inside. Baltizar slipped in behind him. Stoke closed the door with his foot, the creak and moan of the ancient iron hinges sounding like pieces of flint grinding together.

Stoke glanced around at the dank entrance hall. A swell of silence engulfed every stone and dark shadow, making his and Lark's breaths sound like the working of a bellows. Each drip from their clothes boomed against the stone floor. Torchlight flicked yellow shadows along the stone walls and across an alcove, where a marble statue of the Virgin Mother stood, hands clasped, head bowed.

Near his right shoulder, he saw a bell hanging on the wall. He pulled the cord. The sound throbbed down the hallway, transgressing into the tranquility that seemed as eternal and as much a part of the abbey as the stones of which it was built.

"You can put me down now." Lark wiped the water from her face with the back of her hand.

He set her down, trying not to stare at the moisture dripping from her inviting bottom lip, or at the long spiked lashes hooding her eyes.

Footsteps echoed down the hallway.

They both glanced up. A monk paused before them and clasped his hands over his portly belly. Candlelight glistened off his shaved scalp and highlighted many tiny warts. After closely scrutinizing Stoke, he gazed at Lark, at her bare feet, at the water puddle forming around her. His gaze moved to Baltizar and the frown on his face deepened. "Pets are not allowed here. We don't clean up after animals."

"He would be insulted if he knew of what you speak," Lark said. "He is cleaner than you or me, and has never once relieved himself inside."

"Still, he cannot stay here." The brother shook a pudgy finger at her.

She opened her mouth to say more, but Stoke raised his hand and silenced her. He watched the monk's eyes darting back to the pouch hanging from his belt. Something behind the small beady eyes reminded Stoke of a rat. A keen distaste for the good brother rose up as Stoke fished in the pouch hanging from his belt and placed a mark in the round little hand. "Please accept this as a tithe for the church."

The monk stared down at the silver coin and watched it gleam in the torchlight. "Perhaps the rules can be broken this once. You have need of two chambers?"

"One chamber," Stoke said. "This is my wife."

"Believe not that lie—"

Stoke clamped his hand over Lark's mouth. "She is a reluctant bride, not yet used to her duties as an obedient wife."

The monk's small rounded eyebrows pursed at Lark. He looked ready to deny them entrance at all.

Stoke held her mouth with one hand and fished in the pouch again. He thrust another mark into the small, plump hand. "Accept this as a donation for the church."

A greedy light twinkled in the monk's eyes as his sausage-like fingers clamped tightly around the offering. He turned and waved them forward. "Follow me."

"If you keep that mouth closed, wife, I'll take my hand away," he whispered near her ear, pushing her forward.

She nodded.

He dropped his hand, but kept a tight hold on her elbow.

The little round monk paused before a door and opened it. "You'll find a warm fire and linens to dry you. Please be as quiet as possible." He leveled a warning glance at Lark. "We are a silent order here. Vociferous and irreverent behavior shall result in immediate expulsion."

Her eyes flashed.

Stoke knew what was coming. He clamped his hand over her mouth again, cutting off what he was sure would have been a biting retort. "You'll hear not a peep." He shoved her inside and closed the door gently behind him.

Stoke watched her wheel around to face him. "As a husband, you're a paltry one indeed."

"I treat you better than you deserve, wife." A mocking grin stretched across his face.

"I know not why you insisted I be in here with you. You could have tied me in my own chamber."

"You know they'd never have allowed that within the sanctity of the church. You would have escaped in the night."

She grimaced at him. "You gave him too much money too. You could have bribed him with one-fourth of what you paid."

"You nag like a fishwife."

A saucy grin lifted the corners of her lips. "Being around you brings out the best in me."

"Should I gag you again, until you learn to hold your tongue?" He narrowed his eyes at her.

She raised her head haughtily. "That isn't necessary, for I'll not speak to you for the rest of the night."

"Ah, to be granted such a boon." Without taking his eyes off her, he plucked a cloth from a stack on a table. He dried his face and hair, then found her watching him. "Don't stand there, dry yourself."

She grabbed a linen and sat in one of two wooden high-back chairs in front of the hearth. Baltizar curled up near her feet. Lark rubbed his head with her left foot as she dabbed the towel at her face. The mantle around her shoulders opened in the front and he could see the thin gown underneath sticking to her skin, as transparent as wet parchment. He received a view of the hollows of her throat, the swell of her breasts. They were not as small as he had thought.

She noticed him watching her and jerked the mantle closed. With deft movements, she unbraided her hair and wrung the water out of it. As she worked her way down the long length, she inadvertently leaned closer to the fire.

Stoke froze. The flames. Another inch and they would be touching the tip of her hair. The blood drained from his face. His stomach contracted like a fist. His gaze stayed glued to the fire as he grabbed her arm and jerked her back in the chair.

The sight of the flames held him captive, flickering in his eyes. A vision flashed in his mind. Flames leaping up to the ceiling. The screams of people running through walls of fire. The heat burning him. His own scream . . .

"What is it?"

Stoke felt her touch on his hand. Abruptly, he was drawn back to the present. He felt the perspiration on his palms, his heart pounding in his chest, every muscle straining from the memory. A bit late, he realized he was still holding her shoulder. He pried his fingers loose and stepped back from her.

"You almost burned your hair," he said, his voice raspy.

" 'Tis more than that." Her gaze dug into his face. "I saw the fear on your face. You're afraid of fire, are you not?"

"I see the blessing of your silence lasted only a few moments."

"Aye, and I asked you a question." She didn't look at all contrite about breaking her vow of silence.

He stared back at the flames and tightened his lips one over the other. There was no use trying to hide the truth any longer, so he said, "Now that you know the one chink in my armor, will you use it against me?" He turned and gazed into her eyes.

What he saw made him raise a brow in surprise. Understanding gleamed in the golden depths, an open warmth he'd never expected to find.

"Nay, set your mind at rest," she said. "I know what it's like to have fears."

"You have a lot, do you?"

"A few." She gazed pointedly at him. "I wouldn't be human if I did not."

He didn't want to see this warm side of her. She was a woman, not to be trusted. He picked up the cloth that had fallen on the floor and continued to dry his face and neck.

She let the subject drop and went back to separating her thick hair. He cast a surreptitious glance in her direction. Flames gleamed in the wet golden mass as she separated the thick strands and continued to dry them.

He had never noticed the almost delicate slenderness of her fingers, or the small scars speckling the backs of her hands. Her nails looked clean, but worn and chipped like his own. William had bragged of her prowess with weapons, and how she trounced his men in the tilt yard. At the time, Stoke had thought they were the wild imaginings of a doting father, but after she'd so deftly stabbed him, and observing her hands, it was obvious that she'd spent years in learning to kill. It only made him keenly aware that he couldn't turn his back on her. And now she knew one of his deepest secrets.

He scowled at her and said, "Remove your wet clothes."

She narrowed her eyes at him, all the tenderness gone from her expression. She thrust out her chin stubbornly. "I shan't."

"You shall."

"I don't see why I must disrobe."

"As much as you may enjoy sleeping in a soggy bed, I do not. I won't argue with you. Either do my bidding, or I'll rip the clothes from your back." He took a step toward her.

Chapter 14

Lark's hand shot up to ward him off. "Very well, I shall, but must you humiliate me by standing there watching?"

"You need not pretend the modest virgin with me. 'Tis not as if you haven't taken off your clothes ere now. I'm sure you expose yourself for all your many lovers."

"I've had no lovers," she hissed at him, grabbing the mantle from her shoulders and slinging it onto the floor. "How many times must I tell you that?"

"None." He purposely kept his gaze on her face. "You can keep your lies to yourself. And you forget, I've seen you naked. Believe this, should you lie on the bed and spread your legs, you need have no fear I'll be tempted to settle between them. I'd sooner bed an asp."

"Have no fear, you'll never be invited between them." She jerked up her wet gown with one angry thrust and flung it at his feet.

Plop! It hit the tips of his boots.

Baltizar raised his head and eyed the wet article.

A furious blush stained her cheeks. She crossed her arms

over her chest and stared at him with a defiance that, he knew, didn't stop with her expression but went core deep.

The thin tether on his patience snapped. He lifted his hands to grab her, but he made the mistake of looking down at her naked body. His hands froze. Her hair hung in wet spikes down to the tops of her thighs, just touching the golden thatch between her legs. Dusky peach nipples poked out at him from the corners of her folded arms.

His gaze moved lower, past a flat waist to long, slender legs that he'd imagined so many times wrapping around him. They were by no means flawless and dimpled as a woman's should be; a five-inch scar ran down her left thigh and one just as long cut across her right knee. Various small scars covered her thin, yet sinewy shins and calves. Her skin was still wet, and he longed to run his tongue over every scar. Firelight glistened along the alabaster flesh, making it glow yellowish gold, the color of her eyes.

"Do you mean to do something with those?" She motioned toward the hands he still held aloft near her shoulders.

"Aye, but what I'd like to do with them would not please you over much." With every ounce of determination he possessed, he dropped his hands and glanced away. It was the strongest test of willpower he'd ever undergone. Not even when he'd discovered Cecily's betrayal had it tested him like this. But he would overcome this lust. He had to.

He worked open the belt of his scabbard. Out the corner of his eye, he saw that she hadn't moved. All the frustration he felt came through in his voice. "Get in bed."

She looked ready to protest, but must have thought better of it. Turning, she strode toward the bed. Her footsteps plodded on the stone floor and bounced off the bare walls of the small austere chamber.

He couldn't drag his gaze from her. The sway of her small, rounded bottom held him captive, until she yanked back the brown wool blanket and buried herself beneath it.

"I'm sleeping on the right side of the bed tonight," he said, pulling off his wet tunic. "Move over."

"Do you change sides?" She arched a brow at him.

"I never know when another assassin might come. I've learned 'tis best not to be a creature of habit."

"I see." Her golden brows met over her nose. She scooted across the bed.

He sat and jerked off his boots and wet clothes, feeling her gaze boring into the scars on his lower legs. He stood and faced her. "There now, you can get your fill."

She glanced down at the blanket on the bed, looking uncomfortable at being caught staring at him. "How did you get them?" she asked, her voice softening.

"There was a fire at Kenilworth when I was but seven and ten. My mother, father, and brother died it in, along with many servants. I was fortunate enough to escape, but, as you can see, not unscathed." He glanced down at the white raised scars that ran from his ankles to his knees.

"I'm sorry."

"You needn't be." He strode toward the bed and pulled Dragon's Eye from the scabbard. Sleek-hewed metal pinged. He glanced at her and saw her peeking over the blanket at him, her eyes wide.

"Do you mean to use that?" She gazed at his swollen manhood.

"I presume you mean Dragon's Eye?"

Her gaze moved to the sword and she looked flustered. "Aye, the broadsword."

"Fear not I'll use it on you." He eyed her, enjoying her uneasiness. "Since the Holy Land, I've grown accustomed to sleeping with it. 'Tis a good thing, or several assassins would have killed me in my bed." He stared pointedly at her.

"I wish you wouldn't look at me like—" She paused and shrugged. "What is the use? You'll never trust me." She rolled on her side and pulled the blanket over her head.

He thrust back the cover on the right side of the bed and crawled in. A glimpse of her white backside and the curve of her hip made a groan roll up inside him. It took all of his

Take A Trip Into A Timeless World of Passion and Adventure with Zebra Historical Romances! —Absolutely FREE!

Let your spirits fly away and enjoy the passion and adventure of another time. With Zebra Historical Romances you'll be transported to a world where proud men and spirited women share the mysteries of love and let the power of passion catapult them into adventures that take place in distant lands of another age. Zebra Historical Romances are the finest novels of their kind, written by today's bestselling romance authors.

4 BOOKS WORTH UP TO $24.96— Absolutely FREE!

Take 4 FREE Books!

Zebra created its convenient Home Subscription Service s
you'll be sure to get the hottest new romances delivered
each month right to your doorstep — usually before they
are available in book stores. Just to show you how
convenient Zebra Home Subscription Service is, we would
like to send you 4 Zebra Historical Romances as a FREE
gift. You receive a gift worth up to $24.96 — absolutely
FREE. There's no extra charge for shipping and handling
There's no obligation to buy anything - ever!

Save Even More with Free Home Delivery!

Accept your FREE gift and each month we'll deliver 4 bran
new titles as soon as they are published. They'll be yours
to examine FREE for 10 days. Then if you decide to keep
the books, you'll pay the preferred subscriber's price of just
$4.20 per title. That's $16.80 for all 4 books for a savings
of up to 32% off the publisher's price! What's more...$16.8
is your total price...there is no additional charge for the
convenience of home delivery. Remember, you are under n
obligation to buy any of these books at any time! If you are
not delighted with them, simply return them and owe
nothing. But if you enjoy Zebra Historical Romances as
much as we think you will, pay the special preferred
subscriber rate of only $16.80 each month and save over
$8.00 off the bookstore price!

We have 4 FREE BOOKS for you as your introduction to
KENSINGTON CHOICE!

To get your FREE BOOKS, worth up to $24.96, mail the card below. or call TOLL-FREE 1-888-345-BOOK

Take 4 Zebra Historical Romances FREE!

MAIL TO: ZEBRA HOME SUBSCRIPTION SERVICE, INC.
120 BRIGHTON ROAD, P.O. BOX 5214,
CLIFTON, NEW JERSEY 07015-5214

YES! Please send me my 4 FREE ZEBRA HISTORICAL ROMANCES (without obligation to purchase other books). Unless you hear from me after I receive my 4 FREE BOOKS, you may send me 4 new novels - as soon as they are published - to preview each month FREE for 10 days. If I am not satisfied, I may return them and owe nothing. Otherwise, I will pay the money-saving preferred subscriber's price of just $4.20 each... a total of $16.80. That's a savings of over $8.00 each month and there is no additional charge for shipping and handling. I may return any shipment within 10 days and owe nothing, and I may cancel any time I wish. In any case the 4 FREE books will be mine to keep.

Name _____

Address _____ Apt No _____

City _____ State _____ Zip _____

Telephone ( ) _____ Signature _____

(If under 18, parent or guardian must sign)

Terms, offer, and price subject to change. Orders subject to acceptance.

KC0699

4 FREE

Zebra
Historical
Romances
are waiting
for you to
claim them!

(worth up
to $24.96)

See details
inside....

KENSINGTON CHOICE
Zebra Home Subscription Service, Inc.
120 Brighton Road
P.O.Box 5214
Clifton, NJ 07015-5214

willpower to slide the sword between them. The hard, cold steel would remind him of his vow and her devious nature.

He stared at the rounded ridges and valley her side made beneath the blanket as he spoke. "Give me your hair."

"I would like to, but 'tis connected to my head." She glanced over her shoulder at him as if he were a simpleton.

"Give me your hair now, or I'll get it. I vow you will not find it pleasant if I'm forced to gather it."

Frowning, she leaned up on one elbow and gathered the heavy damp mass at the back of her neck. "Here." She wagged her hair at him. "Now what do you intend to do with it?"

" 'Tis merely a precaution." He grabbed the long hair, the thickness matching a sleek horse's tail, and coiled it around his hand until he reached the back of her neck. He left enough length between them so he wouldn't touch her skin. "I wouldn't want you slipping away in the night."

" 'Tis very uncomfortable. I can't turn my head."

"Think you I care about your comfort, my lady?" He snorted under his breath.

Lumps in the straw mattress poked his shoulders and back. He shifted to get comfortable.

"Must you pull my hair?" She turned and glared at him.

"Come closer."

"Being in the same chamber with you is already too close." Careful not to touch him, she scooted closer.

Her thigh brushed his leg. "Can you not lie still?" He stiffened his free arm so he would not reach toward her.

" 'Tis your broadsword. The hilt is poking me."

"Think not I shall move it to please you."

"Heaven forbid it! I did not expect a courtesy from you." She stopped fidgeting and came to rest on her back. In the silence she stared up at the ceiling. Her expression grew bored. As if she couldn't stand the silence any longer, she asked, "What is in the hilt of your sword, anyway? Most knights have holy relics. Yours is the first I've seen with a stone in it. Is it a ruby? I thought it might be, but 'tis the biggest ruby I've ever seen. It must have been costly."

"Leave it to you to think of its monetary value."

Her eyes narrowed at him. "I may be a lot of things, but thief is not one of them."

"Too bad, 'twould have been your best quality." Unable to look in those flaring golden depths without ravishing her, he glanced up at the bedpost and said, "Thief or not, I'll tell you 'tis naught a ruby and not worth a mark. I got it from a peddler in Acre. He swore it was the petrified eye of a dragon and would bring me luck."

"Did it?" She began to sound drowsy.

He watched her eyes closing. Long golden lashes fanned her cheeks. His gaze followed the curve of them as he said, "It gave me luck, until I met you . . ." He grew aware of the healed wound in his shoulder and grimaced.

She yawned. "That proves a talisman has limits. Tell me, did it give you luck in other areas of your life? I've always wondered if there was a talisman that worked for love."

"Naught works for luck in love."

"Surely you had luck with your first wife. You must have loved her."

"Once, a long time ago," he said, regret coming through in his voice.

"What made you stop loving her?"

"She betrayed me."

"How?"

"She—" He caught himself admitting things he'd never told anyone and clamped his mouth shut. An odd sensation hung over him. He wanted to unburden his soul, but why to her?

At his silence, her voice grew huskier and sleepier as she said, "I can't imagine what it would be like to be betrayed by someone you loved. I know my father and Avenall would never betray me. And if they ever did, I would want to die."

Stoke didn't think her capable of such heartfelt emotion. A tinge of unbidden jealousy gnawed at him. He found himself asking, "You love Lord Avenall so much?"

"Aye. I've loved him forever."

He battled a stab of unbidden jealousy and listened to her deep, even breaths. He turned to look at her. She was curled on her side, facing him, both palms together and up under one cheek. His hand holding her hair lay against the edge of her pillow, blocking his view of her eyes. He moved it and stared at the oval face. Her ruby-red lips were parted slightly in sleep, begging to be kissed.

Under the covers, he grew aware of her heat flowing over his naked body. Where the blanket touched him, he imagined it as her hands, caressing him. His fist tightened around her hair, and it pressed against his palm like damp silk. He reined in the desire to run his thumb over it. Worse yet, the womanly scent of her hovered thick in the air, tantalizing his senses. He could feel her elbows touching his arm. The ache in his loins throbbed. Eve, Delilah, Thais, and Aphrodite were lying next to him all in one body. But he was armed with his resolve.

He squeezed his eyes closed. His bare feet hung over the edge of the mattress, and he tried to center his thoughts on the cool air hitting them. But it felt like the flutter of her gown next to his skin. When that didn't get her out of his mind, he touched the hard steel of Dragon's Eye. His right leg rested against it. The sword had absorbed his heat, and if he imagined hard enough, it felt like her smooth, hot skin. Would the misery visited upon him since he'd met the vixen by his side ever stop?

He rubbed his thumb across her soft hair tight against his hand and knew it would increase tenfold ere he was done with her.

An hour later, Lark lay in bed, peering up at the ceiling. The fire had died to dull cinders, casting dark orange shadows on the white walls. One side of her body had fallen asleep and she had lost the feeling in her arm and leg. Afraid to move too quickly, she slowly turned her face an inch toward him. He was lying on his side, facing her. His eyes were closed, and a slight frown furrowed the skin between his black brows, as if something in his dreams disturbed him. She could hear his soft, steady breaths.

Her pulse pounded against her temples as she glanced over at his arm. The hand that held her hair was tucked under the edge of his pillow. She bit her lower lip and slid her hand beneath the feathered edge. Gently, cautiously, she eased his hand from underneath it, a quarter of an inch at a time. She watched his face intently. He didn't move. Didn't blink an eye. With slow determination, she pried open each finger.

As she unwound her hair, it occurred to her how powerful his hand felt next to her own. Just one squeeze could crush her throat. She gulped hard. With the utmost care, she gingerly laid his hand back on the pillow near his cheek. Then she eased over to the bed's edge. One at a time, she lowered her legs over the side.

Creak. The ropes beneath the mattress protested.

Before she could turn to see if the sound had awakened him, a hand gripped her arm.

"Going somewhere?" In spite of the velvety quality in the voice, it grated against every pore in her body.

She felt a tug on her arm and fell across the bed. Her chest hit his, knocking the breath out of her. He pulled her on top of him. Every instinct to fight him dissolved the moment their naked bodies made contact. The smoldering heat of his body touched her everywhere. She grew aware of the hot glow of his skin searing her, the burly arms swallowing her, crushing her to him. A fine film of perspiration broke out on her skin. With each breath, she could feel her breasts moving against the coarse hair on his muscular chest. Her nipples hardened and throbbed.

His manhood, massive and thick, pressed against the sensitive area below her belly. Lower still, the rock-hard feel of it lay against her abdomen and inflamed the sensitive folds between her legs. A searing throb began there and pooled in her breast. She found it very hard not to let her head drop toward his lips, or to run her fingers through the wavy black hair hanging down to his shoulders.

"I sleep very lightly." His hot breath wafted across her mouth like a caress.

"I'll remember that." Her words, whispered softly, were thick with a growing need for him to douse the fire in her.

"I've got to get away from you." He grabbed her arms and froze. His fingers tightened against her skin. His hands and arms began to tremble as if he were fighting an inner dragon.

At any moment she expected him to thrust her away. He didn't. He only stared up into her face, his hands clenched on her arms, that strange coppery glow in his eyes.

"What have you done to me?" The words came from deep within his throat like a lament.

"No more than you have done to me." She moved closer to his mouth.

"We are in no way even, my tigress." The battle within ended abruptly. His hands left her arms, and he crushed her in a fierce embrace. One hand molded to the back of her head as he pulled her face to his.

The moment their lips touched, sparks seared through her body. Every inch of her skin burned. It was an intoxicating feeling, like a floodgate of heat being thrust open inside her. She surrendered to the feeling. He was heaven and earth to her. Now she knew what her father had meant by lust. This was like naught she had ever experienced with Avenall. It was gritty. Corrupting. Indulging. The stuff of Greek myths, Trojan wars, and Roman gods. It was forbidden ecstasy.

Their kiss grew ruthless. His lips moved hungrily over hers. She pressed his mouth with equal fervor, grinding the inside of her lips against her teeth and not caring. His tongue slid across her bottom lip. She opened her mouth, and his tongue drove into it, even as his fingers tangled in the back of her hair.

He pulled back and said against her lips, "Should I be checking to see if you have a weapon hidden on you?"

"No weapons this time, just my hands." She slid her palms over the stubble on his face. The tingle never left her skin as she moved lower, to learn his throat, each tense muscle on his powerful shoulders.

He drew her close for another kiss. His wide hands singed a line down her neck, along her spine. She could feel his calloused palms caressing each bone in her back, leaving goosebumps in their wake. Lower still, he splayed his hands and cupped her bottom, flattening, squeezing. He began to move his hips against hers, pressing her bottom tight against his swollen flesh.

Lark moaned and moved with him. She opened her thighs to better feel him against her aching flesh and ran one foot down the side of his calf. The coarse hair on his legs tantalized the bottom of her foot. Her hair dropped over her shoulders and tangled against his chest. His hands moved along her sides, and then he grabbed her beneath her arms and pushed her up so that she was sitting on top of him.

He raised himself on his elbow and suckled her breast. Lark arched her back and ran her hands through his hair, pulling his face closer to her. His tongue moved over the hard little nub; then he suckled.

She felt his hand slide between their bodies. When his finger touched the center of her fire and stroked her, she cried out and threw back her head.

"Say my name, Lark," he said, his breath burning her nipple. "I want you to know who's bedding you."

"The Black Dragon," she moaned.

"Nay, Stoke is my name. Say it. Say Stoke."

"Stoke . . ." Lark closed her eyes, hardly able to form the words for the feel of him touching her.

"Are you sure you want me, Lark?" His finger eased inside her as he continued stroking her.

"Aye, I do. Please . . ." she moaned. Her hips moved of their own accord against his hand. She exploded in white hot flames. She opened her mouth to scream.

He took her cry in his mouth, then rolled her over and whispered against her lips, "Say my name. . . ."

"Stoke."

As the word left her mouth, he grasped her hips, lifting her off the mattress and plunging into her. His manhood ripped past her maidenhead and touched her womb. Pain coursed through her. Her body tensed. She bit her lip to keep from crying out. The moment the burning cramp subsided enough for her to move, she lifted her fists and beat on his chest. "You hurt me. You did it on purpose! Get off of me, you—you cumbersome oaf!"

He grabbed her wrists, pinning them above her head, while he gazed down into her eyes, his face full of confusion. "You're a maiden? Judas's bones!" He wore the same expression he'd worn when she stabbed in the back, though the fury had turned to regret.

"You look surprised."

"You never acted like a virgin."

"Pray, how does a virgin act?" Resentment came through in her voice.

"A virgin does not go around flaunting herself in threadbare gowns. A virgin holds her tongue, does not look a man in the eye, and knows how to be biddable. A virgin does not lead a man on and stab him in the back."

"It appears I failed all your measures. You and my mother should get together. I can do naught to please her either. Beseems I never measure up or constantly give wrong impressions."

"In this case you did."

"I had only my word, yet you refused to believe it." She tried to keep the resentment out of her voice, but could not. "I told you there was no lover. So we are even. I stabbed you with a dagger, now you've stabbed me with your manhood—a massive thing 'tis too. Believe me, your wound could have hurt no worse than mine. Now get off of me."

"We are not done. I've waited too long to have you. I can't stop now. Had I but known you were a virgin, I'd have gone slower and not hurt you over much."

She opened her mouth to protest, but he silenced her with a kiss. He remained inside her. She could feel her aching flesh throbbing against the hard length of him. He nipped her bottom lip as his tongue eased into her mouth to mate with hers. After a moment, her mind was engulfed by the sensual feel of the kiss. She all but forgot about the pain as he began to move slowly inside her.

Lark began to enjoy the luscious feel of his hardness, how it felt against her tight flesh.

Abruptly, Baltizar growled, his intruder growl, and snarled.

"Can I never bed you?" Stoke ground out in frustration and froze.

She felt every muscle in his body turn to steel next to her skin. The obvious self-control it took him to hold still made her begin to tremble. He clamped his hand over her mouth. The dark, liquid desire in his eyes melted as he glanced toward the door.

He gazed back at her and whispered, "Make Baltizar stop growling—quietly."

"Silence, Baltizar. Come here," she murmured.

Baltizar responded instantly and strode around the bed toward her.

"Mother is coming," she said, using a command her pet knew only too well.

As Baltizar always did when the dreaded "mother" word was mentioned, he crawled beneath the bed.

"Remember, not a sound." Stoke shot Lark a warning glance, then pulled out of her. He grabbed his sword as he rolled onto the right side of the bed.

Cold air hit her body. The loss of the delicious weight of him and the warmth of it caused her to shiver. She pulled the blanket up to her neck, feeling a throbbing between her legs where he'd left her.

The door creaked open.

Stoke's fingers brushed her thigh as he clenched the hilt of his sword.

A dark figure crept into the chamber. Faint flickers of light from the fireplace blinked along a short, portly body. Dim bursts of light gleamed off a tonsure. She could make out the face of the greedy monk who had shown them to their room. Her eyes widened when she saw the dagger in his hand.

Through half-closed eyes, she watched the monk sneak to the side of the bed, surprisingly noiseless for his great girth. He paused and peered down at Stoke's face, making sure he was about to kill the proper person. Without a warning, he raised the dagger and thrust downward.

With lightning speed, Stoke shoved Dragon's Eye upward.

Through the blanket.

Into the monk's chest.

The man let out a gurgling cry and crumpled to the floor.

Stoke pulled his sword out from beneath the covers and turned to look at her. "Get dressed. We should leave here."

Footsteps out in the hall made them both glance past the open door. Light swayed in the hallway, harkening the approach of someone. The tall, slender brother who had answered the gate appeared, candle in hand. His slanted eyes glanced at Stoke, who still held his sword, then at the fallen man on the floor. His eyes looked ready to burst from their sockets and roll down his pointy nose. "May God have mercy on your soul! You've killed Brother Martin!"

"I killed him ere he thrust his dagger in me." Stoke glanced down at the body. "You can see the knife still in his hand."

The brother took a moment and stepped through the threshold. A globe of candlelight followed him into the room. The light below his face accentuated the sharp hollows of his cheeks and eyes, making him appear ghoulish. He bent near the fallen body and lowered the candle. "I do see it now." He clucked his tongue and shook his head. "Oh, the abbot is not going to like this." He glanced up at Stoke, his heavy lids fluttering ever so slightly. "He was new to the order, you see."

"Do you know how he came to be here?"

"Nay, I only know he arrived moments 'ere you came."

"I would like to speak to the abbot." Stoke threw back the blanket to leave the bed, heedless of his naked body.

"Oh, there'll be plenty of time for that."

A cruel smile spread across the monk's face . . . then a flash of metal.

A dagger left his hand, flying directly at Stoke's throat.

Chapter 15

Stoke must have seen the blade coming. With cobra-like swiftness, he snatched up a pillow and thrust it up.

The blade pierced the feather pillow and stuck there.

The monk turned and ran.

Stoke leaped out of bed, snatched up Dragon's Eye, and ran after his attacker. Lark glimpsed a flash of nicely shaped buttock. In awe of how quickly Stoke moved for a large man, she watched him disappear into the hallway. His bare footsteps hitting the stone floor quickly died away.

Lark left the bed and stepped over the fallen monk. She pulled the blanket off the bed, carefully wrapping it around her so as not to touch the fallen man. She peeked out into the hallway, looking for Stoke's dark, scowling face. An eerie silence hung in the air, eclipsing the scurry and gnawing of mice between the walls. One candle burned at the far end of the hallway, but the sphere of light did not touch the dark shadows in between. Half expecting the monk, or Stoke, to appear, she cautiously moved out into the hall.

A hand grabbed her shoulder.

Lark jumped and wheeled around, fists raised. One fist froze near Stoke's nose, the other near his throat.

"Going somewhere?" He glowered at her.

She dropped her hands. "I was going to see if you needed my help."

"More than likely you were trying to escape."

"I must admit the thought did cross my mind. 'Tis dangerous being around you."

"Not really. It could be worse. I've had five come at me at once." He stared pointedly at her, obviously remembering the Scots attacking him. He grabbed her arm and pulled her back into the room.

"Did you find the other monk?"

"The bastard just disappeared into thin air. This place is huge." He stepped over the fallen monk by the bed.

Lark watched his body as he prowled around the chamber, the long muscles in his thighs pumping. As he strode past the bed, her gaze dropped to his behind. She couldn't take her eyes off the most perfect bottom she could ever imagine on a man, rounded and taunt with muscle, nestled perfectly in slim hips. Higher, his torso widened to a broad back and sinewy shoulders.

Between his shoulder blades, a painted dragon spread across his skin. It spanned most of the upper part of his back, the green and black wings touching each shoulder. The sharp spiked tail snaked down to the right, stopping near his right ribs. The red eyes followed her and the wings and tail moved with each ripple of sinew as he walked.

"You can stop ogling me, unless of course you want to finish what we started." He spoke without turning around.

Did he have eyes in the back of his head? She watched him grab his braies from where they were draped over a chair near the fire. Her gaze dropped to the scars on his legs, stark against the tanned skin on his feet and thighs. Red patches, interspersed with white, raised scars slashed across both shins and calves, down to his ankles.

It was a pity to see such perfection marred in any way. Lark had tended burns, and by the look of the scars she knew they ran deep, deeper than any surface scar. She remembered the fear on his face when he'd snatched her back from the hearth.

"You keep eyeing me like that and I might be forced to toss you back in the bed."

Her gaze snapped up to the dragon. Its undulating motion held her spellbound, rippling across his back as he jammed a leg in his braies. She found herself saying, "You should not have put that dragon on your skin if you did not wish to be ogled."

"You weren't looking at the dragon." He finished lacing up his braies and glanced over his shoulder, a slow, perceptive smile spreading across his face.

"Was too." Undaunted by the wry amusement in his eyes, she said, "Well, 'tis true. It draws the eye. I once saw a vendor at a fair with those strange markings all over him, even on his face. He was a dark-skinned man from a country far to the east of the Holy Land. It was common practice among his people to draw on the skin with a needle. The more pictures covering a man's body, the more attractive he was supposed to appear to women.

"It surely worked for him here. His odd appearance had many ladies standing around his booth to stare and buy his wares. I know 'tis your crest, but why did you put a dragon on your back? Beseems a shame to mar your body in such a way." She watched him lift his arms and pull on his tunic. The dragon surged and swelled. All too soon the tunic covered it.

"You speak as if you admire my body." With several succinct tugs, he buckled his scabbard, then shoved on his boots.

Lark stared at his handsome profile, at the aura of masculine power that oozed from him. She recalled running her fingers over his muscular chest, the feel of it like warm steel against her palms. Aye, she admired everything about his body, but she wasn't prepared to tell him that and swell his head. So she said, " 'Tis passing fair."

A black brow snapped up at her, and he didn't look at all taken in by her lie. "Get dressed." He sounded impatient. "I'm going to find the abbot. It is strange that there is no one else about. When I get back, we're leaving. I long to get home." He snatched up his sword from the side of the bed and shoved it down into the scabbard. He grabbed the portly monk's feet and dragged the corpse to the door. Stoke's face showed no more strain beneath the dead weight than if he were dragging a tunic across the floor.

Lark kept her eyes on the gleaming dagger in the monk's hand. His chubby fingers were still tight around it in death. Stoke saw her glancing at it and bent, snatching it up. "I'll be keeping this." He shoved it behind the belt of his scabbard. "And you might as well forget trying to escape. I'm locking the door."

Lark watched him pull the body into the hall. After a warning glance, he slammed the door closed. Several moments went by, then something heavy thumped against the door. She guessed Stoke was making sure she didn't escape.

She heard Baltizar's low whine under the bed. " 'Tis all right, you can come out now." She said the command, "Mother is gone."

Baltizar crawled out from beneath the bed. He sniffed at the pool of blood on the floor.

"Come here." She patted her chest and he leaped up on her. "So you haven't forgotten me totally."

He licked her face while she rubbed her fingers into the thick fur around his neck.

"I'm glad you still remember I'm your mistress. I thought you had forgotten me with the Black Dragon around to court you. At least he finds you tolerable." In a none-too-happy tone, she said, "I suppose I must follow my jailer's orders, or he'll be growling at me worse than Mother."

At the word mother, Baltizar leaped down and cowered under the bed. Lark might have smiled, but she was still shaken by the two attacks only moments apart.

The realization that she didn't want to live in the world without knowing Stoke was alive in it hit her. Escaping didn't seem so important anymore. This was the third attempt on his life since she had met him. No doubt, the assassins would keep coming too, until one of them finally accomplished his goal. He needed protecting, and she might be able to find the person behind the attempts. And when she found this silent nemesis and convinced Stoke of her innocence, he might stop looking at her with that suspicious gleam in his eyes. There had been no guarded look in his eyes when he touched her and caressed her and made her cry out with need.

If she cared to admit it, she wanted to feel his burly arms embracing her again, his lusty mouth devouring hers. She stopped to pick up her damp gown and felt the soreness between her legs. A vision rose in her mind, of Helen sitting by the hearth, sobbing for Stoke when she had thought he was dead. . . .

What had she done?

Lark bit down on the knuckle of her index finger. Helen must not ever know Lark had willingly bedded Stoke, even responded to him. Someone like Helen was too delicate and pure of heart to understand. It would tear her apart. Lark would rather suffer the blows of a mace on her bare back than hurt her sister.

Somehow Lark would have to make sure she never gave in to those carnal feelings again. All she wanted was to prove her innocence, forget this attraction she felt for Stoke, and persuade him to marry Helen as planned. And she could wed . . . Avenall.

"Oh, Avenall." she groaned out his name. How could she ever face him? Her life was ruined. Her worst fear realized: she'd lost Avenall forever.

Out in the hall, Stoke made sure the marble statue he'd slid in front of the door was secure. Then he grabbed a torch from the wall and headed down the maze-like hallway. His gaze searched every shadow, his hand gripping the hilt of his sword.

His footsteps melded with the scurrying of mice as he advanced cautiously around another turn. A muffled sound made him pause before a door. He waved the torch near the door, and saw that it was bolted from the outside.

Dragon's Eye's finely hewn metal twanged in the heavy silence as he eased it from the scabbard. Every muscle tensed for battle. Carefully, he eased back the bolt without making a sound. He raised his sword with both hands and kicked open the door, ready to send another assassin to hell. A loud battle cry followed him into the room.

What greeted him in the small chapel made him blink with surprise. Bound and gagged, ten monks stared up at him from where they were lying on their bellies. Fear burned in all ten pairs of eyes. An elder one with a long gray beard looked up at him. Stoke had seen the same frightened, helpless look in the eyes of does ere he felled them. The elder's jaw trembled below the gag, and his body shook so that his knees knocked against the stone floor.

"Fear not," Stoke said. "I've not come to do you harm." He sliced through the elder's bindings and untied the gag. He helped the trembling elder to his feet, feeling the thin, frail bones of the monk's arm through his cowl.

"Bless you, my lord." The monk closed his eyes as if praying. "We thought you were with them."

"You mean the two who tried to kill me?"

"Aye, the very same."

"How did they come to be here?" Stoke asked. He cut another set of bindings from the wrists of another monk, then handed him the dagger he had taken from the portly assassin.

"They came upon us moments ere you arrived. They bound us and left us here. Are you harmed?" The elder reached out and touched Stoke's arm with a trembling hand.

"Nay."

"How can we ever repay you?" One of the other monks spoke as he cut the bindings of his brothers with the dagger.

"If you learn anything about the two men who attacked me, I would ask you send word to Kenilworth Castle."

"You are the Black Dragon?" the elder said, his beard bobbing on his chest.

"Aye, I'm the Earl of Blackstone."

"Abbot Hadrian at your service, my lord." The elder waved

a gnarled bony hand toward the other monks. "I'm sure our order would be honored to do some spying for you, my lord."

The brothers nodded in agreement.

" 'Twould be of great help to me, since one of the assassins escaped, and I have no time to waste tracking him." A feeling something was wrong at Kenilworth hit Stoke, and he couldn't get it out of his mind.

"You must stay with us a few days."

"Nay, I must leave now. 'Tis almost daybreak, and I'm but a day's ride from home." Stoke watched the veins pulse through the paper-thin skin on the top of Abbot Hadrian's tonsure.

One of the monks handed the abbot a cane. "Come, I will walk you out." He hobbled out of the empty room and into the hallway.

Stoke followed him and listened to the steady tap of the cane on the floor. The Abbot paused and touched Stoke's arm. For a moment he looked torn by what he was about to ask. "This may be an impertinent question, my lord, but why were those men trying to kill you?"

"That, Abbot Hadrian, I know not. I've had many attempts on my life in the past six months. I must find the person who wants me dead."

"Have you enemies?"

"Only one." Stoke thought of Lark and frowned. "I'm unsure of even that now."

"Is this person a woman?" The abbot cut his eyes at Stoke.

"Aye."

"Ah, one can never be sure if they are friend or foe. They're a man's worst adversary, for they know his weakness."

"I have no weakness when it comes to her." Stoke realized he'd over-emphasized his words and they came out as a brusque order.

The elder grunted under his breath, and a smile pulled the blue-veined skin across his gaunt cheekbones. A mouth full of stained, ancient teeth appeared between his lips. "That is what Adam thought, and Samson." He shook his head, sending his long gray beard into motion. "Every man suffers weakness of the flesh. It is the curse of man. May God help you with this Eve in your midst. Fast, pray, keep a vigilant eye. We will try to help you, my lord.''

"Thank you. No need to walk me out. I can find my way."

"Be well, my lord. We'll pray for your safety."

Stoke left Abbot Hadrian gripping his cane, his back hunched. He felt the abbot's eyes on his back as he strode down the hall. The old man had been right about weakness of the flesh. Stoke had lost his resolve when he'd felt Lark's naked heat against him. When he sensed the passion radiating from her, saw the desire burning in her eyes for him, it was more than he could stand.

Her maidenhead had surprised him. The instant he'd thrust through it, a memory had flashed in his mind, of Lark speaking to her brother after she stabbed him. His mind had been blurry, but through the fog, he heard snippets of the conversation, enough to hear she hadn't meant to kill him. He'd suppressed that knowledge until it flooded back to him in that moment.

Stoke thought of the Scot and knew he'd lied about her being a whore. What else had he lied about? Stoke was sure now that she had been telling the truth about the Scots. But he could not allow himself to trust her totally. She was a woman, and as he'd learned from Cecily, women could not be trusted. And too, he wasn't prepared to let her go. Not with the memory of her tight, wet heat, and the throbbing in him to finally possess her still crying out to be appeased. Nay, she was his prisoner and would stay that way.

The next evening, Lark listened to the pounding of Shechem's great hooves on the wooden footbridge at Kenilworth. They'd traveled continuously, stopped only to rest the horse and eat the cheese and brown bread the monks had given them. Stoke seemed impatient to get home for some reason. Lark felt just the opposite, for his castle would be her prison. She shifted nervously in the saddle.

He hadn't spoken four words to her throughout the day, only

stared at her with a contemplative look on his face, as if he were studying a new war tactic and trying to understand it. This suited her. She didn't want to speak to him, for the fact that she was at his mercy struck her hard the moment they'd left the abbey. It still tormented her now and made her stomach clench into knots.

The barbican rose before her, with its high battlements and flanking towers. The massive gray palisade stretched up into the twilight sky, blocking out the moon and stars. Black standards flapped along the parapet walks, the dragons spreading their wings and hissing fire with each wave of the wind. The Dragon's lair. One of the largest castles she'd ever seen.

They passed through an arched portal and out into the fortress proper, where a large, rectangular slope of land held the lists. The quintain stood proudly in the center, silhouetted against the setting sun.

Baltizar trotted beside them as they followed a dirt road that led to another bridge. Lark wrinkled her nose at the fetid odor of human excrement oozing from a ditch near the moat. Two little boys paused on the bank, their frog hunting forgotten. One of them recognized Stoke and waved.

"Master, you're home," he said, grabbing a frog in his hand that tried to wiggle free.

Stoke nodded to them and guided Shechem over another drawbridge.

"Me lord, 'tis glad we are to see ye home," the porter called to Stoke from the parapet. The only thing Lark could see of the man was his round belly protruding over the battlement. He turned, his stomach jiggling, and called to someone behind him, " 'Tis the master home! Open the gates."

Great iron hinges creaked, and the heavy oaken barriers were thrown open.

They passed below the portcullis. The metal jaws on the gate glistened in the soft moonlight, looking ready to bite intruders. She felt like an intruder. The four guards along the parapet eyed her as they would an enemy.

When they finally entered the inner bailey, the portcullis hit the pavement behind them. The hard thud of iron hitting stone sounded too final, like the last thrust of a hammer driving home a headstone. She truly felt trapped inside a very large dragon's den.

She grew aware that she'd leaned against Stoke's chest. Where his body touched hers, it burned her skin. Her spine stiffened, and she leaned forward. All through the day, she'd tried to avoid touching him, but he was so very large. Everywhere she moved, she could still feel him—the rock-hard chest, the sinewy thighs, the burly arms, his hot breath on her neck. How could she keep her resolve to stay away from him when he was so close?

As they cantered to the stable, she frowned and glanced around. The bailey appeared unusually deserted. Torches burned along the walls, bouncing shadows over the gray pavement and the many buildings lining its sides. The courtyard, square and broad, was shaped much like St. Vale's bailey but larger. Unlike at St. Vale, where her father defied custom and swore a hawk would never be found within its walls—he respected the birds of prey and said they did not deserve to be tamed—mews abounded at Kenilworth. She heard a shrill drone from the row of tiny sheds against one wall.

Off from the mews, a massive building caught her eye. The gray stone walls formed a rectangle, fifty feet long and twenty wide. Slate glistened on the roof, from which a large stone chimney rose. A thick chain and lock hung on the door. Lark wondered if that was Stoke's workshop, where he had crafted his sword.

The chapel too was much larger than St. Vale's, and a very costly-looking rose window graced the doorway. Sculpted saints flanked each side of the steps, the white marble glistening blue in the moonlight. It was indeed an impressive holding. And inescapable.

Her brow knit together as she watched a serf boy, no older than ten and six, grab Shechem's reins.

"Todd," Stoke said the first words he'd spoken all afternoon.

"My lord." Todd bowed and blushed at having the attention

of his master, even though Stoke's greeting sounded like no more than a grunt.

Stoke turned and grasped Lark's waist to help her down.

She tried to push his hands away. "Please, I can get down."

"Stop being stubborn." He whisked her down off the horse, letting her body slide along his.

The contact made her nipples harden and her knees grow weak. It would be so easy to wrap her arms around his neck and feel his hungry lips on hers. Instead she stepped back from him. "I can walk on my own."

He gaped at her in stunned silence and lowered his brows. "Walk then, but you had better get used to being here, for you belong to me now." He dropped his hands from her waist and strode ahead.

She blinked at his back, hearing his words, "You belong to me now," rolling over and over in her mind. She dragged her feet and followed him through an enormous oak door. Baltizar strode beside her, his claws clicking on the stone floor. Great boar tusks jutted from the walls of a cone-shaped passage. Torchlight flicked off the many curved, spiked points. At any moment, she half expected the walls to close in around her and stab her for daring to enter the dragon's lair as a suspected enemy.

She felt the chill of the stones against her bare feet. A shiver went down her spine, and she pulled Stoke's mantle more closely around her.

Her gaze strayed to Stoke. He walked several feet in front of her, his broad shoulders swaying with each stiff stride. His hair, black as pitch, gleamed blue in the torchlight. She remembered running her hands through the silken threads. An all-too-familiar warmth seeped over her. Inadvertently, her fists tightened at her sides.

She forced her gaze past him, toward the bright circle of light at the end of the portal. Smells of roasting venison and years of dankness and smoke and body odor permeated the air.

The air lacked the smell of a woman's touch. Until this moment, Lark hadn't really appreciated Elizabeth's efforts to make St. Vale a home. As much as she hated to admit it, there was much to be said for her mother's rushes and the fragrant herbs that she used with them.

Many voices echoed from the hall. But unlike the evening repasts at St. Vale, there was no laughter mingling with the voices, only low murmurs. She guessed the evening meals at Kenilworth were strained and gloomy, very different from the ones at St. Vale. After all, the ease and gaiety of William Mandeville was not present here. Inwardly, she sighed and longed to be home. Even the sight of her mother would be welcome.

Lark followed Stoke into a hall that rivaled many of the grand castles she had heard of in Normandy. The huge vaulted ceiling rose at least a hundred feet, and she had to crook her neck to look up at it. Thickly hewed beams crossed the tall ceiling, darkened by age and smoke.

A wooden gallery, some twenty feet from the floor, circled the room. One wall was covered by a large banner with the Blackstone coat of arms, the same dark, red-eyed dragon she had seen on Stoke's surcoat and on the standards out in front of the castle. Two tapestries depicting dragons in battle covered the other walls, along with a row of antlers. A massive hearth sat on one side, where a short, stocky woman turned a venison carcass. Juices gleamed on the brown skin and dripped into the fire, making it spit and hiss. Smoke spiraled up to the ceiling in a gray, shapeless cloud.

Two cupbearers scurried to and fro around tables circling the room, serving Stoke's men, while young boys deftly avoided the huge trays carried by the serving wenches. A long oak table stood in the center on a dais. Years of stains and scratches glistened beneath a layer of yellowed wax on the surface.

Lark noticed two men sitting at the table, one small, with tawny golden hair, who stared down at his cup. His face was so small, his brown eyes so large, that they gave him the appearance of a frightened chipmunk. The smallness of his features made him look younger than he probably was. She guessed his age at five and twenty. He shared a trencher with a large knight, a nobleman by the expensive green samite of his tunic. He had Stoke's coloring and his same square, proud jaw, but his eyes were blue, not black, and he looked older than Stoke, maybe a score and twelve. He too looked lost in pensive musings as he chewed on a rib bone.

Stoke strode into the hall, his presence filling the massive chamber. Spoons halted. Silence fell over the room. It was so quiet, her pulse grew loud in her ears.

Fifty pairs of eyes turned on her. Their palpable hostility hit her and brought her up short. She paused in the doorway and gazed down at Baltizar. Her hand trembled as she stroked his fur. For the first time in her life, she could not find the courage to meet adversity head-on. It was obvious they all knew she had stabbed their liege in the back. Even if she did try to explain it was an accident, they would never believe her.

"Come, you can't stand there forever." Stoke laced his hand in hers and pulled her toward the dais.

She gripped Stoke's wide palm, the warm strength of it somehow a balm against the animosity directed at her. The knight's blue eyes moved over her face, even more slowly over her body.

Stoke noticed the large nobleman at the table and addressed him. "To what do we owe this honor, Louis?" A hint of dislike came through in his voice. "I have not seen you for five years."

Slowly, a smile distorted Louis's handsome face. The tension between them sizzled. For a moment they stared at each other.

Finally Louis spoke. "Come, cousin, you know I needn't have a reason to visit you. But to tell the truth, I heard you were contemplating taking a wife and was deeply hurt that you did not ask me to come and give my approval. Sir Rowland informed me of what happened. 'Tis a shame all of your plans go awry." A slowly crafted grin turned up the corners of Louis's mouth. He shook his head. "Such a pity!"

"You should have sent word of your arrival."

"Why, so you could welcome me yourself? As much as I missed your presence, I managed very well without you. Ebba saw to that." Louis eyed one of the servitors, a pretty young woman with green eyes and two long chestnut braids down her back. She was of medium height with rounded curves and a large bosom.

A blush crept over the woman's face as she returned Louis's look, then glanced at Stoke.

Lark watched the veins in Stoke's neck pop as he gritted his teeth. His face flushed. A banked fire burned behind his eyes. She watched one particularly thick vein throbbing in his neck and almost felt sorry for the young woman named Ebba. Lark guessed Ebba must have shared Stoke's bed, and more than once, by the frightened way she eyed her master.

Ebba stood his gaze one moment longer, then tears poured down her cheeks. She turned and ran from the room, her sobs following her.

"Ah, cousin, you still frighten the weak with those red eyes of yours," Louis said, sounding amused and pleased with himself. His gaze slid to Lark, slowly raking over Stoke's mantle that covered her. "So this is the brazen lady I've heard so much about. You must introduce us, Stoke."

Stoke's expression remained cryptic as he looked at her. "Lady Lark, meet Lord Trevelyn, my cousin."

Lark glanced at Lord Trevelyn. "I wish I could say I was pleased to meet you, my lord, but under the circumstances and being only a prisoner here . . ." She shrugged as her words trailed off.

"I understand completely." Louis grinned with deliberate politeness, while he looked her over. "So you stabbed the Black Dragon in the back, a considerable feat for a lady."

"I didn't mean to do it." Lark glanced over at Stoke, searching his expression. He gazed at her, that familiar wary light in his eyes. Unable to stand the censure any longer, she glanced back at Louis.

He wore a pleasant, yet cunning smile, the kind of admiring smile one liar bestows upon another. "Pray, how do you stab a man and not mean to do it? How interesting. Did my cousin do something to warrant such a violent attack? You must tell all."

Lark opened her mouth, but Stoke interrupted her. "She will not."

"Come, cousin, let her speak. You must let her favor me with her story. You know how I appreciate such tales of cunning." Louis's lips stretched. A lethal quality flashed in his feral blue eyes, a warning that he could turn on anyone in a moment's notice.

"Cunning is not a virtue, my lord, but a vice." Lark met Louis's gaze.

"Aye, but if we did not have vices, life would be boring. Take my cousin here . . ." He waved a hand at Stoke. "He must have many in order to make you stab him."

"If he has many, I'm unable to find but a few." Lark glanced over at Stoke and saw the bewildered look on his face.

Louis raised a brow at her. "I'm glad to hear you can find little fault in my cousin. I've always thought highly of him." He smiled at Stoke. As if to change the subject, he glanced at Baltizar. "A wolf for a pet, an interesting choice." He reached over the table toward Baltizar.

The wolf crouched, bared his teeth, and snarled.

Louis snatched back his hand. "Ah, I see why you keep him."

"Aye, and he's an exceptionally good judge of character."

A faint ripple of laughter passed around the room.

Louis's eyes narrowed. A bit too late, Lark realized she'd spoken as she would have to one of her brothers. Something in the way he had angered Stoke made her not regret one word of it.

The indifferent facade Louis had tried so hard to maintain crumbled before Lark's eyes. For a moment, she saw a flash of animosity and spite in his vivid blue eyes, but it left quickly. With strained politeness, he said, "I suppose you are correct. I'll have to make a pet out of one myself." He picked up a piece of meat pie and chomped down on it, all the while his gaze saying to Lark, "I'll make a pet out of you later."

Lark had no doubts he would try. She turned and noticed the quizzical expression on the young large-eyed man sitting next to Louis. Their gazes met for a brief moment. A look of chagrin crossed his expression. He looked down at the table and fingered the base of his earthenware cup.

Abruptly, Rowland entered the hall. A priest walked at his side, the gold cross around his neck glistening stark against his brown cowl. The priest's walnut hair was cropped short, and so thick that she could not see the tonsure on his head. He looked young for a priest, perhaps a score and five, and unlike any priest she'd ever seen, he wore a sword. The metal hilt gleamed at his side as he paused near her.

Lark felt Rowland's gaze on her and glanced at him. Censure simmered in his blue eyes. As if unable to look at her, he looked away. Another hostile person to add to the long list, growing ever longer by the moment.

The priest and Rowland paused before Stoke. Both looked eager to speak, but neither did, until Rowland finally said, "Varik took ill just before you arrived."

Stoke's brows lowered over his eyes. "What is wrong with him?" He looked toward the priest for an answer.

"We don't know," the priest said ruefully. "A leach is with him. He assures us Master Varik will be fine . . ." He paused as Stoke grabbed Lark's arm and pulled her toward the stairs.

Rowland watched Baltizar following them and said, "Amory, I thought priests took vows to keep them from lying."

Amory shook his head and stared down at the hilt of his sword. "I admit, I do a lot of things a priest should not do. Lying is indeed a sin and a coward's way out, but I could not tell a friend that his only heir may be dying."

Chapter 16

Stoke pulled Lark up a flight of stairs, heading toward his son's room. He took the stairs two at a time, yanking her with him. Several steps behind him, he heard the steady click of Baltizar's claws.

"If your son is ill, I can help him."

"You've helped me more than enough." Stoke didn't bother turning to look at her.

"Please, trust me enough to let me see him."

Stoke wheeled around, grabbed her arms, and gave her a good shake. "Don't you understand? I cannot let you near my son. Speak no more of it."

The bright gold of her eyes glazed over, not with tears but with something he didn't want to put a name to. Nay, he didn't believe she actually cared enough to want to help Varik. It was only a ploy to gain her freedom.

Unable to look into those golden eyes, he grabbed her wrist, turned, and pulled her down the hallway.

"Where are you taking me?"

"To my chamber."

"Must I stay there? Have you no other place you can put me—a dungeon, a tower?"

"You needn't fear I'll touch you again until you want me, Lark. I'm not in the habit of raping women." He shot her a sidelong look. "If you'd held your tongue with Louis, I could have given you your wish and put you in my dungeon or one of the towers. But you angered him. He is not someone you want to turn your back on or wish to have as an enemy. He would surely get to you ere my back was turned, and then I would be forced to kill him, and Richard would not like to lose one of his largest financiers of the war."

"You would kill such a powerful man for me?" she asked, incredulous.

"Aye. I keep what is mine, and you are mine. I'll not give you up to anyone." He reached his chamber door, thrust her inside, and allowed Baltizar to follow her.

As he pulled the door closed, she grabbed the edge. "I beg you to let me look at your son. A leach will only harm him."

"I told you not to ask that again." He hesitated and stared into her eyes. After a long tense moment, he pushed her hand aside and slammed the door closed.

"I can help him. Please, let me!" Her protests were muffled behind the door.

He glowered at the door and shoved home the bolt on the outside. Her cries rang in his ears as he ran toward Varik's chamber.

The nursemaid, Dalia, a buxom woman with a stern face that looked as if a smile had never touched it, stood in front of the door, wringing her hands. Dalia had been Cecily's lady's maid, and she gravitated into the job of nursemaid when Varik was born. Stoke had been pleased with her up until this moment.

At the sound of his footsteps, she turned toward him. When she saw Stoke, her frown deepened. "Me lord, glad I am to have ye back. Varik's been askin' for ye."

Stoke paused in front of her. "How did this happen?"

"I don't know." She wrung her large hands. "He was fine up until an hour ago. I've tasted Master Varik's food as I always have. If he et' something bad, it would have made me sick too. He's got a rash, and he's burning with a fever. The leach says it's probably the pox.''

Stoke couldn't quell the uncomfortable tightening in his chest as he stepped past her and opened the door. Varik lay on his bed, pale, his black curls drenched with sweat and sticking to the sides of his small, round face. He'd been crying, and his eyes were puffy and red and closed at the moment. A red rash covered his face and arms. The strong odor of fever hung in the air.

A leach stood hunched beside the bed, holding a bowl beneath Varik's tiny arm. Blood oozed down the sides of his elbow. It was common practice for leaches to bleed their patients, but the sight of his son's blood made Stoke lunge toward the man. He grabbed the bowl and shoved the man back. ''What are you about?'' Stoke stared at the leach's pear-shaped head and large, wide nose.

''Bleeding the child. 'Tis the best thing for him. I gave him something to help him sleep. I can do no more for him.'' The leach glanced warily at Stoke.

''Wrap his arm and get out. And if he does not get better, I'll have your hide.''

''Aye, my lord.'' The leach nodded. With trembling hands, he went to work bandaging Varik's arm. After a quick glance at Stoke, he left the room.

Dalia came in and stared down at Varik. ''How is he?''

''Don't let that incompetent fool near Varik again.''

''But he's known for curing sickness.''

''I don't like his methods.'' Stoke stared at the bowl of blood sitting on the bedside table. It looked like an awful lot of blood for so small a child. He stepped over to the bed and sat next to Varik. The mattress dipped, and the ropes creaked beneath his weight.

He brushed back the hair from his son's face, feeling the clammy hot skin on his forehead. ''Leave us. I'll sit with him. And send Amory to me.''

Stoke heard Dalia's heavy footsteps as she left the room, closing the door behind her.

Stoke stared down at Varik. The sound of the door closing forced a memory to the fore:

He stepped into Cecily's chamber. Darkness shrouded the room. A lone candle burned, throwing pointed shadows across the walls over the bed. The scent of tallow, sweat, and the birthing hung in the air like a shroud. Cecily glanced at him from where she lay on sweat-covered sheets.

The emerald eyes staring back at him bore little resemblance to the bright, animated eyes upon which he had loved to gaze. It seemed so long ago when he could look into them and not feel the pain of betrayal. They were not the eyes of the lady he'd courted, given his heart to, and would have given the world to if she'd only asked. These were merely a ravished shell, filled with two years of regret from an unhappy marriage.

Stoke felt a tinge of conscience. He knew she had been faithful to him, yet he'd had her guarded. Many times during their marriage, when she had come to his bed, he thought of trying to start all over, but he could not get past the open wound still deep in him, nor could he ever expose his heart to any woman again—especially this one. His faith in all women had died at the same time as his love for Cecily.

"I didn't think you would come." Cecily's bottom lip quivered. After a moment a tear slipped down her cheek. "Thank you. How did you get Richard to let you come home?"

"I convinced him someone needed to police England and his brother John in his absence, and he agreed."

"Did you see our son? He is beautiful." She smiled weakly, but the smile slowly faded. Another tear slipped down her cheek as she said, " 'Tis the only thing I could give you to make up for the pain I've caused you. Can you ever forgive me?"

He saw the desperate pleading in her weak eyes, watched her lip quivering, the sweat dripping down her pale brow. He found himself saying, "Aye, I can forgive you."

"Thank you. Stoke, you must listen to me. I know I've hurt

you, but you must not let that stop you from marrying again. You must give our son a mother.''

Stoke swallowed past an odd tightening in his throat. He turned away from Cecily and glanced over at his newborn son. The midwife was bundling the squalling child into a blanket. The cries rang loud and clear. Healthy. Full of life. While the light in his mother's eyes was being snuffed out. Birth and death were never fair trades.

He turned back to Cecily and stared down into her sunken, glazed eyes.

''Please, vow to give our son another mother ...'' The desperation in Cecily's eyes bored straight through to Stoke's chest.

He found himself saying, ''I vow it.''

''Thank you.'' She squeezed his hand. Her fingers barely exerted any pressure on his skin. ''Take care of our son ... love him as you could not love me.''

At a loss for words, Stoke brushed back the strands of perspiration-soaked hair from her forehead. He bent and placed a bittersweet farewell kiss on her lips. They felt clammy and hot and barely responsive. Sure that she had gone, he pulled back to look into her face.

Her bottom lip quivered in a smile, a sad rueful smile, then she gazed past him, focusing on nothing. . . .

Varik opened his eyes, pulling Stoke back from his musing. ''Faf-ee, home,'' he said, saying father as best he could, his lips sketching a weak smile.

Something in that smile reminded Stoke of the same expression on Cecily's face before she died. He bent and hugged Varik tightly. ''Aye, I've come home. How are you feeling?''

'' 'Ummy hur's. Bad ache.'' Varik grimaced as if a pain hit him, then gripped his stomach.

''It still hurts?''

''Aye, Faf-ee. Bad.'' He rolled on his side and curled into a little ball.

''You're going to get better. I'm here now.'' Stoke gathered his son up in his arms, wishing he felt as confident as his voice had sounded.

Lark stared at the dragons in Stoke's chamber. They were everywhere. The four-poster bed sported intricately carved dragons in every pose imaginable. On the footboard, dragons flapped their wings in flight and battled knights with fire billowing out of their mouths. Two carved winged serpents stood in the middle of the headboard in an upright position, embracing, their spiked tales entwined intimately together.

Several large tapestries on the walls depicted dragons soaring across fields. Dragons slithered down the legs of a large wooden desk against one wall. A black wardrobe near the hearth depicted a scene of a maiden riding on a dragon's back, all done in inlaid mother-of-pearl. The rushes that most people used on the floors for comfort were absent; in their place there was a large black carpet with a red border around it. In the border were woven the heads of dragons. Dragons haunted the chamber.

"They shall eat us if we are not let out of here soon." She bent to pet Baltizar. She heard someone at the door and turned to glance at it.

The priest came through the door holding a tray of food. His kindly smile was the first warm expression she had seen since coming to Stoke's castle. "Stoke bade me to see you eat. My name is Father Amory, but you may call me Amory if you like."

"What sort of strange priest carries weapons and guards prisoners?" Lark couldn't help but smile back at him.

"I'm afraid not a very good one, nor a godly one. You see, I'm more warrior than priest. I can't make up my mind which I prefer. When conducting services, I want to be a priest, yet I feel no remorse at using my sword for a worthy cause, nor to serve a worthy liege such as the Black Dragon." He set the tray down on the desk.

"But a priest cannot serve two masters."

"So I'm told monthly by my bishop." Amory smiled at her. "He is ready to excommunicate me."

"You could always join the Templars." Lark returned the smile and looked into kind, fawn-colored eyes, a little lighter than the color of his hair.

"Aye, but I cannot see myself in such a zealous order. Nay, if the church excommunicates me, I shall serve the Black Dragon."

"You have been with him long?"

"Since we met in the Holy Land."

"What of your family? How do they feel about you being excommunicated?"

Amory gripped the hilt of his sword and stared down at the floor. He looked unwilling to speak, then said, more to himself, "I have not spoken to my father in seven years. He does not know I took vows."

"I could not imagine not speaking to my father for seven years. I would miss him terribly."

Amory's face tensed and his eyes took on a guarded gleam. "My father and I parted on unhappy terms. He wanted me to marry a lady he'd chosen for me. I refused. He said he would disown me if I did not, so I walked out of his life."

"I'm sorry to hear it."

" 'Tis all behind us now. We'll never reconcile our differences, but life goes on, aye." Amory forced a sad smile.

"I know what you mean. I have a mother whom I cannot please, so I gave up trying."

"I met your mother when I arranged the marriage agreement for Stoke. She's a very gracious lady. I cannot imagine her being irritable with anyone."

Lark smiled wryly. "She reserves her spleen for me. Speaking of Mother, I remember her mentioning you. She thought you were very kind, but the strangest priest she had ever met. When she told me you carried a sword, I was sorry to have been away at another of my father's holdings. I felt sure I had indeed missed a rare treat."

"I know not what sort of treat I am."

"Much more than you think. When Father Kenyon, our elderly priest, heard of you, he ranted so for days about ungodly priests that he was forced to take to his bed. We did not have a service for over two weeks at St. Vale."

"So did you find another to take his place?"

"We did not need to. I went to him and told him you would be giving a service at St. Vale, and there was a miracle—he suddenly grew quite well."

Amory laughed, then sobered. "I would like to have given the service, but I could not. Stoke trusts me to guard Varik and I don't like to leave his side for very long." He stared down at the tray of food. "I feel I failed him."

"You could not help it that he took sick. How is the boy?"

"No better. Stoke refuses to leave his side. He lives for the child. After he lost Lady Cecily, Varik was all he had."

"I know the healing arts. You must persuade him to let me look at the boy."

Amory took her measure for a long while. After a moment, he said, "You do not seem as bad as he said you were, but—"

"Please, I would never hurt a child. And I didn't mean to stab Stoke. I was frightened and did it before I thought."

"But he said you helped the Scots who attacked him."

"I called out to warn him, and he assumed I was with them. Please, for Varik's sake, persuade Stoke to let me see him. He can stay by my side, and I'll take anything I may have to give the boy first, just to prove it will not hurt him. You must convince him, please . . ." Lark's throat constricted and her words trailed off.

Amory touched her shoulders and studied her closely as he spoke. "Very well, if you think you can help him."

"I can but try," Lark said honestly.

Amory nodded, obviously liking her answer, then he dropped his hands. "Eat. I shall see what I can do."

Lark watched him leave. She listened to the bolt being thrown home and glanced at the food. Her stomach growled at the sight and aroma of the roasted venison, oozing with juice. Cabbage sprinkled with parsley nestled beside it. A large wedge of cheese and three chunks of bread filled the rest of the trencher. Steam spiraled up from a mug of spiced wine.

She strode to the desk and sat. As soon as she pulled a piece of meat off the bone and ate it, she grimaced. Though the meat was so tender, it fell off the bone, it tasted like gristle in her mouth. Something told her naught would taste good until she was able to help Stoke's son. If only he would trust her enough to let her.

"Nay, she will never get near Varik." Stoke scowled at Amory. "Did she send you here?"

Amory and Stoke stood in the threshold of Varik's chamber. Amory glanced past Stoke's shoulder and gazed at the bed, where Dalia was busy sponging off the boy's head. He looked paler than ever, his eyes more sunken, the dark circles under them getting darker and larger by the moment. Pain marred his brow. The rash on his face made his skin look burned by the sun.

"Look at him." Amory kept his voice low. "He's getting worse, not better. What harm could it do to let her see the lad?"

"How can I trust her with Varik's life?"

"You must not let your feelings for Cecily guide you in this. I see a genuine need in her eyes to help the child if she can. I beg you to let her try."

"I don't know." Stoke ran his hands through his hair.

"What have you to lose?" Amory continued ruefully. "You must trust a woman sometime, and my heart tells me she is not all evil. She'll try to cure the boy."

"This is Varik's life. If it was mine, I wouldn't care, but 'tis his, and I made a vow to keep him safe."

"He will surely die without her help." Amory shot his friend a look he reserved for the worst of sinners as he turned and strode down the hallway.

Stoke scowled at Amory's back, then at the stanchion, wanting very much to drive his fist through the wood. He heard footsteps and saw Rowland pass Amory. Rowland spoke, but Amory ignored him, looking lost in thought.

Rowland paused next to Stoke. "I've never seen Amory so tight-lipped."

"He's provoked with me." Stoke turned and stared down at Varik's tiny feet poking up beneath the blanket.

"He'll get over it. He cannot stay mad at anyone for very long. I came to see how Varik was doing and to ask you what I should do about Lord Trevelyn. I knew you disliked him, so Amory and I kept a close eye on him. Shall I continue to do that?"

"Aye, I want to know his every move."

Varik coughed and brought Stoke's attention back to him. Rowland, too, glanced down at the boy, looking worried. "He doesn't look any better, Stoke."

"I know. Amory wanted me to let Lark help him."

"Mayhap she can. Evel told me his sister was the finest of healers."

"Lady Helen intimated the same thing to me." Stoke stared at his friend. He grew pensive for a moment, then said, "Would you trust her with your son?"

Rowland ran his hand over the golden stubble on his chin. "Even if I had a son, as your oldest and dearest friend, I cannot answer that."

"Why?" Stoke asked, his voice mounting with frustration.

"If I were to agree, and should you let her near the boy and something happened to him, I could not live with myself. This is a decision you must make on your own."

Stoke clenched his fists at his sides. Then he heard Varik start to wheeze. He turned and saw Dalia giving him a sip of water. Stoke noticed the blood on the rim of the cup and ran toward his chamber.

Lark finished eating and sat counting dragons. One hundred and twenty . . .

The door burst open and made the next number dissolve on her lips.

Stoke stood in the doorway, a pained look etched into his face. He looked torn for a moment, as if what he were about to say was the hardest thing he'd ever expressed in his life. Finally, he said, "I need your help."

"Is he bad?" Lark was unable to still the sporadic thumping of her heart. She didn't know if it was from fear for Varik, or the fact that Stoke had come to her for help.

"Aye, he can't breathe very well, and he's coughing up blood." Anguish softened the hard blackness of his eyes. He clasped his fists at his sides. The tendons in his hand stretched and showed white from the pressure as he added, "I'll give you anything within my power if you can help him."

"I want naught from you." Lark saw surprise flash in his eyes; then hard blackness veiled them. "Think you I would bargain over a child's sickness? In spite of what you think of me, I'd never do such a thing. I pray, as you do, that he lives."

He looked at her, skepticism gleaming in his eyes. Then he turned and left the doorway.

She followed him, watching his shoulders sway, and the stiff line of his back, and his wooden strides. What little faith he had in her! Pressure tightened the back of her throat. She knew desperation had driven him to her. He would never willingly trust her.

Stoke stepped past Rowland and Amory, who stood near an open door, staring into a chamber. As she paused, her gaze flitted between them. Uncertainty still gleamed in Rowland's eyes. At least Amory looked measurably encouraging. She took a deep, fortifying breath, praying she could help the child, and followed Stoke into the room.

She paused near the large woman sitting on the bed and said, "I must examine him."

She shot Lark a glance, then her gaze slid down over Lark's thin gown. Stoke's mantle fell over Lark's shoulders but didn't meet in the front and left a wide patch of gown showing beneath. By the contempt on the servant's face, she knew Lark had been responsible for stabbing her master. Lark guessed every servant and villein for miles must know of her folly. In a huff, the nursemaid rose from the bed.

Lark bent over the child and touched his forehead. His hot skin singed her hand. She drew back and examined the rash on his face. She lifted one of his eyes and peered at pupils so dilated that they almost covered the lens of his eye. His breathing rattled in his chest.

"I know what is wrong with him. I've seen two other children who had the same symptoms. They had accidentally eaten a wild plant." Lark turned to look at the nurse. "Has he been out playing in a wood?"

"Nay, I never let him out of my sight. He just took ill minutes ere the master came home."

"What sort of wild plant could he have eaten?" Stoke asked, coming to stand next to her.

"Nightshade."

"That's poison?"

"Aye, and it's plentiful in the woods. If he has ingested some of the berries or leaves, then someone must have given them to him." Lark watched Stoke's face turn from incredulous to furious.

He leveled his gaze at the nurse.

The large woman backed away until her spine hit the wall. "I swear, me lord, I didn't give it to him. Ye know I'd never hurt Master Varik."

Stoke opened his mouth to speak, but Lark interrupted him. "I believe you're innocent. If you had wanted to poison the child, you could have done it ere he went to sleep, and he would have died no one the wiser."

The nurse looked surprised and relieved by Lark's trust. Some of the censure left her eyes as she said, "Thank ye, me lady."

"You can thank me later. Right now I need your help." Lark slipped into the bed behind Varik and leaned him up against her chest. The wheezing in his lungs lessened a little. "I need you to find some black currants and stew them to make

a syrup for the fever. And we'll need agrimony, sage tea . . .''
Lark paused. She tried not to believe in superstitions, but it
never hurt to guard against misfortune and evil, so she added,
"And a jasper stone, mistletoe, and some elder leaves. Can
you find these?" Lark looked toward the nurse.

"Aye, the mistress kept an 'erb garden afore she died. I
helped her with it. The weeds have gotten to it, but I can find
them. I keep a jasper stone in me room."

"Hurry." Lark watched the woman run past Amory and
Rowland.

Stoke looked at her a moment, then at Varik. In a low voice
rough with emotion, he asked, "Are we too late?"

"I know not, but I will do all I can."

Lark would have given anything to take the despair from
Stoke's eyes. If the saints were merciful, they would spare the
child. But as she knew from caring for sick villeins, naught
could stop Death's toll, not even the saints.

Two nights later, a pall hung over Kenilworth. Silence emanated from the stones in the walls. It blanketed everything with
a kind of hushed darkness. In the stillness, Lark heard her own
heartbeat, pounding, pounding, against the silence. She picked
up a wet cloth from Varik's forehead. The cloth had absorbed
the heat and could not have been any hotter had she picked it
out of a stewing kettle. She dropped it into a bowl of cool
water and rung it out.

She glanced at Varik, as still as a corpse, the only color in
his face from the fading red blisters. Moments ago, his wheezing
had stopped. She could no longer hear the rise and fall of his
chest, nor could she see it at the moment. Her brows snapped
together as she bent and listened for a beat.

"Is he gone?"

At the deep, rueful tone in Stoke's voice, she glanced down
where he sat in a chair near the foot of the bed. He hadn't left
the spot since Lark had come into the room. The worry had
taken its toll on him. His eyes looked sunken, wrapped by

the dark circles under his eyes. Three days worth of stubble shadowed his square chin. The shiny black waves of hair falling down the sides of his face enhanced the hollows of his sharply chiseled cheekbones. His shoulders stooped as he clasped his large hands between his knees.

"I can still hear his heartbeat." Lark kept from him the fact that it was so weak she could barely make it out.

"Should I go and get Amory?"

"Not yet. We cannot give up hope."

"Hope? Look at him." Stoke glanced at Varik. "What hope have we?" His voice grew hoarse and barely above a whisper.

"He'll only be as strong as the hope you have inside you. We owe it to him to believe he'll get better."

"Of the two children you saw eat nightshade, how many lived?"

Lark remained silent, gulped past the growing knot in her throat, and said, "None."

Stoke's jaw tightened. He said naught, only stared at Varik. After a moment, he hung his head and stared down at his clasped hands. "I shouldn't have left him . . ." His voice trailed away.

Lark walked over to him, then dropped to her knees. "Don't blame yourself. You couldn't have watched him every minute."

She lifted her arms to reach out to him, but he raised his head. His gaze locked with hers. The distraught accessible man, whom she had felt the need to comfort only moments ago, was gone; the man before her now alarmed her. The ominous intensity in his eyes made her drop her arms and lean back on her heels.

"When I find out who poisoned Varik, they will think the chief torturer a kind fellow."

The door flung wide.

Amory stood in the doorway, the wooden cross hanging on his chest, swaying. His gaze moved between Lark and Stoke. "I heard voices. Is Varik . . ." Amory's gaze moved to Varik and his words trailed off. He looked unable to finish asking his question.

''He's still alive.'' Lark saw the bone weariness in Stoke's face. ''Please convince your liege to rest.''

Amory opened his mouth to speak, but one glance from Stoke made him pause.

Stoke stared down at Lark, his eyes the color of molten iron. ''You are my last hope.'' Then, as if unable to look at her any longer, he rose.

Lark scooted back on her knees to avoid hitting his legs as he turned and strode from the room, his expression dark and brooding.

When his footsteps had faded down the hallway, Lark felt a burning in the base of her throat. Varik began to cough, and it drew her attention. She ran to the bed and heard Amory begin a paternoster.

Chapter 17

The next morning, Stoke paused before the nursery door, his head pounding from lack of sleep. He'd spent all night in his workshop, crafting a sword for William Mandeville. The work did little to ease the worry of Varik's fight to live.

He listened at the door.

Dead silence.

Amory had not come to him in the night. Was it to spare him the pain of Varik's death? In his mind's eye, he saw Varik's cold, lifeless body lying on the bed, his eyes sunken and closed, his small arms folded over his chest.

Stoke drew himself up, took a deep breath, and opened the chamber door. What he found made him let out the breath he'd been holding. The pressure in his chest eased. For the first time in three days, the tenseness around his mouth and the heaviness that weighed down his brow slackened.

Varik lay on the bed, nestled next to Lark's left side. His head rested on her lap. His eyes were open, and he was sucking his thumb as he held her braid in his hand. His delicate fingers moved over the silken, golden hair.

Lark sat on the mattress, her back against the headboard.

The pillow behind her stuck out on either side of her head. Strands of hair had escaped her braid and whisped down the sides of her face. One strand fell across her eyes and mouth and fluttered when she took a breath. Her eyes were closed, her long golden lashes fanning her cheeks. Her lips were parted in sleep. She had pulled his mantle over her and Varik, and her bare feet poked out from beneath it. She had sleek, long feet, just like her legs. Stoke watched a vein pulsing on the top of her foot and longed to bend and press his lips against the spot. His gaze moved back up to her face and Varik's. At the picture they made, he felt a grin tugging at his lips.

Right away, Varik noticed him. He took his thumb out of his mouth and whispered, "Faf-ee. Va'ik be'er."

"I'm glad you're better." Stoke grinned and approached the bed.

"Aye. Moh-ee make be'er." Varik pointed at Lark's stomach.

"She's not your mother."

Varik's cherub face looked confused. "No' moh-ee?"

"Nay, I haven't found a new mother for you yet."

"Who she?" Varik ran his finger along Lark's braid, the end of his finger dipping along the twined ridges. "Angel, Faf-ee?"

Stoke found himself smiling and it took him a moment to weigh this question. Finally, he said, "Nay, she's not an angel, just someone who knew how to make you well."

"My moh-ee." Varik smiled at him, then possessively put his arm over Lark's hips. He pressed his cheek against her waist.

Stoke didn't have the heart to argue with his son any further. "You've worn Lark out. How about we let her go to bed and rest now. She'll come in a little while to be with you again."

Varik's face screwed up in a frown, obviously not thinking much of the idea. Finally, he said, "A' righ'."

Stoke turned to Amory, who sat up from a pallet in a corner of the room. Baltizar lay beside him and raised his head to glance at Stoke. "Watch him. I'll return soon."

"Aye."

Stoke kissed Varik on his forehead and noticed that his skin was no longer hot. The lingering tinges of anxiety vanished as he said, "Rest. I'll be back."

Varik nodded, and his gaze clapped on Baltizar. The frown turned quickly into a smile, as expressions were apt to do when one so young found his attention diverted. "New dog?" Varik asked Amory.

"Aye, would you like to pet him?" Amory walked toward the bed with Baltizar following on his heels.

With Varik distracted, Stoke pulled back the mantle and eased Lark into his arms.

Her eyes blinked open. "Stoke," she whispered in a voice husky with sleep.

Hearing his name whispered in such a seductive voice, and her hip rubbing against his abdomen, made him hard at once. Her face was inches from his neck. He felt her hot breath brushing against his skin. The ache in his loins grew unbearable.

"I'm taking you to bed." He sounded winded as if he'd run five miles.

"I'm not tired."

"You've been taking care of my son for three days. You're going to bed." He strode out of the chamber and down the hall, feeling her lips a butterfly's wing breadth away from his neck. The heat of her body burned through his clothes. The tear in her threadbare gown allowed his hand to touch her bare thigh. He rubbed his thumb over the silken skin.

"You needn't worry about Varik any longer. The worst is over."

"I am in your debt for saving him." He reached his chamber, closed the door with his foot, and carried her to the bed. He gently laid her down, feeling the soft skin of her bare thigh rub against his palm.

"Consider us even. You saved my life on that cliff, remember? I never thanked you either." She stared up at him, her golden eyes soft, a vulnerable look in them he'd never seen before.

" 'Tis never too late to thank someone.'' His gaze roamed hungrily over the thin gown that did little to cover her body. The slit up the sides showed a wide swatch of seductive creamy thigh. Higher still, he could see the triangle of hair between her thighs, the flat waist spreading out to slender hips, the outline of peach-tipped nipples. The taste of her nipples was so vivid in his mind, he could all but feel the hard little nubs in his mouth. The memory of her hot, tight heat, the same memory that had driven him near insanity since he'd taken her at the abbey, came back to him in a frantic rush.

His resolve to let her rest ere he seduced her again died a quick death. He reached for her and snatched her up into his arms the way a drowning man reaches for a mooring. His lips found hers. She didn't struggle as he'd anticipated. Her arms wrapped around his neck and she willingly kissed him back, the hunger in her lips matching his own.

He took her mouth with such force, it bent her head back over his arm. Starving for the taste of her, he devoured her lips, her cheeks, her neck.

He felt her hands slip beneath his tunic. When they touched his bare chest, he sucked in his breath, every muscle tensing. The torture didn't end there, for then she splayed her fingers and moved them down around his sides. Her fingers boldly kneaded, caressed, burning their way around to the taut muscles of his back. They moved lower to cup his buttock.

A groan escaped deep in his throat. He could feel the heat of her, the fire, her need for him. It drove him. If he did not have her now, he would spill his seed.

She must have felt his frenzy, for she pulled at the lacings of his braies. He drew her hips to the edge of the bed and yanked up her gown. The sight of those long, slender legs, the golden thatch between her thighs, caused his body to tremble.

Her hands shook as she fumbled with the lacings. Driven like a madman now, he knocked her hands away, ripped his braies, and freed his hard, throbbing flesh. He opened her thighs and drove into her.

She arched her back and clung to him.

"Look at me, Lark," he said, feeling her moist flesh so very tight and hot against him that the sensation was like torture, a torture he never wanted to end.

She gazed up at him, her lips parted, her face filled with the sweet agony of lovemaking. He stared into her eyes, mesmerized by the radiant golden flame and the sparks of desire directed at him, burning straight into the very core of his being. At this moment there was no distrust or dissension between them, only their joining by a force much greater than he'd ever known or felt. The potency of it made his heart race. A cold sweat broke out on his body.

He fought it as long as he could, then yielded totally to it. Twice he thrust into her. He bent and kissed her, crying out his release in her mouth as he spilled his seed.

He clung to her, feeling his knees growing weak from the force of their melding. Still kissing her, he lifted her hips and eased her back onto the mattress. Careful not to pull out of her, he moved both of them into the center of the bed; then he settled on top of her.

He kissed a line around her chin as he eased off her gown and tossed it over his shoulder to the floor. Eager to feel her naked skin against him, he jerked off his own tunic and kicked off his braies. He felt her touching him from cheek to toe, the slick film of perspiration between them intensifying her heat until it scalded him.

"Stoke . . ."

"Aye." He slowly moved his chest, feeling her nipples sliding against the moist slickness of his own, while his fingers learned the hollows at the base of her throat. He pressed his lips against the satiny skin beneath her chin and trailed his tongue down her throat, feeling a shiver go through her. The womanly scent of her, braided with the musky scent of sex, tantalized his senses. Never had a woman's scent enveloped him as hers did. He began swelling inside her again.

In an unconvincing voice, she said, "We shouldn't do this again. I have to go home and face my father and Avenall." Her face scrunched up in a frown.

Stoke raised his head from her breast, a nagging feeling of possessiveness stabbing his gut. He gazed into her eyes and murmured, " 'Tis a little late to be worrying about that."

"I know, but I shall have to face him one day. I was betrothed to him."

"Do you still love him?"

"I've loved him all my life. Learning the truth will hurt him, and he'll never recover, for he feels things much more deeply than anyone I've ever known."

Stoke might have grown jealous if Lark had not been kissing his chin as she spoke. Naught in her voice spoke of real affection when she mentioned the weak whelp. Friendly adoration may-hap, but not love. He was attuned to that sound in a woman's voice, for Cecily had lacked it when he courted her, yet he hadn't been wise enough to notice then. Now he could gauge the amount of affection in every woman's voice.

At his silence, she continued, moving her lips up his jaw. "Something puzzles me." She paused in kissing him and stared into his eyes.

"What, my tigress?" He nipped on her bottom lip.

"It is always over so quickly?" she asked in a wistful voice. "I don't know why—I suppose it was hearing my parents making love all night in their bed—but I thought it would last longer. I don't please you, is that it? I know I'm thin and my hipbones poke you. You'd probably rather have someone comely and rounded like Helen—"

Stoke gently put his finger over her lips, cutting off her words. "Should three Helens all enter my bed at the same time, they could not give me the pleasure you do."

"Three?" A blush crept into her cheeks and her expression turned skeptical.

"Three," he assured her with a nod and brushed back a strand of tawny hair sticking to the corner of her mouth. "Surely you must know that you please me much. It was you who made me spill my seed."

"I made you?" She arched a brow at him.

"Aye, it was your fault. If you did not affect me so, and

were not such a tigress in your passion, then I could have held back and pleasured you.''

"Should I not touch you and lie here like a dead stump so you don't spill your seed so quickly again?''

"Nay, you needn't worry about it now.'' He grinned at her, then touched her breast, feeling the high, proud mounds fill his palm. "I mean to pleasure you henceforth every time I take you, and it will be frequent enough so this will never happen again. I'm going to savor every moment I have a tigress in my bed.''

"I'm beginning to enjoy lusty dragons in mine.'' She pulled his head down for a kiss as her long legs slid along the back of his thighs.

The sensual softness of her thighs tantalized him, the long sleek muscles pulsing against his hips. She locked her legs behind him, then he felt the base of her foot gliding slowly up and down the back of his calf, ruffling the coarse hair on his legs. He reached out and spread his fingers along the smooth skin of her legs and remembered the torment this particular daydream had given him. He wanted to drown in the feel of her long legs wrapped around him.

He kissed a line down the center of her chest, resting his lips between the two luscious globes. His tongue flicked out, tasting the salty smoothness of her skin. He slid his tongue up to one of her nipples, then nipped it and suckled. He felt her shudder in his arms, arch her back, and dig her fingers in his hair, pulling his face closer to her.

He began moving inside her. The narrow, hot moistness widened and absorbed him in a sheer sweet torment he never wanted to end. That powerful spell she cast over him took him over. He grabbed her hips and pumped, touching her womb with each deep thrust, unable to stop.

Her hips matched the rhythm he was setting. He could feel her fingers digging into his back. Her hands tangled in his hair as she thrust her tongue into his mouth. Stoke couldn't hold back any longer. In a searing flash of ecstasy that would not let go of him, he came.

* * *

Lark felt him stiffen. He groaned and fell down on top of her, panting. She rubbed her hands over the hard contours of his back and felt his chest moving with each heavy breath.

"Was that my fault again?" she asked.

"By Judas!" he moaned and looked in pain. "The things you do to me. You make me as randy as a pimple-faced lad with his first woman." The pained expression gave way to a pleased male grin; then his lips feathered across her mouth.

"I suppose I should be flattered."

"Aye, for up until I bedded you, I had some semblance of control. Until I gain it back, I shall have to pleasure you 'ere I enter you."

"I'm glad you have a plan of attack." She grinned at him, then ran her fingers over his square jaw, feeling the stubble on his chin.

An abrupt knock pounded on the door, then it opened.

With lightning swiftness, Stoke grabbed the counterpane and threw it over them. Lark peeked past Stoke's large shoulder. Lord Trevelyn's contemptuous blue gaze locked with hers. Lark groaned inwardly as a smirk spread across his lips. He filled the doorway, arms akimbo, standing there as if he owned the world.

"Well, well, cousin, enjoying the morn by breaking in your new prisoner?"

"I should have locked the damned door." Stoke pulled out of her and rolled onto the mattress, carefully keeping the counterpane over her.

"I'm truly hurt, Stoke." Lord Trevelyn clucked his tongue. "Is that any way to talk to me? I came to see how your son was doing, and your priest said you were in your chamber. I came only to tell you how glad I am Varik is well."

Stoke leaped to his feet, heedless of his nakedness, and pointed to the door. "Get out! And next time you enter this chamber without my leave, I might just cut your heart out."

Lord Trevelyn threw back his head and laughed. The smile

faded quickly. "I look forward to it, cousin." He shot Lark a devouring glance and slammed the door closed.

"What an odious man." Lark still felt Lord Trevelyn's gaze on her. She dug her fingers into the edge of the counterpane and waited for the repulsive feeling to ebb.

"He enjoys provoking me." Stoke strode toward the bed.

"Why?" Lark watched the muscles rippling in his stomach and thighs, and felt a familiar warmth glowing inside her.

She frowned with disappointment when he strode to a chest and pulled out a pair of braies. As he put them on, she watched the dragon on his back spread its wings and the fire roll from its mouth. Her gaze dropped to the scars on his legs while he spoke.

"My sire squired Louis and made him into a knight. He loved Louis as a son. When Louis went home to Burgundy to claim his barony, Velda, the lady he'd been courting, threw herself at me. Louis heard of it and came here in a rage. He refused to believe I didn't take the Lady Velda from him. Alas, he did discover her character when he went to court and found her in another man's bed. He apologized to me, but I don't believe he ever truly accepted the fact I didn't seduce Lady Velda." Stoke finished lacing his braies and stared pensively down at the floor.

"Could it be Lord Trevelyn who is trying to kill you?"

Stoke glanced up at her. "He could very well be. I have not seen him in over five years. I find it highly suspicious that he turns up now, at the same time these attempts on my life start." He pulled another clean tunic out of the chest and frowned thoughtfully as he pulled it on.

Lark remembered something and said, "Caring for Varik, I didn't have time to ask you if you found out who gave him the nightshade."

He hesitated a moment, staring at her, reluctant to discuss it. Finally he spoke. "I questioned Dalia again. She swears she doesn't know how he was poisoned. She did admit she'd fallen asleep when he took his nap and someone could have gotten to him then."

"I believe her. I don't think she is the one. Granted, whoever did it had to be someone in the castle, someone able to get close to him."

Stoke's black brows shot together in a scowl. "I've had my suspicions that 'twas someone close to me since the attacks began, I just didn't know how close. Now I know it must be someone living beneath my own roof."

"Does Lord Trevelyn have something to gain by killing you?"

"Aye, he'll inherit my title and lands if Varik and I die."

"But you said he's wealthy."

"Beyond belief, but power corrupts and makes men hunger for more."

"I fear for you and Varik."

"Do you?" Stoke's gaze dug into her eyes.

"Of course I do." The edge on her voice softened. "If you will trust"—Lark stressed the word *trust* and went on—"me, I would like to watch over Varik and see to the preparing of your meals. Then I can be sure you'll not be poisoned."

He stood for a moment, eyeing her with uncertainty, his lips stretched tautly in a frown. A battle raged within his eyes for a long while. Lark didn't flinch from his gaze, for she knew if she glanced away he would deny her request.

"Very well." The words sounded pulled out of him.

Sunlight streaked across one side of the room from the tiny window slit. Dust motes flew through the beam of light as he strode toward her. When he neared the bed, he touched her chin, running his thumb over her lips.

"I'll let you care for Varik and me. Do not fail us, Lark." He bent and captured her mouth in a breath-stealing kiss, then broke it. Desire burned in the black depths of his eyes. "Rest now. You're going to need it, for tonight you'll get very little sleep."

The deep sensual drawl in his voice melted Lark. She wanted to pull him down to her and not let him go. But he turned and left her. She watched the sway of his shimmering black hair on his shoulders as he opened the door and strode out.

His clothes lay on the floor in a heap, beside her own gown. She rose and scooped up his braies and tunic. She froze and stared down at the clothes in her hand. For some strange reason, she didn't mind seeing her own gown balled into knots on the floor, but seeing Stoke's garments so sorely abused bothered her.

Running her hands over the fine linen tunic, she brought it up to her nose and inhaled deeply of his scent, blended with a metallic odor similar to molten steel. Lark remembered him speaking to her father about metalworking. She made a mental note to visit his workshop. In spite of her indifference to him at the time, she was interested in how he had forged such hard steel. Mayhap she could cajole him into making a sword for her, since he had promised to make one for her father.

William. For the past several days, she hadn't a moment to turn her mind to her father, what with worrying about Varik and Stoke. Now a vision of William Mandeville formed in her mind, his bushy gold brows furrowed, the creases at the corners of his green eyes etched with worry. Somehow she had to get word to him that she was unmolested and well. Knowing her father, he would figure out Stoke had come for her and lay siege to Kenilworth. Lark couldn't bear the thought of her father getting himself killed just to free her.

At St. Vale Castle, William Mandeville glanced over at his wife and said, "I'm not worried about Lark." He watched intently as Elizabeth pulled her undersmock down over her rounded naked curves.

"That is very unlike you. Do you know where she is?" Elizabeth's blue eyes flashed suspiciously at him.

"I believe I do."

With each breath she took, her breasts quivered beneath the white linen. He eyed those luscious orbs, could even feel them in his hands. His gaze rose to the wickedly creamy flesh on her neck, the taste of which he knew well. After twenty-five years of marriage, he still found himself awed by the robing of Elizabeth, so much so that he grew hard under the covers. When he saw her about to put on her gown, he threw his legs over the side of the bed and strode toward her.

Her gaze dropped to his erection, and she backed away. "Oh, you'll not get away without answering my question. 'Tis unfair to use passion to change the subject."

"Unfair to you, but I find it very sporting." He backed her up against the edge of the bed. Before she could dart away, he caught her in his arms.

She started to squirm. He ground his erection against her, and she stopped struggling. The anger melted from her face, and her golden eyes softened. She wrapped her arms around his neck and leaned into him. "I know not why I even try to have a conversation with you, for you never answer my questions. Why is it anytime there is something important to be discussed, we always end up in each other's arms? You always manipulate me any way you like. I would just once like to manipulate you—just once get the better of you."

"You manipulate me more than you know." He stared down at her breasts, barely hidden by her undershift, and smiled.

"You are a wretch." She touched her lips to the end of his nose, belying the irritated tone in her voice.

"Aye, I'm convinced of it, but you are just as much a shrew. And you easily have your way with me as much as I do with you. When will you realize there is no winning or losing in love? We are one. You cannot best yourself. Have you not found that out yet?"

"You've adroitly avoided my question." Her dark brows pursed in feigned irritation. "Where is Lark?"

"She's safe."

"I see what it is. You sent her away to shame me, didn't you? That's why you refuse to tell me. I hope you are satisfied. I looked a fool in front of our guests."

"That did not seem to affect their appetites in the least." William moved his hips, feeling his manhood pressing her soft abdomen.

"You and your quips. I hope you are pleased with yourself—

and your daughter. If you had anything to do with this—'' The contemptuous tone in Elizabeth's voice was at odds with the kisses she placed on his chin.

''Think you I would do such a thing, Elizabeth? I would have to be a simpleton to empty my larders and coffers for a wedding, then send the bride away.''

''Then where has she gone?''

''I'm almost positive she is at Kenilworth Castle.''

''But that is . . .'' Elizabeth stopped kissing his chin, and her mouth dropped open, the small wrinkles near her eyes and mouth stretching.

''Aye, the Black Dragon's lair,'' William finished for her.

The shock dissolved from her expression. Her brows snapped together. ''I knew it—I just knew it. I saw him eyeing her in that horrible old gown. It exposed her like a wanton whore. I warned her, but does she ever listen to me? And poor Avenall was devastated when I found her bed empty the morning of the wedding. You must get word to him and Evel. They are out looking for her.''

A grin teased William's mouth and he tightened his hold on Elizabeth. ''Nay, I believe they need to flounder a bit longer.''

''How perverse you are. Do you want her to come home with a bastard in her belly? For that is surely what is going to happen. More shame will be heaped upon our heads.''

''He'll marry her.''

''Can you be so sure of it?''

''As sure as the ocean blue in your eyes.'' He brought his face close and touched his nose to hers.

''William, how can you countenance this and make light of it? She'll end up a whore just like her—''

He clamped his hand over her mouth. ''Let's not speak of her.''

There was a tense moment between them. Unmistakable scorn and pain veiled the desire in Elizabeth's eyes.

Unable to look into those hurt-filled eyes, William stared at the pale skin glistening on her brow and dropped his hand from her mouth.

She turned in a huff and snatched her gown off the edge of the bed. "You may not want to speak of her, but Lark is going to turn out just like her."

William didn't grab her this time, but stood watching the blue linen bunch near her arms as she slipped the gown over her head. "Nay, she will not. Blackstone shall marry her, I'll see to it."

William was silent a moment and said, "And how long must I suffer for one mistake? It's been eighteen years and you still cannot forget."

"How can I forget Lark is your bastard?"

Chapter 18

"Every time I looked at Lark, I saw that woman's face," Elizabeth said, the years she'd suffered etched in her eyes. "It was as if she were living with me. I tried, I truly did, but Lark was not an easy child and every time I saw her I relived the pain over again."

"Aye, and you took it out on Lark. That is why I felt the need to keep her with me. I couldn't bear to see her broken and cowed by your dislike."

"So you made her into a son. That was so wrong of you."

"I made her strong enough to survive your contempt."

"William, you speak horribly to me."

"The truth, my dear, only the truth." William grabbed Elizabeth now and pulled her around to him, clasping her as he would a talisman. "I had so hoped, after all these years, you would know how much you mean to me and not feel threatened. Carmia meant naught to me."

"So you have said, but I cannot forget your infidelity—especially since you brought home a child from it and asked me to raise her as my own." A tear slipped down Elizabeth's cheek. "You ask too much of me."

"So I do. Love asks much from all of us." William kissed her wet cheek, tasting the salty moisture of her tears.

Elizabeth clung to him as she always did when she felt helpless. In spite of all of her bluster, she was a vulnerable woman, almost childlike in many ways. It was that part of her with which William had fallen in love, and still loved.

As he held Elizabeth in his arms, he thought of Lark. She had been a wedge between them since the day he brought her home, but he'd been determined to raise his bastard daughter and not let her come between him and Elizabeth. It was a selfish endeavor, for he knew Lark would have fared better if he'd forced her to go back to the convent and not lived with a daily dose of Elizabeth's scorn. But when she'd looked so forlorn and begged him not to be sent back, he could not bear to part with her. So he kept her near him, in spite of Elizabeth's jealousy. He'd always felt torn between the two of them.

He had been waiting for the right moment to tell Lark of Carmia, but hadn't found that moment in eighteen years. Part of him couldn't bear to see the bright, worshipful light go out of her eyes when he told her, for he'd never had anyone deify him the way his daughter did. But Lark would have Blackstone to idolize now. The little girl whom he'd adored, who had followed him like a puppy, who did everything in her power to please him, was no longer his. She belonged to Blackstone. Had Lark despised Blackstone, William might have gathered an army and freed her, but after talking to her, it was evident she loved Blackstone and didn't know it yet.

He felt a nagging feeling in the back of his mind that Elizabeth could be right. What if he'd misjudged Blackstone? What if he were too stubborn to see he was in love with Lark and wanted only to use her for a mistress? Love never came easy, as he could attest. If Blackstone refused to marry Lark, William would have to force the union. Thoughts of waging war against the Black Dragon brought a frown to William's face as he rubbed his chin against the soft hair on the top of Elizabeth's head.

*   *   *

The next morning, a knock rang through the chamber, waking Lark. By the angle of the sun in the window, she knew it was well into morning. The hinges of the door creaked, and the young woman called Ebba whom Lark had glimpsed on her arrival stepped into the room.

"How long have I been asleep?"

"Since yester morn."

"I suppose I was more tired than I realized." Stoke had let her sleep in spite of his promise. She felt rested, but would rather have suffered fatigue from a night in Stoke's arms.

Ebba wore a cautious expression, but her voice rang with resentment as she stepped over to the bed. "I wouldn't have woken ye now, but the master bade me to bring ye these." She threw a brown wool bliaut, a pair of doeskin boots, and a white linen shift onto the bed.

"Thank you."

"Don't go thanking me with yer ladylike airs. Ye ain't no lady from what I hear, stabbing the master like ye did. Yer naught but the master's prisoner now . . . and his whore." The young woman threw back her head and laughed, a vicious sound that fractured the air.

Lark screwed up her eyes at the woman.

"Have I made ye angry? Well, I only spoke the truth. Yer his whore now and yer welcome to him." In spite of Ebba's malignant tone, tears came to her grass-green eyes and she blinked them back. "He won't come near me now. I don't know if it were ye, or sharing Lord Trevelyn's bed that caused it. I wish ye both were dead."

Lark stiffened and asked, "Did Lord Trevelyn force you to bed him?"

Ebba looked confounded by Lark's poignant question. After a moment, she found her voice. "Nay, there was no forcing done. If ye ever kissed him, you'd know what I mean."

The thoughts of kissing Lord Trevelyn forced a frown to twist Lark's face. "What sort of man is he?"

"He's kind." She fished in her pocket, wearing a pleased-with-herself expression, and pulled out a small pouch. Her fingers dipped into the leather and she withdrew a large emerald. It came to life in her hand, shooting off twinkling green rays. "He didn't have to give me this, but he did. I'm rich now. I can leave here if I want. The master never gave me jewels, and ye won't get 'em either." She sneered at Lark.

Lark bit down hard and asked, "Did you see Lord Trevelyn go near Varik the night he took ill?"

"He'd never hurt Master Varik. He was with me ere the boy took sick." She dropped the emerald back into the pouch and slipped it into her pocket.

"Do you know who poisoned Varik?"

She hedged a moment. "Nay, I don't. Now I've got to get back to me duties." Ebba headed for the door.

Lark watched the sway of her wide hips beneath her home-spun bliaut and knew Ebba wouldn't tell the truth about Lord Trevelyn, not after he'd bribed her. Lark still felt he was the guilty party.

She would have to do more digging. She threw back the covers, then dressed in the shift, the coarse homespun gown, and the boots. The wool itched as she found a comb on the desk and untangled her hair. When she finished braiding it, she headed for the nursery.

She heard a child's laughter echoing from the room and paused in the doorway. Stoke sat on the side of the bed. Varik hung upside down between his father's legs, his dark head almost touching the floor. Stoke pulled Varik up by his hands and set him on his knees.

"Do again, Faf-ee. Make d'awbidge d'op."

"Only if you say Father," Stoke drew out the word father, slowly enunciating each sound for his two-year-old son.

"Faf-eeee."

"Father."

"Faf-eeee."

Stoke grimaced, gave up, and opened his legs. Varik fell

through them. Before he hit the floor, Stoke caught him and pulled his giggling son back up on his knees.

"Do again, Faf-ee! Do again!"

"The drawbridge is closed for now. I have to go and see to the running of the castle." Stoke touched the pouting lip Varik had stuck out. "None of this."

Varik glanced up at Lark. "La'k!" He scrambled out of Stoke's lap and ran to her. He grabbed her gown and yanked twice.

Lark bent and scooped him up in her arms. "I'm glad to see you are feeling so much better."

"Aye, be'er."

She heard footsteps behind her and wheeled around to see the young man whom she'd seen sitting with Lord Trevelyn when she'd first arrived.

"Pardon me, madam." The man bowed slightly. When he raised his face, his already large eyes seemed to grow in his small face. "I came to speak to my liege."

He was a head shorter than Lark, and she had to look down on him. He didn't like having to look up at her, for it was written plainly on his face. "I'll leave you to it then."

His large brown eyes turned to Stoke. "I came to see if we could go over the books, my lord. There are a few problems I must bring to your attention."

"Aye." Stoke waved a hand at the small man. "This is Thomas, my bailiff. Thomas, this is Lady Lark."

"Pleased to meet you. If you'll excuse us, Varik and I must go see to breaking the fast. Would you like that, Master Varik?"

"Aye." He nodded adamantly and clung to her neck.

Lark thought she saw Thomas's eye dart over her person as she stepped past him, but he lowered his head so quickly that she couldn't be positive. She decided then that she didn't care for the little man, or his furtive glances.

An hour later, Rashid, a middle-aged, dark-skinned Saracen, who bawled every word and wore a perpetual frown, shot Lark a contemptuous look. "You not tell me how to cook, prisoner woman. I cook for Dragon for two years. Hear not of complaints." He lifted the spoon from a huge bowl and shook it at her.

Behind him, a young servant boy paused in pumping a bellows and cowered at the hearth.

Lark grasped Varik's tiny fingers before he overturned a mortar and pestle sitting on a table. "I was just saying, my mother always puts more garlic and basil in her Lamprey in Galytyne. It was just a comment. I wasn't trying to tell you how to cook, sirrah."

That he believed not a word she'd said was evident by the arrogant glower on his face. "Then leave kitchen now!" He banged the spoon against the bowl. "Cannot stand more of your chop this way. Mince that way. Don't do this, do that. And your watching like hawk." He jammed his hands into a bowl of onions and threw a handful up into the air. They rained down on the counter, on the floor, and across the sleeves of his homespun tunic. "You nag, prisoner woman."

"I pray that is not so." Lark frowned, hoping she was not turning into a nagging shrew like Elizabeth.

"I not able to work with you gaping at me and offering— what you say?"

"Advice," Lark finished for him.

"Ah, advice." He glanced up at the smoke-covered ceiling. "Allah save me from woman's advice! Take your advice and leave me in peace!"

"Have I been that much of a nag?" Lark stared at a piece of onion that had landed in his dark, wavy hair.

"Aye, large nag. Very large." Rashid stretched his hands out as wide as he could.

"I'm truly sorry." For the first time since she invaded Rashid's kitchen, the tightness around his mouth loosened. "I was just trying to help. And as you know, someone tried to poison Varik. I'm worried about it happening to your master too."

"Not happen in my kitchen." The forbidding lines of Rashid's face came back. He picked up a large butcherknife and said, "I find who did it, I skewer them."

"I believe you would." Lark felt sure Rashid could be trusted, so she added, "And beware should Lord Trevelyn come into your kitchen."

"He never been here. And I not let him in if he come knocking."

"Good."

"Play ho'se, La'k." Varik pulled on her hand. As an after-thought, he added, "P'ease."

Lark stared down at the little face, a round replica of Stoke's. She stared into the bright, sooty eyes. "Very well. I suppose we're done here."

Lark squatted. Varik locked his arms around her neck and crawled up onto her back. She held his legs tightly to her sides as she stood.

Varik pulled on her braid. "Go, ho'se!"

Lark trotted to the door, bouncing a giggling Varik. As she left the kitchen, Rashid's hand darted toward a bowl of minced garlic, then to another small bowl of chopped basil. The move-ments were so quick that if Lark had blinked, she would have missed them. He surreptitiously flung the herbs into the eel mixture and yanked the spoon through the thick mush. With deft swiftness, he slapped the contents into a large iron pan.

She grinned to herself and stepped out into the bailey. The top half of the rising sun peeked over the high gray walls. Squawks from the mews filled the bailey, mixing with the moo of cows and an occasional honk from a goose. The young groom she'd seen when she'd first arrived at the castle was busy forking hay into a large pile by the stable. A dairymaid hurried across the bailey with a yoke over her shoulders. Two buckets of milk dangled on either side of her. Several cats followed in her wake and stopped every now and then to lick up a spill. Baltizar sat, his gaze leeringly trained on their every move. Cats were not his favorite creatures.

Lark stepped past Stoke's squire, a man who looked about twenty, with short-cropped umber hair that rose up flat from his head like a neatly trimmed hedge. He had been leaning against the stanchion watching her every move in the kitchen, but he stood at attention now, prepared to follow her step for step.

"Do you not get tired of following me?" She smiled, but there was no warmth in it, for this squire was just a reminder that Stoke didn't trust her enough not to be watched every moment.

The squire only eyed her.

"Well, I take that as an assent." Lark wondered if the man was mute. Not one word had left his mouth since he'd started guarding her an hour hence, and she'd put three questions to him.

"Assen', assen, assen," Varik repeated in a sing song voice.

"That's assent."

"Assen' "

Lark smiled and shook her head, then noticed Dalia running toward her. When she neared Lark's side, Dalia whispered, "Did Cook eat ye alive? That heathen don't like people near him. I don't like goin' in there." Dalia jerked her thumb toward the kitchen. "All them Saracens are possessed by the devil."

"I saw not one devil hovering about the kitchen. To hear him tell it, I was the only devil there." Lark teased Dalia with a grin.

The continuous frown on Dalia's lips faded. Since Varik's recovery, Lark had confided her fears about Lord Trevelyn to Dalia, and an alliance had formed between them. Dalia rarely scowled at Lark now. On occasion, Lark even teased a smile out of her.

"Yer lucky to escape with only a tongue-lashing. He chopped a man's finger off once."

"Do tell," Lark said, raising her eyebrows, feeling Varik tugging on her braid.

"The man was a kitchen worker. Rashid found him stealing eggs—chopped his finger right off. The man almost bled to death."

"I believe Rashid is very protective of his kitchen." Lark

heard Varik begin to hum as she changed the subject. "Lord Trevelyn has not tried to come near Varik, has he?"

"Nay, not with me keeping watch over the child. I don't let him out of me sight. I'm wise to Lord Trevelyn's tricks now. And the master is too. He's had Sir Rowland watching his every move. I doubt he'll try something sly again."

"I would put naught past him. Where is Lord Trevelyn now?"

"He's in the tilt yard with the master."

Lark's brows furrowed. She knew Stoke would be safe with his men around him, but she couldn't help but worry. Lord Trevelyn's type rarely fought forthrightly or with honor.

"Go 'ilt yard?" Varik perked up.

"Aye, we shall go and find your father," Lark said, sharing a glance with Dalia.

"Faf-ee."

"Father."

"Faf-ee."

Lark gave up and strode beside Dalia, feeling Varik bouncing on her back, trying to get her to go faster. She picked up her pace, and Dalia had to puff to keep up with them.

They passed beneath the portcullis. Lark caught the round little porter eyeing them from the parapet.

After a moment of hesitation, he waved to her. Lark returned his wave with a nod, aware that the servants' attitudes toward her had changed. They no longer viewed her as the prisoner who stabbed their master, but as the lady who'd saved Master Varik. She felt almost welcomed by them, save for the squire behind her.

They strode beneath the opened gates and into the outer bailey. She grew aware of loud shouts and the fevered excitement in them. Her gaze followed the din, past a long stretch of lawn in the outer bailey. Near the far end, Stoke's men had circled the tilt yard and were looking raptly at what was happening in it.

Her gaze scanned the crowd for the tallest man there, but

Stoke's raven-black hair and handsome face weren't to be found. Lord Trevelyn, too, was absent.

"To ya'd, ho'sey," Varik squeezed her neck as he pulled himself up so he could peer at Lark's face.

"Aye, to the yard."

"Ga'op . . . please," Varik wheedled near her ear.

"Only if you say Father. It would please your sire to hear it. Can you do it, my most noble knight, Sir Varik?"

A smile rounded Varik's cherub cheeks. "Fat-he." He stressed each sound.

"A fair try from one so young and so worthy. We'll go ahead, Dalia." Lark tightened her hold on his legs and jogged the rest of the way, bouncing him on her back. She listened to the guard's footsteps behind them pounding the ground and frowned.

Varik's giggles didn't stop until she slowed and neared the men. The smell of male sweat, leather, and horse dung hung thick in the air, an odor she knew well from St. Vale's tilt yard. A tinge of homesickness gnawed at her, but soon faded when another loud bout of cheering drew her attention. She saw the back of Amory's tonsure, stark against his dark, bowl-shaped hair. Rowland stood at his shoulder. She recognized him by the sandy blond hair glistening in the sun. They looked enthralled by what was taking place in the yard.

Lark edged her way up to them. "Please, may we watch?"

Amory stepped aside. "Ah! Lady Lark."

Rowland noticed her. "Pray, what is that on your back?" His face glowed with a handsome smile. He, too, had warmed to her since word of Varik's recovery.

" 'Tis the noble knight, Sir Varik."

"And his trusty steed?" Rowland's grin grew wider as he looked at Varik.

"Aye, and the steed has run her last mile."

Amory smiled and said, "Come then, Varik, give your destrier a rest and sit upon my shoulders. You can see much better too."

Lark watched Amory lift Varik onto his shoulders and asked,

"Where is Sto—" Her words trailed away when her gaze traveled over the soft, sandy loam of the yard and paused on Stoke and Lord Trevelyn.

Their arms were locked in a fierce wrestling hold. Each leaned into the other, chests touching, arms twined and locked on their shoulders. Neither moved, their arm muscles tensed, glistening with sweat. They must have been holding this pose for a long while, for she could see their sinewy arms trembling. They wore only loincloths, and though Lord Trevelyn's physique was taunt with muscle, he was not as broad of chest as Stoke.

Lark couldn't keep her eyes off the bronzed, pulsing muscles covering Stoke's body. His male frame was perfect in every way, save for the scars on his lower legs, which she barely noticed with so much glorious masculine flesh elsewhere. He had not an ounce of extra weight on him. He was all knotted sinew and sharp-hewn lines, like a marble statue. Lark remembered running her hands over his body, the way her fingers dipped over the steel contours of his muscles, the heat of his skin burning her hands. Warmth washed over her, pooling deep inside her. She fought the feeling and watched the dragon on his back expand with each heavy breath. The dragon's gaze, piercing in intensity, stared directly at her. Something about those eyes reminded her of Stoke's.

"Faf-ee! Faf-ee!" Varik pointed to his father.

At the sound of his son's voice, Stoke lifted his head. His gaze found his son, then Lark. A sensual grin teased the corner of his mouth.

Lord Trevelyn grinned wickedly, aware that Stoke's concentration was broken. His leg whipped toward Stoke's right side.

"Watch out!" Lark yelled.

Chapter 19

Stoke felt the impact against his knee. His leg buckled. He cursed as he fell on his back in the dirt. Louis dived on top of him.

"I could have stabbed you, cousin," Lord Trevelyn said between his teeth as he tried to pin Stoke's arms to the ground.

"You could have tried." Stoke stared into the keen blue eyes, then freed one arm and wrapped it around Louis's neck.

"You act like a besotted fool around your prisoner. I wouldn't get too attached to her. You never know when she'll escape you."

Stoke jammed his foot in Louis's stomach and flipped him backwards over his head. Before he could move, Stoke fell across him, pinned his arms, and said, "I doubt she'll be escaping any time soon."

Louis growled and struggled the way a man pinned by demons would struggle. But he couldn't break free. Stoke heard the shouts of his men at his victory. Lark screamed the loudest of them all. The enthusiasm in her voice made him smile inwardly.

"A fine match." Stoke rolled off of him, eager to get Lark alone.

"But it will never be over for us, will it?"

Stoke looked hard at him a moment. "Only if you want it that way." He turned and strode toward Lark, leaving Louis to glower at his back.

The glow in her eyes, the proud smile lighting her face, seeped over him. For some reason her smile made him feel as if he swallowed sunshine, warming him from the inside out.

He felt his men slap him on the back as he strode toward Lark. Stoke's gaze never wavered from those vivid golden eyes. Her gaze dropped to his loincloth. The smile faded and a blush stained her cheeks.

He glanced down at his protruding loincloth, his swollen manhood jutting out beneath it. A wry grin turned up one side of his mouth. Rowland and Amory wore knowing smiles on their faces.

"Faf-ee win."

"Stay with Amory for a moment. I'm going to show Lark the creek." He ruffled his son's hair, then swept Lark up into his arms and strode toward the drawbridge, leaving Amory and Rowland grinning like simpletons.

His squire began to follow them, but Stoke waved his hand through the air. " 'Tis all right, Jamus, I want some privacy."

Jamus nodded and strode back toward the tilt yard.

"Must you embarrass me in front of your men like this?" she hissed.

" 'Tis no embarrassment for a man to want a woman."

"Aye, it is when the woman is your prisoner, not your wife. And you have your squire watching her every move."

"He's there to keep you safe from Louis."

"I don't believe you. You don't trust me. Must I suffer more humiliation in the eyes of your men? You can't just carry me into the woods with your manhood jutting out of your loincloth." She waved her free hand toward his erection. "You might as well be flying a standard."

He grinned from ear to ear. "I'm not ashamed of wanting

you, Lark. I've counted the hours since the last time I touched you."

"You have?" Her irritation melted behind the incredulity in her voice.

"Aye, visions of your sleek, naked body next to mine and delving into your hot moist heat distracted me. I made several mistakes in the tilt yard because of you—you saw one just a moment ago with Louis."

"And that was my fault?" A wry grin turned up her lips, setting to life the dimple in her cheek. "Beseems I get the blame for an awful lot of your failings."

"Aye, you cause all my troubles." A lopsided, sensual smile slowly moved across his lips.

She appeared to remember something and glanced over his shoulder at the tilt yard. "As much as I enjoy causing all your troubles, I cannot go with you, my lord, I must keep an eye on Lord Trevelyn. See, he's talking to Ebba."

Stoke paused and turned enough to glance at them where they stood, huddled, heads bowed, away from everyone. "She let him talk to her?"

"She showed me a very large jewel that he'd given her. I think it was to bribe her to say that she was with him when Varik was taken ill."

"I know of this jewel."

"How did you know?" Her radiant golden eyes widened in disbelief.

"Ebba showed it to me, trying to make me jealous," Stoke drawled nonchalantly.

"Do you not think that is suspicious?"

"She would be an idiot to lie for Louis, then go around presenting the evidence. I have Rowland and my men watching Louis and Ebba. Forget about them. What was that about you liked causing my troubles?"

For a moment, she looked undecided about dropping the subject of Ebba and Louis. But her gaze fell on Dalia and the indecisive look left her expression. She sighed loudly. "I suppose I could do my best to trouble you." Her arms slipped around his neck, and she began placing tiny kisses along his chin.

Stoke felt her warm breath feathering down his neck, the tenderness of her lips against the coarse stubble on his chin. Her fingers twined in the hair at the back of his neck, sending gooseflesh down his spine. He grew aware of her side pressing against the top of his erection. The same unnerving, overpowering throbbing that he always felt when he was near her erupted in him.

"I'm warning you, if you keep troubling me in this manner I may keep you in the woods for days," he drawled, his voice husky.

"Is that a promise?"

She grinned a siren's grin that shot directly through Stoke. He groaned inwardly and increased his strides.

"May I make a confession to you?" Lark asked, nibbling on his ear.

Stoke grunted, hardly hearing her for the ache in his loins.

"I like being in your arms. 'Tis nice. I've never been carried by a man until I met you. Plenty of knights have thrown me over their backs and knocked me to the ground, but none carried me—Avenall tried once, but his face turned blood-red, and he huffed as though lifting a full-grown milking cow. I made him put me down for fear he might hurt himself."

" 'Tis obvious you've never had a real man hold you."

"The things I have missed in my life." An impish gleam lit Lark's golden eyes and the dimple in her cheek winked at him.

Stoke smiled at the teasing taunt, for he would wipe that grin off her face soon enough. He neared the stream. Moisture hung in the air, redolent with the earthy scent of moss and dried leaves. Water gurgled and eddied and glistened like hammered silver. He watched the water's swirling reflection in Lark's eyes as he gently set her down on the creek bank, keenly aware of the way her coarse russet gown felt against her lithe body.

He let his hands slide along her thighs and the rounded curve of her back. He felt a small shudder go through her and grinned at her response to his touch.

Shadows from the canopy of leaves overhead flitted across her comely face, darkening the gold of her lashes. Sunlight shot through the leaves, throwing tiny diamond-shaped rays of brightness across her legs and the top of her head, just touching her rosebud mouth. Her thick braid lay across one shoulder and cascaded down to her waist like a multicolored golden rope.

She reached over to touch one of the many wild ferns dotting the bank and said, "If fairies truly live, this is their home." Awed by the beauty, she glanced around her. " 'Tis beautiful here. I'm glad you brought me." She smiled up at him, the welcoming hunger in her gaze calling out to him.

He answered it by dropping to his knees before her. "I thought you would like it, but I would rather have your attention on me."

Determined to prove to himself that he could conquer this mad lust and make slow, passionate love to her, he wrapped his fingers around her thin ankles. Slowly, he moved his hands up her shin, raising her gown and shift as he went.

She shivered, even as he felt the gooseflesh rise on her skin. "I believe you have my attention," she said in a whisper.

"Not your undivided attention, yet. Give me a moment." Grinning, he lowered his mouth to that enticing spot on the top of her foot. He ran his tongue over it, feeling the pulse throbbing. Higher, he brushed his lips over the arc between her ankle and leg, letting his tongue follow the wondrous curve. He gave equal attention to both legs, moving his lips up the velvety skin on her shins, her knees.

The smooth edge of a scar on her right knee brushed his lips. He touched it with his finger and asked, "How did you get this?"

"Harold pushed me out of a tree when I was eight."

"I hope you pushed him back."

"A few years later, I gave him the scar over his eyebrow."

When he reached the top of her thighs, he paused over another scar on her thigh. He placed kisses along it and said against her skin, "And this one."

"That came from not paying attention with a lance. The quintain got me the first time I rode against it."

"Think not that you will ever enter my tilt yard." He eased open her legs and ran his fingers through the golden triangle of curls between her long, slender legs. The musky scent of her filled his senses.

"Would you deprive me of so much pleasure?" she asked, arching her hips at his touch.

"I'll manage a way to make it up to you." He opened the soft pink folds and lowered his mouth to her.

She tensed and dug her nails into his shoulders. "Nay, Stoke, you cannot. I prefer the quick way." She pulled on his shoulders, trying to pull him up to her.

"Nay, I mean to take my time and pleasure you." He touched his tongue to the center of her desire.

She moaned and writhed beneath him. Her hands dropped from his shoulders and she dug her fingers into the ground at her sides. He stroked her with his finger and tongue until her body quivered all over and she was calling out his name in fevered gasps. Abruptly, her hips arched. She cried out her release.

With the alluring taste of her still in his mouth, his self-control held only by a thin thread, he kissed his way up to her belly. Her muscles quivered against his mouth as she tensed. He tasted the salty perspiration slick against his lips.

"Stoke, please come to me." She pulled at his shoulders with trembling hands.

"All in good time, sweetling." His manhood throbbed with gorged blood, the ache shooting all the way down to the soles of his feet. But he was determined to go slow. He made the mistake of glancing down the length of her body, at the shining alabaster skin gleaming along her tiny waist, the barely flaring hips, the golden woman's mound between those wickedly long legs.

"You are so tempting . . ." He forced his eyes closed, kissing his way up to her breasts, inching her clothes up her arms.

He took one hard nipple in his mouth and suckled. She tried to touch him, but he pulled her clothes up to her elbows and trapped her arms above her head.

"Stoke . . ." she cried out in frustration, arching her back when he touched his mouth to her other nipple. "This is torture."

"Aye, for both of us." He ran his tongue up between her breasts, along the silken skin of her neck.

She moaned and frantically jerked her arms free of her clothes. The moment her hands delved into his hair and she forced his face up to hers for a kiss, he knew he was close to losing the battle within him.

She opened her mouth and her tongue dove deeply into his mouth, exploring, driving him to the edge, while she wrapped her long, sleek-muscled legs around his hips, writhing against his manhood.

"Take me, Stoke . . ." Lark begged softly, digging her nails into his back as she arched against him.

"God! I'll take you, tigress. I'll take every inch of you . . ." His words came out strangled in the back of his throat.

Wildly, greedily, he kissed her, while he thrust into her, savoring the tantalizing feel of her moist heat embracing his hard flesh.

Her hands went imploringly to his buttock. "Stoke . . ." she gasped out, pushing at his buttock.

"Aye, my tigress, I know what you need." He picked up her hips, driving his flesh into her, touching her womb.

Each thrust came furiously now, his thighs pounding against her again and again. Lark's soft whimpers of passion drove him to the precipice of his control.

"Come with me . . . Lark."

Lark's claws dug into his shoulders as she gave way to the

raw ecstasy of her own passion. He groaned deep in his throat. There was no fight left in him. His whole body began trembling.

He felt the shudder of her release and heard her cry out. It was the moment he'd died a thousand agonizing deaths to obtain. Trembling, every muscle clenched from restraint, he pumped one last time, hard, deep, driving to her womb. He surrendered to his own shattering release, feeling bit by tiny bit of him giving over to the power she wielded over him.

He collapsed on top of her and stayed that way, momentarily paralyzed by fatigue and the all-encompassing force that had just flowed between them. His breathing finally returned to normal, and he rolled off her, pulling her close.

For a long while they lay there, enmeshed in each other's arms, the sunlight dancing luminous shadows over their naked bodies. They clung to each other, daring not to break the spell by uttering a sound, listening to the timeless mating hum of the cicadas, crickets, and frogs as lovers must have done centuries before them, by this very creek, on just such a summer day as this one.

"I'll always remember this place," Lark said wistfully.

"You need not commit it to memory. You and I will come here often." He tightened his hold on her and pushed her bottom tighter to his side.

She lifted her head from his chest and stared at him behind long, golden lashes. Strands of straight hair that had come loose from her braid hung in her eyes. She shoved them back with her hand and her expression turned grave, determined. "I'll not stay here as your prisoner forever."

"I'll never let you go." Stoke realized he'd squeezed her so hard that she had winced and he loosened his hold. "You may be carrying my son." He spread his hand over her belly, feeling his fingertips gliding along her silken skin. The thought of Lark having his babe made him grin.

"Why do you keep saying that?" Lark knocked his hand away and pulled back from him. "I'm not with a babe. And wipe that ignorant grin off your face."

"You could be." Stoke smiled at her, then wrapped his arms

around her and eased her on top of his chest. He'd never had a woman who fit so snugly in his arms, her head just reaching the top of his chin. It was easy enough to kiss her by hardly bending his head. Her legs were long enough that her hips were almost aligned with his own, and he could feel the golden curls at the apex of her thighs rubbing against his manhood.

"Let me go . . ." Belying her plea, she lay her head on his chest and didn't try to pull away. "I'll never be able to face Helen or my father—Sweet Mary!—what of my mother?" She tried to raise her head, but Stoke held it against his chest with his hand.

He turned her face so she would have to look him in the eyes. "You needn't worry about her."

" 'Tis easy for you to say such, for you have never had to live with her." Her face screwed up in a thoughtful frown; then she appeared not to notice him as she blurted, "If I find I'm carrying your child, I can never go home. I'll leave the country—aye, that is what I'll do. My Uncle Egbert will let me stay with him. He would not care that I carry a bastard child. His daughter was abducted by his enemy, and he took her back after the lord had raped her. Aye, my uncle has a kind heart—"

Stoke clamped his hand over her mouth. "Lark, you're rambling like a lost leper. You're staying with me. Think you I would let your uncle raise our child?" He tore his hand away from her mouth and replaced it with his lips.

She stiffened and kept her lips tightly closed. He softened the kiss, running his tongue along her bottom lip, then sliding his lips across hers. He slipped his hands down over her back to cup her buttock, all the while continuing his invasion of her mouth.

A little moan harkened her yielding to him and she melted in his arms, kissing him back. Stoke ground his hips against hers. She gasped, and he was lost in his desire for her.

As he sheathed himself in her hot flesh and drove his tongue into her mouth, feeling her hips moving with his, he knew she had power over him, and he never meant to give another woman that again. But the temptation was too great, the physical attraction too overpowering to fight. He felt her move against him and it drew all his thoughts back to their lovemaking.

Forty yards away, a figure stood huddled behind a thick stand of brambles, watching Stoke and Lark. A branch rustled slightly as the figure melted back into the forest.

Chapter 20

A long time later, Stoke and Lark entered the bailey, hand in hand. Save for two washerwomen hanging up clothes on a line, the bailey was empty. Squawks from the mews melded with the whinny of a horse in the stable.

Lark felt her damp hair slapping against her bottom and saw Stoke's wet hair gleaming in the sun, from their bath in the creek. It was the most luscious bath she'd ever had. Stoke had kissed and fondled her through most of it.

Footsteps brought Lark's gaze around to Jamus as he strode over to Stoke and bowed before him. As usual, he said not a word, only handed braies and a tunic to Stoke and stared at his liege for orders.

Stoke turned to her. "I'm going to my workshop and finish work on a sword I promised your father. I'll leave Varik in your competent hands."

"May I come with you? I would love to watch you work," Lark said eagerly.

"Nay, I allow no one to enter my workshop."

Lark felt the excitement leave her in a gush, taking with it the smile on her face and the warm bloom from their lovemaking. She flung her next words at him. "Admit it, you don't allow those people whom you don't trust in your workshop." She turned and stepped away from him.

He grabbed her arm and pulled her back to him. "That is not true, Lark. No one has ever stepped foot in my shop but me."

Abruptly, Varik's giggle echoed through the bailey. Lark glanced past Stoke and saw Varik riding on Amory's shoulders. Amory ran a few steps and stopped suddenly, which caused Varik to pitch forward. Amory caught him ere he fell. Varik broke out in another gale of laughter.

"Do again." Varik tapped the top of Amory's head.

"All right." Amory ran three more steps and the whole process started over again.

Dalia hurried behind them, watching Varik with a careful eye, her hands out in front of her as if she expected to have to catch him at any moment. "I don't think ye should be doing that, Father Amory. He could fall."

"I wouldn't let him fall." Amory shot her an indignant look.

Stoke grabbed Lark's chin and forced it up so she would look at him. "We are not done discussing this yet."

" 'Tis done as far as I'm concerned." Lark stared back at him, not flinching beneath the penetrating black gaze boring into her.

Amory paused in the game and came to stand near Lark. Varik reached out his tiny arms toward Lark. "La'k, take?"

Lark pulled Varik off Amory's shoulders and held him in her arms. "How have you been, Sir Varik?"

"Miss you?"

Lark stared into the bright little face. Varik wrapped his arms around her neck in a fierce hug, and she felt a tug on her heart. One day she would have to leave this child. And his father. In a guarded voice that belied the emotion brewing inside her, she said, "I missed you too."

This discourse did not go unnoticed by Stoke. The frown on his face melted to a pensive expression.

"I was just going to give alms to the poor. Would you and

Varik join me?'' Amory asked. ''Mayhap you could tend some of the villeins as well. The healer we have is—as you know—not worth a grain of salt. And he charges outrageous prices. With your healing talents, I thought—''

''Say no more.'' Lark raised her hand to stop him. ''I shall be glad to help—if a prisoner is allowed such freedom.'' She glanced ruefully at Stoke.

Stoke frowned. ''You may go. Take care you do not stay over long.'' He eyed Jamus, silently reiterating the order.

Jamus nodded, then focused his stoic gaze at his charge.

''Very good,'' Amory said, pleased. ''I'll go retrieve the cart from the kitchen.'' He strode away.

Without another word, Stoke headed for his workshop, the clothes Jamus had given him swaying in his hands.

Lark watched the muscles writhe in his back, the dragon flapping its scaly wings. He still wore the loincloth.

Lark leaned over toward Dalia and kept her voice low enough so that Jamus would not hear her. ''Did you happen to see what Lord Trevelyn did after he left the tilt yard?''

''Went to his room, me lady. Called for a bath and Ebba. I heard the wench and him ...'' Dalia paused and stared at Varik, who was listening intently to everything being said. She shot Lark a knowing glance and said, ''Laughing. Aye, they was laughing.''

''I see.'' Lark nodded knowingly.

''They'll probably be laughing for some time.''

''Then we can help Father Amory without having to wonder what mischief your master's cousin is about.''

''Aye, and Sir Rowland has his eye on him too. I saw him standing near Lord Trevelyn's chamber door. Ain't likely he'll be getting out of there without Sir Rowland seeing him.''

''So long as someone knows his whereabouts.''

Lark turned and spotted Stoke pausing at the door to his workshop. He bent and pulled a key out of his boot. As he jammed the key in the lock, he turned. Their gazes clashed. His expression was full of guarded suspicion.

Unable to stand the brunt of his distrust any longer, Lark

glanced across the bailey. Her gaze fell on the bailiff, Thomas. He stood in the doorway of his office, his gaze on Stoke.

Something made Thomas glance at Lark. He looked chagrined at being caught staring at his master, then turned and darted back into his office, slamming the door behind him. There was a swiftness in his retreat that made Lark blink hard at the closed door.

As she turned back around, she found Dalia and Amory watching Stoke too. So the master's secret workshop was a curiosity for all. As she turned and followed in Amory's wake, she couldn't help but wonder what was in there that he had to keep hidden from the world.

'Twas well past sunset when Lark stepped out of a hut in the village. She raised a brow at the stars winking at her. It must be later than she'd imagined. The odor of dung, animals, stewing eel, and bodies in need of cleaning wafted beneath her nose. The smell of a village.

Dalia and Varik had left some time ago so Varik could take his nap. Lark reminded Dalia to keep the door locked until she returned, for she knew Dalia would probably fall asleep and she didn't want someone to poison Varik again. Amory had left an hour ago to give the Vespers service.

She had always liked the sunset service at St. Vale, for it signaled the closing of a day and usually gave her an hour of reprieve from Elizabeth's constant harping. How a sword-carrying priest such as Amory presided over a sacred service would be something to see, but she could not get away from the village. So many needed tending—so many wounds to heal, boils to lance, fevers to cool. All the villeins she tended had offered their blessings for her kindness, but Lark enjoyed making people feel better. Healing was the only other thing, besides knowing how to use weapons, that she felt confident doing.

She heard Jamus's footsteps behind her. All afternoon he had stood with silent diligence outside each hut she had visited, never making a sound, but always there. Silence pervaded him like a thick fog now.

It settled over her too, until she said, "I had hoped, since you are my second shadow now, that you would speak to me on occasion. I wish I knew whether 'twas your dislike of me, or some other reason you'll not speak. I know your name is Jamus. I hope 'tis all right if I call you that."

Nothing but footsteps, though his footfalls hit the ground a little harder than before.

"I wonder if you know who is behind these murder attempts on your liege. One must watch the silent types. My father once had a retainer who never spoke—I take that back, he did grunt when he wanted food—but two words never came out of his mouth together. One night—oh, about six years ago—horses started disappearing, and what do you know, my father found Rattle—that's what we used to call him—stealing another retainer's horse out of the stable."

"I d-d-don't kn-kn-know."

At the sound of his voice, Lark paused and looked at him. He stared down at the ground, his face tainted with a blush. The bantering tone left her voice as she said, "You needn't be ashamed of stuttering."

"P-p-p . . . eople m-m-make jest of it." Jamus forced out the last words in a rush.

"They are ignorant knaves. I know what it is to be made a joke of—my twin brothers have teased me since I can remember. Many a day I felt sure they could not be my real brothers. When I was but a wee thing, I used to think wicked fairies brought them and dropped them at our doorstep. I kept going into the forest to ask the fairies to take them back, but they never came to get them. Finally I gave up and decided the fairies probably put them there to torment me, for my father always said, what didn't kill me would make me stronger. I believe he was right."

Jamus grinned sheepishly at her. The moon silhouetted his frame, his short hair a stark, straight line against the soft roundness of the blue sphere behind him. He had a pleasing smile when he used it.

Lark grinned back at him, until a queer feeling rose in her, as if someone were watching them. They had reached the gates of Kenilworth. Her gaze strayed along the battlements, the peculiar sensation making her skin crawl. There was no sign of anyone, but the feeling wouldn't leave her.

Hinged metal grated against metal. Her gaze dropped to the bailey's inner gates as they swung open.

Abruptly, the thunder of hooves met her. All she could see was twenty-five-hundred pounds of black destrier bearing down on her. Stoke's destrier.

The horse swerved.

She leaped to the side and plowed into Jamus. They both careened to the ground. The horse reared and its huge hooves pawed at the air, horse and rider one massive black shadow in the darkness.

Before she could untangle herself from Jamus, she heard Stoke dismount. His feet hit the ground like two solid boulders. Seconds later, his fingers bit into her arms and he hauled her to her feet. Jamus scrambled to stand behind her.

"Where have you been?" he said, his fingers squeezing her arms. "I was just coming to look for you. Amory said you were at the village tending the sick, but I did not expect you to stay so long." He eyed Jamus. "I thought you would have brought her back by now."

"Don't growl at Jamus." Lark knocked his hands away. "I couldn't leave the village. There was a sick elderly woman, who could not fix her dinner. I stayed and made broth for her."

"You should have sent word to me."

"I thought you would still be in your *workshop.*" Lark couldn't help the hint of jealousy tainting her voice. She noticed the leather apron that covered his tunic and braies. Metal splatters dotted it, along with many small burned spots.

"I left it a moment ago to come and find you, but you were gone."

"Mayhap that is a good thing, for now you know what it

feels like not to have me as your prisoner and under your watchful eye, for one day I'll leave here.''

Stoke turned toward Jamus. ''Leave us.''

Jamus shot Lark a sympathetic glance, then grabbed Shechem's reins. Horse and squire disappeared through the gates, the slow thud of hooves trailing them.

She waited until the sound had died away and rounded on Stoke. ''You didn't have to be so terse with him.''

''So now you've suddenly found compassion for my squire. Could it be possible you have spent too much time in his company?'' He stared down at her, enough moonlight hitting his face for her to see the jealous glow in his eyes.

''So now you not only don't trust me, but you think I seduce the guards you have set upon me. Well, let me tell you something.'' Lark shook her finger at him. ''I'm not in the habit of seducing men—save for you, and it was not me who did the seducing. At first. And I'll tell you something else. If I wanted to leave here, no number of guards could stop me. So you can find other duties for your squire rather than following my every move.''

Lark felt Stoke's hot, rapid breaths hitting her face. When she saw his hands whip toward her, she realized she might have goaded him a bit too far.

He grabbed her around the waist and tossed her over his shoulder.

''You cannot treat me like this. I'll leave.'' Lark didn't tell him she wouldn't leave him even if he let her go. She had to stay and watch Louis. That didn't mean the infuriating man shouldn't know she didn't like being manhandled, so she hit his back for good measure. ''Let me down. I might look like a bale of straw to be tossed about, but I'm not one.''

''How well I know that, but throwing you over my shoulder gives me great pleasure.''

''Where are you taking me?''

''To my bed.''

''Don't take me there,'' Lark said in frustration.

''Why not?''

"I'm trying to argue with you, and if you take me to your bed, then I won't be able to."

"Precisely why I'm doing it."

" 'Tis not fair," Lark protested again.

"Life is never fair."

Lark rolled her eyes at the derisive tone in his voice as she stared at the tie on his apron. Somehow she had to get his attention. Her arms were long enough to reach his bottom and she gave it a good tweak. It was hard enough getting her fingers into the rigid muscle there; worse yet, he didn't flinch.

"If you continue to tempt me with your caresses, I may be forced to take you right here," he drawled.

"It would be preferable than lying in your bed."

One moment Lark was on his shoulder, then next her feet hit the stone floor of the bailey. He grabbed her and pulled her into his embrace. "Now, say that again while I'm holding you." His dark eyes bored into her face.

"You heard me." She stared up into his black eyes, eyes she could lose her soul in if she were not careful. Her hands were on his chest, her palm over his heart. Strong and steady, the beat thumped against her hand. The heat emanating from his massive chest seeped through his black velvet tunic, seemingly intensifying the pulsing.

"You seemed to like my bed only hours ago."

Lark felt his words rumble in his chest and said, "I lost my wits—I do that when you make love to me. And I'll tell you something else. You ruined my life with Avenall, and now you keep insisting I must remain your prisoner and mistress. Well, I'll not be subjugated by any man—especially you. I don't even like you."

"Listen well, for I'll not say this but once again. If you ever try to leave me, Lark, I'll find you and bring you back. I've left my mark on you—you belong to the dragon now. You'll always belong to me." He kissed her, a powerful, mind-stealing kiss that dipped her backwards over his arm, so far that her braid touched the ground.

The fire in his lips claimed her. She could feel it burn all the way down to her toes. In spite of what she'd just said to him, she did care for him, more than she wanted to admit.

She shouldn't give in to his lust so readily, but sweet Mary! To spurn him would be like not being able to breathe. She felt his large hand cradling her head, the feel of his powerful arms embracing her, the searing ardor of his lips and tongue invading her mouth.

Her arms tightened around his neck, and she drank him in, committing to memory the irresistible feeling of how it felt to be totally consumed by not just a mere man, but one as torrid and ravaging as the Black Dragon. Stoke was correct; he had branded her. Every time he touched her, his mark on her went deeper. Soon it would envelop her if she wasn't careful.

A long time later, Stoke and Lark strode into the hall. Stoke listened to the voices drifting from the hall, Rowland's and Louis's among them. His men were already milling about the tables, waiting for him. Servants scurried about the room, filling trenchers and goblets. Jamus stood near a wall, mooning over Ebba as she floated about the tables, her hips swaying, breasts bouncing, attracting the notice of every man in the room. By the furtive glances she aimed Stoke's way, it was clear she was trying her best to make him jealous. More than likely, she still brooded over the fact that Stoke would never take her to his bed again.

Rashid came hurrying into the hall, his arms laden with a tray of food. He saw Stoke, paused, and bowed slightly. "Master."

"When did you start bringing food from the kitchen?" Stoke asked, frowning.

"Since that." Rashid nodded at Lark.

Stoke raised his brows at Lark.

She shrugged. "I only paid him a visit in his kitchen."

"Stay too long, too." Rashid scowled at her.

"I was only worried about your master's food." Lark peered

at the food on the tray. "If that is for Varik and your master, then I should taste it."

Rashid nodded and shot her an indignant look. He shifted the tray to his right side, out of her reach. "You not offend me by tasting my food. I taste it in front of you. That please you? Oh, Allah!" He rolled his eyes heavenward.

"I do not wish to offend you." Lark frowned at him. "I trust you, Rashid, but one of your kitchen helpers could put something in the food."

Rashid snorted under his breath. "No one put anything in my food. Food get cold, no time to argue." He hurried over to the dais and set down the tray at Stoke's table.

Stoke leaned over and grasped her hand. "Try not to offend the best cook I've ever had. I'd like to keep him."

"Offend him? All I wanted to do was taste your food. We can't be too careful."

"A strange behavior for someone who said a short while ago she didn't like me."

"I don't want Varik to be without a father."

"I appreciate your concern for Varik." He felt her trying to pull her hand out of his, but he tucked it beneath his arm and held on tightly. Grinning from ear to ear, he felt her hip brush his as they made their way across the hall. Her stride was almost as long as his, and he didn't have to slow his pace, as he had to do with most women.

The moment the laverer saw Stoke, the young boy hurried over to him, sloshing water over the sides of a bowl. The boy paused before Stoke, his bright red curls bobbing around his face.

"Me lord." He bowed, the freckles on his face stretching in a subservient smile.

Stoke unwound his arm from around Lark's and washed his hands and dried them on the cloth the young man presented to him. As he was about to untie his apron, Lark stepped over to him and said, "I'll do that. You can't see behind you."

She pulled it over his head without him having to bend over.

Made of stiff leather and suede, it was not a lightweight article, but the burden of it didn't seem to bother her at all.

"Beware. You're acting submissive. Are you trying to work your feminine wiles on me?" Stoke cocked a brow at her.

"If I had any feminine wiles, then I'd certainly know better than to use them on a man as suspicious and distrustful as you. I'm certain you would be impervious to them." She thrust the apron against his chest and walked away.

Stoke frowned at her back and shook his head. This rebellious attitude, he knew, came from her resentment at being held against her will and, no doubt, her sense that he couldn't fully trust her.

After she had saved Varik's life, he felt sure she was not involved with his nemesis, yet in the back of his mind there was still a minuscule nagging of doubt that was firmly fixed by Cecily's deception and the uneasiness he felt around all women. No matter how hard he wanted to dash this uncertainty from his mind, he could not.

To further complicate his relationship with her, he had feelings for Lark that he had never wanted to feel again. He needed time to come to grips with them. Exercising caution was the prudent way to deal with Lark, for he would never lay bare his heart to another woman—especially one he wasn't even sure how she felt about *him*.

Sexually he pleased her, but never once in all their lovemaking had she spoken an endearment to him. He had a feeling she still mooned over that scrubby sapling, Lord Avenall. More than likely, she wanted to leave and go back to him. But Stoke wasn't prepared to let her go. Not now. Not ever.

Still frowning, he watched her long, coltish strides swishing her wool gown around her ankles, her arms swaying at her sides like a man's. Not one bit of sway in those small hips. Not that he cared any longer about rounded curves and large bosoms. Her long, lean lines tempted him as no plump woman ever could.

She strode past Jamus. The squire noticed her, then glanced at Stoke. A blush colored his cheeks when he saw his master standing there holding his apron. He hurried over to him, bowed, then reached for the apron.

"I'll t-take that. S-s-sorry, m-my lord." Jamus flinched as if expecting a reproach.

Stoke handed him the apron, hardly noticing Jamus. His eyes were on Louis, who had paused in speaking to Rowland and Amory and eyed Lark like a new mare he was about to break in.

Lark moved toward a place at table well below the salt, where the servants ate. In six steady beats of his heart, Stoke crossed the hall and grabbed her arm. "You're eating beside me."

"Why? I'm only your prisoner. As such, I should eat here. Do not embarrass me further by having me eat at your side." Her eyes held unveiled pain.

"Lark, I—"

"Please, your men are staring. Let it go." She glanced down at his chest, a despondent look in her eyes. When she moved her head, a long strand of golden hair fell down over her brow.

He fought the temptation to push it back out of her eyes, turned, and walked to his chair, a frown etching its way across his brow. He took his seat and watched Rashid taste a bit of eel from his trencher.

Rashid leaned over and said, "She proud, master. Not like other women."

"Aye." Stoke kept his gaze on Lark.

"Proud women like a mare, need gentle handling and much stroking."

"I'll take your worldly advice under advisement."

"Your servant, master. Just come to Rashid when you need help with women." Rashid winked at him, finished tasting the rest of the food, then executed an exaggerated bow in Lark's direction.

She nodded, and a weak grin spread across her cheeks but didn't touch the sadness in her eyes. She sat along with all the other servants and his men, the scraping of their chairs the only sound in the hall now.

"You try eel, master," Rashid said.

Stoke took his spoon and tasted it. " 'Tis interesting. Something different."

Rashid did not look pleased with his master's assessment. "New recipe. I try to make better."

"No need, 'tis perfect."

Rashid exchanged a glance with Lark. She looked smug about something. In a petulant tone, Rashid said, "I go back to kitchen now. Work to do." He hurried from the hall.

He passed Dalia as she crossed the room with Varik in her arms. When Varik saw Lark, his voice carried around the room. "La'k! La'k! Eat wi'h La'k!"

"Nay, with yer papa," Dalia said.

Forthwith, his bottom lip stuck out in a pout. He glanced at Stoke, then back at Lark, looking torn between them. "La'k eat wi'h me and Faf-ee?" He addressed his question over Dalia's shoulder to Lark.

"Your place is with your father, Varik, not with me." Lark kept her voice firm, though the strength it cost her to keep it so showed in her face.

If Varik's lip stuck out any further, it might have touched his chin. Dalia set Varik down in the tiny chair Stoke had fashioned for him, curtsied, and strode over to Lark and sat beside her.

Rowland took the seat on the other side of Stoke, while Amory, Thomas, and Louis occupied the chairs next to Varik.

"I see you found your wayward Persephone in the village." Rowland grabbed a plump chicken breast from a trencher. Grease dripped down his hand as he took a bite of it.

"Aye, I found her." Stoke kept his voice low. "What did Louis do all afternoon?" He glanced at his cousin and found him staring at Lark. The hungry look in his eye made Stoke's brows snap together.

"He stayed in his room with Ebba. She could be involved in this. She may have been the one who poisoned Varik. And displaying the stone could be a ploy to keep us off track."

Stoke watched Ebba brushing her breasts against Jamus as

she poured wine into his cup. "Aye, I've thought of that. Keep an eye on her too. I trust her about as much as I trust Louis." Stoke handed Varik a spoon, all the while scowling at Louis. "While I was away, did you find out anything?"

"Nay, not a thing, but 'twas not for trying. Amory, Jamus, and I have kept watch on the servants and your retainers, yet still someone managed to poison Varik. I think we are fighting a losing battle, until we find out who is behind these attempts."

"We'll find the bastard." Stoke gritted his teeth.

"Soon, I hope."

Varik dropped a piece of bread in his lap, and Stoke bent over and picked it up, then threw it to Baltizar beneath the table. The sound of Baltizar's jaws clamping shut made Varik peek beneath the table and smile.

Rowland took another bite of chicken and swallowed. "What will you do with Lady Lark now?"

"I know not."

"Do you believe she's still involved in this scheme to kill you?"

"Not any longer."

"Have you informed her of that?"

"Nay, and I don't intend to."

"Have you forgotten she's a lady, whether you like to think of it or not? You cannot keep her here for very much longer against her will."

"I'll keep her as long as I like." Stoke grabbed his chalice. His hand tightened around the base now with such force, the hammered gold twisted in his hand. Elderberry wine dripped down over his fist and into his lap.

"Then we had better order more chalices to be made." Rowland handed him a corner of the tablecloth and grinned at the scowl on Stoke's face.

Across the room, Lark felt Stoke's eyes on her and ignored him. She bent closer to Dalia. "Which of Stoke's people do you believe capable of working with Lord Trevelyn?"

"I know not, me lady."

"What do you know of Thomas, the bailiff?"

"A wily little man. Never liked him meself, but he does his job. Worked for the master for over a year now." Dalia shrugged and jammed a large piece of meat pie into her mouth.

Lark felt Amory's and Rowland's gazes on her. "And what of Father Amory and Sir Rowland. Could they be helping Lord Trevelyn?"

"Nay, not Father Amory, he's good as gold. And Sir Rowland, well, he's been the master's neighbor for years. Known each other since they were in swaddlings. Nay, ain't Sir Rowland."

"I wonder who else it could be besides Ebba? Surely, there is someone else. Ebba said she was in her room with Lord Trevelyn when Varik was poisoned. I spoke to Father Amory, and he confirmed her story. There must be someone else besides Ebba."

"Speak of the she-devil . . ." Dalia motioned over at Ebba as she left Rowland's side and stood near Stoke, bending just the right way to brush breasts and hips against him.

Lark watched Ebba bend to speak to Stoke. One full breast almost pressed against his cheek as she ran her hands through his hair, smiling a coquette's smile. Something Lark had never been able to master.

Lark's gaze landed on a bowl of fruit sitting in front of her trencher. She reached out and plucked a nice red hard apple from the top, glanced hard at Ebba, and drew back.

Chapter 21

Dalia saw what Lark was about and grabbed her hand. "Oh, ye can't, me lady."

"But I want to." Lark narrowed her eyes at Ebba's head, judging the trajectory and how much strength it would take to send the apple smashing against that comely face.

"I know, but ye can't."

Lark's shoulders sagged as she dropped her hand to the table. "I suppose not. It would set a bad example for Varik." Lark opened her hand and allowed Dalia to pull the apple from it.

" 'Tis written all over yer face, ye care for the master."

"Nay, I do not," Lark said, a little too adamantly.

It earned her a raised eyebrow from Dalia. Unable to look at her, Lark stared down the food in the trencher. A fly landed on the side of the hollowed out bread. With a languid swat, she batted it away.

Dalia nodded and dropped the apple into the bowl. "There is no harm in admitting ye love him. Lord knows, he needs the love of a woman. Me mistress treated him bad and turned him bitter against loving. Ye might be able to change that. 'Tis clear he wants ye."

"What happened between them?"

"I didn't like it, not even from the start. I knew me mistress was doing wrong, and he so loved her at the start. She was a comely thing. Men worshiped at her feet."

"What did she do to him?"

"She fell in love with the son of Lord Breeden, her father's enemy. Lord Breeden had tried to take her father's land and war raged between them for years. Her father wouldn't let her see Lord Breeden's son, so she snuck out at night. The very week they planned to run away, he up and was thrown from his horse. Broke his neck, it did. She mourned so, her father arranged for the master to marry her, thinking it would cheer her. I begged her to tell the master the truth about her maidenhead being gone, but she wouldn't. Wouldn't even admit it to me—me who'd raised her. I knew her like I knew the back of me hand, and I knew she wasn't a virgin."

"So he found that out on the wedding night. It was stupid of her to lie to him."

"Aye, well, she reaped what she sowed." Dalia shook her head. "I'll never forget that night. 'Twas horrible. Never heard such ranting and raving. He wanted to send her back to her father, but she begged him not to. Oh, she got what was coming to her that night. Any other lord would have slit her throat, but he didn't. He took pity on her. Didn't touch her for a year just to make sure she wasn't with another man's bastard."

"Did she betray him again?"

"Nay, believe it or not, she grew to care for him, but 'twas too late. He could never love her back. He only wanted an heir off her. Went to her bed until he got her pregnant; then he stopped going at all and left for the Holy Land. I believe it was just to get away from her. Many a night, I'd hear her crying from loneliness. And I couldn't feel sorry for her, for she'd brought it all on herself. He got what he wanted though. 'Fore she died she gave birth to Master Varik."

"How tragic."

"Aye, but he loves that child."

Lark watched Stoke helping Varik butter a piece of bread.

He was such an attentive father. Lark glanced down at her own belly and frowned.

Dalia glanced at Lark. "You could be with child."

"Do not even think it. I cannot be carrying his child. I intend to leave here once Lord Trevelyn's guilt is proven and Stoke and Varik are safe."

"Ye may be wanting to leave here, but the master's mind is made up on ye. And once his mind be made up, he doesn't change it."

"He must, for I'll not remain the mistress of a man who only looks on me as his enemy and prisoner."

"What if he forces ye to marry him? Yer a lady. He's taken your maidenhead. 'Tis likely he'll be doing the proper thing and marrying ye."

"He hasn't mentioned marriage." Lark grimaced over at Stoke, who stared broodingly down at his trencher, then back at Dalia. "I'll not marry a man who doesn't trust me."

"It ain't in him to trust women." Dalia sighed. "After me mistress finished with him, he lost all faith in women. He guards his heart well now, but I do know he looks at ye the way he used to look at me mistress 'fore he married her."

"Only when he wants me to warm his bed, and for no other reason." Dalia's brows rose at Lark's blunt observation, but Lark ignored her and continued. "I'm only his prisoner and that is all. But I shall leave one day and he'll not stop me."

A worried frown marred Dalia's brow as she glanced at Baltizar. "Looks as if ye'll be leaving alone, me lady. You're wolf has taken up with Varik."

Lark glanced beneath Stoke's table at Baltizar, sitting beneath Varik's feet. "He does seemed confused these days about whether to stay with me or Varik and Stoke. I've always believed animals had an innate sense of danger—especially wolves, and I believe Baltizar's protector instincts are at work. He'll leave with me when the danger has passed."

Abruptly, the porter came running into the hall, his portly middle jiggling, his chest heaving.

The twitter of conversation died, the only sound the hiss from the coals in the hearth.

The porter paused near the dais, so out of breath that he had to bend over and clutch his knees to speak. "Me lord, there's a messenger at the gate, bearing the king's standard. Should I let him in?"

"Of course." Stoke waved the man away.

A few moments later, three mail-clad men entered the hall, their tabards striped with three gold lions on a red background. Their faces were partly covered by the nasal of their helms. The middle one bowed and spoke. "My lord, I've a missive from King Richard." He handed Stoke a piece of rolled parchment, the golden seal of the king gleaming in the candlelight.

Stoke took the proffered missive and motioned at the tables. "You must share our bounty."

The men nodded in agreement, then strode over to find a seat at the tables. Stoke bent behind Rowland's back and handed the missive to Amory. Not many lords could read, even Lark's father. Skills of a good lord meant he must have superb manners so as not to offend at court, know how to fight with honor and knightly prowess, and how to hunt. The lowly task of reading was left to priests and women. Lark had thought it a lowly pursuit as well, but she needed to be able to keep logs on her potions, and she begged the St. Vale priest to teach her.

Another challenge was finding a secret place, away from Elizabeth's harping, to pursue the art. Elizabeth thought Lark should spend her time on learning to spin, manage servants, and embroider. Since Lark failed miserably at all of those attributes, reading became one of her secret passions.

Amory cleared his throat in the silence, jarring Lark from her musing. He raised his head. All forty people in the hall leaned forward in their seats, eager to hear the news.

Amory seemed to know this, and he rerolled the missive with intricate slowness, taking his sweet time, as any priest would who held a captive audience. He cleared his throat and said to Stoke, "It says here, you are to be Richard's champion at a royal tourney to be given on the day after his second coronation in London Towne.''

"I see he favors you over me." Louis cut his eyes at Stoke.

"It appears so."

"There is no accounting for taste."

Stoke glowered at his cousin for the remark. They looked ready to pounce on each other. In her mind's eye, Lark could see Louis pulling out a weapon and bludgeoning Stoke. It would be just like him to attack unexpectedly, just as he had when Stoke wrestled with him in the tilt yard. But would he attack himself, or would it be the person working with him? Lark had to find out who else was involved with him besides Ebba.

Something else bothered her too. She could not forget the way Stoke had forbidden her entrance into his shop. A memory had haunted her all day, that of hearing her father and Stoke speaking about Dragon's Eye. Her father had said Stoke could be a rich man if he started an armory. The metal he had used to craft his own sword must be exceptional if it was hard enough to cut through German steel. She shouldn't pry. She had no right in the world. If he ever found out, he would probably explode into a rage, but her pride was still stinging and her curiosity kept calling out to be satisfied.

One little peek couldn't hurt. She glanced down at the pouch hanging around her waist. Earlier, Amory had fetched the sleeping draught the leach had left for Varik in case she needed it in the village. The vial was still half full.

Later that evening, Lark leaned back in a chair, her long legs crossed at the ankles, listening to the hiss of the fire. She felt Stoke's eyes on her and glanced up to the table where he sat opposite one the king's emissaries, a chessboard between them.

Firelight flickered off Stoke's raven hair, shooting grayish-blue highlights along the waving mass. A wolfish look gleamed in his eyes. It was obvious he was growing impatient to take her to his bed.

The man Stoke played against sat studying his king and

scratching the red stubble on his chin. He appeared unaware of his opponent's restlessness.

Rowland and Amory and Jamus watched the game from their chairs. Thankfully, Louis and Ebba had retired for the evening, for Lark was sure if Ebba had flirted with Stoke much longer, she would have attacked the wench.

Lark glanced back at the pitcher of wine left on one of the tables. Her hand touched the pouch at her waist and she impatiently fingered the suede. To hurry the game along, she yawned and graced Stoke with a coy come-hither smile.

Stoke's gaze raked over her body. He shifted impatiently in his chair and scowled at his opponent.

"It looks as if you'll be here for a while," Lark said, holding back a grin. "Shall I refill your cups, my lord?"

He scrutinized her for a moment, nodded, and frowned at his opponent. "Are you going to make a move by Michalmas?"

The redheaded man grunted, then moved his king.

Lark knew the game would be over soon, for the move was a stupid one. Her hand trembled ever so slightly as she grabbed the cups and hurried over to the table. Making sure her back was to them, she reached in the pouch, eased out the vial, and dumped the sleeping draught in the wine. She stuffed the empty vial back in the pouch, then swirled the cup. Satisfied that the powder had dissolved, she hurried back to the table.

By the time she reached it, Stoke had checkmated his opponent's king.

"By damn, you're a wily one." The redheaded man bowed to Stoke.

Lark thrust the cups in their hands. "Here you are."

Stoke and the man set the cups down at the same time and stood. "A good game, sir. I'm for my bed." He grabbed Lark's hand. "Come with me."

Lark glanced at the cups on the table and snatched up the one she thought was Stoke's. The wine sloshed over on her hand as she allowed Stoke to guide her across the hall. When they reached the stairs, Lark paused and held the cup out to him. "Your wine, my lord."

"Better be careful, Lark, you are beginning to make yourself indispensable to me—not that I'm complaining. I like this caring side of you. What has brought it about?"

"I just thought you might be thirsty."

"I am." He brought her hand up and licked the wine off the back of her fingers, his tongue hot and rough against her skin. "But I'd rather have you," he whispered, eyeing her over the rim of the cup.

Lark felt her insides warming at the look in his eyes. "I've heard my brothers say wine excites sexual desire. What do you say, my lord?" A teasing grin stretched her lips.

"I say, I need naught to excite me when you're near me," he drawled, cocking a brow at her.

"Then I'll drink it." Lark pulled her hand out of his and turned up the glass. She drank a sip, though if anyone looked at her they would swear she was drinking the whole thing.

Stoke snatched it from her. "Here, you'll fall asleep ere I get you to my bed." He turned up the glass and guzzled it down.

Lark watched him, wide-eyed, as he set the glass down on a step. He clasped his hand in hers and guided her up the stairs.

When they reached the top, Dalia came striding toward them. "Master Varik won't go to sleep until the both of you tell him good night."

Lark frowned at Stoke. Would he make it to his chamber ere he collapsed? They followed Dalia down the hallway, their footsteps keeping time with her pounding heart.

They found Varik sitting up in his bed, blowing on a flute. Every off-key note made Baltizar's ears flinch.

"You should save your practicing 'til morn." Stoke took the flute away, hugged Varik, and ruffled his hair. "Good night, little liege."

"Nigh', Faf-ee." Varik glanced at Lark and raised his hands toward her. "Nigh' nigh', La'k."

Lark stared down at the chubby little arms opened wide for her, at the black curly hair falling down a diminutive brow and along a face no wider than her splayed hand. Sweet innocence radiated in the smile stretching his cheeks, the small gap between his baby teeth showing. Two-year-old little boys should not be so adorable, nor so easy to love. She felt a lump growing in her throat as she bent and hugged him.

"Good night, Sir Varik, take care of your dreams. Do not slay too many dragons." She felt his arms tighten around her neck.

"Me won'."

"We should go," Stoke said behind her back, impatience in his voice.

She meant to just pull away, but she felt Varik's soft cheek brush her face and she could not help but place a tiny kiss on it. As she rose, Baltizar hopped up onto the bed.

"Well, I see where you are spending the night." She rubbed her hand over his muzzle.

He nudged her hand with his nose, licked it, and settled down beside Varik's legs.

"That wolf shouldn't be on the bed." Dalia spoke from where she stood holding a candle near her own cot.

" 'Tis all right." Stoke slipped his hand in Lark's and eased her toward the door.

"And he'll protect Varik," Lark added. "Make sure you keep the door locked."

"Aye, miss, nary a soul will get in here."

After one more glance at Varik, who was busy smiling and getting a hand washing from Baltizar's tongue, Lark and Stoke slipped out of the room. They waited for metal to clank against wood as Dalia threw home the bolt; then Stoke led her down the hallway.

Muted yellow shadows from a torch flicked across the walls and floor, making the black velvet of Stoke's tunic glow with a golden hue.

Lark glanced at his face. Not a sign the draught was working. Did she pick up the wrong cup? She listened to their footsteps melding together, and asked, "What of this tourney? Surely you're not contemplating going."

"How can I refuse the king?"

"It is an honor," Lark said, her voice full of pride for him. "But you will be an easy target."

"Are you worried?" He searched her eyes.

"Of course I am."

"That is good to hear, for you'll be going with me." His gaze slid down her body, taking in the unbecoming brown wool gown hanging loosely on her. "We should have Dalia make some gowns for you."

"Nay, I can't go to court."

"You'll go where I go." He bent so he could peer into her eyes. "Do I detect fear in you?"

She swallowed hard. " 'Tis just that I've never been to court."

"Your father never took you?" Stoke asked, his tone incredulous.

"My mother said I was not fit to meet the king. Which suited me, for I was sure I would do naught but offend him and probably have my father's lands confiscated by a usurper. So when my father was forced to go, I stayed home with one of my brothers to mind St. Vale. It didn't bother me, really. There was a time when I would have liked to go to see what it was like, but hearing Helen's stories of the gabby ladies-in-waiting and their dour sewing parties cured me of that notion quick as a wink. It would be like hell to be trapped in such a circle for all of an afternoon. Do you not think so?"

He laughed, a deep, rich sound, the first laughter she had heard from him in hours. "I see your point," he said, sobering.

Before Lark knew it, Stoke had swept her into his chamber. It seemed so natural to walk into his chamber, feeling his strong arms around her. It almost felt as if they were married and had been so for a lifetime. But they were not. They were strangers in every way except physically. He knew every inch of her body, but he did not know the real Lark, the person worthy of his trust and love.

He closed the door and pulled her into his arms. One of the servants had lit a candle and left it in a candlestick on the mantle. The glow from the candle set the tarry blackness of his hair ablaze. Light flicked over his chiseled jaw, making the skin beneath the stubble there glow golden. His dark lashes hid his eyes from her, for he was gazing down at her body, caressing her with his eyes.

He didn't have to touch her. His gaze was enough to cause that familiar stirring way down deep in the pit of her belly. If she had her wits, she should pull back from him.

Wits.

Those had left her the moment they entered his chamber.

The saints help her, but she would lie with him again. She would steal these few moments of bliss. One day she would have to leave him, for she wouldn't remain his prisoner or his mistress.

He bent and captured her lips. Never breaking the kiss, he swept her up in his arms and carried her to his bed. Gently, he laid her down and with maddening slowness eased down on top of her.

The weight of his body settled down on her, pushing her deeper into the feather mattress. She groaned inwardly at the sheer hardness of him, touching her everywhere, the very fiber of her skin aware of every inch of him.

He cupped her breasts, kneading, teasing her nipples into hard nubs beneath her gown and shift. She wrapped her legs around his thighs and her arms around his waist, then pulled him as tightly to her as she could.

His lips pressed harder against her mouth, while his hips undulated against her. She could feel his hardness pressing against her, sending wave after wave of heat coursing through her. He plunged his tongue into her mouth, all the gentleness gone from his lips. They took possession of her now, urgent in their need. One of his hands left her breasts and he yanked up the hem of her gown.

With clumsy fingers, she freed his manhood. He thrust into her. Their lovemaking grew to a fevered pitch, each clinging to the other. She glanced up at him and caught him staring down at her, his eyes searching hers for something. But what?

Any moment she felt she would break apart. All coherent

thought left her mind. She squeezed her eyes closed and forgot about the draught she'd given him and that probing look in his eyes.

Fifteen minutes later, Lark's fears that she'd given Stoke the wrong cup finally dissolved. He drifted off to sleep. She could hear his heavy breathing above the pop of the fire in the hearth. It wasn't one of his light sleeps, for he was snoring. His burly arms cuddled her as they lay spooned together on the bed, his chest against her back, the triangle of black hair there rubbing against the top of her spine. This is what she would miss most of all when she left—lying beside him, feeling him close to her, the heat of his hard body melding with her own, the pulsing of his heart. A heart that would never love her.

She grimaced, rose on her elbow, and shook him. He groaned and rolled onto his back, his snoring growing louder. She glanced down at his boots. Firelight softly flickered along the leather edges where they lay on the floor.

Sure that he wouldn't wake now, she eased her hair from beneath his arm and crept out of bed. Cool air in the room hit her warm, naked back, and she immediately missed the heat of his body. Watching his handsome face all the while to make sure he stayed asleep, she slid over to the edge of the bed and gingerly left it. She glanced back to see if he'd awakened, but he hadn't moved, still wearing a sated male smile.

She slipped on her gown, then tiptoed over to his boots. When she looked inside, she could find naught but his dagger. No key. But she'd seen him pick it out of his boot. Curious now, she turned the tops of the boots down, but couldn't find a secret compartment, nor was there anything in the soles. He had to have gotten the key from somewhere. After searching his clothes thoroughly, she snatched a candle and a tinder box from the mantel and left the room.

It didn't take her long to reach the bailey. Torches burned on the walls, and she could see two guards pacing above her. The cold stones brushed her bare feet as she moved along the walls, her senses attuned to any sound. Something large and white padded across her path. She froze. So did a large white cat. They eyed each other with marked suspicion, two prowlers in the night, each on her own mission.

The cat didn't stop to be petted, but darted into the mews. Lark eased over to the workshop, listening to the flutter of wings from the mews. She couldn't help but grin before hurring to the workshop door.

She had only a few moments before the guards made another pass. She ran her hands along the stanchion, looking for a hidden compartment. Over the top. Down along the bottom. Abruptly, the sound of footsteps grew louder. The way she was standing, the light from a torch flickered on the hem of her gown, a beacon for the guards.

Frantic now, she dove beneath the shadows of the eaves and pressed her back against the wall of the workshop, holding her breath. The uneven stones pressed through the wool of her gown, the coolness of the granite seeping into her shoulders and back.

The heavy tread of the guards' footsteps sounded like wet clothes slapping against a rock. Then they faded.

She almost gave up, but as she pushed back to stand, her hand brushed a loose stone near the base of the door. It moved freely against her fingertips. Something flat and smooth poked out between the cracked mortar joints and brushed her palm. She recognized the feel of the slender metal. A key.

Footsteps echoed, getting closer. The guards again. With trembling hands, she worked the lock and slipped inside. The hinges of the door creaked. She grimaced as she pushed it closed.

The acrid odor of molten metal and smoke filled the air. She struck the flint and lit the candle. A globe of light flooded the room. A workbench ran along the length of the walls. Iron tools of every description stood on pegs over it. Vises, casts, spools of thread, pots of wax, and large chunks of iron ore cluttered the bench. In the middle of the room sat a huge caldron and over it a pulley. Lark saw what she knew was a potter's kiln off in a hearth in the corner. She strode toward it.

Abruptly, the door flew open.

Lark jumped in mid-stride and dropped the candle, catching a glimpse of the fury on Stoke's face before the flame went out.

"What the hell are you doing in here?" His speech was slurred, yet the words came out with the same intensity of a sword slicing through the air.

Lark backed away from him. Her bottom hit the edge of the bench and she froze. "S-since you wouldn't let me in, I was just curious about your shop."

"Your curiosity satisfied?" Stoke staggered over to her, grabbed her arm, and pulled her outside. He slammed the door, then fumbled with the key Lark had left in the lock.

When he couldn't master it, Lark shoved his hands away, locked the door, and handed the key back to him.

He snatched it from her. "You drugged me, didn't you?"

"Evidently not enough." A wave of dizziness must have caught him, for he fell against the door. "What woke you?"

"I'm immune to such trickery. The moment you left the bed, I woke and knew you were up to something." Lark tried to steady him, but he shoved her hands away. "How did you find my key?" he growled.

"It was an accident, really. You have the perfect hidey hole for it."

"Evidently it's not hidden well enough to keep dissembling, meddling wenches like you out of it." Stoke grabbed her arm and pulled her toward the hall, half leaning on her to stay up. "I knew I should have chained you to my side. I shall in the future, and I'll know better than to drink anything you give me."

"I only—"

"I know what you wanted."

"Please don't be angry with me. I just wanted to see where you spent so much time. I thought you were afraid of fire. How is that you can work in there around it? You must need an awful lot of heat to melt the ore.''

He hesitated a moment, then said, ''I force myself to face my fear. Once I start to work on a piece, and the metal is melted, I forget about the fire.''

''Why is there a potter's kiln in your workshop? You're not a potter.''

''Ask another question, and I'm going to make it impossible for you to sit for a month.''

The scathing ire in his voice made Lark clamp her mouth closed. After a moment of feeling him dragging her across the bailey, his strong fingers biting into her wrist, she said, ''I'll not tell anyone what I've seen in your workshop, if that is what is bothering you.''

''I know you shall not, for this seals your fate.''

''What do you mean?'' He jerked Lark through the door into the hall.

The door slammed closed behind her.

He paused and glared down at her. ''This means we'll have to marry.''

''Marry?'' Lark blurted the word so loudly, it echoed through the hall. Positive she'd awakened the sleeping servants, she lowered her voice, hissing at him, ''I'll not be joined to a man who doesn't trust me.'' She didn't add, *or love me.* ''Being your prisoner was bad enough. Why not keep me as your prisoner?''

''Your father will eventually come for you. I'll not give you over, so 'tis best we marry to avoid a war. You'll do what I say.'' Belying the words uttered between his clenched jaw, he pulled her against his chest and squeezed her until she couldn't breathe.

''I won't,'' she gasped.

''You will. We'll marry in the morn.''

''You can't make me agree to it.''

''I'll find a way to change your mind.'' He bent and kissed her.

Lark struggled, aware of his powerful arms crushing her, the heat of his lips against hers, the way his chest rubbed her breasts with his deep, angry breaths. She couldn't think. He was using her passion against her, but she couldn't give in to this demand. She wouldn't.

"I do." Lark uttered the words so softly, Amory was forced to lean forward to hear her.

Stoke merely glowered at her, looking impatient.

Lark stared down at the altar. She felt as if this were her funeral service rather than her wedding day. A storm raged outside. Rain battered the rose window in the chapel. A pall hung in the vast empty space, a clap of thunder breaking it every now and then. Stoke allowed no one else in the chapel save Rowland, Varik, and Dalia, and they stood behind them.

Lark felt the tight grip Stoke's hand had on her fingers, knowing it wasn't because he loved her, but because she'd seen his workshop and he wasn't about to let her get away. She couldn't put up a fight, for she knew if she went home, Stoke would not give up until he'd caused a war with her father. And what if she were with child as Dalia had so recently pointed out? Lark had wanted to deny it, but it could happen. If she were to bring a bastard into the world, she could not bear to see the disappointed and shamed look on her father's face. She could not have that on her conscience.

Before Lark realized it, Amory had finished the wedding service. Stoke eased her up to her feet, wrapped his arms around her, and kissed her. Lark's heart wasn't in the kiss, but in the tortured years ahead of her, of loving a man who could never return her love.

He pushed back from her and whispered, "You may not like this, but get used to it, Lark, or 'twill be only strife between us."

Another bolt of lightning flashed through the chapel. Thunder rolled, shaking the very foundation. Lark closed her eyes against the omen.

Abruptly the doors to the chapel swung open.

Chapter 22

Lark gasped. That repressed superstitious voice in her half expected to see Satan at the door. She gazed at the cloaked figure. No devil, just a monk. She let out the breath she'd been holding and watched the clergyman's cloak blow around his square frame and face.

He stepped across the threshold and closed the heavy door behind him. It banged, the sound at odds with the pounding of rain and hail against the chapel roof. He shook the rain from his hood and strode toward them, his brown cowl dripping around his sandaled feet. A dark trail of water followed him down the aisle. He paused in front of Stoke and bowed. "Forgive this intrusion, my lord, but Abbot Hadrian begs that you come to him right away. We've found two men you need to question."

"So soon," Stoke said, pleased. "Abbot Hadrian has indeed been busy. I'll come right away."

Abruptly, the door opened again.

Jamus ran into the chapel. Lightning flashed behind him, freezing his frame in a flash of light for a moment. He slammed the door closed and could hardly speak through his rapid breaths. "M-my l-lord, I'm s-sorry, but Lord T-Trevelyn j-just left the c-castle."

"Follow him, Jamus."

Rowland stepped toward him. "I'll go with him."

"Nay, I need you to go with me. I'm taking Varik and Dalia to the abbey."

Dalia turned, her expression incredulous as she held Varik in her arms. Varik looked mesmerized by the sight of the monk.

"You're taking Varik because of me." Lark fought the tightness forming in her throat.

"I'm taking him because the last time I left him, someone poisoned him. If something should happen to him again, 'twill rest on my shoulders and not yours."

"I don't believe that. You still don't trust me. You never will," Lark said, hiding her pain beneath a tone of resignation.

He stiffened from the accusation. "Believe what you will, just be here when I return."

"I'll make no promises."

He gripped her arms and peered down at her, his eyes scouring her face. "You'd better be here ere I return."

"I may go for a long visit to see my father. He hasn't been told yet, you know."

"You'll not leave here without me to escort you. You'll wait and we'll go together." He scrutinized her a moment longer, then kissed her and hugged her with a fierceness that crushed the air from her chest. Wearing a solemn expression, he stepped back from her and strode away.

Lark watched his shoulders move with each of his stiff strides. When he reached the door, Lark called out to him, "Watch your back."

He glanced hard at her, his expression inscrutable. Then he turned and followed the monk outside.

Lark watched Amory, Rowland, Dalia, and Varik all leave the chapel. Amory smiled sadly, a look of compassion and regret on his face. Rowland, too, looked more solemn than she'd ever seen him. Varik was humming and playing with

Dalia's braid. He paused and waved to her over Dalia's shoulder.

"Come, La'k."

Lark shook her head. "Not this time." Lark watched them hurry out into the storm.

As she watched the rain blowing in through the chapel door, a knot began forming in the back of her throat. If it was the last thing she ever did, she would gain his trust. Somehow. Someday.

She heard footsteps behind her and saw Jamus striding down the aisle. "I'm going with you," she told him.

"N-nay, y-you c-can't d-do that. You heard him."

"If you don't let me go with you, Jamus, I'll sneak out and follow you. I want to help you keep an eye on Louis. I know he's the person trying to kill Stoke, and he'll try again soon."

Jamus gazed at the determined look on her face, shook his head, and shrugged.

After Stoke had ridden out, Lark and Jamus took their leave of Kenilworth. Up in a tower, Ebba stood at the window, her eyes on Lark. She smiled as she moved away, the soft tread of her footsteps whispering down the stairwell of the tower.

Several hours later, Stoke left Rowland, Amory, and Baltizar guarding Varik in the abbey garden. Abbot Hadrian ambled beside him, his cane making a sucking sound in the mud. The rain had stopped, and a rainbow arched across the sky.

Stoke listened to his and the abbot's footsteps slush through the mud. The elder beside him, back hunched, cane swinging, moved with a swiftness that belied his age.

"We have the men, my lord. They are in our prison," Abbot Hadrian said.

"And how did you capture them?"

"God's hand has a wide reach—you should know that after fighting infidels in the Holy Land." Abbot Hadrian turned, an almost wicked grin on his face.

"How did you find them?"

"I sent out the brothers and we questioned everyone we encountered about the two men posing as monks. The trail led us to a village. The villagers knew of the two men and said they had seen them talking to the men who hired them. As God would have it, those two men who hired the killers were raised in that village and had family there. We found them in a nearby inn, over-imbibing and wenching. The village is not too far from your own Kenilworth."

Stoke followed the abbot out into a courtyard. In the center was a round fish pond. Large golden carp darted among lily pads. They passed a group of monks carrying hay rakes on their shoulders. Abbot Hadrian nodded a greeting to them, then finally came to a small conical building. He waved his staff toward it. "You'll find them inside. I regret they are none too happy about being here, so be careful."

"I shall."

"You'll find the key to the locks hanging by the door." The abbot turned and strode back toward the fish pond.

A small window, no wider than a man's head, was set into the side of the prison. The stench of perspiration, human excrement, and dampness emanated from the small portal. Impatiently, Stoke grabbed the keys hanging from a large iron ring and opened the door.

He was forced to bend down to step into the cylindrical room. Straw covered the ground. Pairs of manacles hung around the curved walls. The last two sets imprisoned the wrists of two men. They glanced up at the sound of his footsteps. Stoke recognized the droopy eye and scarred face of the two men he'd dismissed for badgering Lark at St. Vale.

"What have we here?" Stoke said, jingling the keys in his hand.

"Me lord, we didn't do it." Sills spoke, his droopy eye twitching.

"Aye, we're glad ye come. These monks are crazy." Sweat poured down Torr's scarred face.

"If you think these monks are insane, you haven't seen what

I'm capable of doing." Stoke pulled his dagger from his boot and ran his hand along the edge.

"We didn't do naught, me lord." A drop of sweat ran down Torr's nose and dropped onto his tunic.

He glared at Torr. "I hope you keep lying. I haven't tortured a man since the Holy Land."

Torr flinched under Stoke's gaze. Then his mouth screwed up into a grimace.

"It was all his idea." Sills motioned toward his companion, the chains on his wrists clanging against the stone wall.

"Shut up, you dolt!" Torr yelled.

"Nay, I ain't dying for ye."

"You'll die anyway when I kill ye."

"Try it."

"What was his idea?" Stoke said, breaking into their argument.

Both men clamped their mouths shut. Then Sills said, "Taking the money for hiring those two murderers."

"Who gave it to you?"

Torr saw Sills open his mouth and blurted, "The person will have us killed if we tell ye."

"I'll kill you if you don't." Stoke thrust his dagger beneath Sills's neck and had the pleasure of seeing him flinch and jerk his neck up.

"All right, me lord, we'll tell!"

"Better be the truth, or I'll know your lying."

"'Tis the truth."

"Then tell it." Stoke glared at Torr, keeping the anxiety from his expression.

"Will you spare our lives?" Sills asked in a wheedling voice.

"We'll see. I'm not in the habit of allowing my enemies to live, but if your story proves true, I might feel more tolerant toward you."

" 'Twill, me lord." Sills nodded.

"It better." Stoke's weariness of tracking this silent nemesis came through in his voice. Now he would have him.

" 'Twas Ebba, me lord."

Stoke's eyes narrowed at Sills. "You'd better not be lying."

"For God and all, I be tellin' the truth. She gave us the money to hire those two killers and said if we didn't keep our mouths shut about it, she'd see we were killed too."

Stoke scowled as he remembered that Ebba was at the castle with Lark. He whipped around and ran out the door.

Two days later, Lark slowed her roan near Jamus. They had followed Lord Trevelyn here, to the banks of the Thames. Redolent of moss, fish, and fresh water, the odor of the river wafted beneath her nose. A thick line of trees blocked her view of the water, the smell letting her know she'd been downwind of it for the past twenty miles, all the way from London Towne.

Something large and white caught her eye. She glanced at the round tower of Windsor Castle. It rose above the castle's white heath-stone walls on a central mound. Laid out like a butterfly, the castle's round tower and its circular walls formed the central body, the upper and lower baileys rising from either side like misshapen wings. Square turrets rose from the two baileys at strategic intervals. She could see the royal colors of the king flying along the walls on tall poles, letting everyone know His Majesty was in residence.

Beyond the moat, a city of tents stretched for what looked like miles. Lark guessed the king had probably ousted his troops in order to make room for his many loyal vassals.

When Lark spotted the long line to get into Windsor Castle, she jerked hard on the reins. Horses, knights, servants, and wains of every description snaked in a curving line to the gate. The bright, expensive samite and shimmery sendal silk of the noble ladies' gowns and veils checkered the winding mass. Servants tending livestock hovered around their masters' wains. The two servants in front of her were sitting on the ground with their charges, a pair of black swans and a peacock. Lark listened to their discordant squawks and thought them fitting gifts for the king. It appeared everyone in Christendom was eager to wish their king well in his second coronation.

Lark kicked her destrier and trotted to the end of the line, Jamus at her side.

" 'T-tis a jumble," Jamus remarked.

Lark studied the line of people. "Do you see Lord Trevelyn?"

Jamus nodded and pointed. "That's his st-standard there, with the t-two d-dragons on it."

Lark followed the line of his finger, past the other pennons flapping on poles, to a bright red square striped with two rearing dragons. Through the mass of humanity and livestock separating them, Lark spotted the backs of a group of knights, their red tabards bright on their shoulders.

"I really don't wish to meet the king, Jamus, but I suppose we must if we are to follow Lord Trevelyn and see whom he speaks with. Let us move a little closer to him?"

Jamus nodded. "M-mayhap I should r-ride ahead. T-two will m-make him s-suspicious."

"Very well, I'll wait here. Let me know the moment he moves." Lark watched him ride off and noticed the lists in a far field.

Large tents of various sizes lined both sides of the field. Hammers rang out in a discordant beat as workmen constructed a long wooden gallery, the stepped seats rising twenty- and thirty-high into the air. In the middle jutted a dais for the king. Tapestries bearing the Plantagenet red and gold flew over the fenced sides. The spectacle of a royal tourney awakened the excitement of battle in Lark. Never having seen one, she had dreamed about what the royal lists would look like. The grand scale of it far surpassed anything she'd ever imagined.

"By my teeth! Look at this. We should have stayed in London."

Lark's head perked up at the sound of the voice. She had loved the deep timbre of it since she'd first recognized it as a young child. William Mandeville's voice. She began to turn around, but the next voice made her freeze.

"But we are nobility." Lark cringed at the sound of her mother's words. "We have every right to be entertained by

Richard. He'll not turn us away. We should have arrived sooner. I told you we should have, but you wanted to wait in case she returned with . . ." She sounded too angry to speak and her words trailed off.

"Don't worry, Elizabeth, Helen will find a new hasty-witted beau soon enough." Leather creaked as her father turned in the saddle. "Just take care, Helen, to drag him to the altar ere he runs off again—though if he leaves my coffers as full as Lord Blackstone did, I could easily make a living by your suitors changing their minds."

"I don't want a husband, Father. I'm never going to marry."

Lark almost turned around at the petulant tone in Helen's voice. Had that really been her biddable, meek sister uttering such sharp words? Lark wanted to applaud her, give her a look of encouragement, but she couldn't risk discovery.

"Don't let this one little mishap with that horrible beast Lord Blackstone taint your life forever," Elizabeth said, her voice having an unfamiliar pleading tone in it. "Once the eligible lords see you at court, we'll certainly have you married off by May Day."

"I don't want to be married off. I've decided never to marry. I'll take the veil first."

"Nay, you cannot," Elizabeth screeched. "It would kill me to see you in a convent. I'll never see that hoyden sister of yours married now, but you'll marry, that's all there is to it."

"I'll not. I'd rather be roasted alive."

"Speak to her, William."

With fatherly wisdom in his voice, tainted with a bit of dry wit, William said, "Beseems a waste if your mother dies if you go to a convent . . . then again, I would hate to see you roasted alive. Though, I must admit, it pleases me no end to hear you give voice to an opinion of your own. I thought never to hear one. I give you leave to do what you like, my daughter."

"William, you did that on purpose!" Elizabeth screeched.

Lark could feel the warmth of a grin on her father's face. How she'd missed him.

The line advanced, and Lark watched as Lord Trevelyn's

group moved toward the gates, ahead of everyone. A rider bearing the king's standard lead them forward. She heard her father mumble a curse about the king's favorites.

If she could just ease away unnoticed, she'd be free to join Jamus. She gathered the reins and guided the roan around a male servant holding a peacock.

"Lark, child, is that you?" Lady Lucinda's round face poked out of the window in the closed wain. Her eyes widened. "'Tis you. Bless my feet!"

Lark gestured frantically at her to be quiet.

"What are you doing, Lark? Are there flies hereabout? I hope not. I thought the king would try to control those horrible pests. I was just telling Sir Joseph I thought I heard your mother. Where is she?" Lady Lucinda glanced behind Lark and waved frantically. "There she is. I see her—and dear sweet Helen. Such a horrible bother about her marriage. And you my dear—how bad of you not to come to your own wedding. But we didn't let any of your mother's food go to waste." Lady Lucinda turned back and glanced inside. "Did we, husband?"

She didn't wait for answer, but whipped back around and said, "What luck meeting you here. I thought I should die without anyone to speak to. Sir Joseph doesn't listen to a word I say. You must come in here and keep us company. Why are you in your armor, child?"

Lark hoped the armor she had borrowed from one of Stoke's retainers would have given her cover, but that was not to be.

"Pigeon!" William's bellow drowned out Lady Lucinda's voice.

Lark cringed at her father's bellow, and the back of her helm clanged against her armor. She turned and saw William, his golden brows meeting over his eyes.

"Lark!" Helen cried as she hopped down from the wain, where Marta sat staring at Lark, her parchment-thin skin stretched across her gaunt cheeks in a look of disapproval. But her expression looked jovial compared to Elizabeth's countenance.

Helen paused near Lark and blurted, "I've been so worried about you." She reached up to touch Lark's hand.

"You needn't have been." Lark grasped her hand tightly, looked down into her large, doe-like eyes, seeing the worry there. The guileless trust in Helen's eyes went right to the quick of Lark's heart.

"What is wrong, Lark?" Helen looked at her. "Are you unwell? Your face is flushed. You must get that armor off. 'Tis a hot day for March."

"Truly, I'm fine." Lark shifted nervously in the saddle. No doubt Helen had decided not to marry for the simple reason that she still wanted Stoke. How could Lark tell her they were married?

"I know something must be wrong. Will you not tell me what it is?"

William cleared his throat.

Lark glanced over Helen at him. Keen, knowing eyes met Lark's. There was no escaping the green sternness in them; it bored right through her.

She shifted in her saddle and swallowed hard. The thumping of footsteps made her glance over Helen's head to see Elizabeth, her blue veil flapping near her shoulders with each stiff step. For the first time in Lark's life, she welcomed the sight of her mother—until she looked into Elizabeth's eyes. A winter wind off the fells couldn't have struck Lark any colder.

Her mother paused next to Helen. "Where have you been all this time? Do you know the shame you heaped upon our good names? I die when I think of having had to face all those guests. It was horrible, just horrible—so wicked of you."

Before Lark could answer her, Elizabeth continued with her tirade. "Have you stopped to think about the trouble you caused? We heard not a word from you. Your father had his suspicions where you were, but the least you could have done was sent word that you were unharmed. I have been worried sick." Elizabeth paused. That her own words surprised her showed on her face.

Lark, too, raised her brows. It was the first time Elizabeth had ever openly expressed any worry over Lark. She had harped enough, pointed out every fatal flaw in Lark, but never had she said, "I was worried about you."

The unprecedented moment was tainted by Elizabeth's next words. "Did you think to appear before King Richard dressed like that? We'll all be tossed off our barony. Have you naught a care for even the king's opinion of you? What were you thinking, Lark, coming here in armor?"

"Evidently I don't think." Lark sighed under her breath, feeling the hope that her mother actually loved her dying a quick death.

"We must find you a gown."

"I could help," Lady Lucinda said from her window. "Please allow me to do that. I would love it. I've seen several other ladies I know with young daughters. Mayhap they can help us, though I don't think any of them are as tall as Lark."

"Lady L, how kind of you. I did see the Marquis of Lor's wife. I know she has a daughter almost as tall as Lark. We could borrow a dress from her, until I find suitable material and make a gown for her to be presented to the king." Eager to find the lady in question, Elizabeth glanced down the long line.

"She did not come here to meet the king." William rested his hands over the pommel of his saddle and eyed Lark for an explanation.

"Why did you come here?" Helen asked.

"I came to trail the man who . . ." Lark paused, the sound of hooves drawing her attention. Her insides clenched as she watched Evel, Avenall, and the twins gallop toward her. The moment she'd dreaded was fast upon her.

Avenall reached her first. He reined in next to her father and stared at Lark, his handsome face with the hardest set to it she'd ever seen. "Why did you run away on our wedding night?"

Lark opened her mouth to speak, but Evel cut her off. "Do you realize we've been scouring the countryside for you?"

"How did Harold and Cedric find you?" This from Helen.

"We were helping a young woman on the road, who was accosted by ruffians. Harold happened to spot the fray.

'Tis a good thing too, or we'd still be out there looking for Lark." Evel cut his blue eyes at her. "I thought I might find you here."

" 'Tis just like her to cause mischief," Cedric and Harold spoke at the same time. "If we had not gone into London Towne for a visit, we would have never found Evel, and Avenall."

Lark glowered back at them.

"Where is Blackstone? Surely he is with you." William surveyed the crowded line for a sign of him.

"Blackstone! What would he have to do with this?" Avenall never took his eyes off Lark as he spoke.

"I believe Lark was about to tell us that." William leveled a pointed look at his daughter.

Lark wrapped the reins around one palm, until her hand turned white and her fingers felt numb. She couldn't bear to look at Avenall, so she gazed down at her hands and spoke. "Well, I . . ."

Her voice was drowned out by thundering hooves, a pounding so loud that Lark felt the vibration in her chest. She clamped her mouth closed and turned. Ten knights on horseback filled her vision, all in black tabards. A red dragon hissed and flapped on a black pennon carried by one of them. In the fore, a massive knight rode, decked in all-black armor, dull in the sunlight. It was armor made for killing, not for exhibition. The nasal of his black helm hid his nose, only two eyes gazed out at her. Stoke's eyes.

Chapter 23

He drew closer, his aura saturating the air as darkness saturates the night sky. Sunlight hit the stone in the hilt of his sword and glinted in her eyes. Momentarily blinded, she blinked and moved her head, watching people scramble to get out of his way. She'd never seen him in full armor. He looked invincible.

Lark swallowed hard as Stoke's destrier came to a stomping halt beside her. Helen and Elizabeth stepped back near the wain, giving him a wide berth. Behind him, his entourage paused, Amory and Rowland among them. Another six knights surrounded Dalia and Varik's wain.

Varik spied her and called out, "La'k! La'k!"

She waved to him. "Hello, Sir Varik."

"Miss you!"

"Take him inside." Stoke motioned to Dalia and the knights.

The wain rolled past her on the way to the castle. Varik turned around and waved his little hand at her. Rowland and Amory acknowledged her with a nod as they passed. Baltizar's head popped up from the back of the wain. He rested his chin on the side and stared at her. The sight of her old friend brought a smile to her face, but it disappeared the moment her gaze clashed with Stoke's.

His expression remained inscrutable, save for the fire in his eyes and the pulsing of a jaw muscle. He said not a word to her, but turned and addressed her father.

"I must inform you, sir, your daughter is married to me." Stoke threw the words out like fireballs. They sizzled through the air.

Elizabeth gasped, breaking the drought of words. Tears glistened in Helen's eyes. Unable to look at her, Lark stared down at her chain mail.

"I'll not ask your reasons for marrying my daughter without my permission, for I already know them," William said.

"You've known about this all along?" The look Evel leveled at William could have singed his eyelashes.

William didn't sound at all contrite as he said, "Aye, I've known he had her."

"Why did you let us go looking for her?" Avenall asked, his voice tight.

Evel and Avenall narrowed their eyes at William and waited for his answer.

"I had my reasons." William ignored them, turning back to look at Lark and Stoke. No amusement gleamed in his keen green eyes as he scrutinized Stoke.

"If you've known that I've had her, you must know I had no choice but to marry her."

"I'm glad you did the proper thing." The scowl on Elizabeth's face brightened.

"How could you marry him?" Avenall looked incredulous.

"It was not of my choosing." Lark felt a knot growing in her throat.

"It matters not. She's mine now." Stoke glanced at Lark, the anger that had been in his face masked by a strange, unreadable look.

"How dare you claim her?"

"This is not the time to wax gallant." Lark grimaced at Avenall. She'd never seen such emotion on his face. What had gotten into the passive, gentle man she had known? Whatever it was, it would get him killed. "Please, stay out of this," she said. " 'Tis done, and you can't change it."

"Nay, I shan't," Avenall said, never taking his hate-filled eyes off Stoke. "He had no right to take you and force you to marry him."

"I have no quarrel with you. 'Tis best you keep it that way." Stoke's words were uttered with calm evenness, though a lethal storm brewed in his eyes.

"I'll not back down from you. You abducted Lark, didn't you? She didn't leave as we thought. I knew she would never run away from me. By God and all the saints, I'll see you dead before I let you get away with this!" Avenall lunged for Stoke.

With lightning swiftness, Stoke deflected Avenall's fist. Lark saw a blur. Heard knuckles connect with a chin. Then Avenall tumbled out of the saddle and landed in the dirt on his back. Before Lark could leap off her horse, Helen ran to him and fell to her knees beside him.

She lightly stroked his cheek. "Are you all right? Please say you are all right."

Avenall's eyes opened. For a moment he just stared up at Helen with a confused grin on his face. The cloudiness faded from his eyes as he rose on his elbow and shook his head. He worked his jaw, testing to see if he could open it. All the while staring up at her, he touched Helen's hand, still on his cheek. After a moment, he said, "I'll live." He dropped his hand and glared at Stoke. "We'll finish this in the lists."

"You cannot!" Helen grabbed his shoulder. "Please, don't do this—you mustn't. You'll die!"

"He's a scoundrelly knave. First he hurt you, now look what he's done to Lark. Nay, I'll meet him in the lists."

Tears gleamed in Helen's eyes as she glanced at Stoke. "Please, do not fight him."

" 'Tis up to him, my lady."

Evel had leaped off his horse and was helping Avenall up. "She's right. You can't challenge the Dragon."

"I have, and I shall," Avenall said as Evel and Helen helped pull him up to his feet.

Lark had never seen such passion in Avenall's eyes. Did he still care for her? She didn't ponder it long, for Stoke grabbed her. In one quick jerk, he sat her down in front of him on the saddle, the added seventy pounds of her armor naught to him.

He was about to kick his destrier, but the firm timbre in William's voice stopped him. "Hark you well, Dragon, I'll let you keep Lark, but if she is unhappy or you mistreat her, you will answer to me." William leveled a determined glance at Stoke.

"I'm happy, Father."

William looked into Lark's eyes, searching to see if she'd spoken the truth. It was clear by the scowl growing on his face that he didn't believe her.

"You needn't worry, Lord Mandeville, she'll be treated as a wife should be treated," Stoke said, his arms tightening possessively around her waist, her armor clanking against his. After one more glance in William's direction, Stoke galloped toward the gates, leaving her father staring after them.

Lark felt the anger in Stoke, boiling like a cauldron, and said, "I suppose you mean to beat me now for leaving Kenilworth?"

"Nay, but I should beat Jamus." His voice was a low growl near her ear.

"Please, do not." Lark turned and looked at him and regretted it as soon as his gaze scoured her face. " 'Twas my fault. I forced him to let me come with him to keep an eye on Lord Trevelyn."

"I didn't want you near him. That's why I sent Jamus. I wanted you to stay home, where you'd be safe. I should have known you do just the opposite."

Lark quickly changed the subject, hoping to assuage his anger. "What did you find at the abbey?"

"I found out that Ebba is working with the person who wants me dead."

"Did you speak to her?"

"Nay, she'd disappeared when I returned to Kenilworth."

"Stoke, you must be careful here. With all these people about, you could be easily killed."

"Take care, you're sounding like a worried wife." He looked deep into her eyes, searching for something. "Did you miss me?" He bent down to kiss her.

"Nay," Lark lied and turned back around in the saddle, watching the horse's ear flick as a fly landed on it.

Turning away from his kiss was the hardest thing she'd ever had to do. Over the past two days, she had missed his lusty embraces, the kisses that warped her thoughts, the way his large, calloused hands felt on her body. Every moment she'd thought of him and worried whether he was all right. But she would never let him know it. Neither would she ever confess her love for him, for he didn't love her, nor trust her, and she'd learned from trying to love Elizabeth that it was better not to open your heart to attack. Nay, he'd never know how she felt.

She felt him stiffen and his hold on her tightened. Lark felt the sting of tears and bit her lip.

Windsor's lower bailey teemed with mass confusion. Lords and ladies dismounted; their retinues of servants and livestock ran about looking lost. One of ten grooms hurried toward them to take Shechem's reins. Stoke noticed the strange glance the groom shot his bride. He obviously couldn't decide whether a man or woman was beneath the armor. And if a man, why was he sitting on Stoke's lap? Stoke ignored the groom, leaped off, and turned to help Lark down.

She knocked his hands away. "I don't need your help."

"I think you do." In spite of her protest, he grabbed her waist and put her down on the ground. She looked up at him. He saw the despondent look in her eyes and knew it came from being forced to marry him. He'd never forget the way she'd shunned his kiss moments earlier. He was sure she thought herself still in love with that baby-faced puddle, Lord Avenall.

"*Bonjour,* Dragon!" a deep voice bawled across the bailey.

"Sire!" Stoke called out.

Stoke followed the voice to a high window in the round tower. King Richard stood there, his golden hair and vivid blue eyes gleaming in the sunshine.

"What have you brought me?"

"A wife, sire." Stoke pulled off Lark's helm. Her long blond braid uncurled down her back. He grabbed her arm. She dug her heels in, but he pulled her forward for the king's perusal.

Rich, booming laughter burst across the bailey. "She does not look the part of a wife, but bring her up and let me have a look at this prize." Richard moved away from the window.

Lark turned on him, her yellow-gold eyes flashing. "I can't go with you. I should go and find Jamus and Lord Trevelyn."

"You'll do no such thing. I have men scattered about watching his every move."

"Still—"

"Say no more. You're going to meet the king."

"But I can't meet him wearing chain mail. Did you not hear my mother? I'll shame my family and you."

"I believe he'll be more offended if you make him wait to change. Nay, you'll meet him just as you are."

"But—"

"You should have stopped to think of it ere you put on armor. I'll just introduce you as my rebellious bride."

"You'd like that, wouldn't you? I have a very good reason for wearing this suit. I thought I might have to battle Lord Trevelyn, and I'd rather meet him suited than wearing a gown."

"Now you can battle the king, should the need arise."

"Sometimes I could hate you."

"Only sometimes? I'm hurt, Lark." He grabbed her hand and pulled her toward the bailey.

Ten minutes later, Lark stepped onto a lush carpet as she followed Stoke into the royal chamber, a large, high-ceilinged room. Wide beams buttressed the circular ceiling. Tapestries covered the stone walls, depicting scenes in the Holy Wars. A huge desk sat off to one side. Near it, posts, as wide as her waist rose from a massive mahogany bed.

The king leaned his elbow against the mantel and eyed her with the shrewdest blue eyes she'd ever seen. Short, golden curls framed his sharp-planed Plantagenet face. Even with his six-foot-five frame on a slant, he looked the giant of a man he was.

Feeling someone's eyes on her back, she turned and gazed into Louis's face. He sat, sprawled in a chair behind her, and had the audacity to wink and leer at Lark, while a woman sat in his lap—a beautiful woman at that. She appeared some years his senior, about her father's age. The wrinkles near her eyes were just starting to show. A smile stretched across her wide mouth. Her bright scarlet dress was stark against the long, thick multi-colored blond braid that fell to her waist. Lark knew respectable ladies never wore scarlet. The woman was a courtesan, and a wealthy one by the gold circlet on her head and gold bracelets dangling on her wrists.

"Well, well, what have we here?"

The sound of the king's voice brought Lark's gaze back to him.

He stood up straight and clasped his hands behind his back. The movement sent the burgundy velvet mantle on his shoulders flapping against his elbows. He stared straight at her, his expression unreadable.

A fine sheen of sweat broke out on her forehead. In her mind, she kept hearing Elizabeth's words, "You'll shame us all." For the life of her, she couldn't find the words to speak.

Richard raised a bushy golden brow at her as if expecting something from her.

"May I present Lady Lark, sire." Stoke touched her shoulder, then leaned close and whispered, "Give the king his due."

Lark realized she'd been standing there, staring back at the King of England like a simpleton. She thrust back her leg to curtsey—which she'd never quite mastered properly in Elizabeth's eyes—but her knees were trembling. Under the added weight of her armor, she found it impossible to bend without falling on the floor. So she did the only thing she could do, she dropped to one knee and bowed her head.

"Forgive me, your highness, I've not yet learned the art of curtseying in armor." Her voice sounded shaky.

"When you do learn such a feat, I want to be the first to see it."

Lark felt a wisp of hair sticking to her mouth. She shoved it back with her hand and saw a ghost of a grin on Richard's face.

He strode over to her and held out his hand. "Give me the great pleasure of helping a lady in armor to rise." Lark placed her hand in his large palm and allowed the King of England to pull her to her feet. When she was steady, he touched her chin and moved her face from side to side, studying her profile.

"Have you ever been presented to me, *mademoiselle?* Surely not, for I would have remembered such an interesting face as yours—a face full of life and character." He traced the edge of her jaw with a long finger. "Hmmm, quite a stubborn-looking chin you have. The young gallants must have found you a challenge—and my friend here." He motioned to Stoke.

Stoke's gaze was locked on the king's hand as it touched Lark's jaw. He looked ready to attack Richard at any moment. Instead he stepped up to Lark, pulled her back a step, and locked his arm through hers.

An amused grin stretched across Richard's lips. His shrewd eyes twinkled as he studied Stoke.

"Aye, you are correct, your highness." Lark broke the uncomfortable moment. "The few times you have held court in England, I was at home, tending my father's lands. But you've met my sire, William Mandeville, Baron of St. Vale. one of your trusted vassals."

"Aye, I remember your father well—a good man."

Lark heard a little gasp from the courtesan sitting on Lord Trevelyn's knee. Right before Lark's eyes, the woman's face drained of color. She unwrapped her arm from Lord Trevelyn's neck and stared at Lark the way one would look at a specter rising from a grave. Abruptly she stood, the scarlet gown rippling along her rounded curves. She appeared unsteady on her feet and gripped the back of the chair. It was a rare occasion when Lark could look a woman directly in the eyes without dropping her gaze, but this woman stood as tall as she.

Richard followed Lark's gaze and said, "Allow me to introduce to you. Lord Trevelyn, who just arrived, and his, um"—he paused, searching for a word—"friend, Carmia. As you can see, Lord Trevelyn and Carmia are long acquainted."

"Fortunately for me." Lord Trevelyn smiled at Carmia, who ignored him completely, her gaze locked on Lark's face.

"So, tell us," Richard said, eyeing Lark. "Do you know how to use weapons to go along with your armor?"

"Aye, your highness, but only sword and lance."

"Not a bow?" Richard raised his brow, an amused look on his face.

"Nay, I couldn't shoot a straight arrow if my fate depended upon it."

"But you use a lance?" Richard looked incredulous.

"Aye."

"Will you ride in my tourney, then?"

"Nay, she will not." Stoke spoke up, cutting off Lark.

"May I know why not?" Lark glanced at him through narrowed lashes.

"I have spoken."

"Ah—for a moment, I forgot I'm your wife. Of course you have every right to order me about. Forgive me, my lord." Lark used her most cutting tone, and bowed to him.

"I'm glad you finally understand your place."

Golden eyes battled black ones for a moment, until Richard broke the silence.

"Aye, that is settled. Then I hope you will consent to keep me company when your husband is out on my field. We'll discuss weapons at length."

"It will be my pleasure."

The gracious smile faded from Richard's lips. "Stoke, Lord Trevelyn tells me there have been many attempts on your life."

"I know not how he should know." Stoke looked askance at Louis.

Louis grinned contemptuously. "Why your mistress, Ebba, told me. You must have forgotten she was in my company a great deal at Kenilworth."

"This worries me," Richard said. "I should let Lord Trevelyn champion me at the tourney."

A smug smile spread across Louis's face as he crossed his legs and drummed his fingers on the side of his chair.

"Nay, I'll not give up the honor," Stoke stated.

Richard was silent, seeming to weigh the two men. After a moment of contemplation, he said, "Very well, since you feel this way."

Lark saw the smug look drop from Louis's expression; then she cast a worried frown in Stoke's direction.

"You must sit with us at the banquet this eventide and we can speak at length of this. You are too good a friend to lose." Richard clapped Stoke on the back. "It has been too many years since I've seen you."

"Aye." Some of the tension left Stoke's face. "I hope Henry treated you well in his prison."

"Not as well as he could, but better than I would have treated him." Richard smiled wryly. "Speaking of treating me, I've yet to receive that replacement sword you promised me over two years ago. I had to fight the heathen Saracens with naught but an inferior German blade." He wrinkled up his nose. "Not at all close to the steel you make."

"I'd thought you would have forgotten about it when you were captured."

"Forget about a weapon as good as your own? Never. I expect it within the month."

"You'll have it, sire."

"While you are casting them, I would be honored if you presented me with one," Louis said with a derisive smile.

"Unfortunately, I only make a few a year, and after the king's I've reached my limit." Stoke ignored his cousin's indignant gaze and turned to Richard. "I'll leave you to my cousin, and we'll take our leave. My bride here has yet to be fitted with a proper wardrobe. As much as she may enjoy wearing armor, I do not enjoy seeing her in it."

"I see your point." Richard threw back his head and laughed.

Lark scowled at Stoke as he bowed to Richard, locked his arm in hers, and guided her from the room, leaving the king with a white-toothed grin on his face.

One of two guards standing in the hallway closed the door behind them.

Lark waited until they cleared a corner, then tried to jerk her arm free of Stoke's grip. "Let me go!"

"Nay. I should beat you soundly for acting like a shrew back there." With one quick jerk, he pulled her around and into his arms.

She hit his wide chest. Their armor clanked together. She gazed at his square chin, at his lips, at the long hair curling around his shoulders, at that devilish peak on his brow. She remembered placing kisses on that peak, remembered the way the tip of it brushed against her lips. She knew exactly how the stubble on his chin felt against her naked breasts, belly, and thighs, the roughness of it sending shivers through her body. Her heart began banging in her chest, while her body came alive with yearning.

She thought he would try to kiss her, but he only stared down at her, as if waiting for her to make the first move. If only she could throw her arms around his neck and kiss him. But she wouldn't. She couldn't let him know she loved him, so she said, "I won't be ordered about by you." She tried not to think of his arms around her and that hungry look in his midnight eyes.

"You're my wife, Lark. You'll do my bidding, and I'll not have you parading around in armor and riding in tournaments."

"Go ahead—order me about like one of your churls."

"I'm only thinking of your safety."

"Why do you worry over someone you can't trust?" Lark searched his face.

"You're my wife. 'Tis my duty as your lord and master to

care what happens to you." He stared down at her and rubbed his thumb across her lips.

"Can't have you shirking your duties." She jerked her face back from his hand and felt a choking pressure in her throat.

The sound of footsteps made them glance behind them.

Carmia appeared, a flustered look on her face at having caught Stoke and Lark in each other's arms. "I'm disturbing you."

"Nay, you are not." Lark stepped back from Stoke, breaking the hold he had on her. An impatient scowl darkened his expression as he glanced at Carmia.

"My Lady Lark."

"Aye?"

"May I have a private word with you in my chamber?"

There was such pleading in the woman's voice, such a look of entreaty in her bright blue eyes, that Lark found herself saying, "Aye, I'll speak with you."

"My chamber is across the bailey in another hall. Please come too, my lord. This concerns you as well. Please, follow me." She turned and led the way.

Lark stared at the tawny blond braid hanging down Carmia's back. A strange feeling tugged at her. She remembered the woman's reaction to her name only moments ago and began to regret agreeing to speak her.

Stoke slipped his hand in hers. She remembered what he'd said about his duty to care for her. No mention of love. Just duty. She wanted to pull her hand back, to never touch him again, but for some reason the feel of the powerful warmth of his fingers next to her own was comforting. She couldn't draw back.

In the bailey, William dismounted, the stench of an eight-foot-high dung pile hitting him. He grimaced and stared at the confusion about him. There were people everywhere. Some grumbling about their accommodations and the poor planning of the king for his second coronation. A knight's horse was rearing, scattering people, other horses, and a flock of chickens that happened to be near his hooves.

The knight's squire jerked on the reins and tried to control his mount, with little success. The knight grew impatient, berated his squire, and finally gained control of the frightened animal. As the squire trotted the horse off to the stable, William spotted Lark. Blackstone strode beside her,

and . . .

He gulped hard at the tall, buxom frame, the scarlet dress, the bright blond hair. Carmia.

His gut churned at the thought of Lark discovering the truth from Carmia and not him. The sound of Elizabeth's voice tore into his thoughts, and he wheeled around, remembering her. His wife and Carmia in the same country was courting danger, but both of them in the same bailey could prove disastrous.

Elizabeth was speaking to Lady Lucinda and Sir Joseph, looking enthralled by what Lady Lucinda was saying. If only she would stay that way for just a few moments longer. He tossed the reins to a young groom and dashed across the bailey, his gaze flitting between Elizabeth and Carmia.

Carmia noticed him first. She paused and looked almost frightened at having been caught with Lark. "William," she said, her voice huskier than he remembered, made so by her apprehension.

He remembered how that voice could woo a man senseless. And she still looked like the siren she was. "Hello, Carmia," he said, his displeasure at seeing her coming through in his voice.

"Father, you know this woman?" Lark stepped up to him, her golden eyes searching his face.

"Aye, I do." William remembered Elizabeth and turned to glance at her. At that moment, Lady Lucinda pointed directly at him, her mouth never ceasing its incessant chatter.

The moment William had dreaded for almost a score of years came. Elizabeth spotted Carmia.

Chapter 24

William watched the smile on Elizabeth's face fall. Her jaw clamped, her fingers knotted into fists at her sides, and then she stomped toward him, leaving Lady Lucinda still talking to her back.

"Mother is coming, and she doesn't look happy. We'd better go," Lark said, turning to Blackstone.

"Stay where you are, Pigeon. She's not angry with you."

"Who then?"

"With me," William said, eyeing Elizabeth.

She came at William with the force of a battering ram. She didn't stop until she stood nose to nose with him. "How dare you bring that woman here?" Her screech echoed around the bailey, causing a hush to fall over it. A death knell could not have brought more silence more suddenly.

William heard his own heartbeat pounding in his ears. "Now, Elizabeth—"

"Do not Elizabeth me."

"Let me explain."

"What is there to explain? I knew you'd not stopped seeing this—this"— Elizabeth jabbed her hand at Carmia and blurted, "this creature! I knew it in my heart." She pounded on the region near her heart, tears glistening in her eyes.

"You are mistaken, my lady," Carmia said, her voice tight.

Elizabeth turned and glared at her. "How dare you speak to me! Do you expect me to believe the likes of you?"

The last vestiges of politeness left Carmia's voice. "You're ignorant if you think I have seen William. I haven't spoken to him in years."

"That's a lie. A lie, do you hear!" Elizabeth charged Carmia.

William tried to grab the edge of Elizabeth's gown, but it whipped past his fingers.

Elizabeth collided with Carmia.

They both went down.

Elizabeth attacked full force, pulling hair, clawing, trying to get her hands around Carmia's neck. In all the years he'd known his wife, William had never seen the full force of her ire. Eighteen years of anger drove Elizabeth's fury. He took a step to break them apart, but paused as Carmia wrestled his wife to the ground, pinning her arms there.

Elizabeth glared up at Carmia, chest heaving, tears flowing down her face. "You've won," she said, sobbing. "Now get off me."

"I've won naught, my lady. 'Tis you who've won everything. For years I've envied you every moment, every hour of the day. You had everything that ever mattered to me. How I've longed to be you for just an hour."

"Nay, you don't want to ever be me. She's never loved me. All I've tried to do for her—she's never appreciated it. She's done everything in her power to vex the soul from me. I could never reach her. You should have raised her, you were her mother. . . ." Elizabeth's sobs choked off her words.

William turned and saw Lark. She stood frozen, her trembling hand clutching Blackstone's.

Finally, she knew. It would end now. William felt the weight of the lie he'd carried around with him lift—until he glanced into Lark's visage and the heaviness hit him again. Her face was so white, it looked chiseled from marble. Her nostrils flared, the black centers of her eyes mere pinpoints, the lids unblinking. Those dark centers pierced him as no sword could ever have done, and he felt it down to the quick of his heart. Gone was the idolizing light in the golden depths. All that remained was emptiness and pain. She stared at him a moment and gulped deep in her throat.

"I'm sorry, Pigeon. I meant to tell you. I tried so many times." William stepped toward her.

"Now I know." Lark turned and ran through the bailey, parting the staring crowd as she ran.

William turned to go after her, but Blackstone grabbed his arm. "I'll go to her."

William watched Blackstone go after her. In spite of the added weight of her armor, Lark had already cleared the length of the bailey. Her long braid swayed down her back as she rounded the corner of a stable.

How could he ever make it up to her? The telling shouldn't have been like this. He had always envisioned the moment, just the two of them, in the tilt yard—her favorite place. He would set her down on the fence rail, climb up beside her, and break it to her gently. So many times during his life he'd had that vision. It had faded quickly when he imagined the disillusioned look on Lark's face when he told her the truth. It was the same expression he'd just witnessed. God help him! All his life, he couldn't bear the loss of her adoring glances. Now look what had happened. His own selfish weakness would make his pigeon hate him.

Elizabeth's sobs broke into William's musing. He saw Elizabeth curled up on her side, lying on the bailey floor. Her hands covered her face, while sobs shook her whole body. It was as if she were letting out all the years of anger and pain inside her. William felt his own eyes glazing over as he bent to comfort his wife. He had hoped all the strife would be over; instead it was just beginning.

* * *

Stoke found Lark huddled behind the stable. Her back was pressed against the wooden planking, her arms wrapped around her bent knees, and she was staring straight ahead, seeming not to notice anything. The blank, pale look on her face made an anxious feeling tug at his chest.

"Stop right there," she said, without bothering to turn and look at him.

"I came to see if you needed me."

"Why should I need you?" she said, her voice dead. She turned and looked at him, her eyes as hollow as empty pits. "I don't need or want your comfort. Do you understand? Just leave me alone. You've done enough to me already, forcing me to marry you, ruining what happiness I could have had with Avenall."

Stoke blinked at her, absorbing the words she'd hurled at him. Without another word, he turned and left her.

As he rounded the corner, he bumped into the servant, Marta. She grabbed his arm. "Oh, me lord." She gazed at his face, taking in the dark scowl, the raw emotion that must be blatant in his eyes, and said, "Please, me lord, don't be angry with her. She's had a blow."

"Aye, we all have." Stoke strode past her.

Marta shook her head and watched his stiff strides across the bailey, then turned and hobbled behind the barn.

It was Lark's way to brood alone, but when Marta watched Lark raise her head, and she looked into Lark's face, she knew this was not brooding. It was devastation.

"Go away, Marta." Lark laid her head back on the barn wall and gripped her knees until the knuckles in her hands whitened.

"Nay, I won't." The moment Marta touched the top of Lark's head, the steely control slipped from Lark's face. Her bottom lip trembled as tears flowed down her cheeks. Marta gently stroked to the top of her head. "Ah, me child, me child."

"Oh, Marta!" Lark threw her arms around Marta's legs and buried her face in her dress. "He could have told me. All those years she berated me. I tried when I was little to please her, but I could do naught right. It was because she hated me. If I had but known the truth, I could have understood. I should have known. When they argued, it was always over me. Why didn't one of them tell me?''

Marta felt Lark's body shaking against her bony knees. She wanted to find words to ease the ache in this child, but a lifetime of pain could never be erased by words, so Marta let her cry it out.

It took a long while before Lark stopped sobbing. Marta stooped and wiped Lark's face with her apron, as she had done countless times when Lark was a child, but she'd been only wiping away dirt then, not tears.

''Why didn't Father tell me? I'll never forgive him.''

''Lark, if ye can't find it in your heart to forgive him, then you be not the child I raised.'' Marta leveled a reproachful glance at Lark. ''Don't ye dare look at me like that. He's your father and the kindest man in the world. Don't ye see—he didn't want to hurt ye.''

''But he did!'' Lark cried, before her words choked off.

''He did naught but love ye, all yer life. He favored ye above all the others—even above his sons, and ye bein' a bastard child. So he should have told ye. There are weaknesses in all of us. Weaknesses are to be forgiven.''

''You knew. Why didn't you tell me?''

'' 'Twas not me place.' ''

''What of Elizabeth? I would have thought she would love to rub it in my face.''

''I'm ashamed of ye, child, speaking of the mistress like that.''

''Why? She's not my mother.''

''She may not've brought ye in the world, but she be more a mother to you than that whore. Don't ye ever let me hear ye say different.'' Marta shook her finger at Lark.

''She's never acted like a mother.''

''But she has. Do ye think she doesn't love ye? If ye think that, then yer a fool, child. She sewed gowns for ye whilst ye be away. Many a time at it, I caught her crying, silently. I knew she be crying over ye.''

Lark frowned, feeling a lump forming in her throat. "Why would she do that?''

"Why do ye think?''

"She's never loved me. I could never please her, so I gave up trying.''

"Don't ye see that she was hard on ye 'cause she loved ye. That was her trouble. She didn't want to love ye, 'cause she knew where ye came from. But she did and it galled her.''

"Oh, Marta, I don't believe you.''

"One day, ye'll know what I'm sayin' is the truth.'' Marta waved her thin hand angrily. "And I be tellin' ye one more thing—if ye be not careful, ye'll drive yer husband away sure as I'm standin' here. Ye should have seen the look on his face when he left here after ye turned him away.''

"I don't care. He forced me to marry him. He doesn't love me. He only wants to make me his prisoner for the rest of my life.''

"I don't believe it for a moment.''

" 'Tis true. I saw his workshop, and he forced me to marry him so I could not go and spout off about it.''

"Well, if ye be believing that, ye are stupider than those twin brothers of yers. The question is, do ye love him?''

"I don't,'' Lark blurted.

" 'Tis Marta ye be talking to, child. I know ye like I know me own insides. If ye love that man, ye'd best let him know it and stop protecting that heart of yers. Ye've always guarded it, but ye may find ye've no need to when 'tis all over and done with. 'Tis plain he's been hurt by another woman, and he needs time to learn to give his love. And a man like that will take only so much. I've said me piece, and I've always spoke plain to ye. And I'm speaking plain now. But ye'll hear no more about it from me. Beseems ye need to search yer own soul.'' Marta turned back around, stiffened her spine, and hobbled away past the stable.

Lark stared after her. Tears streamed down her face again and she buried her face in her hands.

Meanwhile, Ebba stood hidden in the shadows, peering behind a tall hayrick, watching Lark. A devious smile spread across her full lips. She waited until Marta strode away, pulled the hood of her cloak over her face, and darted out into the bustle of the bailey.

A little while later, after she'd cried until there were no tears left, Lark stepped out from behind the stables. She didn't want anyone to see her red nose and swollen eyes, so she kept to the edge of the bailey, watching the bustling castle servants running past her. She scanned the bailey for any sign of Elizabeth and William. They were gone, along with Marta. She didn't think she could face her father yet. The hurt ran too deep. And Stoke was nowhere to be seen either.

Marta's warning plagued Lark, but she could not find the courage to tell Stoke she loved him. How could she lay open her heart like that? It was easy for Marta to admonish her, for it was not Marta's heart that would be crushed.

"Lark! Lark!"

She turned and watched Helen run across the bailey toward her, dodging chickens and servants. She paused before Lark and clamped her hand over her chest.

Heaving, she said, "Oh, Lark, I've been looking everywhere for you since Mother told me what happened." She noticed Lark's eyes and clasped her hands. "How wretched you must feel. If I'd known—"

"I know. 'Tis all right. I'm glad I know now. At least I know why mothe—Elizabeth hated me." Would she ever get used to not calling Elizabeth Mother any longer?

"I have to confess something to you." Helen dropped her head and lowered her gaze, her long lashes hooding her eyes.

"I hope 'tis not to tell me another deep, dark family secret. I've had my share of those for one day."

Helen answered Lark with tears. They slipped down Helen's cheeks and dropped from her chin.

"What is it?" Lark touched her chin, lifting her face.

"Oh, 'tis a wicked, wicked lie." Helen's bottom lip quivered for a moment; then she grabbed Lark and hugged her so tightly that Lark couldn't breathe. "You'll never forgive me."

"I shall." Lark pried her sister's arms from around her neck and looked at Helen. "Now tell me."

Helen hiccuped and said, "I've lived a lie for so long."

"What, Helen? Don't tell me Mother had an affair and we're not even half-sisters."

"Nay, something much worse."

Lark grabbed Helen's shoulders. "What is it?"

" 'Tis Avenall. We can't let him fight Lord Blackstone."

"Because you care for Lord Blackstone?" Lark asked, a tinge of jealousy in her voice. She didn't want Stoke until he trusted and loved her, but she didn't want Helen to want him either. "Is that what you're trying to say?"

"Nay, nay!" Helen said between sobs. "I love Avenall, Lark. I've loved him for years, since the day Father brought him to St. Vale."

Lark's jaw dropped open.

At Lark's silence, Helen blurted, "Please don't hate me. I never meant for it happen. He's so gentle and kind."

Lark clamped her jaw together and stared blankly at Helen. Lark felt as if any moment she would explode from the pressure inside her. Suddenly uncontrollable laughter erupted from her. She bent over, tears rolling down her cheeks. She grabbed her middle, her chest convulsing wildly.

"Lark, are you all right? I'm so sorry—can you ever forgive me? Lark, please stop. Are you having a fit? I'll go and get Lord Blackstone." Helen turned to leave.

Lark grabbed her arm and said between gasps, "Nay, do not. I wouldn't want him gloating over the fact that I've been a stupid, blind fool all these years. Why didn't you tell me, Helen? You of all people—I thought I could trust you." Lark wiped at the tears streaming down her face with the back of her hand. She looked at her beloved sister, who she never thought would betray her. But she had believed that of her father also. Real tears stung her eyes, and she blinked them back.

"I couldn't. I didn't want to hurt you. Avenall couldn't hurt you either. He tried to tell you."

"Did he? Well, he royally blundered it." Lark couldn't keep the bitterness from her voice.

"When he couldn't tell you, I begged him not to."

"How long have you two been in love?"

"I think I've always loved him, but he didn't realize he loved me until after he'd asked you to marry him. Only a year ago did he declare his love to me."

"Only a year ago?" Lark frowned.

"You must understand. We didn't plan it. I remember he came into the garden to get me for the evening repast. I fell on a stone and he caught me. We kissed, and . . ." Helen's words trailed off as if she were too embarrassed to say more.

"Would you have let me marry a man who didn't love me?" Lark asked, her tone incredulous and filled with disappointment.

"I would have, for I could never hurt you. I knew how much you loved him." Helen's bottom lip trembled, her wide brown eyes glistening with tears. "I would rather have lived without him, than to hurt you."

"Oh, Helen." Lark couldn't help but hug her sister. "I always felt that he could have been a bit more passionate. Kissing him was like kissing a dead fish."

"Lark!" Helen drew back.

Lark saw the indignant look on Helen's face and amended, "I'm sure he's more passionate with you."

"You love Lord Blackstone, do you not?"

Lark evaded the question. "Speaking of Lord Blackstone, why did you act so upset when he cried off? I thought you cared deeply for him."

"It was pure selfish jealousy. Since Avenall had to marry you, I didn't want to be alone all my life and pining away for

Avenall, knowing he shared your bed. I had to have someone, even if I didn't love him. Do you understand?''

"Aye, I do. Avenall was not the right man for me. I couldn't see that until Marta and Father pointed it out.'' Lark paused, feeling a sharp ache in her breast. Every time she thought of her father now, the ache appeared to get stronger. In spite of Marta's scolding, she didn't think she could forgive him.

"Lord Blackstone suits you.'' Helen scrutinized Lark's face. "He must love you, if he married you.''

"Only to make me his prisoner for the rest of my life.'' Lark frowned.

"Surely he must be in love with you.''

"I've seen not a shred of evidence of it—other than he's more than willing to take me to his bed.''

Helen's cheeks turned the color of beet juice.

Lark stared at the prim, shocked look on her face. A wry grin touched Lark's lips. "You needn't look so offended. Your time will come with Avenall. Tell me, has Avenall spoken to you of marriage, now that I'm no longer to be his bride?''

"Nay, he won't until he faces Lord Blackstone.'' Worry plagued her expression. "He thinks he'll be wounded or maimed and I'll not want him. Lark, I just cannot let him face Lord Blackstone. He'll kill Avenall. You know yourself, you're better with a lance than he is. I asked Evel and the twins to help me, but Evel refused, and the twins—well, you know how they can be.''

"Why does he insist upon this? He doesn't love me—surely he's not doing it to defend my honor.''

"He hates Lord Blackstone. I'm sure 'tis jealousy, pure and simple. He thought I cared for Lord Blackstone, and he hated to think I would be his bride. He looks upon you as a sister and can't bear the thought of what Blackstone did to you.''

Lark raised a brow at Helen. "Admit it, you wanted to make him jealous, didn't you?''

She hedged a moment, then said, "Aye, I did. I was jealous too. I tried not to be, but I couldn't help it.''

"You're human,'' Lark said, matter-of-factly.

"Aye, and selfish. I want Avenall now that I can have him. Alas, what good does it do me now? Avenall has made up his mind to ride against Lord Blackstone. He'll be killed, and I'll have naught." Helen's eyes glazed over with tears again.

Lark's expression was pensive. Then she turned back to Helen. "Fear not, I'll think of a way to keep him safe."

After Lark sent Helen back to be with Avenall, she went in search of Carmia's chamber. She paused before the woman's door, her fist raised. After a moment of struggling with indecision, she finally knocked.

Carmia's voice sounded muffled and unsteady behind the door, "I don't wish to see anyone."

"Not even your daughter?"

Lark heard the muted sound of footsteps; then the door opened. A stranger, her mother, stood staring at her, her eyes puffy and red from crying. She reached out to touch Lark's arm.

Lark pulled back, not knowing why; she just knew this woman had not wanted her and she didn't want her touch now.

Carmia frowned at Lark for an awkward moment. A sad smile barely touched her lips. "I hoped you'd come. Please come in."

The small, bare room held only a bed, two chairs by a hearth, and a trunk. Carmia waved to one of the chairs. "Please sit down."

"Thank you, but no."

"Please let me explain."

"What is there to explain? I know the truth now."

"I wanted to keep you, I did." Tears blurred Carmia's bright golden eyes, so much like Lark's. "But I knew you'd become a lady in William's care. What did I have to offer you? Moving from court to court, a prostitute for a mother. Nay, I couldn't bear to give you that kind of life."

"I thank you for that." It surprised Lark that there was no bitterness in her voice. Her next words amazed her even more.

"I wouldn't have known my father, and that would have been a terrible loss for me."

"He is a wonderful man. I wish he had loved me, but it was just one night here at court. Your mother was not with him, she was with child. He had over imbibed, and I admit, he was devilish handsome and I wanted him. I lured him to my bed—"

Lark raised her hand to stop her. "Please, I don't need the sordid details."

"But I want to tell you, to try and make you understand."

"I really don't want to understand. I just want to forget it."

Carmia's expression fell. She stared pensively down at her hands, the whisper of her palms brushing together the only sound in the deafening stillness.

Finally Carmia broke the silence. "Are you not curious about my family?"

"Mayhap," Lark said begrudgingly.

"My father was a cobbler. I had no brother and sisters. He beat me constantly. Finally, I'd had enough and ran away. I learned to speak properly and made my living as a courtesan. I've not regretted one moment of my life. If I lived it all over again, I would do it just the same. But I'm so proud of how you turned out. You're so beautiful. You do credit to Lady Elizabeth."

"I wouldn't tell her that."

"But you are a sparkling gem, and your Lord Blackstone sees it—and, I'm afraid, so does Lord Trevelyn."

"That reminds me—what do you know of him?" Lark raised a suspicious brow.

"I've known him for years. He's gallant, charming when he wants to be, and never makes demands on me." Carmia smiled, a smile that revealed the extent of their relationship. "Why do you ask?"

"No reason, other than he's Lord Blackstone's cousin." Lark knew she would get nowhere questioning Carmia. She was caught within Lord Trevelyn's deceitful charms. He was, after all, an attractive devil, much like his cousin.

" 'Tis obvious you did not come here to make small talk with me. Why then did you come here?''

"I need your help."

"My help?"

"Aye, on the morrow at the tourney. I'll need your help. I'll gladly pay you."

Carmia looked indignant. "Are you trying to insult me?"

"Nay, I just thought—"

"Well, I'm sure I can do something for my own daughter without payment."

"I'm sorry to have mentioned money."

"I forgive you." Carmia smiled weakly.

As Lark confided her plan in Carmia, she studied the older woman, seeing herself in the oval face before her. It was a little older, more weathered by age and life, but the resemblance was uncanny. No wonder Elizabeth couldn't stand the sight of Lark; she must have seen Carmia staring back at her everyday of Lark's life. Lark closed her eyes and sighed. Then Marta's words came back to haunt her; "Don't ye see that she was hard on ye 'cause she loved ye. That was her trouble. She didn't want to love ye, 'cause she knew where ye came from. But she did, and it galled her."

"I had better go." Lark cast Carmia a quick glance and left her chamber.

As she strolled through the bailey, another one of Marta's admonishments came back to her: "If ye love that man, ye'd best let him know it and swallow that pride." Lark hurried her pace. She wanted to find Stoke and beg him to forgive her for the callous way she'd turned him away when he'd tried to comfort her.

"Well, well, well."

Lark froze and looked up into Louis's face.

Chapter 25

"Lady Lark, I've finally got you all to myself."

Lark tried to step past him, but he blocked her path. She tensed, taking up a defensive stance, and said, "We had to meet sometime."

"Aye." His sky-blue eyes gleamed with a wicked, unrelenting look. "You've been on my mind since I met you. Do you know how much I enjoy fire in my women? And you have fire. Would you like to go to my chamber and burn me?"

"I would rather be thrown in the middens than lie with a murdering scurvy knave like you."

"Think you I'm trying to kill my cousin?" His lips parted, his white teeth gleaming in a wicked smile. " 'Twas not me who plunged the knife in his back, and let me say I know not how you got him to marry you, but what a conquest for you."

"Don't try to change the subject. You are behind these attempts on his life. You have the most to gain from his death. Know that I'll foil any further murder plots you devise for Stoke and Varik. I'll protect them with my life."

"How noble you are. I'm sure Stoke would have a good laugh at a woman protecting him."

"Don't underestimate me, my lord. Many a man has done it and regretted it." Lark glared back at him.

"I'm sure of it. There is no fear in your eyes. 'Tis dangerous for a woman to show no fear—I would much rather face a man without fear than a woman."

"Why is that?"

"I can be sure of what a man will do, but I have no idea how a woman will react. Women are capricious creatures"— his voice grew derisive—"particularly when they are in love. Please say this need to protect my cousin comes from love. What a good jest that would be. You must know he'll never love you—his first wife saw to that. Now, should you come to me . . ." He stepped toward her.

His outstretched hand never touched her arm. Stoke grabbed his hand and shoved him back. "If you ever come near my wife again, I'll see you in hell."

"I was just wishing her well on her marriage." Louis smiled that taunting smile of his. "I was not invited to the wedding. Can I not kiss the bride?"

They glared at each other, the tension sizzling. Lark pulled on Stoke's hand. "Please, leave him."

Stoke cast one more long look at Louis and allowed Lark to pull him away. It took all of her strength to get a few steps out of him. Then he turned and grabbed her hand, pulling her through the bailey. She caught a glimpse of Jamus, who stayed clear of his master's rage, standing near a well with sympathy in his eyes.

"I should have known you'd get into trouble the moment I turned my back on you."

Lark's earlier resolve to tell him she was sorry melted. "You must know he'll never love you—his first wife saw to that."

Louis's words echoed in her heart. As Stoke pulled her through the bailey, she felt a sinking feeling drowning her heart.

* * *

In the wee hours of the night, Lark sat combing her hair in Stoke's chamber. She glanced at the high-backed chair near the mantel, at the large bed, down at the comb, the only things she'd had to look at besides the four walls. Half an hour ago, four seamstresses left her room after they'd fitted her with a new wardrobe and shoes. They were the only people she'd spoken to in two hours. Stoke must have ordered the gowns made, and she might have appreciated them had he not treated her so wretchedly.

Earlier, he had left four guards at the door and ordered her not to leave the room, using the excuse that it was to keep her safe from Louis. But she knew better. This was a tactic to exert his dominance over her, to put her in her place. As his prisoner and wife, he had every right to subjugate her with his edicts. The very thing she'd dreaded in marriage had come to pass. Well, he'd find out she wouldn't be treated like chattel.

And who was to keep him safe from Louis? He must have gone to Richard's banquet and forgotten all about her. The thought that Louis might be there had worried her all night. Lark glanced over at the fireplace and stared at the flames. She could set the room on fire, distract the guards, and leave. That would teach Stoke a lesson. As she was about to rise, she heard voices.

Stoke's deep baritone, raised high in song, boomed in the hallway. What sort of song was beyond her kin, for it was slurred and muffled behind the door.

She slapped the comb down. Quickly, she blew out the candle and hopped into the bed, pulling up the covers. She would not give him the satisfaction of letting him know she'd sulked the night away.

The door burst open.

"Where the hell is the bed?" She recognized the voice as her father's.

"Over there," Rowland said.

"I've no need for a bed yet." Stoke's loud voice boomed through the room.

"Shhh! Do you want to wake my pigeon?" Lark raised her

brows at the sound of her father's voice. His voice grew low and thick. "She's angry with me. I hurt her. She'll not forgive me. I'd do anything to have my pigeon forgive me."

Lark felt his words down in the pit of her heart. She wanted to run to her father and ease his guilt and tell him she forgave him.

"Don't count on it. Her heart is as tough as shoe leather," Stoke drawled.

Lark frowned and rolled her eyes at the wall.

"Damned silly name, Pigeon," Stoke said. "Where'd you get it?"

"When she was little, I found her in the pigeon coop collecting feathers so she could put them on Harold and Cedric and convince them they could fly off the roof—they'd given her a nasty trouncing the day before." William chuckled.

"What'd you do?" Rowland asked, curious.

"I let her go to it. If the twins were ignorant enough to believe her, they deserved to fall off the roof."

"And did they?" Rowland asked.

"I found them both hanging by their hands on the edge, covered in tar and feathers. Lark was below them, enjoying their distress. They've been leery of her tricks since. And the name Pigeon stuck after that," William said, his voice filled with thoughtful tenderness.

"Why am I not surprised by that story?" Stoke slurred.

"I'll tell you more on the morrow." Lark felt a thump against the mattress; then it sank as Stoke's weight hit it. "There now. Do your duty and give me plenty of strong grandsons."

"Can't. She hates me for making me marry her."

"You've got it backward. You made *her* marry *you*," Rowland said. "And there's always a way around hate in a bed, old friend."

"Aye, hate heats the blood. Use it, man, use it." This wise advice came from William.

Lark heard a thump that sounded as if her father had slapped Stoke's arm. Rowland and William broke out in song again. She heard unsteady footsteps. The door slammed shut.

"Lark." Stoke's deep voice was wheedling. He touched her arm.

Lark felt a shiver go down her arm and ignored him. She couldn't let him know how lonely she'd been without him, nor could she give in to her desire to have him make love to her, especially after he'd locked her in this room.

"Lark." He scooted over to her. She'd left on her shift, and he ran his hand along it, sliding it over her breast as he kissed her neck.

In spite of the tingle shooting down her neck and the heat growing in her loins, Lark grabbed his hand and shoved it aside. "Leave me alone. Go to sleep."

"Very well. I hope your side of the bed stays warm."

Lark heard his loud grunt as he rolled away from her. A few moments later, his deep breaths told her he slept.

He wasn't going to touch her again.

Lark felt a kind of loneliness she'd never felt in her life. Everyone she'd ever loved had betrayed her. William. Elizabeth. Helen. Avenall. Now Stoke didn't even care enough to try a second time to touch her. She wanted to have him hold her in his strong arms and whisper, "I love you."

Louis's words came back again, like a bad dream. "You must know he'll never love you ..." They echoed over and over in her mind as she hugged her middle and felt tears stinging her eyes.

The next morning, Lark woke and felt the bed beside her. No Stoke. Only cold sheets. Well, she was glad he was gone. Wasn't she?

A knock sounded on the door.

The muffled voice of a guard called, " 'Tis Lady Helen to see you, my lady."

"Let her in."

Helen stepped through the connecting door, a bright yellow dress in hand. "Lark, Mother bade me bring you your wedding dress."

Constance Hall

"Could she not bring it herself?"

"Nay, she said she couldn't show her face outside the chamber, after attacking that woman." Helen glanced at the frown on Lark's brows and added, "I'm sorry."

" 'Tis no matter. But I would have liked to thank her for it."

"I'll tell her." Helen smiled down at the dress. "Is it not lovely? You're going to look like a princess when you go to the tourney."

"I'm not wearing that."

"But—"

"If you want to keep Avenall safe, you'll do as I tell you and not protest. Now take that dress to Carmia."

Helen looked at her, unsure. "What will Lord Blackstone say when you don't come to the tourney? Lord Rowland told me you were to sit with the king himself."

"Worry not, I'll be there."

Helen looked confused and asked, "What are you going to do?"

"I'm going to stop Avenall. And I need you to go and distract the guards."

"How can I distract them?"

"Just bat your eyes and tell them you need their help down the hall. They'll follow you with their tongues hanging out."

"All right. I'll do it for Avenall."

Lark frowned and wondered if he was worth all this trouble after the way he'd lied to her. But Helen loved him, so she had to see that he wasn't harmed.

Lark's gaze flicked through the throng of people for any sign of the guards, but they were nowhere in sight. She hurried by the gates leading to the field. Rowdy spectators, eager for the tourney to begin, filled row after row of the sloping wooden galleries that lined both sides of the field. Tent-like canopies shaded one side, where the nobility and the rich sat. The other side was uncovered, and there the poor serfs and freemen took their places. The onlookers who couldn't find seats stood behind the fence, some with children perched on their shoulders trying to get a better view. A roar of voices filled the air and added to the hum of excitement.

Beyond the fences, Lark scanned the row of tents on either side of the field. One side of the field housed the king's vassals, the other side the challengers, knight errants for hire, with little coin but stalwart hearts.

Gaily-colored heraldic banners waved in the afternoon breeze. A steady stream of squires and pages ran in front of the tents like ants who just had their hill stepped on. Knights stood nearby, arrogantly barking orders at them.

Amid the chaos, she spotted her father's emblem, a roaring dragon on a white field. Lark slipped past the crowd and headed for the tent. A group of men gathered near a drainage ditch and stared down at something. Harold, Cedric, Evel, and Avenall were among the men.

Lark paused near Evel. "What are you looking . . ." Her words dissolved as she stared down at a body in the ditch. Sewage swirled past the corpse, dotting the pale arms and the brown gown with bits of excrement. Long strands of chestnut hair slashed across a pale face. Eyes stared up at naught. Those eyes. That face. Ebba. Lark caught sight of the bruises at the base of her throat as she turned away.

"Sweet Mary," she mumbled.

"Do you know her?" Evel raised his brows at her.

"Aye, she was a serving maid at Kenilworth. Stoke said she was involved with the person trying to kill him."

"We must get word to him."

"Would you worry him ere he rides in the tourney? Nay, have her body sent back to Kenilworth for burying and tell Rowland to send out some men to question everyone around here. Someone might have seen or heard something."

"What will you be doing?"

"I must speak with Avenall."

At the sound of his name, Avenall turned, noticing her. The

twins dragged their gaze away from the morbid sight and turned around too.

"What are you doing here? You're supposed to be sitting with the king." Harold narrowed his eyes at her, the scar on his face livid.

"No doubt she's worming her way into some mischief."

"You shouldn't have seen this," Avenall said.

"I've witnessed worse. I must needs speak to you."

"Aye, I need to talk with you too," he said, looking almost afraid of her.

Lark watched the men lifting Ebba's body out of the ditch. They laid her out on the ground, and Evel took off his mantle and draped it over her face and body. He gave orders to the men, then called to Avenall. "We shall meet you on the field. Father's waiting for us."

Avenall nodded.

Lark saw one of Stoke's men striding toward her. His gaze was on Ebba and he didn't notice her. She grabbed Avenall's hand and pulled him forward. "Come, we'll speak in Father's tent."

He allowed Lark to drag him into the tent; then he stood before her, clutching his hands in a white-knuckled grasp. "I'm truly sorry, Lark. I meant to come and explain to you, but I was at a loss for words."

"How about, I'm in love with your sister. That would have worked. You did have a whole year to choose your words."

"I couldn't bear to tell you."

"I've forgotten how noble you can be." Lark's tone held just enough acid to make him flinch.

"You have to believe me, I never meant to fall in love with Helen. And I do love you—just not the way you would like." Avenall turned his back on her and fingered a mace sitting on top of a chest. "I'll always love you in my own way."

Lark noticed her sword sitting in its scabbard next to her father's. He must have brought it for her. She eased over to it and drew it out, watching Avenall's back.

"That is very comforting." Lark kept her tone derisive, so

he would feel like a heel and keep his back turned. She crept toward him, the hilt of her sword raised.

"I hope one day you will get over me."

"I intend to." Lark brought down the hilt of her sword on the back of his head.

He collapsed on the ground with a loud *thunk*. Lark smiled down at him. "You may not know this, but you're already forgotten. Helen is welcome to you." Lark bent and began taking off his armor, knowing that if she didn't ride in the tourney, Evel and the twins would come looking for Avenall.

She didn't relish facing Stoke in the lists. A memory rose up in her mind, of him riding toward her outside the castle, his black armor covering his hulking body, the massive, ominous look of him. She frowned, left the tent, and strode past the guard, unnoticed in Avenall's armor.

Lark trotted Avenall's gelding down to the challengers' side. She stayed well back from the other knights. Through the slit in her helm, she could see the small pennons on their lances, sporting their brilliant colors. Some lances held bright streamers made of sleeves, stockings, and ribbons, tokens of some lady's affection. Lark thought of Stoke and wondered if he would have a lady's token on his lance.

A loud cheer went up.

She glanced toward the middle of the canopied lodges. Just below a royal coat of arms emblazoned on a banner, she spied the Coeur de Lion just taking his seat. The height of the dais and the tallness of his frame added to his regal bearing, his very presence hovering loftily over everyone's head, making him appear larger than life.

Lark held her breath as Richard leaned over and spoke to Carmia, sitting in a chair next to him. A veil covered her face, so only her eyes showed. The vivid yellow dress Elizabeth had made for Lark made Carmia stand out among a group of ladies, stark against the burgundy cushions of her chair. Her hair, the same tawny blond as Lark's, fell to her waist like a golden waterfall. The king didn't seem to notice that Carmia had taken Lark's place, for he leaned back in his seat and motioned to the field marshall.

Behind Carmia, Varik sat on Marta's lap, petting Baltizar. Amory and a guard of four, wearing Stoke's colors, surrounded Varik and Marta. Lark breathed a little easier knowing Varik was protected should an assassin try to harm him.

"All comers to the field."

The field marshal's bawl brought her gaze back around to the lists. Two knights in front of her rode out onto the field, the other staying back to wait for the melee to begin. Six others entered the field from the vassals' side.

An abrupt silence settled over the lists, a silence of awe.

"Look, Da, 'tis the devil himself," a child's voice rang out in the hush.

Lark glanced down the field at Stoke, an imposing figure in his dull black armor, astride his coal-black charger. An ominous air hung about him like the quiet before a storm, filling the whole field. Only the whites of his eyes showed against the cold blackness of his helm.

Shechem pranced to a halt in front of the king.

"Your champion, sire, Lord Blackstone of Kenilworth," the marshal's voice cut through the silence.

Carmia took out a red scarf and tossed it to Stoke. He caught it in midair and pulled back on the reins. His destrier dropped down onto his front knees, bowing before her. Stoke bowed too as the horse righted himself. The crowd cheered at the trick.

Not so Lark. She mumbled, "Ostentatious fool," and with a grimace watched Stoke tie the scarf to his lance. He must have been pleased by the offering, or he wouldn't have entertained the crowd so. Lark didn't think he'd be too pleased if he knew it was Carmia who had given him the scarf.

Lark noticed the other knights riding toward the field marshal. Much to her chagrin, she realized she'd been sitting there like a dolt watching Stoke. She galloped up to the other knights and paused near them. Straws were being drawn to see who would face the Dragon first. She drew the last straw from the field marshal's hand.

"All right, let us see who's first."

Lark held out her gauntleted hand with the other knights. The field marshal looked them over and pointed to her. "You've the longest rod among them. You'll take the first pass. You're a might small—hope you can keep it up against the Dragon. I've never seen him lose. See that your mount doesn't piss on you when they drag you off the field."

A bout of laughter issued from the other knights.

Lark eyed the marshal and the other knights. Lowering her voice, she said, "I don't mind a little dampness, 'tis the dung and wind that I cannot abide."

The other knights and the marshal grinned at her. Lark heard the crowd begin to chant for the start of the tourney. Evel jogged toward her, a lance and shield in hand.

"Here, Avenall. You'll need these. 'Tis a stupid thing you're doing."

Lark took the lance and shield and remained silent. She kept her helm down so Evel couldn't see her eyes.

"I still say you shouldn't do this. Let me take your place. I can ride against Blackstone."

"Nay."

"Avenall, what's wrong with your voice?"

"A tickle in my throat." Lark wouldn't look at Evel.

"Avenall?" Evel hesitated a moment, then grabbed her arm. "Damn you, Lark. Look at me."

Lark turned and gazed down at him through the small opening in the helm. She could only make out the upper half of his body and face, flushed with rage. "What the hell have you done? You can't do this. I'll not let you."

"Be quiet, Evel. Do you want the marshal to hear you?"

"The king will have you hung if he finds out."

"I promised Helen to see that Avenall didn't fight Stoke, since you and the twins wouldn't help her."

"I could not stop him. He's my friend. This was a matter of honor for him."

"Where was his honor when he was going to marry me and loved Helen? You men and your honor. You turn it on and off when it suits you. By the by, did you know about him loving Helen?" Lark hefted the lance onto her hip, a motion she'd done many times in her life.

"Nay, but see here—"

"I'll not argue with you. I can do this and without anyone the wiser, if you hold your tongue." Lark kicked the destrier forward, leaving Evel staring opened-mouthed at her.

She trotted to the start of the list. At the opposite end of the field, Stoke sat at the ready, a mountain of black, the red scarf Carmia had given him the only color near him. Lark prayed her usual prayer before combat, "Dear Mother Mary, give me swiftness of limb to dodge the lance, the strength of a pure heart, and a lucky opening." She gripped the shield and lance tighter, feeling her palms sweating against the gauntlets.

Richard stood and raised a flag to shoulder height. "Are you ready?" his deep voice rang out in the field. He glanced at Lark, at Stoke, watching for their nods. . . .

The flag dropped.

Lark heard the roar of the crowd in her ears and spurred the destrier forward, keeping her eyes on Carmia's dangling red scarf. Twenty-four-hundred pounds of horse and knight came at her. She braced herself, feeling the pounding of her mount's hooves vibrating through her whole body.

Lances and shields met.

With reflexes that had always been her saving grace, Lark dipped to the side. The end of Stoke's lance barely grazed her shield and veered off. He moved too quickly for a man of his hulking size, and she missed her mark. Her lance didn't come close to him.

Cheers grew louder. Hands clapped; feet stomped. The excitement reached a fevered pitch.

Lark pulled back on the reins. As she turned her mount, a bright flash caught her eye, and she spotted the monk who'd escaped after trying to kill Stoke at the abbey, though he wasn't wearing a cowl this time. He sat on the front row of the lesser galleries, a crossbow raised in his hands, an arrow tip glinting in the sunshine.

The crowd yelled at her to ready herself. Frantically, she turned and saw Stoke already riding toward her. With a sharp nudge, she sent her mount into a gallop. Stoke drew closer. Her gaze flitted between Stoke and the monk. Stoke didn't appear to notice the assassin, and it was too late to warn him. The man aimed the bow.

Seconds before she and Stoke clashed again, she veered to the right, heading straight for the man.

Boos from the crowd rang in her ears.

The assassin glanced away from Stoke and saw her heading directly for him. He turned the bow her way. Before he could fire, her blunted lance plowed into his middle. Man and bow careened back against the crowd behind him. As the man fell, he loosed his arrow. It left the bow and came straight at her.

Chapter 26

Lark raised her shield, but not fast enough. Pain ripped across her thigh. She glanced down and saw the arrow embedded in the saddle, still wobbling. Near it, blood oozed from the front of her thigh and dripped down the arrow's shaft. The point had ripped through her chain mail, just grazing her skin.

Loud shouts brought her gaze up to the gallery. The crowd had surged upon the fallen man. Frenzied by their own sense of justice, they pummeled the fallen man with fists and feet.

Lark shouted at Stoke, "Save him—you need him alive."

He looked at the mob. "It's too late." Stoke gazed into her eyes and growled, "I should beat you soundly." He threw his lance and shield to the ground, then reached for her.

She pulled on the reins, backing away from him. Her lance snapped up again and she jammed it against his chest. "You'll keep your distance, my lord," she yelled above the roar of the crowd.

"Don't be a fool. You'll cost us both our heads for making a mockery of the king's tourney." He grabbed her lance and yanked it out of her hands. With an angry toss, he threw it down, along with his lance and shield. He yanked off his helm, and strode toward her.

At the thunderous expression on Stoke's face, Lark backed the destrier further down the field until it hit the side of the galleries. She couldn't go back any farther. Stoke grabbed the reins and lead her horse across the list.

"I can guide my horse. I've had worse wounds than this fighting the twins."

"Be still. I'm taking you to my tent."

"You should know something," Lark said, hoping to get his mind off his anger.

"What?"

"Ebba was found strangled near my father's tent. I asked Evel to tell Rowland so your men could question everyone."

"A wise idea, though I'm sure they'll find no one saw or heard anything." Stoke's eyes narrowed. "I suppose Louis is tying up loose ends. She was my last lead."

"Have your men been following Louis?"

"Aye, and he remained with Carmia all night. Jamus saw him leave her chamber this morning, and he's remained with his men, in plain sight, since. If he did it, he paid someone to do it, probably the same bastard who hurt you."

Lark heard the field marshal bellowing at the crowd for order. They left the chaos behind them and reached the tent. Stoke lifted Lark from the horse and carried her to his cot. Her chain mail rattled against the wooden sides.

"Are you in much pain?" He frowned down at her.

"Nay, I told you, it's naught."

He shot her a dubious look, pulled off her helm, and tossed it on the ground. He bent and peered closely at the wound in her leg. "I should turn you over my knee for disobeying me, but I think this wound will be punishment enough."

Lark plopped her head on the cot and stared up at the top of the tent. "I suppose I need punishing for saving your life."

"You shouldn't have been out on that field. You think I want you wounded on my account? Here, sit up and I'll get this armor off."

Lark allowed him to help her sit up. As he pulled off her hauberk, she said, "You should thank the saints I was there, but I suppose you don't want to be in my debt, lest you have to feel some faith in me."

"I do, Lark. How could I not after you saved my life?" He unbuckled her chausses and eased them off.

Lark gritted her teeth as he lifted the torn chain mail off the wound and pulled it down over her braies. "There will always be doubt in your mind that I was with those Scots. Not until your nemesis is found and I've truly cleared my name will you ever believe in my innocence."

He remained silent, the strain between them growing tenser by the moment. He turned and threw the chausses on the ground behind him.

Thunk. They hit the ground sounding like the clink of iron pans.

"I shan't argue this with you. I have a tourney to finish. I'll send for your sister to tend the wound." He stood and turned to leave.

"That's right, go. You cannot defend your true feelings, for we both know what they are. I'm sick to death of trying to right my honor in your eyes." *And get you to love me.* Yet she didn't say that. She lied and said, "I don't care now one way or the other."

"Beware of your words, Lark, for you can't take them back." With that parting shot, he turned and left the tent.

Lark fought the tears welling up in her eyes and the ache in her chest that made it hard to breathe. She wanted to tell him how much she loved him, but she knew he had no love to give. She couldn't risk exposing her heart and having it destroyed as Cecily had destroyed his.

She heard Stoke berating his men for letting her get out of their sight. He growled orders at them to stand guard over her, and if they let her get away again, he would have them both flogged. The guard Lark remembered seeing following her earlier, a thin man with a bean-shaped head, came in and stood in the corner eyeing her. The other took up a stance in front of the tent.

Lark shrugged apologetically as she swung her legs down from the cot, the ache still pulling at her chest. She didn't know which hurt worse, the wound in her leg or the one in her heart.

The guard looked warily at her.

Abruptly, William and Elizabeth came through the opening in the tent. Elizabeth pulled off the veil hanging down around her face and looked at Lark. "I saw it all. I guessed it was you. I came to see if I could help." She saw the guard in the tent and pointed to the entrance. "Out with you. I can't tend my daughter's wounds with you gawking at her."

The guard frowned, then stepped out.

Elizabeth set down a pail of water and a small box of herbs and bandages. She sat on the cot next to Lark. "I think this needs a few stitches," she said, probing the wound with her finger.

Lark flinched as a sheen of sweat broke out on her forehead.

"I thought you were not coming out of your room."

"I had to come see your father and brothers ride in the tourney."

Lark turned and looked at her father, the apprehension in his eyes going straight into her heart. She raised her hand and reached out to him.

He stared at her trembling, outstretched arm for a moment. His eyes filmed over as he said, "Can you forgive me, Lark?"

"There's naught to forgive." Lark felt tears sting her own eyes. He bent and hugged her so tightly that she could hardly breathe.

"I'm so sorry, Lark. I meant to tell you sooner."

"I know, Father."

"Get away now." Elizabeth pushed him back. "I need to tend this wound." She blotted at the blood with a wet cloth. "I was very proud of what you just did, saving Lord Blackstone like that." Elizabeth's words held no malice or contempt, but were uttered flatly with a bare hint of feeling. For the first time in her life, Lark saw a gleam in Elizabeth's eyes when she addressed her—a proud gleam.

She gazed at Elizabeth, unable to speak past the knot in her throat. Lark had waited her whole life to hear those words from Elizabeth. The knot seemed to be getting larger by the moment. Any minute it would strangle her. She could hold back the tears no longer, and they streamed down her face.

Elizabeth looked at Lark, tears forming in her own eyes. She clasped her arms around Lark. "I should have said it sooner, I know, but I could not."

"I know, and I didn't make it easy for you." Lark hugged her tightly, feeling Elizabeth's shoulders shaking against her own.

"Oh, Lark," Elizabeth said between sobs. "I've tried to be a good mother to you, but the harder I tried, the more I failed. I just couldn't get past the anger and resentment. I could never forget you were that woman's daughter, but though you vexed me at every turn, it didn't ever stop me from loving you."

"I realize that now."

Lark and Elizabeth stayed that way for a long time, rocking and crying.

William watched the two women he adored most in the world. A pensive smile spread across his lips. Eighteen years of hell was finally over for him. If Lark and Blackstone could only realize their love for each other, William's peace would be complete. Only time would tell there. Love could be a brutal soul mate at times—especially between two such guarded hearts. He knew about Blackstone's first wife; Rowland had told him the story. Also he knew how Lark shielded her heart behind a hard exterior. Sometimes there wasn't enough love between two people to bring down the walls around their hearts. Could that be the case with Lark and Blackstone? Had he misjudged them both?

Fifteen minutes later, Helen, Avenall, and Evel stepped into the tent.

Helen cried, "Lark! I saw what happened. Are you all right?"
Helen stared at Elizabeth stitching up Lark's leg and turned
pale.

Avenall, rubbing the back of his head, glanced at Lark. He
frowned as his gaze slid over his own armor heaped on the
ground. "You were wounded on my account. I should have
been out there instead of you." His irritation came through in
his voice.

"It was my own stupidity. I should have reacted faster and
the arrow would never have touched me." Lark gritted her
teeth as she felt Elizabeth bandage her leg. William had cut
the leg off her braies so that only the lower part of her thigh
and leg showed, which Lark thought wise, since practically
everyone she knew was in the tent.

"Helen and Evel told me what happened. I'm going out
there to face the bastard myself this time," Avenall said. "I
don't need you fighting my battles, Lark."

William glowered at Avenall. "If you step one foot onto the
lists, I'll personally kick your arse the length of it." He'd never
spoken to Avenall in such a manner, and Avenall's jaw dropped
open. "You needn't look like the put-upon one here. I know
why Lark did this, and it was for your sake."

" 'Tis my fault. I should have stopped her," Evel said.

"You couldn't have stopped me." At Evel's frown, Lark
smiled at him until she felt Elizabeth pull the bandage over her
wound and secure it.

"Nay, Father, it was my fault. I asked her to do it," Helen
blurted.

William stared at the pair and pursed his lips. "Oh, I see
the way of it now. Well, it's taken you two long enough to
declare yourselves. I hadn't seen it before, but you'll suit. Now
don't speak to me again until you've set a date for the wedding."

Loud cheering thundered from the galleries. "I wonder what
is going on out there," Evel said. "Come, Avenall, let us have
a look." Evel left, followed by Avenall and Helen, hand in
hand.

"I wonder myself what's happening." Lark tried to stand,

but Elizabeth pushed her back down. "Now, don't be stubborn like your father. You should rest."

"But 'tis only a scratch."

"So it is, but 'twill be sore if you don't stay off it." She picked up a bowl and dropped the bloody cloth she used to clean the wound into it. "I'll go and dump this outside, then your father and I shall go and see what is happening and report back to you. And don't think to move from that spot—I know you too well." She shook her finger at Lark.

Lark smiled at the reprimand. She could now. Elizabeth loved her. She could stand almost anything from her, knowing Elizabeth cared.

Elizabeth disappeared through the tent opening. Her father paused, then beamed a grin at his daughter. "Don't you just love her when she's overbearing?" He rolled his eyes and left the tent.

Lark chuckled in spite of the pain in her leg.

Forty-five minutes later, the twins had words with the guards and stepped into the tent, their eyes full of mischief. "You missed a good tourney, little sister," Harold said in his chiding way. "So sorry to see you taken out."

"Aye, I would have liked to see you finish with Blackstone," Harold said.

"Well, she ain't finished with him." Cedric elbowed Harold, and they both snickered.

"What do you two want?"

"We came to give you a message and tell you about the tourney you missed. It didn't last long enough. It only took one pass for every challenger. The Dragon burned them all. Left one man unconscious on the field."

"He wasn't happy."

"Did you see the scowl he leveled at the woman posing as you sitting with the king?" Cedric snickered and elbowed his brother.

"That woman had me fooled for a while. You do have a bit of wits in you to come up with such a devious deception."

"Thank you for the compliment, Harold, but what message did you have for me?" Lark looked at Harold and knew he was dying for her to ask so he could tease her a little longer. So she closed her eyes, leaned back against the tent, and ignored him.

"Tell her, Harold."

"Now, how did he put it? He said"—Cedric deepened his voice—" 'Tell your sister we'll be leaving for home as soon as the melee is over.' "

He couldn't come order her about himself, so he was sending her brothers to do it.

The sound of muffled footsteps made Lark glance at the tent entrance. Carmia put her head inside. "May I come in?"

"Aye," Lark said.

Carmia stepped in, carrying the yellow dress in her hands. She'd changed back into a scarlet dress, with a daringly low neckline. The twins couldn't take their eyes off her cleavage.

"Please go," Lark said to them.

Harold eyed his sister. "Don't forget what we said. You'd better be ready to leave with him."

"You know our perverse little sister—she'll probably not be ready and get beaten for it." Cedric added his part, shooting Lark a snide look.

"You can leave any time." Lark pointed at the tent flaps.

They shot her an identical look, eyed Carmia with an equal amount of contempt and interest, then left.

Carmia stepped over to her. "Did you have to grow up with those two?"

"Aye, every day of my life," Lark said, her voice weary. "Father tried to squire them twice, but my uncles sent them back, complaining they were unmanageable knaves."

"I'm sure you managed them well enough."

A small grin turned up Lark's mouth. "Aye, the keenest pleasure in my life was my daily fray with them." Lark realized she'd been rambling on to Carmia as if they were old friends. She grew quiet.

Carmia frowned at her. "I just brought back your dress."

"Was the king very upset with you?"

"Aye, though he was more provoked with you." Carmia smiled. "But your husband smoothed his temper by winning the tourney. Richard said he was going to make a point of visiting you at Kenilworth."

"Oh." Lark grew silent again. After a moment, she said, "Thank you for risking Richard's wrath on my account."

"I wanted to do something for you." Carmia looked anxiously at Lark. "Do you think . . ." Her words trailed off.

"What? Ask me."

"I'm going to be leaving on the morrow to go back to Normandy. I wondered if you would send word to me of how you are doing. I won't clutter your life with the likes of me, and you surely don't need me now, but I just want to how you are faring."

Lark stared at Carmia a moment, wanting to resent her, to send her away for leaving her as a babe and never coming to see her. But she could not hurt this woman. Though she was a complete stranger, Lark felt a connection with her, a bond that try as she might to ignore, she could not. She lifted her hand and touched Carmia's arm. "I will write. And I would welcome a visit from you."

Lark saw a glimmer of light in Carmia's eyes that she'd put there. She smiled until she thought of Stoke, of going home, seeing him, sharing his bed, and knowing he didn't love her. Physically he was attracted to her, but as she knew from her brother's lusty appetites, that would soon wear off and he'd take a mistress. Or several. Lark felt a horrible emptiness inside her, getting larger by the moment.

Chapter 27

That afternoon, Lark sat in back of the wain with her arm curled over Varik's shoulder, feeling the cart bumping beneath her. She didn't know which felt worse, her leg or her head from being jarred over the ruts in the road. Baltizar had his head on her shoulder, panting. His breath smelled of wild onions and rotted meat. She shoved him away. "Go and lie down."

He turned, saw Elizabeth behind him sitting on the straw, and crouched. Elizabeth sighed resignedly.

"You needn't think I'm going to hurt you. I can make room."

Elizabeth extended her hand. Baltizar crawled toward her, sniffed her hand, then moved back.

"All right, but one day I'll pet you," Elizabeth said. "Lie down, you flea-bitten creature."

Baltizar sat next to Lark's legs and rested his head on her knee.

Lark looked at Elizabeth. "Are you comfortable?"

"I cannot complain—my teeth have not rattled free yet." Elizabeth smiled at her.

"I'm glad you and Father decided to come home with me for a visit."

"You know your father. When Lord Blackstone mentioned the sword he would give him, I knew he couldn't say nay."

Lark glanced at Amory, who drove the wain, then at Stoke. He rode next to her father. The breadth of his shoulders seemed to dwarf her father. She had yearned so to run her hands over them, to feel him take her in his arms, but he hadn't made a move to touch her, not since she'd been wounded and they had quarreled in the tent. And if he preferred to ignore her, so could she ignore him. But she was finding it increasingly harder by the moment.

Lark listened to the steady clop of Rowland's horse behind them, along with the wooden wheels of a second wain, which carried supplies and tents. Sixteen knights flanked the two wains, forming a walled guard of armored men. Helen and Avenall had gone back to St. Vale along with Evel and the twins, so Harold and Cedric were not there to annoy her, though she might have welcomed the distraction to get her mind off Stoke.

"Wee, Moh-ee." Varik pulled on the sleeve of Lark's new gown, a beautiful blue sendal. Varik smiled at the little pearls on the sleeves and ran his fingers over them.

"Ye just went not too long ago." Dalia turned from where she sat next to Amory and looked down at Varik.

" 'Tis all right, I think he needs to stretch his legs, as we all do." Lark ruffled his dark curly locks.

"Oh, dear, I believe my legs have fallen asleep." Elizabeth rubbed her thighs. "I cannot say I enjoy this pace your husband has forced upon us."

"I believe he wishes to get home as soon as possible, my lady," Amory said, pulling back on the reins. "He fears there may be another attack."

"That is ridiculous. No one would attack us with such a large guard."

Rowland leaned over to Elizabeth. He flashed her a handsome smile, but it faded into worry as he said, "Begging your pardon, my lady, but this villain doesn't seem to stop at anything."

"For once my friend is right." Amory grinned at the indignant look on Rowland's face. "Yet I don't think 'tis all worry that's made his disposition so foul over the past few days." Amory eyed Lark pointedly.

"Could you not grace him with one of your sweet smiles, Lady Lark? I feel sure it will improve his spirits a hundredfold." Rowland grinned at her as he trotted his horse up to the front of the wain.

The other knights had been listening. They shared a glance and nodded their heads in agreement.

Amory called to Stoke as he pulled the wain to a stop. "Varik needs to relieve himself."

Elizabeth leaned forward and whispered, "Rowland is correct, Lark. You should be ashamed of yourself. You cannot continue to ignore him. He's your husband. Show him a little attention and you'll have him eating out of your palm. Look not at me like that. Just observe your father. He'll do anything for me."

"There's a difference—he loves you," Lark said, biting her lower lip and turning to look at Stoke.

At that moment, he turned. His gaze searched the wain until he found her. The hard look in his eyes softened just a little, as if he were pleased that she was looking at him.

"You can draw a bear quicker with honey than vinegar," Elizabeth whispered.

"Thank you for that bit of wisdom. If I ever want a bear, I'll remember it." Lark frowned and leaned back against the wain, remaining broodingly silent.

Stoke left the main road and paused in a clearing near a thick wood. Behind the woods, a hill rose, covered with tall grass. The last edge of the setting sun peeked over the top and lit the sky with deep indigo and magenta and dusky rose.

Stoke hopped down and helped Elizabeth and Varik out of the wain. Varik smiled up at him. In a clear voice that carried, he said, "Thank you, Father."

"You are quite welcome, little liege." Stoke grinned proudly down at him.

Varik glanced up at Lark. "Did good?"

"Aye, better than I could say 'father'."

Varik smiled broadly; then clutched Dalia's hand and dragged her toward Baltizar.

Lark made a move to jump down. Stoke's smile faded as he reached for her. "Let me help you down."

"I'm fine, really." He ignored her protests and lifted her out of the wain. She felt his hands slip beneath her and reveled in the feel of them on her again. It seemed like ages since he'd last touched her.

He didn't set her down right away, but carried her to a spot near a large oak. Lark felt his breath on her face, the heat of his body seeping through her clothes. Her resolve to keep him at arm's length was dissolving quickly. But then she heard Louis's voice taunting her, "You must know he'll never love you . . ."

Lark couldn't settle for anything less than his love, so she said, "Please put me down. I can walk." Lark watched his jaw tense at her words.

His strides grew stiff, each one jarring her against his brawny chest. He set her down near a large tree. "Now you'll not have to suffer my touch." He wheeled around.

Lark opened her mouth to stop him, but he was already halfway across the camp, barking orders to his men.

She leaned her head back against the tree trunk. Through a wash of tears, she watched Varik squirming in Dalia's arms. He pointed to where Baltizar was sniffing a blackberry bush. "Down! Play Ballie."

"All right, go play with the wolf." Dalia set him down, held his hand, and walked with him over to Baltizar.

Baltizar stuck his head beneath the bush and flushed out a rabbit. He took off running after it into the woods. "Ballie! Ballie!" Varik followed, pulling Dalia behind him. Amory and two other knights ran behind them.

Abruptly, two of Stoke's men came striding over to guard Lark.

She couldn't stand to be near his men, or Stoke, not with this sinking feeling dragging her down. With little difficulty, she pulled herself up. "I'm going to relieve myself. And I wish to do it alone."

"Don't go far, mistress." The bean-headed guard gave her a warning glance.

She nodded and hobbled off into the woods, the ache deep inside her worsening as she thought of the days ahead of her at Kenilworth, with a husband who would never care for her.

Stoke watched his men setting up his tent and William's. Lady Elizabeth was busy badgering the men to get it straight and not on damp ground. William stood back, sipping ale from a flagon. He turned to look for Lark and saw her hobbling off into the woods. Since his men weren't following her, he supposed she was going to relieve herself.

Stoke turned to go after her, but he felt sure it would just anger her. He scowled at her back as Rowland strode up to his side.

"I see naught has changed between you and your wife."

"Nay." Stoke watched her tawny blond hair flash behind tree trunks as she went deeper into the woods.

"Give her time. She'll get used to being a wife."

"Aye, but I'm losing patience with her." Stoke's fists clenched at his sides.

The sound of horses' hooves made Stoke and Rowland turn. Louis came galloping through the woods, leading Jamus's mount, while Jamus sat trussed and gagged on the saddle. Louis threw the reins at Stoke. "I don't appreciate your little spies following me. This one has become very annoying."

Jamus mumbled and struggled against the bindings to no avail. Rowland strode over to him, drew a dagger from his boot, and cut him free.

"I have good reason to have you followed."

"Now, cousin, do you think I would have tried to kill you over a bloody woman?"

"Aye, I think you'd kill me over a halfpenny."

Louis grinned contemptuously. "The trouble with you is,

you are suspicious of everyone. Believe me, should I kill you, I wouldn't do it behind your back."

"What made you come all this way to bring back my squire?"

"I came to invite you and your wife to my holding for a visit. You left so suddenly after the tourney I never got a chance to speak to you."

"Why do I not believe you?"

"To be truthful, I really didn't want to see you, but your wife."

Stoke's arm snaked out. He gabbed Louis by the front of his tunic and jerked him off his horse. He drew back and plowed his fist into Louis's face. It happened with such speed that Louis didn't have a chance to defend himself.

Louis's eyes crossed as he collapsed to the ground.

Stoke stared at Louis. Abruptly, the same perception of danger that had kept him alive in the Holy Land prodded him now to find Lark.

He ran across camp and into the woods. As he passed the tree where he'd last seen her, he saw something shiny flash in the corner of his eye. He paused and saw a dagger stuck to the tree. A note hung from it.

Stoke pulled out the knife and examined the inlaid pearl handle—Lark's dagger. His hands trembled slightly as he slid the note off the blade. He saw a long smear of blood slashed below the last line. He ran his finger over the smear. It was damp. It was Lark's blood.

He had been through dark alleys where Saracens lurked as thick as cobbles in the streets, where he never knew if a stray arrow or sword would find his back; he had faced hundreds of men in battle, never afraid of fate and what it might hold for him. But he felt a bone-chilling fear now. Fate would not curse him by taking Lark. He wouldn't let it.

He yelled over his shoulder to Rowland. "Tie up my cousin. Don't let him leave here." His fist crushed the parchment as he headed for the woods to find Amory.

* * *

Lark knew she was dreaming. Stoke was in her dream. He stood in a vast space of darkness. She could only see the whites of his eyes and the grayish cast of his skin. The rest of him melted into the blackness. She called to him. He didn't answer. Again she called, screaming this time, but he looked right through her. She stepped toward him. His mouth opened as if to speak to her.

Instead of words, a huge wave of fire rolled toward her, straight at her face. All she could see was a red cloud of flame. The heat burned her. She felt her eyelashes being singed away, her lips . . .

Lark woke with a start before the fire consumed her. Her head was leaning against something hard. A pounding sound wouldn't go away. She realized the pounding was coming from her temples, and she recalled being hit on the back of her skull.

She turned her neck slightly and glimpsed the thick iron bars of a cage encompassing her. She tilted her head slightly and glanced through the iron bars. Above her, the cage hung suspended by a chain, wrapped around one of the many rough-hewed oak rafters spanning the ceiling.

She tried to move her arms, but there was barely enough room to turn her head, the tiny cage no bigger than one from a mews. Someone had stuffed her inside it with little care, her legs bent tight against her chest, her shoulders pressed against the sides. All her weight was on one side of her hip and wounded thigh.

In an attempt to relieve the pressure on her wound, she pushed against the cage with her elbow and again tried to move. The cage rattled against the chain holding it and began to sway. A woozy sensation hit her. She closed her eyes a moment to keep down the bile.

When the swaying stopped, she opened her eyes and tried again to move, this time more gently. She felt leather thongs on her wrists. Her hands were squashed between her chest and her bent knees, making it almost impossible to move them.

Dried blood covered her thumb where someone had cut her. The wound was long but not deep. At least the person used a dagger to cut it. The pain it afforded didn't come close to her throbbing thigh and head.

She peered past the bars at her surroundings. It was an old workshop of some sort, a shop that looked very much like Stoke's, the same hammers and punches, not neatly displayed on pegs, but thrown haphazardly on a bench. As in Stoke's workshop, black smoke covered everything; the acrid smell of iron ore and charcoal blanketed the air. But this shop was larger, and by the sound of running water she heard outside, it was an abandoned mill.

Sharp beams of sunlight shot through the holes in the old thatch ceiling and between the weathered planking on the walls. A large number of beams met, cubing the room with mosaic lines of light. She watched the dust motes in the smoke-filled air spiral through the sunbeams for a moment and knew by their angle that the sun was setting. How long had she been unconscious?

The sound of whistling made her peer over her bent leg, down at the door. The high, discordant trill came closer, blending with the light crunch of footsteps.

Someone opened the door.

Thomas the bailiff stood in the doorway, his small frame silhouetted by sunlight. A pair of brown woolen braies covered his short legs. The green tunic he wore hung on him, too big for his squatty chest and arms. His keen eyes darted up to her. He smiled, a weasel's smile.

"Well, well, I see you're awake." He strode into the barn, slamming the door behind him.

"You! So it was you all along."

"Aye, 'twas I." Thomas pointed to his chest, looking proud of himself. He strode farther into the mill and stood below the cage, peering up at her. "I enjoyed watching you chase after Trevelyn. Blackstone's plan to trap you kept your prying eyes off me and on his cousin. I couldn't have planned it better."

"Why did you get Ebba to poison Varik?" Lark asked, voicing her suspicions aloud.

"I wanted to keep you guessing about Lord Trevelyn. When Blackstone came home with the story that you'd stabbed him and you were in league with the person trying to kill him, I was ecstatic. You kept Blackstone's mind off finding me. Then I learned he meant to bring you back as his prisoner. I needed to find out if you were as devious as I hoped you would be."

"Did you think you could recruit me as you did Ebba?"

"Aye, until you saved the boy. Then I heard you speaking to Dalia about Lord Trevelyn being the guilty one."

"You must have relished that."

"Aye, I had many a good laugh over it." A vicious grin lifted one corner of his mouth.

"Did you laugh when you killed Ebba too?" Lark almost hated to ask the question, for she had a feeling she already knew.

"Aye. The little slut threatened to expose me if I didn't give her more money." Thomas flicked a piece of dirt from beneath a fingernail.

"Why do you want Stoke dead?"

"For the secret."

"What secret?"

"The secret he's stumbled upon working with metal."

"You didn't have to kill him to get it."

"He would have come for me the moment he knew I'd stolen it."

"What is the secret?" Lark stared at him, puzzled.

"It's all in the kiln."

"I don't understand."

He looked at her as if she were a simpleton. " 'Tis the kiln that is his secret. I tested it here. If you melt the ore in a kiln, it makes the metal stronger. I don't know why, but it does."

"How did you get into his shop to find the secret?"

"I found the key as you did, by fumbling upon it."

"You know about that."

"Aye." He smiled a too-knowing smile. "I know a lot of things about you. I've been watching you very closely."

Lark remembered making love to Stoke in the woods by the lake. A blush spread down her face. In a hurry to change the subject, she said, "So you mean to use Stoke's secret to become wealthy?"

"Aye, as soon as he's dead. I can't have him killing me, now can I? I want no interferences when I start my own armory. Kings from all over the world will pay any price I ask. They'll bow before me." His eyes gleamed with hatred. "I've never had anyone look up to me. Well, they'll be looking up to me one day. There will be no more working for arrogant lords, doing their bidding, taking care of land that should be mine."

The door burst open.

"Me lord—Blackstone! He's comin'." A grubby-faced man stood in the doorway. His gaze darted up to Lark, his eyes gleaming with anticipation of a coming kill.

"Is he alone as I bade him in the note?"

"Aye, looks like it."

"Very good."

Lark watched Thomas put on a pair of heavy leather gloves, pick up a pair of thongs, and walk to the hearth.

"What are you doing?"

"Heating things up a bit. I'm going to make sure he dies this time. He's managed to avoid the bungling fools I've hired, but I'll see it done properly this time." He picked a burning log from the fire and tossed it out into the room. Then another. And another. He grabbed a bellows and fanned them.

Whoosh.

Flames licked out from the logs, consuming the old and rotting wood in voracious squalls. Flames erupted and crawled along the floor.

" 'Tis time for me to go." He held up his arm against the heat hitting his face and ran from the mill.

Lark's eyes stung from the billowing smoke; every breath bit at her throat. Heat surged up in great gusts. The iron bars

beneath her grew hotter by the moment. She could feel them
warming against her bottom and feet.

She covered her mouth and coughed, twisting her body so
she could see the small door on the cage. Her gaze landed on
the chain and lock. She watched the flames spreading up the
walls to the ceiling, and below her, shooting across the floor.
Sweet Mary, don't let Stoke come in here.

Stoke paused on the path to the mill. New saplings from the
nearby forest hid it from view, but he could see smoke rising
above the tops. His blood ran cold at the sight of it. He knew
it was a trap by the note Amory had read to him:

Come alone to the old mill at Kenilworth. I have her.

As he galloped up a rise toward the mill, he saw the flames
leaping along the thatch roof. Grinding his teeth, his heart
pounding in his chest, he headed straight for the stream. He
leaped off Shechem's back, thoroughly doused himself, then
ran through the brush that had grown up around the abandoned
building.

He tried not to look at the flames flicking out at him around
the door. If he looked, he would freeze. He needed to concentrate on Lark's face instead of the fire. It took every bit of
willpower to pull his wet mantle over his head and leap into
the furnace of flames. The heat hit him like a blow.

"Lark!" he yelled above the roar of the fire. The smoke,
the flames overwhelmed him. God in heaven, where was she?

Instantly, he was back at Kenilworth, battling flames, listening to screams of his father and mother. The heat was all
over him, searing his legs. He ran and ran. He had to get out
of the castle . . .

Stoke turned to run back outside the mill, but then he heard
Lark's voice.

"Stoke! Don't come in here. You'll be killed. Get out!"

Lark. He had to find her. He had to. Fighting every festering
memory in his mind, summoning all the courage within him,

he beat the fire back and moved farther into the mill, all the while screaming her name, "Lark! Lark! Answer me!"

Through a wall of smoke and leaping flames, he saw the tiny cage hanging from the ceiling, then Lark, stuffed into it. Below her, flames leaped across the floor.

His gaze followed the chain that held the cage. It was tied around a flaming beam, but haphazardly, one end of it hanging loose down past the cage. If he could only reach it! Determined to do so, or die with her, he ran through the fire. It hissed against his wet boots and braies.

He leaped for the chain. One hand missed its mark, but the other caught. The scalding heat of the links burned his hand, yet he held on and swung over to the cage, coughing as the smoke filled his lungs.

"Save yourself! Don't be a fool."

"If you die, I die too. You're my life." He saw the lock holding the door. Still suspended by one hand, he withdrew Dragon's Eye. "Watch out!"

She crouched and dipped her head between her bunched knees.

He brought down Dragon's Eye with all the strength in his body. Sparks flew as the metal collided. Dragon's Eye drew up short. The vibration shot all the way up through his arm. The chain refused to give. Now he knew the reason for all this. He knew. It was made of same metal he'd used to make Dragon's Eye.

The smoke grew worse; he could hardly see Lark through it. The heat scalded his lungs. Could he hold on much longer? He heard a loud crack and felt the beam overhead give way.

Frantically, he glanced at the lock. It was worth a try. He brought Dragon's Eye down again. It hit the base. He heard a loud crunch. Then it fell open and crashed into the flames.

He jammed Dragon's Eye back in its scabbard and jerked open the door. With his free hand he grabbed Lark's bound hands and pulled her out. Her eyes looked ready to close on him, and she looked as pale as chalk.

"Stay awake for me, Lark."

"I'm trying." She coughed violently between each word.

He felt his insides churning as he gazed at the flames below them, the flames he must face to get out. But he had Lark. He could make it. He had to. He grabbed her around the waist. "Hold on!" Holding tight to her, he closed his eyes and dropped from the chain.

He hit the ground with both feet, still holding Lark. The heat burned the soles of his boots and lapped at his body as he stumbled through the flames.

Another crack from the beam.

He staggered through the smoke and fire, unable to see, letting his instinct guide him. He saw the light from the door, a grayish black haze before him.

A loud creak.

The beam holding the cage gave way.

Abruptly, he leaped through the doorway. A great burst of heat propelled him out of it. Bits of burning debris hit his back and head as he rolled down the sloping yard of the mill.

He clutched Lark tightly to his body. They whirled through the tall underbrush, coming to rest near the stream bank. He lay there, trembling, clutching Lark to him like a talisman. He had held his breath through the last few moments, and now it came out in a loud gush.

Lark had landed on top of him, her face on his chest. He felt her body convulsing and heard her deep hiccups.

He grasped the sides of her face and gently eased her chin up so he could look into her eyes. Tears streamed down her cheeks, making long rivulets through the black smoke on her face. The tear-stained whites of her eyes showed stark against the golden lashes. Her blue gown had turned an ugly sooty-gray. Her hair too was filled with soot and smoke, the tawny gold now a lackluster brown. She looked beautiful. Beautiful and alive. And crying.

"What is the matter?" He ran his thumb over her tears and smeared the soot across her face.

"All this time, I thought you didn't love me, but you do. You really love me," she said, in between hiccups.

"Are you just figuring that out, my tigress? You're everything to me . . . everything." He tangled his hands in her hair and brought her face down to his for a kiss. When their lips met, he felt the fiery passion in them as she wrapped her bound arms around his neck and clung to him. His tigress was back.

"Well, well, well."

Stoke and Lark broke the kiss at the same time. Thomas stood ten feet from of the mill, flames leaping up behind him. He held a crossbow, pointed between Stoke's eyes. "I'm glad I've got your attention. Damned if you don't have a hundred lives. Just killing you is becoming a life's work. Get up. I want to see your face when I kill you."

"Kill me, but leave her alone." In spite of her gripping his arms, Stoke shoved Lark off him, stood, and faced Thomas. "I see I owe my cousin an apology."

"Aye, and he won't even get the pleasure of killing you for your mistake." Thomas snickered and aimed the bow at Stoke's heart.

It all happened at once. Lark screamed. Baltizar leapt from the woods and attacked Thomas from the side. Wolf and man hit the ground. In trying to ward off the attack, Thomas lost the crossbow. Baltizar attacked with the relentless feral strength of his kind.

Abruptly the roof of the mill began to collapse.

"Baltizar!" Lark scrambled to go after him.

Stoke grabbed Lark around the waist as the building surged forward, a huge, crumbling tower of flames.

It hit the ground, spewing a cloud of fire and debris out around it.

A blast of heat hit Stoke in the face, and he pulled Lark back. He heard Thomas's scream die away. Then there was only the roar of the fire.

"Oh, Baltizar," Lark said, sobbing. She turned and clung to Stoke, burying her face in his smoke-blackened tunic.

He held her, feeling her body shaking, reveling in the feel of her turning to him for comfort. Over the top of her head, Stoke saw something dark emerge from behind the flames. He pulled back and turned her so she could see what he was seeing. "Look."

Lark's sobs stopped as she gazed at Baltizar, trotting toward them. "Sweet Mary! He's alive." Lark ran to him and petted his singed fur. His nose looked burned, and the whiskers on his face were gone. "I'll have to mend you, old friend."

"I didn't know he followed me," Stoke said, eyeing the wolf with awe. "I thought he'd gone off hunting."

"Wolves can sense danger."

"Aye, and a lot more than that, to my thinking." He stared at her a moment, watching Baltizar licking her face.

"Do you think he knew you'd have to save me and I'd know you finally loved me?"

Stoke looked into the keen eyes of the wolf. "Aye, I think he knows a lot more than we shall ever know," he said, bending to cut the bindings on her wrists with his dagger.

"Just think, I might have gone through my whole life never knowing you loved me. Can you forgive me for turning you away?" She touched his jaw, running her fingers over the stubble.

"It has been like torture not being able to touch you. I've wanted you every minute of the day." He gazed down into her eyes and tightened his arms around her.

"I'll make it up to you." A sultry grin spread across her lips.

"You had better." Stoke bent to kiss her, but she drew back.

"May I ask a question?"

"What?"

"Can we get married again?"

"We are already married."

"Aye, but I want to do it again." She smiled at him, the dimple in her left cheek beaming.

He grinned at her. "I'll agree only if I have your heart at the altar this time."

She stood and wrapped her arms around his neck. "My heart has been yours since the first time we kissed. I was just too frightened to admit it.'' She murmured against his lips, ''I love you, Stoke . . . I love you,'' then kissed him.

He took fierce possession of her mouth. Lark buried her hands in his thick hair, kissing him back, welcoming his possession. He slid his hand up and put his palm over her heart, feeling it pounding against his fingers. It was strong and steady and belonged to him.

Epilogue

The chapel at St. Vale was full to capacity. The King of England occupied one side of the front pew and eyed the couple before him with relief and amusement in his eyes. Varik sat next to the king, stroking the ermine fur on his mantle.

Louis frowned over at them and touched his swollen nose. Rowland gazed at Louis with a jaundiced eye, then at Amory, whose voice filled every corner of the chapel. His sword knocked against his thigh as he raised his hand and emphasized the Latin words.

Baltizar sat next to Amory's legs, his gaze trained on Stoke and Lark. If anyone in the chapel were to look at the furry beast, they would swear he was smiling.

Sunlight beamed through the small rose window over the altar, casting a rainbow of colors over Lark, Stoke, Avenall and Helen. Stoke wore all black velvet, the embroidered dragon on the back of his mantle eyeing the crowd.

Stoke turned and with his gaze traced his bride's thick, tawny hair flowing down her back, her perfect oval face and pouty lips. His gaze dropped to her sky-blue silk dress that flowed around sleek curves. The blue of the dress matched the bright vivid periwinkles in the circlet on her head.

As if feeling his eyes on her, she turned and stared over at him. She smiled at him, an unusually sweet, pliant smile. He squeezed her hand tighter.

Avenall was holding Helen's hand. He gazed down at her with a look that he'd never bestowed on Lark. Helen blushed as she stared into his eyes. His gaze dropped, devouring her curves, displayed so well in a blue sendal dress, her dark, walnut-brown hair flowing in waves down to her waist.

Lady Lucinda bent over and punched her sleeping husband. Sir Joseph cracked open an eye.

"You're missing everything. Look at Lark and Lord Blackstone, dear," she whispered. "He hasn't turned her loose since we came in. See how he's holding her hand, as if he'll not let go of it. I'm sure he doesn't intend to let her go, for she's led him a merry chase." Lady Lucinda chuckled softly under her breath. "Ah, but who would have thought Lark would show so well. I've never seen her look so comely, more so than Helen. Oh, aye, I'm sure of it. Who would ever believe that? Oh, and how those two got together is beyond me, but such a love story. Did you not think Helen's blue dress just a tad darker than Lark's? I'm sure it is the light color of it . . ."

Sir Joseph rolled his eye, closed it, and left his wife to whisper on.

While Father Amory spouted on in Latin, Elizabeth leaned over to William. "Oh, William, I thought this day would never come. Did you ever think that we would finally get those two married?"

"I didn't worry about it at all, my dear." William slipped his hand in hers and squeezed it. "They just had to find the right partners. That should teach you not to meddle."

"I, meddle?"

"Aye, you do. I've no doubt you'll be doing the same with my sons."

Elizabeth glanced over and Evel and the twins. The twins

were eyeing Sir Blanton's twin daughters, sitting a pew behind them.

The young ladies looked disgusted by the twins' attention. Evel seemed preoccupied and stared up at the rose window. A curious expression settled over Elizabeth's face.

"I see you, and I know what you're thinking. No more meddling," William said in a chiding whisper.

Lark could hear William whispering to Elizabeth, for their pew was right in front of the altar. She grinned and glanced over at Stoke. He stared down at her, his eyes consuming her with bright fire. How she loved that fire in him. There was no doubt about it. He was her own special dragon.

Dear Reader,

Just a little note on the metal-working techniques Stoke had stumbled upon in my story. His discovery was far ahead of his time.

Iron ore is what Stoke melted to make his swords. Carbon is a constituent of iron ore, which is not steel until it goes through a long process. The smelting procedure that removes impurities from the basic iron ore forms steel. The more carbon, the harder the steel. The use of the potter's kiln in the story provides a reducing atmosphere that is mostly carbon monoxide and carbon dioxide from the burning fuel (which in this case is charcoal). This process contributes to the strength, but Stoke also had to temper the heated metal, and then reheat it in contact with a carbon-based medium such as charcoal or wood to get the kind of hardened metal used for his sword.

Blacksmiths who made chain mail and weapons for knights guarded their secrets of smelting for centuries. The use of closed ovens for melting iron ore did not come into use until the eighteenth century. Steel was very expensive to make and up until the steel age, cost prohibitive. Not until our century were true advances made in steel products.

I hope you enjoyed Stoke's hobby as much as I enjoyed researching it and writing about it. Please look for my short story, "Fate's Little Miracle," part of *Baby In A Basket*, an April, 1999, Zebra release, as well as my next historical romance, *My Wicked Marquess*, to be published in November, 1999.

I would love to hear from you. Please write me at: P.O. Box 25664, Richmond, Virginia 23260.

Happy Reading!
Constance Hall

BOOK YOUR PLACE ON OUR WEBSITE AND MAKE THE READING CONNECTION!

We've created a customized website just for our very special readers, where you can get the inside scoop on everything that's going on with Zebra, Pinnacle and Kensington books.

When you come online, you'll have the exciting opportunity to:

- View covers of upcoming books
- Read sample chapters
- Learn about our future publishing schedule (listed by publication month *and author*)
- Find out when your favorite authors will be visiting a city near you
- Search for and order backlist books from our online catalog
- Check out author bios and background information
- Send e-mail to your favorite authors
- Meet the Kensington staff online
- Join us in weekly chats with authors, readers and other guests
- Get writing guidelines
- AND MUCH MORE!

Visit our website at
http://www.zebrabooks.com

ROMANCE FROM FERN MICHAELS

DEAR EMILY   (0-8217-4952-8, $5.99)

WISH LIST   (0-8217-5228-6, $6.99)

AND IN HARDCOVER:

VEGAS RICH   (1-57566-057-1, $25.00)

YOU WON'T WANT TO READ
JUST ONE—KATHERINE STONE

ROMANCE FROM GEORGINA GENTRY

COMANCHE COWBOY   (0-8217-6211-7, $5.99/$7.50)
Cayenne McBride knows that Maverick Durango is the perfect guide to lead her back home to her father's Texas ranch. And when the fearless half-breed demands that she give up her innocence in exchange for his protection, Cayenne agrees, convinced she can keep her virtue intact . . . until she falls in love with him.

WARRIOR'S PRIZE   (0-8217-5565-X, $5.99/$7.50)
After spending years in Boston at a ladies' academy, the Arapaho maiden Singing Wind returns to Colorado. Ahead of her lies a dangerous trek into the Rocky Mountains . . . where a magnificent warrior dares to battle for her body, her heart, and her precious love.

CHEYENNE SONG   (0-8217-5844-6, $5.99/$7.50)
Kidnapped by the Cheyenne warrior Two Arrows, Glory Halstead faces her captor with the same pride and courage that have seen her through hardship and bitter scandal. But as they make the brutal journey through the harsh wilderness, Glory and Two Arrows discover passion as primal and unyielding as the land they are destined to tame. . . .